THE FIFTH GOSPEL

COMPLETE SHORT FICTION

Farrukh Dhondy was born in 1944 in Pune. After graduating in physics from Wadia College, he won a scholarship to Cambridge to train as a quantum physicist, but ended up reading for a BA in English. He is the author of a number of books including *East End at Your Feet* (1977), *Poona Company* (1980), *Bombay Duck* (1990), *The Bikini Murders* (2008) and *Prophet of Love* (2013). He has also written screenplays for film and television, including *Bandit Queen* (1995), *Split Wide Open* (1999) and *The Rising: Ballad of Mangal Pandey* (2005).

THE FIFTH GOSPEL
COMPLETE SHORT FICTION

Farrukh Dhondy

HarperCollins *Publishers* India

This edition first published in 2014 by
HarperCollins *Publishers* India

Copyright © Farrukh Dhondy 1976, 1978, 1982, 1993, 2014

Page 633 is an extension of the copyright page

P-ISBN: 978-93-5136-446-7
E-ISBN: 978-93-5136-447-4

2 4 6 8 10 9 7 5 3 1

Farrukh Dhondy asserts the moral right
to be identified as the author of this work

HarperCollins *Publishers*
A-75, Sector 57, Noida, Uttar Pradesh 201301, India
77-85 Fulham Palace Road, London W6 8JB, United Kingdom
Hazelton Lanes, 55 Avenue Road, Suite 2900, Toronto, Ontario M5R 3L2
and 1995 Markham Road, Scarborough, Ontario M1B 5M8, Canada
25 Ryde Road, Pymble, Sydney, NSW 2073, Australia
10 East 53rd Street, New York NY 10022, USA

Typeset in 11/14 Stempel Garamonds
By Saanvi Graphics Noida

Printed and bound at
Thomson Press (India) Ltd.

Contents

EAST END AT YOUR FEET

For the pupils of Archbishop Michael
Ramsey's School

1.

Dear Manju

MANJU WAS A REAL INDIAN beauty and Bhupinder was her younger brother. Their aunts envied Manju and told her mother that she ought to use a firmer hand with her. Bhupinder, on the other hand, was a favourite and was encouraged to do what he liked. He hardly remembered their father, for the boy had been only three years old when his father died, and though Manju was older and could recall what her father was like, she didn't spend any time thinking about him. She spent much more time thinking about herself and the way she looked and about films and film stars and clothes and about the boys of Brick Lane.

'Pinder, go see where your sister is,' their mother would say and Bhupinder would have to go around the houses of Manju's friends and fetch her in. He didn't like doing it and Manju didn't like him following her around saying, 'Mummy says it's nine o'clock and come home just now with me.'

Bhupinder had been constantly told that he was Manju's guardian, that he had the responsibilities of a brother, and that good brothers didn't take these responsibilities lightly. Manju did take them lightly. She didn't seem to want to

3

acknowledge that he was now fourteen years old and his voice was cracking and the little hairs just sprouting on his chin marked an approaching season of authority. She pinched his cheeks in front of her friends, she disgraced him by making fun of his cracking voice.

Bhupinder knew he had to be patient with her. She didn't seem to realize how much a girl's honour meant, especially in the Indian community where everybody gossiped about everybody else. He would hear the elders discuss other girls.

'She's picked up English ways,' they would say. 'She goes swimming with white boys ... no respect left for her elders ... if she was my daughter ... nobody will marry second-hand girls ...'

And Bhupinder was conscious that Manju was pretty, very pretty. She had long black hair which shone like a river by moonlight, and a broad mouth and a small, straight, perky nose and almond-shaped eyes and light brown skin. Her mother called her 'my fair one'.

When Manju was forced to come home, she would sit in front of the telly and grumble or sulk.

'You should become a dog catcher,' she would say to Bhupinder, 'you're always sniffing around after me.' And to their mother she would say, 'How do you think it makes me feel having this big baby trailing around after me? What will my friends think, that I can't look after myself? I wasn't eloping or something, I was only watching telly at Ritu's place.'

Her mother would look at her softly, without getting into an argument. Manju was difficult, but she was the light of her life. She was clever and she was considerate and would help their mother around the house with cooking and sewing and keeping the flat clean and reading and writing letters that had to be written, and she would even help with Bhupinder's school. She would go instead of their mother to the parents' evenings and speak to his teachers, who thought she was charming.

Bhupinder was proud of walking around with her when they went shopping, or when the community gathered at someone's house, or when they went as a family to the temple a few times a year and met other Punjabi families at religious festivals. But in their own area, or around the school it was different. The boys, the Indian boys of their locality, weren't nice. They would stare at Manju in that dirty way and pass remarks and make him feel, if he was with her, like a weak and scared bodyguard. He knew that Manju was quite aware of the things they said, and it made him a little ashamed to know that she understood their remarks and didn't seem to mind. She liked having admiring eyes on her, looking her up and down, and she even liked their grins and the competition they seemed to have to say rude things. They would imitate the language of the movies: 'What a piece of merchandise,' and, 'The opened lotus is thirsty for rain,' in Hindi.

It was all right to say things like that about girls you didn't know, about English girls who wouldn't understand, but when it came to your own sister it wasn't to be tolerated. It was the language of show-offs and loafers, Bhupinder thought, and it made him mad. In his heart of hearts he knew that looking after his sister meant facing up to them some day. Everyone said England was a civilized country, but he knew these boys, they were uncivilized rogues and how can a man protect his family's good name with such people around?

Yet Bhupinder envied them. A few of these lads, some from the fifth and sixth form in his school, made it a habit to hang around the Nishat Café in Brick Lane. They'd be there every day after six, having changed out of their tatty school uniforms and wearing their check jackets and flared trousers, their hair thrown back in a rolling puff like the heroes of the Hindi movies. They'd play songs on the juke box and three-card flush at the tables and drink endless cups of tea, and tease the girls who passed. Some of them were Sikhs, but they didn't grow their hair and they didn't even wear turbans any more. Their families either didn't care or had lost control of them, Bhupinder thought. They were the sort of Indians who gave the community a bad name, swearing all the time, getting into trouble with teachers and the police, carrying knives and wasting their time on talk of money and sex and horse racing, singing loudly in the street as though they owned London or something. Most of the other Indian boys Bhupinder knew kept out of the way of this gang, and yet they talked about them and their latest doings, how they bought up all the tickets at the cinema when a good movie was showing and sold them for double the price to the families who had come from all over London to see *Bobby*; or how they had thrown six white girls into the swimming pool with all their clothes on after some argument.

One of these boys was called Manjit. He was in the sixth form at Bhupinder's school and he was the king of the Nishat pack. He had a particularly bad reputation in the area, and a worse one at school. One of his teeth had been knocked out in some long-forgotten brawl and it gave his nicotine-stained grin a look of rotting evil. Even the teachers were afraid of him because he'd do the most vile things. He was known to expose himself in the playground at school and call the younger boys over to where his gang was to have a look. One of his older brothers was in jail for stabbing a man in a fight over a woman, and Manjit boasted about it. There were gangs of white boys in school too, but they kept away from Manjit's crowd and kept to their own sorts of entertainment.

For some reason, Manjit had been made a prefect at school. The teachers always talked to him as though they were addressing someone their own age. So when Manjit and two of his tough cronies were given prefects' ties at assembly, and the headmaster announced the arrangements for parents' day that year, Bhupinder got the uneasy feeling that the time had come.

'Our new prefects this year will help out with the Indian parents who attend the function,' the headmaster said and Bhupinder knew that it would mean bringing Manju to the school and facing the Nishat gang.

Bhupinder's mother received the note about parents' day and passed it on to Manju.

'You better go and have a good talk to his teachers.'

'I don't need anyone to come and talk to the teachers. I'm getting the maths prize again so you can see I'm doing all right.'

'Don't be such a baby,' Manju said, ruffling his neatly combed hair with teasing fingers, 'I won't tell them that you mutter in your sleep and Mummy wants them to know that we have to chase you all round the house with a cake of soap before you'll have a bath.'

'She's only three years older than me,' Bhupinder protested.

'She's passed all her jeezees,' his mother said. She couldn't pronounce the English letters too well. She earned her living by taking in stitching from the firm that brought pre-cut jobs in a van once a week, and most of what went on at school was a mystery to her. 'But if you want,' she added, 'I'll come and leave Manjula behind and then all your teachers and friends will know that your mother is a villager and can't speak English.'

'I don't want her wearing all that war-paint in my school. Mr Crawley is a big Christian and he thinks girls with make-up are prostitutes.'

'Your tongue will get boils if you talk about your sister like that,' his mother said.

'Go and wash your mouth out. I don't know where you kids pick up these long words,' Manju said.

'Well, it's true,' Bhupinder said. He knew now that there was no way out of it, that he'd have to let Manju come to the school. 'If Daddy was alive he'd never have let you make a disgrace of the family by painting up like a dancing girl.'

'Tht tht,' his mother said, 'your father would have been very ashamed to see you always fighting.'

'Who's fighting?' Manju said. 'The little one is just showing us what a big man he is.'

'You'll get one in the face just now,' Bhupinder said, holding up his fist. Manju grabbed his fist in one hand and kissed it lightly and bounced back before he could take a swipe at her.

'Coming to think of it,' she said, 'I'd better tell your

form teacher that Mummy's very worried about you wetting your bed when you get into a tantrum.'

'Manju, go and get a bottle of milk before the shop closes,' her mother said, and Manju, seeing that Bhupinder was really getting the needle, blew him a sarcastic kiss and with mischief skating round her face, went out of the door.

On the evening of parents' day Manju wore a black salwar and black kameez with a red border round the neck and hem. It was a tight kameez and, as she emerged from her room, Bhupinder suspected that she'd chosen it carefully because it showed off the curve of her hips and the firmness of her breasts. She had rouge on her cheeks and wore bright-red lipstick, and she had extended the line of her eyes in an upward slant in black. She wore a tikka, a plastic dot in the middle of her forehead.

'Look at her, Mummy. I'm not going with her, people will think I've come to auction her.'

Their mother came out of the kitchen.

'Your sister looks very pretty. Now don't start the fuss again, go along, or I swear I'll put on Manjula's clothes and make-up and come myself and shout all over the school that my son may be clever at adding up but he doesn't respect his poor illiterate mother.'

Bhupinder knew it was no good protesting. They mustn't be late for the occasion and someone had to go. He didn't want Mr Crawley including him in the list of boys whose families didn't care about them. That was the way he put it. 'We are proud of the families in our school,' he said, 'and we are sure they are interested in their children's welfare.'

'Tell her not to talk to any strangers,' Bhupinder said, making ready to go.

'Look, next time for my birthday you can buy me a spacesuit, then nobody will be able to see me and you can be proud of being a purdah-wallah family. Really, anyone would think I'm going naked to your wretched school.'

Just as Bhupinder feared, Manjit was there at the gate of the school, surrounded by three or four of his cronies. They stood leaning against the gate and guiding parents to the appropriate place in the school, the juniors to the year rooms and the seniors' parents to the hall.

'Good evening, Bhupinder,' Manjit said in a funny voice, as though he was teaching a parrot to speak. Bhupinder pretended he hadn't heard. He looked at Manju to make sure she was following his quickened pace, pointing out that they had to go round the building.

As they passed, one of Manjit's mates said in Hindi, 'That would do me for a mattress.' Bhupinder's ears turned red. Still he pretended he hadn't heard. He saw that Manju had, and that she was smiling to herself.

'If I had a mum like that it would drive me to sin, Einstein,' one of the others shouted after them, calling Bhupinder by the name they used for him in school.

'They are filthy bastards,' Bhupinder said to Manju in a hoarse voice, trying to prevent his throat from squeaking.

'Doesn't the tall one have a sister called Sheila?' Manju asked. She turned as a voice behind them said, 'Yes, but not as pretty as you.'

Manjit had followed them silently for a few metres.

'I know the way, thank you,' Bhupinder said.

'I'm being polite to your sister,' Manjit said.

'You can clear off, thanks,' Bhupinder said, not turning to look at Manjit.

'Ugly boys have pretty sisters,' Manjit said.

'I know Sheila, she's quite pretty,' Manju said, and she smiled at Manjit. Bhupinder felt like grabbing her by the arm but he restrained himself.

'Why have you been hiding your sister, Einstein?' Manjit said as they got to the door of the hall. Bhupinder waited till they had walked safely into the hall which was filling up with parents and teachers. 'You mind your own business,' was all he could think of shouting back at Manjit.

Now he felt that the eyes of the women were on Manju. They went around and talked to the various teachers. Bhupinder collected his prize, a book by Kipling, and as they walked out he saw that Manjit and his mates were now lounging around the back of the hall talking to the headmaster.

'So Einstein strikes again,' Manju said as they walked home. She wanted to make friends, she knew Bhupinder was nervous because of the possibility that the gang may follow them. Still, she couldn't help stealing a glance backwards to see if they were.

The next day in school, during the break, one of the Indian boys in the fifth came up to Bhupinder.

'Oi, Bhupinder, Manjit wants a word with you, you'd better come.'

'He can come here if he wants me, I'm not allowed in the sixth form area.'

All morning Bhupinder had been expecting some such approach and now he felt a claw of nervousness grip his guts.

'They're saying things behind your back,' the boy said.

'Tell Manjit to get himself stuffed,' Bhupinder said.

'I don't want to be held responsible for sending you to hospital,' the boy said.

'I don't care,' said Bhupinder thinking that he could never find the right reply, something smart to say, in time.

When school finished he wanted to bolt home, but he felt that the word that Manjit was looking for him had spread through the school, and he didn't want his form-mates to see him rushing.

Manjit and his gang were at the gate before him. Being sixth formers they could hop it before the bell. 'Make way for mastermind,' Manjit said. He held out a packet of cigarettes as Bhupinder passed. 'Have a fag,' he said.

'I don't smoke,' Bhupinder replied and tried to pass, but his way was gently blocked by one of the others. 'You shouldn't talk to your sister's lover like that,' someone said.

'No, look, we don't want anybody to get hurt, do we?' Manjit said. 'Come on, Bhupinder my brother, tell me your sister's name.'

'What business is it of yours?' Bhupinder said, looking straight ahead of him.

'Oh nothing much, I'm collecting new names for my budgie, it's called Bhupinder and it's just had a sex operation so I want a girl's name.'

Bhupinder felt his blood speeding to his temples. He turned around. There were no teachers about and some boys had gathered at a safe distance, smelling trouble.

'Give the password and we'll let you go,' said the boy blocking his path.

Bhupinder was sure that they knew her name already. Then it struck him that they wanted him to say it: 'Manju' … and 'Manjit' … perfect.

'It's Raquel, isn't it?'

'No, it doesn't begin with "R".'

'Or could it sound something like Manjit? Your father must have been good at reading horoscopes.'

'Get out of my way,' Bhupinder blurted, raising his arm on to the shoulder of the boy who stood before him. The boy smiled, confident that Bhupinder was half his size; the smell of aggression came off him.

Bhupinder was close to tears and knew it; the rest of them were making filthy comments now. 'You can drive an express train through a girl who has known so many men,' one said.

Bhupinder wheeled on him and his right hand struck out at the boy's face, obeying some command from deep within him, some demon that came flying out. And in the next instant, as his hand weakly connected with the boy's head, a cold shiver came over him. Manjit grabbed his wrist. At the same time he pushed the other boy away. The tears hung just behind Bhupinder's eyes now, and he blinked them away. He held his breath to prevent it from coming out in jerks and to stop himself trembling in confusion. There was what looked like a jungle of faces around him. Manjit's firm grip on his wrist steadied him.

'I'm not scared of you,' Bhupinder said and the boys laughed as the last word strained into a squeak.

'Go your way, my friend,' Manjit said, pushing the other lads aside and taking total control. Bhupinder walked forward out of the circle of hazy faces. He felt humiliated and the fear dug into his heart and liver as though it had carved a hole in his insides.

He grabbed his books tighter under his arm and he was thinking on the way home of the karate lessons he should have taken, of the gang he should have joined. They had made a fool of him and his own reaction to them scared him. He hadn't faced up, they would all know that he had backed down. He couldn't look after himself, leave aside being his sister's guardian. When his mind turned to her, he felt that his revenge was somehow tied up with her, tied up with revenge against her for putting him in this situation. If he had no sister, or at least if she didn't throw herself into the bitchy game of attracting their filthy attention, he would never have got into this.

As he lay in bed that night, a net of thoughts spread out and came together, swirling through his mind to form a plan of revenge. He couldn't reason with wild animals, he thought. The only way to deal with them was to shoot their leader. He had heard that somewhere, but where could he get a revolver? His thoughts ran away with him. He saw himself facing Manjit with a loaded gun pointed at the bastard's heart and saw the look of terror and repentance on his face as Bhupinder tore off his mask and revealed himself to be the man Manjit had wronged, the man whose sister had had her honour stained. But Bhupinder would show no mercy, he'd work his awful revenge and he'd walk around the city after that with a magic circle of dread around him. He would be marked as a dangerous man, and good at maths. And then the boys in the Nishat Café, leaderless, would elect him and beg him to take charge of them.

Or maybe it wouldn't work out so smoothly. Maybe the police would get him and he'd sit in death row for weeks while his appeal to the prime minister was being heard and he'd walk, followed by his mother and Manju, to the electric chair, and she would swear never to dress like a cheap tart again.

In the morning he said nothing to Manju or to his mother. He went to school knowing that if it came to a fight, he would have to take the challenge and accept a beating. He'd point out to all those who came to watch that he was smaller than Manjit, but he wasn't afraid of him. In the corridors he saw one or two of the boys who had been at the gate with Manjit, but they passed him as if nothing had happened, as though they weren't aware of his existence.

In a sense that was reassuring, maybe they'd forgotten the whole thing. Still, some emptiness remained in Bhupinder. He knew that words would have to pass before he could get rid of the ticklish fear in his spine. His pride had taken a knocking, it had been forced so low, pushed down his throat and curled up somewhere, restlessly inside him.

Two days passed without incident. On the third, as Bhupinder was settling down to a game of chess in the lunch hour in his form room, Manjit walked in. This was unusual as the sixth formers stuck to their own part of the building and were never seen on the fourth-year floor.

'Bhupinder,' Manjit said, with what seemed to Bhupinder to be a note of regret and even respect in his voice. Bhupinder looked up from his game, blinking as though a bright light had been suddenly switched on. For an instant he thought that Manjit had come to ask his forgiveness, because somehow he knew of the mountain of venom that had piled up inside Bhupinder and in his dreams he had seen this mountain explode like a volcano and come down in dreadful lava on his head.

'Just come outside one minute, man, I want to talk to you.'

Automatically Bhupinder got up from the desk and followed Manjit to the door. As they walked out he felt the eyes of the boys on them. Manjit led him to a quiet spot in the playground.

'Listen,' Manjit said, taking the forbidden cigarette out of his pocket and lighting it, 'you have to do something for me.' His eyes were searching for feeling in Bhupinder's face. They were also telling Bhupinder that he was sorry for what had happened the other day but it wasn't his fault and he wanted the younger boy to forget it, man to man.

'I've got only fifteen pence,' said Bhupinder.

'Look, I don't want to borrow money,' Manjit said with a hurt expression. Then, making a resolve to himself to continue, he said, 'Your mother is very strict, isn't she?'

Bhupinder looked at him with amazement. 'What if she is? My father's even stricter, and he works in the foundry and he's nearly two metres tall,' Bhupinder said. He didn't know if Manjit knew he was lying.

'Look, forget it, just give this to your sister, will you?' Manjit said, pulling a pink envelope out of his pocket. His eyes were pleading.

Bhupinder didn't take the envelope.

'Look, she knows, I swear by God I'm not mucking about. Take it.'

'What does she know?' Bhupinder wondered and his curiosity fought with the sense of shame that was coming over him. He took the envelope.

'If she sends a reply, you bring it to me,' Manjit said and Bhupinder looked up from the neat handwriting on the envelope into the anxiety in the hard eyes. Surely she hadn't any dealings with this son of a bitch, he thought; she has more sense.

'You never come to the Nishat, do you?' Manjit was saying.

'I have a lot of work to do. My father doesn't like me going around with loafers.'

Manjit ignored the remark. 'You could come to my house any time. I always take my friends there to eat and we go to all the movies free, I know all the cinemawallahs. Have you seen *Pakeezah*? It's coming next week.' Manjit's tongue gave a quick lick to his lips. Bhupinder could see that he was trying to chat him up, and he felt a sort of transference of power. The king of beasts was wondering what he could say to be friendly.

Bhupinder put the pink envelope in his pocket. 'All right,' he said, 'I'll think about it.'

He no longer felt nervous. He was thinking about Manju and wondering if this fellow had really made any contact with her. He could tell his mother, he could tell his uncles when they came on Saturday and Manju would almost definitely be sent back to Jalandhar, away from England, and she'd learn to behave like a decent Indian girl. 'I've got to go and take the register up for my form teacher,' he said and as he turned and walked back Manjit walked behind him as though to offer him his protection. For the first time, for those hundred paces back to the fourth-year floor, Bhupinder felt the eyes of the school on him with respect and wonder. It was not the sort of respect that winners of maths prizes get, it was more the sort that counts, that you can trade on. And yet there was something not quite right about it, Bhupinder felt, something that whispered to his mind with every step that he was trading a bit of his self-respect for his feeling of belonging to the gang, this feeling that Manjit was following him like a puppy and that other boys in school would think twice before they said anything to a member of Manjit's mob.

When he got home, Manju was already there. She seemed to be waiting for him. Her face was expectant. 'What did you do in school?' she asked, her eyes darting all over him.

'Maths, English, drama, physics and GS,' he said. 'Do you know what the central problem of the Third World is?'

'Listen Pinder, I can only go out today if you tell Mummy you're coming with me. I'll give you sixty pence for the films if you want.'

'Keep your bloody money,' Bhupinder said. 'Besides, I want to watch *Star Trek*.'

He walked out of the room and went into his bedroom. Taking the pink envelope out of his pocket, he pushed a chair against the door and sat on it and opened the letter. It was a pink sheet of paper with a flower motif and it said in the corner in print: 'Khalsa Transport Co. "In God We Do Have Trust",' and then an address and phone number. The letter said:

My Respected Manjula,
You must forgive my writing this letter. I am asking your good brother Bhupinder to deliver the same. It is very good of you to say that we can meet each other far from other people's jealous eyes. I must tell you you are very beautiful, better than all film actresses, and you must not believe all things that people in this East End are saying about me, especially Punjabi people, because they are full

of jealousy for good fortune. But I am not writing for bad purposes. You are more educated than me, but my father has a big truck company and your uncleji and your mataji all know my father and know he is a respectful person. I will ask your brother to make my introduction to your family and then we can stop meeting secretly. Still for just now I have to see and talk with you so please say when you are vacant and I will let you know through a letter via Bhupinder where to meet. This is just a quick note to let you know I am thinking of you always.

    Yours
    Manjit Singh

Bhupinder stared at the piece of paper. So she has seen him, he thought. He went to the kitchen and fetched a box of matches and, locking himself in the lavatory, he burnt the letter and the envelope and flushed it away.

For an hour he sat on his bed wondering what he should do. He could tell his mother that Manju was deceiving them, or he could confront her straight. He hit upon another plan. Manjit must be taught a lesson. The letter was obviously serious. He must do something. He went to the drawer and pulled out a sheet of paper. Then in his best hand he wrote:

Dear Manjit,
Meet me tomorrow in the corner of the school grounds at seven-thirty – your school, the place where there is a hole in the wall by the side.
    Manju

He put the note in an envelope and put it into his school bag. As he thought of the details of the plan, his hands began to sweat. He must kill Manjit or at least wound him seriously. He would lay an ambush for him, and yet he didn't know how it could be done. At least this way, Manjit would be alone and he had a chance. I'll have the element of surprise on my side, he thought, remembering the words their history teacher had used when talking about the British landings on the French coast. He'd have to go armed, he thought, and the idea gave him a weak shudder. He knew nothing about knives. Maybe a stick, a cricket bat or something on Manjit's head.

As he turned the problem over in his mind, Manju came into the room. 'Will you come with me?' she said, 'I just want to go down to Brick Lane and get some jelabees for after dinner.'

'I suppose you want to go into one of those filthy restaurants?' Bhupinder snarled.

'What's the matter with you Pindy, it'll only take fifteen minutes, and you like jelabees don't you?'

'I can't just now, I've got to write my letters and solve an important problem.'

'Don't talk rubbish, there's no one you can write letters to, or have you found yourself a little girlie?'

'Don't bother me, I've got business to do with some characters you don't know of.'

'You watch too much telly, I must tell Mummy to get you to bed before the gangster serials.' Manju could see that he wasn't going to help her.

'You can go by your bloody self, and don't think I don't know about your jelabees.'

'Mummy says you have to come with me.'

'You can fool Mummy, but you can't fool me,'

Bhupinder replied. He sat at the table and pretended to be getting on with some work. He could hear Manju complaining that he wouldn't go with her and pleading to be allowed to go alone.

'Pinder, go with your sister,' his mother shouted.

'I'm not going anywhere with her,' Bhupinder shouted back. 'She disgraced me the other day in school, so she can paint up and stare in the mirror.'

He could hear his mother telling Manju that if she really wanted sweets so badly she'd make some herself, she had everything in the house. Bhupinder listened. He felt like letting Manju know that he knew she was deceiving their mother and that it wasn't sweets she was after, but it would only lead to a lot of crying and fuss. He would have to handle this thing a man's way. The burden was not his mother's to bear, it was his and it was heavy.

The letter lay like a little time bomb in his bag. The next day at school, he felt he ought to tear it up and throw it away and forget the whole business. How to deliver the letter?

The problem was solved for him by Manjit who appeared at the door of his form at lunchtime. Bhupinder was putting away his stuff in his desk.

'You've had Bentley for geography?' Manjit said. 'He couldn't teach me a thing, poor fellow tried very hard.'

Bhupinder didn't feel like making school conversation. He took the envelope out of his bag and held it out to Manjit. Manjit grabbed hold of it and said, 'Hey thanks, I'll talk to you after lunch.' Then he was gone.

Now the whole thing had been put in motion. After school, Bhupinder went to examine the appointed spot.

He hadn't exactly challenged Manjit to a duel, but he felt something of the excitement of having put out a challenge. There were boys playing penny-up against the broken wall in the corner of the playground and Bhupinder thought it would look suspicious if he prowled around looking for a good place to hide and spring an ambush. He would come early and mark out the territory. There'd be nobody about and he could leap out from the shadows and deliver a few blows before Manjit even realized what was going on.

He went through the breach in the wall. The streets around this side of the school were derelict and boarded up, waiting for demolition. At seven-thirty they would certainly be empty.

He decided that he'd take a stick and tie a metal spike to it. It wasn't like carrying a knife, you couldn't kill a man with a stick, but you could make him beg for mercy. The problem was of course that he couldn't make his preparation or build his lethal weapon at home.

He skulked about his bedroom for a couple of hours. At six he changed into a sweater and his heaviest pair of boots and told his mother that he was going down to Inder's to fetch a textbook.

He sped out of the house and made his way by the back streets to the deserted block. There was a lot of garbage about. He could certainly pick up a stick and string and anything else he wanted here. Even if he didn't win against Manjit, he thought, the other would have to respect his guts and that would make him leave Manju alone. It must have been near seven when he finally found a light metal pipe and decided it would be sufficient. He didn't want to cut the enemy too badly. He approached the breach in the wall and looked about. As he had anticipated, there was no one, not a stray cat about. Somewhere in the evening sky he could hear voices, the beat of a reggae record thumping through the thickening air. Just opposite the school wall were the empty houses, gutted and bare as skeletons. He could go in there.

Bhupinder walked into one of them and took up what he thought was a good position. He could see the breach in the wall and he couldn't be seen. He'd dash out and do his dirty work as Manjit stood around, or sat down on the spilt bricks. His boots crunched against the broken plaster and brick in the house. It was getting dark and he tried to ease himself into a position of complete silence. He could hear his own breath. Half an hour passed and no one came, no footsteps, no sound. He felt his body tightening as it did when he was about to jump into the cold water of a swimming pool. Inside the warm huddle of the sweater he was cold. And still no one came. It must be past seven-thirty now, Bhupinder thought. Maybe Manjit wasn't coming, maybe he'd seen through the challenge and wasn't man enough to accept it.

Just as he was thinking this, Bhupinder heard the rumble of a car engine and saw the lights of the car picking out a path in the deserted street. The car slowed down and stopped on the opposite side a few metres from where Bhupinder was hidden.

He's come in a car, Bhupinder thought. Why hadn't he thought of that? What should he do now? He waited to see if Manjit would get out of the car. He couldn't see into it from where he was and it was getting dark fast. He waited. The car door didn't open. Ten minutes passed and they seemed like an eternity to Bhupinder. He must do something. He put his head round the open doorway. The car's lights were switched off and he was sure the person in the car couldn't see him. He walked towards it. He'd call out for Manjit to climb out of his armour plating and face him like a man.

'Manjit,' he said, stepping forward, 'come out. It's me.'

Bhupinder stood in the middle of the road, his heart beating uncontrollably. Nothing happened. He walked closer to the car and bent down to the window to look in. On the front seat were two people, clutching each other, sprawling under the level of the windshield, the man on top of the woman. Bhupinder turned, not knowing what to do. It was an awful mistake.

The window of the car came down. 'Oi, you, mate, what the hell do you want?' a voice said, and the man's head poked out of the window.

'Not you,' Bhupinder said. 'I thought …'

'Well don't think, mate. Does a man have to go to the North Pole to get a little privacy?'

Bhupinder turned and walked away. Then he began to run. Just as he got to the corner of the derelict street, where it joined the main road, another car pulled into the street. He thought he saw Manjit at the wheel, but it was no use turning round now. As he made his way home he felt, well, if Manjit really wanted to take up his challenge he would have been there on time.

In a way he was disappointed. He had never been in a hand-to-hand fight before, at least not a serious one. He could remember when a boy in his primary school had set upon him and banged his head on the paving stones four times after sitting on him. That was a memory of having lost, and he had now lost the chance to have won. He would have proved himself, he was sure, and yet it was terrible. What would the man in the car think? That he had been prowling around trying to get a peep at lovers? It brought a blush to his cheeks.

He looked back, half expecting to see Manjit following him. He didn't want that. This way, at least he could feel that his challenge had been refused, or that Manjit had seriously thought that Manju was offering to meet him and had turned her down. Either way the problem was solved. Walking home, he remembered he'd told his mother that he was going to Inder's for a textbook. He hurriedly stopped over at Inder's place and picked up a book.

'You look like you've seen a ghost,' Inder said.

'No, my mother will be a bit worried. If it's after eight she thinks the world has closed shop.'

He walked now with his head high and his step light. The burden had gone, he had somehow proved to himself that, even if he was terrified of disturbing the lovers in the car, he hadn't been scared of Manjit. Perhaps men only fight to prove to themselves they aren't afraid, to unload their dread, he thought.

He opened the door and as he entered his mother said, 'Where's Manju?'

'How should I know?'

'I sent her after you to Inder's. I thought you'd got into some talk with him, and you haven't even eaten this evening.'

'What time did you send her?' Bhupinder asked. 'About seven. You went out and said you'd be getting a book.'

'She'll be back,' Bhupinder said. 'You shouldn't have sent her after me, I can look after myself.'

'What could have happened to her? Are you sure you went to Inder's?'

Bhupinder looked at the clock on the mantelpiece. It was nearly eight-thirty.

'Look Mum,' he said in Punjabi. 'We're both grown up now. How old do you imagine we are? We don't have to go chasing around after each other. She can go where she damn well likes, I'm not running around town looking for her. She's a big girl now, you shouldn't worry about her. This house needs some new rules.' And then, seeing the pained expression on his mother's face, he added, 'Maybe she's gone round to her friend's after. She's seventeen, you know. Does a girl have to go to the North Pole to get some privacy?'

❧

2.

Pushy's Pimples

SAMIR AND PUSHPA SOMETIMES CALLED their father 'Daddy', and they sometimes called him 'Pitaji' according to Indian custom. It depended on his mood. If he was angry, or lecturing them about how Indian girls and Indian boys should behave or not behave, how they could so easily spoil his good name in the town, then they said 'Yes, Pitaji', 'No, Pitaji'. But if he came home from the shop with presents for them, or when he announced that the family were all going to the Hindi films on Sunday, or to their uncle's place in Southall, or if he was just plain nice and didn't insist on switching off the late night movie and ordering them up to bed, then they called him 'Daddy'.

They knew he preferred the English word, especially in front of white customers in the shop. His face would compose itself in pride when he was called 'Daddy'; especially if it was Pushpa. He would ask her to get the extra bottle of milk from the fridge in the back for a late and regular customer and his eyes would shine with pride when she replied in her London accent.

Pushpa was still the baby of the family and got most of their dad's attention. Samir, now that he was in college and Pushpa was still in school, was out and about with his mates, and he didn't care. Girls need that extra bit of care, especially Indian girls, he thought.

When Daddy passed his driving test there was general rejoicing at home. He would at last be able to drive them all to Leicester to his brother's place; and they could see their cousins over the weekend. He'd been promising the trip since he bought the van and began driving lessons with the Recommended School of Motoring. Samir was happy about that. He always said to Pushpa that their dad was tight and he was only taking them up by car because he wanted to save on the rail fares.

Pushpa, whom her friends at school called Pushy, should have been just as delighted. She had been looking forward to seeing Reena and Geeta, her twin cousins who were the same age as she was. She'd spent her childhood with them in the big house in Baroda, in India before they all came over to England. She loved being with the twins. They were the only ones in the family who understood all the things that were on her mind. Better than her English friends, and better than all the other Indian girls she knew. They met regularly at half-term and in the holidays, when they came down to London and Pushy showed them around. This time it was to be different. Their uncle, the twins' father, had written to say that since they'd be doing their CSEs that summer and had extra classes in the holidays, they had better stay in Leicester, and that they wouldn't come down to London. There was an important reason why Pushy didn't want to go with the family this particular weekend. She now had to make an excuse. She waited till she got her dad alone in the front room.

'Daddy, I can't go.'

'Everybody's going,' he said, lifting his eyes from the Gujerati newspaper he always settled into after work. 'But I can't, Miss Burntwood has got my ticket and we're going to *A Midsummer Night's Dream.* I can't miss it.'

'Too many dreams,' he said.

'It's not a cream, silly,' Pushy said. 'It's a play by Shakespeare and it's on our syllabus and we have to go.'

Pushy was pleading. She was amazed at the ease with which she told him this lie. She hadn't exactly planned the story, but once she got going it came to her. He can't find out, he'll never find out, she was thinking, and when the real reason for her wanting to stay blotted out the lie in her mind, a stony lump of spit gathered in her mouth. When you tell a lie you have to swallow a lump to clean your mouth out. Her hands began to sweat. This was the first step.

'I'll ask your mother if you can be left alone for two days. It's too long by yourself. How can I face my brother and say I've left Pushpa all alone in the house?'

'I won't be by myself, Daddy. I'll be with Miss Burntwood on Friday and then I'll go down to Chacha's on Saturday by train.' She looked at his face and knew that it was working. 'It's on my O-level syllabus. All the kids in the class are going.'

Mr Patel shouted across to his wife in the kitchen. Pushpa wasn't going with them. There was no comment from the kitchen. Pushpa knew that it wasn't the sort of argument that her mother would get into.

Pushpa's heart began to beat faster and she ran up to her room. It was at the back of the house on the first floor. If her mother saw her face, she thought, she'd know that something was on Pushpa's mind. She was sharp; you couldn't lie to her.

Pushy went up to the mirror on her dressing table. She stuck her tongue into her cheek to push the skin out. She looked at the pimples on her face. They made a heavy pink rash from under her eyes to the bottom of her jawbone, on both sides. Like a volcano, she thought, exploding like a volcano. She was beyond crying about it. For the last year she'd fought a battle with these pimples, this stain on her otherwise beautiful face. She saw that the door was shut and pulled the tube of Skintex out from under her mattress and gently rubbed smears of cream on to the ugly spots. She hated them, they weren't part of her body, they were an invasion. At last she'd have the chance to wipe them out.

All-out attack, she repeated in a whisper. She'd heard a man on the telly say it. Pushy knew, the Skintex was no good. Some mornings she woke up having dreamt that the curse had gone, but she would look in the mirror and see that it was redder and more bloody-looking than ever. She'd tried everything, and still the spots seemed to multiply. It was like those science fiction movies in which some fungus or plant or vine or something begins to creep all over the face of the earth and no power can stop it. She'd bombarded her face with lotions from every chemist she knew of. She'd written, without letting her dad know, and under a false name, to the beauty parlours and the women's magazines. Nothing. It would bring tears to her eyes. If she had just one wish, like the girls in the fairy stories did, that would be it. To lose this blight. She longed to have the smooth silky skin of the girls in the magazines, the girls in the street, the girls at school, the girls on telly, that girls anywhere and everywhere seemed to have. Except her. Maybe there was some truth to her mother's belief that sins in your past life have to be punished in your present life. She wanted to cast off this skin, if necessary to cast off her body, like a snake or a spirit, and coil into something else.

Everyone noticed. One girl in school had said that Indians bring disease into the country, and even though Pushy knew it was just something in the class discussion, she wanted to bury her face in the desk. For the white girls, having spots and pimples meant something else. They never made fun of her directly, but they had a joke about pimples. Denise had said something that gave her a hint about it. It was awful to think of, and yet she'd been thinking about it. A hundred times since.

She asked Michelle, her best friend in school, to explain what it was they were giggling about. When she was alone with Michelle she could ask her anything, about bras and underwear and the things she didn't dare ask her mother. When they were with their other classmates, Pushy knew that Michelle wanted her to pretend to know as much as anyone else. Michelle didn't want them to know, she felt, that it was she who told Pushy about boys and sex and private girl things, what she called 'the facts of life'. When they were alone, Michelle wasn't shy about these things, even though Pushy blushed when she used certain words.

'Don't be so damn silly,' Michelle would say. 'You have to know, haven't you? You can't remain innocent all your life, can you?'

It was true, Pushy thought, and thanked God for Michelle and her concern to steer her out of innocence. Still, about this latest thing, Pushy wasn't sure. It frightened her and she preferred not to think about it. She wasn't sure that she'd even understood Michelle correctly.

'It's in your blood,' Michelle said, 'hormones and that. They get to boiling and then you've got to let the heat out. Once your blood gets the heat out, you'll be all right. Married women don't get pimples, see?'

Pushy tried to test this theory on the street, but she had no way of knowing who was married and who wasn't. She looked from their ring fingers to their faces. She thought of all the teachers who weren't married and she pointed out to Michelle that none of them had acne. 'Them teachers,' Michelle said, 'the amount of heat they let out they ought to have cold sores instead.' Pushy dropped the subject but she wanted to know if Michelle was serious. When they were walking in the park at break she brought it round to pimples again.

'You should try it,' Michelle said. 'After all if you've used Tampax, you know the job's already done so I don't know what all the fuss is about. Look at me, I don't have any pimples. I reckon most of the girls in our year have had it, at least once. Except Annette and she's a weed.'

Pushy thought of Annette. She was a plump girl in their form and she was the only white girl who had a faint trace of spots on her face. She and Annette, they were marked, she thought. Everyone knew.

Pushy knew that Michelle had done all sorts of things. She always told Pushy about what her boyfriend and she had done the previous evening, and how he'd wanted it and how she hadn't been in the mood.

'You should stand up to your dad. After all, it isn't India, and the old man had better change his little ways.'

Pushy didn't want to tell Michelle that it wasn't her dad. Boys never asked her out. There was a magic circle of Indianness around her which stopped a boy from getting close. There were the boys at the Asia Club, but they were Indian boys and knew that drinking coke at the bar and sitting together at concerts was as far as they could go. Sometimes they took some of the girls for a spin in their cars, but they never asked her. Pimples again. She didn't blame them.

Then Michelle had made her an offer. She said that if one day Pushy could get away, Ron's friend Steve would like to take her out.

'You wouldn't mind trying it with him, would you, he's ever so nice. And he's Ron's best mate.'

Pushy didn't know what 'trying it' meant, but she suspected that Michelle just meant going out with him, maybe, hold hands, maybe allow him to kiss her. Ron was Michelle's boyfriend and he'd brought Steve to the fifth-year dance. They, Ron and Steve, worked together, and since they didn't know the other kids in school, they had formed a foursome under Michelle's management. Pushy told Steve she didn't know how to dance, and he said he didn't care, it was just an excuse to grab hold of girls anyway.

Of course Pushy was flattered that Steve wanted to see her again. He had asked Michelle about the 'Paki girl'. Michelle said it in a matter-of-fact way and added, 'He's not prejudiced or nothing, just a bit flash and carries on like that, but he really fancies you.'

When Pushy told Michelle that the house was going to be empty that weekend, she hoped that Michelle remembered about Steve. She didn't want to ask outright. 'Can't face Leicester and all that Indian family scene,' she said. Michelle understood all right.

'Right,' she said, 'what the stars foretell. We'll go out in Ron's car and end up at your place. Don't be scared, it'll be all right. All you have to do is relax and let him talk and I'll take care of everything else.'

Pushy knew what Michelle meant by 'everything else'. She got a sinking feeling in her stomach. Babies, she thought. If you have it you can get pregnant, but Michelle obviously knew how to avoid that.

Pushy didn't give Michelle a definite answer, but she knew that Michelle would now plan the whole thing. She looked in the mirror when she got home from school on

Thursday. Mirror, mirror on the wall … Pushing back her long hair, she thought, yes, I've got nice eyes, and delicate small ears and my skin is soft brown and … her fingers touched her cheeks. Tomorrow, she thought.

'Pushpa,' her dad called.

'I'm doing my homework, Daddy.'

'We are motoring tomorrow so we are sleeping early,' he shouted.

'Blimey,' she heard Samir saying, 'you'd think we were going round the world in eighty days, the way you carry on.'

Pushy sat late into the night after the house was dark and everyone else had gone to bed. Her family must never find out, she thought over and over again. And then her mind turned to Steve. But she didn't think of him as he was, she thought of him as a sort of ghost, but not white in colour, brushing against her body and his hand on her cheek. What Michelle said must be true, it had to be true. If she did this one thing, just once, she might get rid of the pimples forever. It was as if her prayers had been answered, but not by God she thought, by the Devil. It didn't matter; she was determined to do it. She'd shut her eyes. Would it be worth it? What had she to lose? What if she found she liked it? Could you become addicted to sex like an animal, or like people get addicted to cigarettes, and then not be able to live without it? If Daddy found out he'd kill her, he couldn't stand that, it would be the end.

On Friday morning she left for school, thinking that she'd tell Michelle it was all off. The morning passed. Pushy kept looking at Michelle all through the English lesson. In the lunch break she went up to her.

'Michelle, about this evening, I don't want to do it.'

'You're a baby. You don't have to do anything you don't want. I'll be there to tell him off if he gets out of control.'

How could he get out of control, Pushy asked herself, would he tear her clothes off, and his face get fixed in a cruel mask? No, she couldn't do it.

'C'mon, it'll be a nice evening, he may never ask you again, you know.'

When the bell rang at the end of the afternoon and Michelle and Pushy walked as usual to the corner together, Michelle touched her on the cheek with one finger and said, 'The Secrets of Sex from Mademoiselle Michelle. Look, it'll be all right, we'll just have a spin in the car.'

There was no one at home when Pushy got back. Dad had said they'd make an early start to avoid driving in the dark. Pushy felt cold in the house. She put on the front-room fire and she went through all the rooms checking to see if they were tidy. She went to the corner of the street and bought a few cans of coke and some beer. She had to go through with it now, if only to show Michelle that she wasn't as babyish as Michelle imagined. She wouldn't allow them to stay all night. That way she wouldn't be actually sleeping with a man. She may allow him to touch her or kiss her or something in the front room, but she wouldn't even let him know where her bedroom was. Michelle could go up there with Ron if she liked. If only she could have the same attitude as Michelle had to men. Life would be so much easier. But that would mean her father would have to have different attitudes, and Samir, and her mother, and that was impossible.

It wasn't that she was innocent, she knew everything. Miss Burntwood had talked about it in class, in front of the boys. She'd even said dirty words, the one with 'f' and the one beginning with 'c', and she said they were perfectly good words because D. H. Lawrence used them, only you had to know when and where to use them. The girls had laughed. They listened carefully to her. There was not a whisper in class and some of them said afterwards that she was a frustrated old cow, she must have had it once in her lifetime and was celebrating the anniversary of the event by talking filth in class. Pushy liked Miss Burntwood and thought that the girls were just jealous of her. After all, she was being frank and teaching them what she was paid to teach. Still, it was no good Miss B saying that it didn't matter if a girl was not a virgin, that many girls lost their virginity through physical exercise and horse riding and sometimes naturally during periods. Everyone knew men didn't have respect for girls who were too easy. If an Indian boy ever found out about a girl not being a virgin, he wouldn't marry her. Yet there was no sure way of knowing, a man could never be certain, and mature people should always be honest about their experiences. I'll never be honest about this, Pushy thought, I'll never tell the man I marry. I'll do it once and try and forget it. Time dulls the memory, she had heard, also that time cures all wounds, except her stupid pimples. If she carried them around, nobody would marry her anyway. By some miracle this boy Steve fancied her. Maybe she would eventually marry an Englishman, maybe even him. He and Ron were partners in a moving business, they drove a truck and were making their way, Michelle said.

If it didn't work out and he just wanted her for her body, she would have a bath after and forget him. She'd drink some beer and then she could say that she didn't know what he'd done to her and it wouldn't be her fault. She'd pretend she didn't remember a thing.

As she dressed she looked at herself in the mirror, naked, whole. She'd let the man who married her have a good look. Steve wasn't to be given the impression that she was what the English girls called a 'slag'. If she let him, only if, then she'd let her skirt down just a little and shut her eyes and he could do the rest. As she climbed into her only non-uniform skirt, she practised loosening the buttons and her heart thumped like a drum.

Ron and Steve were already at Michelle's place when she got there. They suggested they go to a pub, and when they got there they left the girls with Babychams and went off to play darts. Steve had been very attentive to her in the car. He was tall and had short blond hair and he showed her where he'd had his ear pierced to put on an earring.

'Long John Silver with a brass,' Ron said, but Pushy didn't get the joke and Michelle coiled up to him as he was driving and tittered. He didn't touch her, even though Ron and Michelle were kissing each other as though they each needed artificial respiration every time they'd stop at the lights and when they climbed in and out of the car.

'He says he really wants to,' Michelle said to Pushy when the boys were out of earshot. Even hearing that made Pushy's stomach go funny. Michelle was dressed as usual for the evening with a tight, low-cut T-shirt and jeans. 'We can go round to Pushy's place,' she said, as though the boys didn't know. 'There's no one there, her family are away.'

'I'm a removal man,' Steve said when they got talking.

'Girls' knickers mainly,' Ron said. But Steve didn't even laugh. He kept his distance and made funny remarks of his own. He was very clever, Pushy thought, and wondered if he really fancied her or whether Michelle had just told her that so she and Ron could have a place for the night. She was surprised at herself when she found herself wishing with all her heart that he would touch her, just to show that he did fancy her, that she was not repulsive to him, that he could look past her pimples with his gorgeous green eyes.

Steve was talking to her about the Indian films he'd seen. He said he went because he used to have a school friend from the East End called Pat, and did she know him? But he found the people in the films beautiful. Then he turned to talking about how he'd been with this friend Pat to curry places and Pat had made him eat something which burnt the tongue out of his head and made his body feel like it was on fire. Indians must be very hot-blooded, he said, and Pushy wondered if Michelle had told him anything at all about her problem.

'I never eat curries,' Pushy said. 'That's only in restaurants.'

'I told Pat it was a black power plot to kill whitey,' Steve said. Pushy's mood was slowly changing from being worried to being amused and very interested in how his mind worked and how he acted out with his hands the stories he told himself.

Michelle directed Ron to Pushy's house. It was almost twelve by the time they'd finished driving around and Pushy was relieved, because it would mean the neighbours would be asleep. She was thinking that she felt a bit drunk anyway and she wouldn't have to pretend so hard. I'm going to let him, she thought. And then it struck her that he may not want to. As the car stopped, she felt herself breaking into a sweat. This was it. They were out of the car. Her feet seemed to move automatically. She felt Steve's hand next to hers and his fingers, without warning, reached for hers. She pulled her hand away.

'Not here, the neighbours,' she said, and he smiled and nodded vigorously. Pushy walked up to the house, wanting to seem casual. She'd put the reading lamp on the floor so anyone passing wouldn't see the front room lit.

Gaskarth Road was deserted. She must be silent in case the snooping neighbours … walls have ears.

The blood was pounding in her temples. Once they were inside, everything would work like in a play. If I don't do it now, I'll never do it, I have to, I have to, she kept thinking and a knot gathered in her tummy. She pulled the key out of her handbag and put it in the lock. Just as she did that a light went on behind the curtain in the upstairs room. She heard footsteps inside the house. Michelle and Ron saw it too.

Pushy's heart sank.

'Someone's doing your place,' Ron said.

The front door opened before Pushy could push it and Mr Patel's figure, in the act of reaching for the hallway light stood framed in the door. He took in the scene at a glance.

'It's twelve o'clock,' was all he said.

Pushy's mind raced and the words came without her thinking.

'Michelle and Miss Burntwood's brother brought me home from her place,' she said.

Pushy didn't know if Ron and Steve would understand.

'Thanks, Michelle, thank you, Mr Burntwood,' she said, turning to them, telegrams of panic in her eyes, her face trying to keep cool. Michelle nudged Ron who was the only one whose puzzlement showed in his face.

'Not at all, Pushpa, and now I'd better see the other young lady home,' Steve said, and Pushy noticed that he'd changed his accent and put on his best posh voice. Her eyes said thank you, but Steve was smiling at Mr Patel. 'Very nice meeting you, Pushpa. Goodnight, Mr Patel,' he said.

Pushy watched the performance as if she were watching something on television. Her father was uncertain, but he muttered a goodnight.

Samir came downstairs in his pyjamas as they shut the door behind them. 'You should have seen it,' he said. 'Dad was dead scared of the motorway. He stopped three lanes of traffic single-handed.' Mr Patel grunted and went upstairs. 'How was the play?' Samir asked.

'I liked it,' Pushy said.

'We're going by train tomorrow. The old man won't save on the fares anyway, he's decided to keep off the motorway. It was really funny, he went five kilometres up and came right back. You can come, can't you?'

'I'd like to see Reena and Geeta,' Pushy said, 'but old Burntwood is having us round to discuss the play tomorrow and I haven't decided whether to go or not.'

~

3.

East End at Your Feet

A TALE OF TWO CITIES, that's what I'd call it if the blinking title hadn't been bagged by somebody else. I remember the story, and Miss Mullins's voice reading and the girls listening as though they were in love with every rascal whose head was chopped. I remember the part about the guillotine, and catching the head in a bucket. She told us that the fellow who invented that got the chop himself. Must have felt weird, like getting your hand caught in the mouse trap that you're putting cheese in for the little devils. No, not quite like that, more like the other story she told us about a fellow who invented a maze and put a monster in the centre of it, and then got trapped in it himself and couldn't find the way out. I feel like that, only I didn't invent the damn maze, only my own thoughts. I invent those all the time and get lost in them.

Charles Dickens wrote the first story of that name, about Paris and London, but my story can't be about Paris because I never got further than Boulogne on a school trip. I remember that trip, drinking one whisky after another in the bar on the boat and all the lads running about the streets and playing silly boys with the mademoiselles we met. 'How about a bit of the *autre,*' and all that crap. And then one of them says to me: 'Go on Cashy, show them the rope trick, pull it out and make it stand up by whistling "God Save the Prime Minister" in Indian.' I never took no notice. I used to think them things myself, but I never said them.

My story's got to be about Bombay and London. Not that I know much about Bombay, I haven't even started school here yet. My uncle says I'm the head of the household, but I feel like its arse, everyone sitting on me and kicking me around. Not my mum and Sheila and Shobha, my sisters. They just mope around and my mum cries, God she can cry, she's a champion at it. Every day there's priests in the house. They turn up regular as the milkman, and start muttering their nonsense, and then Mum cries even more. She starts howling and my aunts come and say 'There, there' and bull like that.

I can't take it. Not that I'm not sad or hard-hearted or anything, but I prefer to be with myself, and I sit on the balcony and watch the seagull and the cars crawling along the sea road. Sometimes there are sails out on the water, fishermen, the same blokes who pull their nets up on the beach and dry out kilometre on kilometre of the stinking Bombay Ducks. If the breeze is this way, the pong comes in and you have to shut the doors and go in.

It's Saturday, I checked it on the calendar in Grandad's room. Nobody knows what day of the week it is here. If you have something to do, then you count the days to the weekend, because you always want them to hurry up, or to slow down. Days are like money, my dad used to say. They are like loose change now that I've got nothing to do but spend them.

The lads are in the park now. We put down our jackets as goalposts and the teams divide automatically. Same teams from day to day and week to week. I'm the best goalkeeper in Hackney, I reckon. Juniors, I'm talking about, I'm not that big-headed to think I'm professional standard. Not yet. Maybe never now. But I play in the first eleven for the school. I never let one past the day we played Dalston Grammar, even though they said it was a hard team and they'd score off us as easy as giving candy to a baby. (I like to say it that way, because babies are getting tough nowadays and you can't *take* stuff off them as easy as you could.) This big black bloke was playing centre forward for them and he charged the ball right up. He was hanging around and wouldn't take a shot, wanted to bring it in safe. If I was ref, I'd have given him offside at least three times, but them old geezers are blind, at least blind to what grammar school teams do on the field. I fell on the ball at his feet. I took a dive, like I was going off the deep end. He kicked me in the mouth but I'd got the ball. I showed my lip, cut and bleeding, to Mr Knights, our coach, at half-time but he said it was too late to do anything about it.

'Kashyap, boy, we've got to win this game, we want goals not hospital cards.'

'All right,' I said, 'all right.' I stopped him two more tries in the second half. He thought he could elbow it past me if he tempted me out of the goalposts. He tried to get his shoulder down and into my chest, but I jumped on the ball. I didn't care if he tossed me around like a bull with a rag stuck on its horns. The kids from our school went wild. They rushed on the pitch. 'These bastards want to play rugby,' Rob said to me. He was our fullback.

Mr Knights tells me he's going to send me for the West Ham trials. I can see myself in light blue and claret, those are our colours, and all the girls sending me messages through my mates. Sharon wants to go out with you, and are you corning to the fourth-year dance, because Diane fancies you? Nah, I've got the trials coming up and I've got to practise. Become impenetrable, like the bloody Wall of China past which nothing can get.

To be a good goalkeeper you have to practice. It's even harder to be good at than kung fu is, even though some blokes in our year reckon that that's the most difficult game. Skills. I reckon that's a load of cods, because no geezer's going to play fair with you just because you've got your black belt on. They're going to thump you first and look at your certificates after. That's if you're still alive. Best way is to get a stick or a chain, or a knife, or best of all a gun, like all the villains in the East End. I heard once that the Kray brothers hired a tank to attack a lad that grassed on them. They'd heard he had a machine gun and didn't want to take no risks. They drove it right down Mile End Road and the public thought it was the army carrying out manoeuvres. You hear a lot of stories like that in London and I reckon half of them are only three-quarters true or half true. Which makes the level of truth in London half of half, or three-quarters of half, whatever that is. That's more than Bombay, I can tell you that, at least from the things that have happened here. My uncle said at the airport that it was a modern building they lived in. When we get here, it's all falling to bits, and he said there was a beach in front of it, but the bloody rocks he was talking about are nearly a kilometre away even though you can see them from the balcony if you've got your specs on.

He was going to look after us, he says, when we get off

the plane in Bombay, all sleepy and full of food because they give you a meal every half-hour on them flights. He said to my mum not to worry about a thing and next day he brings in these sharp lawyer blokes to get me to sign all sorts of papers. They put a cross against an empty space and say sign here. My mum looks on and says I'd better sign where my uncle says, and I tell her to get away from the papers or they'll have to put them in the drier before they can use them in court or whatever they're doing. The lawyer blokes, all in black coats like scarecrows, all look at my uncle as though I was an animal or something getting out of control.

These lawyers don't look as smart as the one I had when I was up in the magistrates' court in Bow. That customer was really flash. I was sitting on this plush chair in his waiting room with his secretary typing away with a mini-skirt covering what was good above her blue tights. She says, 'Put your jacket on before going in to see Mr Big himself.'

'I'm hot,' I said.

She looked me up and down and said, 'Impatient to get in the cooler?' Smart bird.

'Why don't you go on telly?' I said. 'You'd run Frankie Howerd out of business.'

The solicitor says, 'I'm going to take a statement on the tape recorder, but before we switch that on, I want you to tell me if you actually intercepted the merchandise.'

I said I don't know and he began speaking to me like I was deaf mute, encouraging me to lip-read him.

'I'm sorry sir, I may be Indian, but I speak perfectly good English, but I haven't swallowed a dictionary and I was just wondering if you'd clarify your inquiry.' I like that: 'clarify your inquiry'.

'You're a cocky young fellow.' If he'd said that to Mel or Tony, they would have fallen about.

I was given a year's probation, we all were. Mel had actually driven the van full of sugar packets, millions of 'em, and he was charged heavy and sent down to Stamford House.

'That's where you'll end up, and the game won't touch you, they won't have a can in any of the teams from here to Lisbon,' Mr Knights said. He was giving me a lecture on going straight for the sake of the game. Now I don't know where Lisbon is, but I guess it's far enough for me not to want banning from here to there, so I said I'd go straight. And apart from nicking sweets and a few things from Woolworths for Christmas, I never joined the lads in the game. Knighty said I had a chance, and I hung on to it like they say a drowning man holds on to a straw. Only I never figured out how straw got on the sea in the first place. It's all a load of bollocks – I could make up better proverbs than that. Like spitting on a forest fire, I said once. I got a pat on the back for that. One remark like that and the dumb teachers remember it till the end of the term. 'Kashyap shows creative talent in his English lessons.'

'What's that?' my dad asked, looking at the report.

'I'm good at poetry,' I said. But my dad obviously thought that poetry was only good for poofs. Chances are he never knew what poofs were. But he knew what mattered. His eye would check on the physics and chemistry and maths reports.

'Your father had a lot of hope and ambition for you,

Kashyap. You must try and live up to his faith in you, and fulfil his life's wishes.'

But I was thinking about my own life's wishes. I wanted that blue-and-claret shirt, West Ham forever. If I'd been given two more years in London, that's what I'd have done.

I don't know much Hindi, but I have to speak to my grandad in Hindi 'cause he don't know nothing else. I'm young enough to learn, but he ain't, and that's the reason I suppose I could learn to like Bombay. They say I will, I'll forget London. It's not London I'm worried about, it's just the whole idea of changing your life. At my age kids don't normally have plans for their lives, but you can see how you're going to grow up, you have a pretty fair idea. Now it's India and starting all over again, with friends, with the language and even getting used to the stinks.

I used to pretend I couldn't speak Hindi when I was with the lads. We are on a street corner and the rest of them are deciding whether we ought to go up the West End and tease the prostitutes and play the pin balls. We're outside the café and nobody has a penny on them. A Paki geezer comes along. He's got this fuzzy hat and a long coat and tight trousers. I can tell he's a Muslim, but they can't. I don't see him approaching. He stops by John and he says, quite polite like, 'Could you please directing me, one address ...' and all this, and he sticks out a grubby little bit of paper. Only one problem, it's not in the East End. The address he's got scribbled is down in Blackheath or some place. So John says to him he can't go straight there and Mel says, 'Yeah, you have to turn yourself at the corners,' putting on what he thinks is an Indian accent. Then he says, 'Shall we roll him?'

The rest of them are looking at me. They were staring in my face to see how I was taking it, because Mel wasn't thinking when he said that, just naturally taking the mick. So John says, 'Shut your yapping mouth, you Irish git, so what if the geezer's not English, you got something against Cash and his lot?' And then he hands the bloke over to me. OK, so I'm Indian and I go up to the bloke and talk to him in Hindi, whatever I can manage and I tell him to go down to the Elephant and then take a 53 bus. He smiles all over and puts out his hand and taps me on the shoulder to show he's grateful.

When he's gone, Mel says, 'Say something again in Indian.'

'Not for you,' I says.

'Go on, Cash, I didn't mean it, you know I was just larking about.'

'That could have been my dad,' I said, 'and how was he to know you're Mr Humorous himself?'

'Keep it on,' he says, 'keep it on, son, it's windy today.'

So I cussed him with all the Hindi swear words I could think of, and they all fell about holding their guts and doubling up right there on the pavement. I taught them a few of the best, and they went around shouting them at all the Indian faces they met in the street and at school in the next few days.

I said I get the stink of the drying Bombay Duck and with it I can imagine the smell of cod in batter at the local chippy. That's the worst of it. What I wouldn't give for a real fry-up from down Kingsland Road. It's vegetarian food in my grandad's house. All dal and rice and bhindi and enough yogurt to drown an elephant in. Ugh, yoghurt down your throat three times a day, or starve. I can't complain. It isn't even our house, and Mum's in mourning so I feel selfish if I even think of my turn, but I can't help it.

My uncle keeps telling me to think about taking up my studies where I left off, but he doesn't know that I never left off, I hardly got started. I'll confess that I'm worried about that now, I keep thinking of O levels or whatever they have here, and how I wouldn't get a job without them here. It's not like London where you can go on the dole, there isn't any dole here. They just let you die in the street, them loving Indians, and I've seen it, I tell you. There's people sleep on the streets all over the city and some of them are just skin, like plastic bags stretched over their bones.

My uncles say they'll look after us now. They're always in and out of the house and Christ I have to remember all their names and the right names to call everyone each time they ask you something. Sometimes I feel I have to get out, because all these uncles just talk about 'the future' all the time like it was their favourite subject. I make excuses to get out. I say I'll get a new toothbrush and they say they'll send the servant out for one. So I say he won't know the West Ham colours and they look at me as though I'm barmy. It must seem a bit doolally looking for West Ham coloured toothbrushes in Bombay. I get down the elevator like a shot. Blokes always touching their heads in salaam here. My uncle's a big shot. Dad used to tell us about him sometimes in London, say he'd go into partnership with him once he'd saved enough money. You'll never save a bean, we used to say and I believed it.

I am down in the park. It isn't much of a park, just a huge empty space with a few palm trees tucked in a corner.

Plenty of people about, all playing cricket and chucking stones about. There's a game of football too. If you're a goalie, you can't just ask for a game, everyone has to trust you before the game starts. It's not like playing anywhere else on the field, where you can join in and tackle someone and dribble past them and do your stuff. These kids are playing without shoes.

If I get into a school I'll get in their team. I asked about football. They don't even have a blooming league. You've got to join the army if you want to play football; it's good exercise, good for the young to take exercise. That's my grandad, a bit behind the times, but what can you expect? He's never been out of Bombay in his life.

'Humans are the same everywhere.' That's Miss Mullins. She thought she ought to feel sorry for me. 'You've taken it very well. I was wondering what had happened to you. I've been to India and it's absolutely wonderful. It'll be better for you of course. They're your own people. All this confusion of the East End will disappear. You will think of us, as we shall think of you, won't you?' And then the girls throwing their arms around me. 'Cashy, don't forget us now.' It was as if I'd stopped a hundred for West Ham juniors already.

I heard the headmaster saying to Mullins when I was standing outside the door, 'He'll be better off, wisest thing,' He didn't say that to me. He said, 'Kashyap my boy, you've had one or two scrapes with the law but all is forgotten and we'll always be proud of you.'

It was only then I began to think about the whole thing, going away. Like dying, really. Mullins said confusion, but there was no confusion before. My dad was no big shot, he was a tailor and the confusion only started when he kicked it. Died, I mean.

He worked at one of them firms that made you do all the stitching and cutting and then took the profits and gave you twenty-five a week. Peanuts. And our house showed it. After he died, the hire purchase man came and took the telly and the fridge and the damned plastic-covered couches in the front room.

'Leave that stuff alone,' I said.

The trucker said, 'Argue with the bailiff, mate, I'm doing my job.' I'd have laid one on him. Right, I'm smaller, but I'd have hurt him as much as he could damage me. But Mr Dayal, my dad's mate, he said to leave them, they had a right because my dad hadn't kept up the payments and we wouldn't need the things because we were packing up to go anyway.

It was two weeks before it was all over and fixed. The social workers came and all our Indian neighbours. They knew my parents but they wouldn't have anything to do with me and used to tell my dad to whip me and keep me in line like they did with their sons. He never beat me once, though. He lectured me about how hard he'd worked, and how he'd saved money for three years to go home and get married.

'Was it worth it?' I used to ask, and he'd scowl at me and say that my mum was the jewel of the East.

'Ever seen a hundred-kilogram diamond?' I asked him, but he never hit me.

He said, 'Kashyap, Kashyap, all boys are disgraceful. It is their nature, but it is bad to joke with your elders.' I agreed with him. It wasn't him at all that bothered me.

And it was all true about how he'd worked. I know because he had a buttonhole machine at home and he'd do extra work after hours, and that meant till two in the bleeding morning, his fingers like Olympic spiders crawling all over that nifty machine. I told him there was better work for quick fingers to do. Actually, he knew all about me. When he looked at me with dark eyes it was as though he could see right through me. And he was proud of me, like they all are, proud of his eldest son.

They all stare at you in the same way. The beggars in the street, the people in the trains. Boy, they said the East End was a slum but anyone who says that ought to have a look at this place, even without glasses on. Half the houses aren't even houses, they're just tin and wood boards and stuff. Not our house. I'm sitting in the front room and the fan in the ceiling goes round like a helicopter, like the whole place is going to take off or maybe come crashing down, but my mum said it's been there for years and made the same noise before I was born. The flies aren't scared off by the racket it makes. They are my grandad's mates. His game is grabbing a few of them. He shows me how to grab them by bringing your palm up slowly and snatching at the air above them. I'm an expert now.

I go to school and I come back, and then out with my mates in the evening. I don't mind doing a few things for Mum in between, but after seven my time's my own. You should see the stuff they have on telly here, cor blimey, no *Kojak,* no kung fu. Not that I miss the telly. I miss the lads. It warn't nicking and that, leastways not always, sometimes it was just walking down the streets and chatting up the girls, or going up the youth club. And in our fourth year at school everyone begins thinking about jobs, then it's lectures and parents' meetings and everybody making up their minds. It's a miracle in that bunch. A thieving lot, Mel and John and Mo. Now Mo's going to drive his father's trucks. With a couple of trucks to back you, you can fart on O levels, he says. And John's going into the docks on account of his old man. And Gordy'll be a bloody butcher's assistant. Can't read so he'll be chopping out best New Zealand to someone who asked for English Lamb. He says he can tell by the colour. So Mo says, yeah, stamped with Union Jacks.

I never tell them I'm going to be a doctor. Dad goes on at me about it and I know he writes home regularly and always there's something to mention about how well I'm getting on with maths, even though I've torn my book up in front of the maths teacher and got sent home and suspended till Dad comes up and begs.

'I've never known any of your lot behave as badly as you do Kashyap, but Mr Knights here is willing to put in a good word for you, and only on his say-so we have agreed to give you a further chance to fit into our community.'

I couldn't give a monkey's for his community and all that, but I want to stay in the team, so I just swallow my pride, like a spoonful of castor oil that my grandad thinks is good for you. Makes you fart something rotten. My dad doesn't care for it, not the castor oil, the football I'm thinking of, and Knights says I stand a chance. I'm down in front of the net and the best shooters in the school taking shots with three balls and I'm diving and dancing like crazy, like a maniac with ants in his pants.

So I think to myself that even if he's not seen Indians like me, he hasn't seen them in his first eleven or in goal either. Sure, they play cricket, they do good maths, the teacher's pets. All crawling and in the sixth form, to be lawyers and accountants. Some from Uganda who are called Asians. With hair like poofs, trying to look like Brian Ferry or some crumb from the hall of fame. They'll never have the East End at their feet. You know, that's the saddest thing about it. All of them, crawlers, were looking to clear out from the East End. Go and work in the City and live in Kensington or some posh place and dress up in pinstripes and say 'toppung' and call their mates 'old chap'.

My dad wanted me dropped from the team, and he even came up and told old Knights, but Knights wanted to win the league so he says he'll keep his tidy mouth shut as long as I keep coming to practice. It used to come to me that the only way I would ever become a pro was if my dad died. I hate the thought now, but I'm being straight, and I'm even thinking it wasn't what I thought, I'm not Uri Geller or one of them magic blokes who can think things and they happen. That's what I thought when he refused to buy me my kit and Knighty had to beg it off of the school. It was rotten. I couldn't even take my cup home. John was on the team and he said your dad's a nutter, because his old man took his down the local to show his mates.

I heard a lot about India this and India that from my mum, but it was never my business, because I reckoned on dying a cockney. It's what fourteen years can do to you. I thought the East End would do for me like it did for my dad, when it choked him up and they brought him home on a stretcher and Mum and I spent the whole night at the hospital.

We sat in the corridor on a bench and I put my arm round my mum. She was howling something terrible. The doctor comes in with a nurse with a face looking like half past six, and they call me aside. 'I'm awfully sorry.'

And I couldn't think of nothing to say so I says, 'It's not your fault.' Then I can't get my mum away from the doctor. She never touched a white man in her life, not even to take change in a shop, and she's hanging on to the doctor like she was drowning and he'd come in to save her. Talking Hindi and trying English and crying all the time. So he leaves her with the nurse. Brushes her off, his jaw drops down to his waist, he can't handle this mad Indian woman who's begging him to do something, do anything.

Then the crematorium and the priests and relatives I didn't know existed, and mutterings and prayers in the house, all streaming in from Leamington Spa and Bradford and God knows where, with all their grubby children, all wearing Bri-nylon shirts and saying what a good man he was as if they knew the first thing about my dad. And they vanish the next day and it rains and England is shutting down.

I go down to the firm where Dad used to work and the manager talks to me for a good half-hour. They can't employ me, I'm too young. Just two years more, so I'd better do what my uncle says. He came all the way from India. Nothing for you here he says, cold climate no good. I'd have given my dad half my life if it could be done, just to stay in West Ham.

He could talk about the climate, it's like a bloody oven here and raining half the time. I'm sitting on the balcony and there's a blind beggar with a little girl guiding him. Letters from England. John says West Ham are playing Leeds and West Ham are favourites for the Cup. They've dropped Clyde Best for the game, and the lads send their love and kisses. One day … but no good thinking about that. The beggar's opened up his harmonium and his blind eyes looking like white marbles are pointed towards me. He's beginning to sing his song and the little girl is just standing there waiting to start wailing for money when he's past the first verse. I don't care much for Hindi songs, though some of the words are good. This one says,

'Go away, fly away, bird
Go to the home of singing choirs
There's nothing for you here, my beauty …'
Or something like that. My Hindi's improving.

~

4.

The China Set

MY NAN IS MUCH WISER than my dad. He says she's so smart she can imagine a stick with only one end. Not that my dad's stupid, he must be quite smart to make up a thing like that, but he doesn't take time to think as he's always telling us to do. He's a postman. Sometimes he says he should have stayed in India and become a goldsmith like his father and his grandfather. It makes you feel rich playing with other people's gold, he says, but the gold ran out or something and he had to leave Bombay and come to England and send money back to keep his brothers and sisters.

He's lovely, my dad, though I think I love my nan best. She only came to live with us last year and she still doesn't speak a word of English. She gets along though, goes down to the shops by herself, a little old Indian lady in a sari, not even the sort Mum wears, but black or brown because her husband's dead, and tied round in the old-fashioned way with the loose flap coming over her shoulder from back to front. She travels by bus and tube all over London, and my brother and I teach her to say 'I'm a senior citizen' instead of 'No English, no speaking' like she does, and to say 'Sorry, I don't speak English so please speak to me in Gujerati or Hindi'. My brother taught her that, though I think it's silly because if she really did go around saying that, they'd think she was daft.

She's only been in London for a year, and she never complains about the cold or anything like that. She says, 'Where my grandchildren are, there I want to be, their faces make the sun shine,' and funny rot like that. She's always telling us stories about when she was a girl in India. We've given her a room on her own, the back room on the first floor of our house in Ealing, just near where the BBC studios are.

Anyway, this story really starts with a song. No, it starts with this boy in school – I might as well be frank since I'm writing this down, and I don't care if Dad or Mum gets to see it. The boy's name is Ralph and his dad's an actor. If you've seen the play *Canterbury Tales* in the West End, or on telly, then you've seen his dad, because he's in it. Ralph's very sweet. I'm the only Indian girl in our class at school, and even though all of them are very friendly, Ralph is the only boy who ever talks to me seriously. He once asked me if I was going to get married to an Indian boy, somebody my dad chose for me. I said maybe I will, but that the ideas in my family are changing, that we are really not superstitious or anything like that.

'Why does your dad get so jumpy every time I come round? He puts on a face like I was going to rape you or something.'

Until about two weeks ago he used to be going with this girl called Andre. She's also in our class at Goldhawk Comprehensive. (The boys always call it Colditz Comprehensive.) Andre was his girl, but he used to still sit next to me in class and make her jealous and behave as though he didn't notice that she was staring. If the teachers don't have enough texts and we're sharing books, he always gets one between us and touches my hand when he turns the pages. She's always watching, Andre, but pretending that she's not. He calls me Minihaha because he says I'm small, Indian and funny.

Ralph's going to be an actor. He always gets the highest marks in English and takes over the drama class whenever he's feeling like it. He's clever. He can play the guitar and I think he tries to look like a pop star, with shaded glasses and a sort of smart haircut, long at the back and short on top. He brings the best records to school, not all that reggae rubbish and Donny Osmond and Slade. He listens to David Bowie and the Rolling Stones and all sorts of new groups that no one's ever heard of. He says he's learning to play the sitar from the lead guitarist of a group he's going to join.

One day, about a week ago, he said he wanted to listen to some Hindi pop and I said my dad's only got film songs and he gets them straight from India so he won't let them out of his sight. 'In that case I'll have to listen to them up your house, won't I?' he said.

To tell you the truth, I was very glad he said that, and I told him I'd tell him when he could come because my dad had to be got in the right mood. If Ralph came too often he'd start getting ideas and making a fuss.

I talk to my nan about my friends, so I told her about Ralph and she asked if he was from a good family and whether I liked him. I said that I did like him a little, and there weren't any good or bad families in Britain, they were all the same. She said that that could never be, there was always a difference between gold and lead and the older you get the better you could tell.

My dad has the same sort of ideas. You can't blame him because he must have got them from her. He lectures us on and on about such things. When we went to pick up Nan from the airport, he was saying he hadn't lost respect for his own dad, even though he was dead. My brother's quite cheeky and he said, 'Neither did Hamlet,' but my dad doesn't understand about Shakespeare so the joke was no good on him.

Dad always says that English people put their parents in old people's homes because they have no shame, but we Indians know how to look after our own. Sometimes when he talks that way I like it, it makes me feel different and also better than the rest, because it's true, I suppose, they don't have any old folk's homes in India. But there are beggars and hungry people all about the streets and when I point that out my dad says it's true, but what can one do, there are rich and poor everywhere and poor people may be starving but they have good hearts.

'Can't pay the rent with good hearts,' my brother says.

When Dad speaks like this it frightens me too, because I don't really know anything about India. Since I was four I've lived in London and now that I'm fifteen I often think of going to India. My mother always says we're going next year, but Dad says there's not enough money saved and next year never comes. If I start earning my own money I'll save up and go, just for a visit.

The day Ralph came Dad was on the evening shift, Ralph turned up, as always with books and LPs in his hand. We sat in the front room where the record player was and where Mum could have kept an eye on us while she cooked next door in the kitchen. Ralph had been there a few times and he always sat politely, not like at school where he sprawls out on the desks and sits with his trousers pulled to his shins, cross-legged on the cement flower pots in the school playground.

Nan was in the house when he arrived, and Mum had just nipped out to the launderette with two loads. Nan came and sat in the front room with us while we played the discs and talked in English. I kept watching the door for Dad, knowing it wouldn't really matter, if Nan was in the same room. She wanted to know why Ralph wore a necklace – he had a chain and pendant, the sort you buy for a few bob in Shepherds Bush Market. She wanted to know if he was a prince of some sort, or whether he was a dancer. I translated for her and Ralph said that he was the Prince of Darkness, but Nan didn't get the joke and said he was so white, he shouldn't say that about himself.

After we played through some of Dad's LPs, Ralph wanted to put on his own and asked if it was all right. 'There are Indian bells on this one, remind you of the cows tinkling home in the sunset, listen,' he said.

Now I don't listen much to pop, but I was relieved that Dad wouldn't come home to find us playing with his records. So Ralph put on the Stones and we listened. We sat through it and talked. Then he said, 'What about all the old Indian hospitality then, you haven't even offered me a bleeding cup of tea?'

I wished he hadn't said that, because I didn't want to ask Nan to make it and if Mum had been there it would have been all right, but according to Hindu custom you only serve up tea to a young man when your dad has brought him home to look you over as a marriage proposition. I said to Nan that there were cokes in the fridge and she got the hint and perhaps she understood that it was awkward for me so she went and got them herself, and she did a very sweet thing, she brought them on a tray with a can opener. Ralph said it was a good idea and began to open the can with the can opener and I split myself laughing because Nan didn't understand what she'd done wrong. She began talking to Ralph in Gujerati as though he understood every word and he just smiled at her.

'Hey, listen to this one,' Ralph said as one song came to an end and another started. 'Are you sure your nan doesn't understand English?'

I didn't know it was going to be a rude song. Personally, I don't think there's anything rude about that song or any other. It's about this girl who likes going out with pop stars and film stars, and I think girls dream about that, at least lots of them in our school do, but this song puts it in a slightly different way. I might as well be frank and say what the song actually says. The words are something about 'star-fucker, star-fucker, star-fucker, star …' and about missing her two-tongued kisses and wrapping his legs round her thigh, and making her scream all night. We listen to that sort of thing every day in school and there are much worse songs on the radio which have two meanings, like the one about 'my ding-a-ling', which is not really about a bell at all. Even so, I knew that my dad would feel that this was his house and no filth should be brought into it.

I was going to say that to Ralph. I could see from his face that he wanted to see how far he could go with me, he had that sort of defiance, pretending that he was listening to just some old love song. But it was too late. Dad came in taking his grey jacket off, and Ralph said,

'Hello, Mr Desai.'

Dad grunted and he went into the kitchen, asking Nan for the house keys which she kept tied to her sari, in a big bunch on her waist. When she first came from India, Dad made a big thing about it and handed them all over to her, saying that she was the boss of the house. He was just going upstairs when he stopped in the doorway and turned round with lines on his brow, crumpled like crushed paper. It was as though someone had said, 'stick 'em up' from behind and he didn't quite understand. He was standing in the door, his body half going out and half coming back, listening to the words that came out of the loudspeakers. I knew he was too shy to say anything in front of Ralph. Still, there was a silence and Nan pushed her way into it, speaking to him about the letters she had to write to India and saying that Mum had the one from her youngest son, Dad's brother, and he could see it when she came back from the launderette. The record was saying something about 'giving it to Steve McQueen' when Dad decided to leave it and went upstairs.

'Can we put something else on?' I asked Ralph. He changed the record and as he looked round at me he grinned slyly, as though he knew that he'd done some mischief and that the thunder behind Dad's frown would soon come crashing down. He finished his can of coke and said he was going straight to his evening job.

'I'll leave the records for you, you can bring them to school tomorrow,' he said.

'Why don't you take them with you? I might forget,' I said. I wanted him to get them out of the house, but I also wanted him to leave them so I could show the others in class that Ralph had been at my house when I took them back. I felt that he wanted to show them, and Andre, that too.

'No, bring 'em in tomorrow. I can't take them to work, they'll most likely get nicked.'

When Ralph had left I wanted to know what sort of a mood Dad was in. So I went up to his room and he was sitting on the bed, still looking angry.

'I'm going to help Mum down the launderette,' I said.

'What kind of boys do you bring into my house?' he asked.

'Oh Dad, don't be so sticky, there aren't any other kind of boys, at least not at our school, and Ralph is best at work, he gets top marks all the time, and you're always telling me to make friends with the top ten.'

Dad didn't reply, he just made a face.

When I came back with loads of washing, the records were still on the player, so I picked them up, intending to take them to the room I shared with Lekha, my sister. I went through the records and found that the Rolling Stones one was missing. I shouted all round the house, but nobody could tell me where it was. I knew that Dad had taken it, so I crawled all round the front room and pretended to be looking for it under the table and behind the couches and under the newspaper. Dad just put on his glasses and began to read the letters my mum gave him, taking not the least bit of notice of me.

I didn't want to start an argument, because I knew he was waiting for me to ask him to give it back and then he'd start on about how English people were different from us, and some words should never pass a girl's lips or ears. I was fed up of telling him that I was Indian but also English, because where you live matters, even more than the blood you have in you, and that my mind was English in a way because I had two sets of ideas, one for the English people I knew and one for the Indians.

When Dad settled down to eat, with Mum fetching him his food, because he ate before all of us, I went up to his bedroom and looked all round. The record wasn't anywhere, but his cupboard was locked. And this is where my nan comes in, and her story, the one she told me.

I saw Ralph in school the next day and told him that I

was still listening to his wretched records and my brother wanted to tape them so I'd bring them back later.

'Your old man looked like Geronimo yesterday,' he said. 'I thought hang on, he's gone to the kitchen for his tomahawk.'

'He's funny sometimes,' I said, but I couldn't tell him about the record. It was the same for two days. Ralph would make silly jokes, he'd say I was making record curry and all that. He knew I felt rotten about it.

I went up to Nan's room and sat talking to her that evening. She didn't ask me what was on my mind. I think she knew. So she began telling me her story.

She said that when she was my age in Bombay, which must have been long before the First World War (I can't even *think* that far back except in history lessons), they used to live all together in a big house, nineteen brothers and sisters and cousins and four sets of parents, her own and her uncles and aunts, and her grandad. He must have been my great-great-grandad, and they were all scared of him because he was the chief of the household. He was a kind of tyrant, but he earned the first pay packet in the house, and that made him lord and master. He always wore a turban, and he worked as a goldsmith and she said he was a very good artist and made the most fabulous earrings and bangles and things.

One day when the men were all out at work and the boys had gone to school with their slates and chalks (they didn't send girls in those days) the women and girls trooped out of the house to their local market. It was called Grant Road and was spread out under a huge railway bridge near their house. The women had heard that there were all sorts of new things at the market, just off the ship from England and they'd better go fast. Like the sales in Oxford Street, I suppose. She went along with the rest, because she said one thing that girls were taught to do by their mothers and aunts was to bargain with tradesmen and bring the prices down and pretend you weren't going to buy and walk away and come back and keep your face straight to show you didn't really like what they had to sell.

Only the wives of the house, that's Nan's mum and her sisters-in-law, had any money. When they got to the market, there was a huge crowd gathered round a particular street stall. You know what they were selling there? China – English tea sets and dinner sets and vases. My nan laughed when she told it. She was remembering the delight with which they looked at these things, because they hadn't seen crockery for home use before. They looked at the coloured patterns and the salesman let them handle the cups and plates. Well, she said, they had seen them before but this was the first time they'd got so close. There was a dinner set there with a Chinese pattern on it, with bamboo branches and beautiful birds, all red and blue and yellow, in the branches, the same pattern on each plate and dish. They asked the price. They could manage it, they decided, if they pooled their money. Her mum made the decision. Yes, they'd buy them, they'd use all their own money and not touch the housekeeping. When the man wrapped them up in tissue paper and put them in a box, they carried them home like they'd won a trophy in the World Cup or something.

That evening, without telling any of the menfolk, they laid the dinner set out as a surprise.

'You wouldn't get any like it nowadays,' she said. 'It was all little patterns, carefully done like a silversmith had been working on it.'

They sat down to dinner a little uncertain and very excited. Then the storm broke. Her grandad came in from work and hung up his turban and took off his work shoes and put on his slippers and walked into the dining room, where the women were supposed to serve the meal to the sitting menfolk. His daughters and daughters-in-law watched his face as he saw the china set instead of the silver and brass trays that they normally ate off. They were proud of their display and had even put a table cloth down, 'like the memsahib's house', Nan said.

Her grandad took one look at the Chinese bird crockery and his eyes went blazing mad. He grabbed the table cloth and before their eyes, as they held their breaths, he picked up the lot, took it to the window, and flung it crashing downstairs, two floors down to the courtyard. The crash brought the neighbours to their windows and they caught the last act of the play.

'We are Indians, high-caste Indians,' he shouted. 'I won't have this foreign mud in my house, shiny mud that's all it is. Trust women to be fooled by pictures of parrots. I won't eat off shiny mud plates and nobody from my house is going to waste my money on heathen inventions.'

That was the end of that. The women folded their arms before them, and not one of them dared go out to pick up the pieces till he gave the order. The table was set as usual with metal trays in a matter of seconds. Nan said they were always scared of a beating in those days.

'That was sixty years ago, or something,' I said, 'and our

dad he still thinks the same. He's thrown away my friend's record, just because he doesn't understand the songs.'

'Sshh, he hasn't thrown it away,' she said, and she giggled like a little girl. 'He was listening to your record when you went to school yesterday, and he locked it up in his cupboard, but I've got the key, so I stole it.'

She pulled the LP out from under her bed.

'What about Dad?' I asked, worried that he'd blame me for going through his cupboards.

'Thieves can't complain about stealing,' she said. 'What happened about the crockery?' I asked her a few days after that. 'Did you ever get to eat off china?' 'Not when my grandad was alive,' she replied. 'It was really different in those days. Men were gods.'

~

5.

K B W

TAHIR'S GONE NOW. NO ONE to play chess with. I ask my dad for a game and he says he has a union meeting to attend this evening. 'Young Habib would've given you three in a row with one hand tied behind his blooming back,' he says as he goes out.

My dad says they're going to move an Irish family in. He knows that I shall miss Tahir. 'Maybe young Paddy will know some chess,' he says.

Their flat was exactly like ours, except the other way round, like when you see a thing in a mirror. Like twins growing out of each other our two flats were. And I was Tahir's best friend. The windows are still smashed, but the flat's been boarded up, like some others on our estate. It goes for kilometres. You must have heard of it, it's called the Devonmount Estate, Borough of Hackney. I shan't go to cricket practice today. I dropped out after Tahir left. We joined the team together so I think it's only right that we pull out together.

My mother don't understand. She says, 'Go on out and do something. Go and play cricket, you can't help the way the world is. Don't sit there looking like a month of wet Sundays.'

Dad understands. 'Son, you're right. Don't have no truck with racialist swine.' He always talks like that. Mum still needles him about being a communist and he always replies that he's a Red in her bed, and the day she tries to put him under for his political views, he'll leave. They all know my dad on the estate. Twenty-two years he's been here.

I was born here and went to school here, to Devonmount Juniors and then Devonmount Comprehensive, no less. Tahir came here eight months ago. His dad came from Bangladesh, because they was driven out by the riots. That's what Tahir told me. He came straight into the fourth form. I took him to school the first day. My dad introduced himself to Mr Habib as soon as they moved in, and he said to me at dinner that day, 'My boy, a Bengali family has moved in next door, and I've told mister that you are going to take master to school. He's in your school and I want you to take him in and stick him outside the headmaster's office.'

That's how I met Tahir. I asked him what games he liked and, he said cricket so I took him to Mr Hadley, the local vicar who runs the cricket team, and Tahir bowled for us. He was great. He lit up when they said they wanted to try him. Mr Hadley gave him the bat and bowled to him, and Tahir struck it hard to mid-off and was caught first go. Then Hadley gave him the ball. Tahir stroked it like it was a pigeon or something and when he looked up there was a shine in his eyes, same as you get out of the toe of a shoe when you put spit on the leather. He took a short run and bowled that ball. It spun at an amazing speed to leg side.

'What do we have here?' Mr Hadley said, and his glasses gleamed. Tahir was our best spin bowler. He took four wickets in the match against the Mercer's Estate. When we won that match we were sure to get to the finals with the Atlanta Atlases. They were the best estate club going. If we beat them we'd be champs of Hackney. If you don't live in Hackney and don't live on the Devonmount, you don't know what that means. But I'll tell you what it means. It means Vietnam, North Vietnam that is, beating America in a war. That's what it means, a little country with a lot of determination, and without two ha'pennies to rub together, beating what my dad calls the biggest military machine ever built by man or money. Because ours is the worst estate. The flats are filthy and the stairs and the courtyard are never cleaned. There's coal dumps in the yards and half the places are boarded up. You should have seen the Habibs' flat. Water pouring down the wall of one bedroom, the wallpaper all peeling off like scabs, and the roof plaster all torn to bits. My dad said that it was nothing less than a crying shame for a workers' government to treat the workers so. My mum said she remembered when she was a little girl, and they ought to be thankful for a bathful of water which was hot.

The door of their flat has been forced open and the young ones play in there. That's what they call kids who still go to primary school on the Devonmount. I'm not a little 'un any more, I'm twelve and I'm not interested in climbing the garbage carts and pulling bits off people's cars and playing cowboys and Indians or hide-and-seek or cops and robbers in the empty flats. I used to be, and in those days I couldn't see why everyone on the estate complained about it. To me the empty flats were space. They gave you the feeling not that you belonged there but that the place belonged to you so you could never leave it. Last year they built an adventure playground for the little 'uns on an empty site, and they went in hordes there, but after a while they didn't like it, they stopped going and started back in the empty flats again. There was nothing to nick in the adventure playground but the empties. You can find and flog all sorts of things around here. There are some blokes on the estate who'll give you quite a few pence for a load of pipes or even for boards and doorknobs and toilet seats and that, and the kids on the estate break in and rip everything up. It's only when a flat has been completely ripped up that it becomes a place to play in. It gets cleaned out like a corpse gutted by sharks. I walked through their flat yesterday and it's been done over.

When Tahir's family first moved in, the people around didn't like it. They didn't go to the trouble to worry them, but the boys from C Block came to our building and painted 'Niggers Out' on the landing. My dad said it was a shame and he gave me some turps and a rag and asked me to clean it off, but I couldn't, it wouldn't come off. He said it was an insult to coloureds, and I know it was because the lads from C Block don't like coloured people – they're always picking on Pakis and coons when they're in a gang. My mum says they only do it because they're really scared of them, but I don't think they are. When Tahir and I came home from school together they used to shout, 'Want to buy an elephant?' and all that bollocks. Tahir never took any notice. He always walked looking straight ahead, but even though he didn't understand what they were saying, he'd become very silent and not say a word to me all the rest of the way. I still think I was his best friend. There was always six of them and they was bigger than us. Sometimes they'd even come to our block and shout from downstairs. If Tahir's father heard them he'd come out on the gallery and shout back at them. I think he was a very brave man. He wasn't scared of anyone and he'd say, 'Get out, swine,' because those were the only swear words in English that he knew. He didn't speak English very much and when my dad met him on the stairs or invited him round for a cup of tea, he'd just say, 'It is very kind, don't trouble, please don't trouble.' Tahir told me once that his father was a karate expert and could break three bricks with one hand. And he was strong. One day when I was in their flat, he lifted a whole big refrigerator all by himself from the bottom of the stairs.

The trouble all started with the newspapers. There was a story in the *Sun* one day which said that two people in London had died of typhoid. My mum and dad talked about it at home and Mrs Biggles, my mum's mate, said that a girl in C Block had been taken to St Margaret's Hospital and was under observation there. The girl was called Jenny and we knew her 'cause she used to go to the same school as my little sister Lynn.

The story went around the estate that there was typhus in the East End, and everybody was talking about it. Then a funny thing happened. We play cricket down in Haggerston Park and after the game, when Mr Hadley has locked the kit away in the hut at the corner, he takes us all to the vicarage and he gives us bags of crisps and cups of cocoa, and lets us listen to his records. Well, this last Saturday, we had a lot of kids turn up for cricket practice. Usually there's only the team, about thirteen lads, but this time there was eighteen because Mr Hadley said we had to have proper trials for the juniors team. We all sat around while James and Mr Hadley made the cocoa. He peeped around the door and said, 'There's only seven mugs, so you'll have to share the cocoa.'

We said, 'Right ho, umpire,' because that's what he likes to be called. Sometimes he tells us, if he's feeling like talking about church, that vicars are umpires from God and that life is like a test match between good and evil. I think Mr Hadley explains things well, but I still don't believe in it. My dad says that Hadley should stick to cricket and not brainwash the team, because my dad's dead against the Christians. He's an atheist but our mum tells us not to take any notice of him, because she believes in God.

Anyway, on this Saturday, James brought in the cups of cocoa to the team and gave them to every second person, as two people had to share. We were sitting in a circle on the carpet and Nick was changing the records. Every now and then someone would get up and there'd be an argument about whether to have David Essex or the Slade on next. Tahir never said a word. He was holding his steaming cup of cocoa and you could see the gaps in his teeth when he smiled. The lads would ask him to whistle and he'd always try but he couldn't do it on account of the big gap in his front teeth.

Next to Tahir there was a boy called Alan, and when Tahir had taken a few sips of the cocoa after it had cooled, he passed it on to him. The rest of us were fighting for the mugs, just mucking about sort of, and eating crisps at the same time. I was watching this boy Alan, who had freckles and a thin face which looked scared most of the time, and I could see that he didn't want to take the cup from Tahir.

'Have it, I've finished,' Tahir said.

Alan said he didn't want any cocoa, so Tahir turned to try and give the mug back to James.

'Everyone's got one,' James said. 'They're sharing if they haven't.'

'You didn't get,' Tahir said, smiling upward at James. 'I'll share someone's,' James replied, but when Tahir tried to give him his cup, he said, 'No, that's all right, you have the rest, I'll get some later.'

Tahir put his cup down in the middle of the carpet. All the cocoa from the other mugs was finished, but no one wanted to pick up Tahir's mug. Then it struck me. Mr Hadley shouted from the kitchen that the milk was finished, and there was a sort of silence in the room.

Tahir was searching the other faces. 'Anybody could drink it,' he said.

Nobody picked up the mug. It stood on the carpet, not even half drunk. I looked at the others. A second before they'd been laughing and talking, but now there was only the sound of the record player. I think Tahir understood. I looked at Alan. He had a look on his face like a dog that's been whipped. The others were looking at him too.

'I don't want any,' he said.

Mr Hadley, his red face shining still with the sweat of the game, came in and said that it had been a damned hard selection and if we put in a bit of practice we could beat the Atlases. 'Fine cricket,' he said, and he rubbed his hands as usual. 'With fine weather it'll be finer.'

Tahir was silent on the way home. He kept looking at his feet as we walked, and he looked thinner and even smaller than he normally looked.

When I got home, Mrs Biggles was there in the kitchen. 'They suspect typhus, the girl's shaking with fever and the poor dear didn't even recognize her own mother,' she was saying. She was asking Lynn questions about the girl Jenny who was in hospital. 'It's not known here,' the doctor said to her mother, 'it's the foreigners have brought it in, that's for sure, from Istanbul and Pakistan and now from that Ugandan Asians' place. We've never had these things here,' he went on.

'It's the blacks bring these things in here …' she said. My mum went dead silent. After Mrs Biggles had left, my dad put his mug of tea on the table and said he didn't want Mrs Biggles and her filthy mouth in his house, but Mum pretended she didn't hear and kept looking at the telly screen.

Another odd thing happened, on the following Monday. I woke up and dressed for school. Usually by the time my cornflakes are on the table, Dad's gone to work, but I found him in the kitchen that morning. He looked worried. He was sitting at the kitchen table with his hair brushed back and shiny with hair oil. He was talking to Mum, and then he took his coat and left. Mum said the people on the estate were rats and they needed poisoning, or leastways they deserved it. 'He took him to the pub once,' she said, 'just once as far as I know.'

'Who?' I asked.

'That Mr Habib from next door, your Tahir's father, even though the poor man couldn't drink on account of his religion, he had to drag him along just to show everyone.'

'Who took him?'

'Them people from C,' she said, 'they've painted things on our door. I wish Dad would call the police.'

As I walked out to school I turned to the door and it said 'K B W' in big black letters.

Dad was furious with Mum for telling me about it, and they had a right row that evening. Mum had scrubbed it off the door with sandpaper.

'Did you come back with Tahir?' she asked.

Tahir had been at school that day, but he behaved a bit strange. He wasn't there for the last lesson and I reckoned he must have hopped it.

'What does it mean?' I asked my dad, remembering the letters.

'It means your dad is poking his nose into other people's business,' my mum said.

'You know what they painted on our door, son?' my dad asked.

'I saw it,' I said.

'It means Keep Britain White,' Dad said. He looked grey in the face and serious. You know what that means, son. It used to be the Jews in the thirties, now it's bleedin' Indians and Pakistanis. Some people have seen you with Tahir.'

'More like they've seen you chatting like old friends to Habash, or whatever his name is,' Mum said.

'I've seen a lot of it and I hoped you wouldn't grow up in a world with these anti-working-class prejudices. I don't care what your mum says, but we've got to fight it. I've been fighting it, and I hope my son and grandson will fight it too.'

'And a lot of good it's done you,' Mum said.

But I was kind of proud of my dad.

'They are fascist scum, lad,' he said. He always, calls me 'lad' when he gets to lecturing about his politics.

'Don't go putting your ideas into the boy's head, you leave him to think as he pleases.'

Dad ignored her. He sat with his palms on his knees and with his tall back pushed against the chair, the way he always did when he thought he was teaching me the facts of life.

'You know this typhoid, lad,' he said. 'People are blaming the Habibs for bringing it in. But any law court in this country knows they're innocent. It's ignorance and superstition. This girl Jenny went to Spain on the school trip with our Lynn, didn't she?' This was said more to Mum than to me.

I hardly slept at all that night. The next day the papers said that the girl Jenny was worse and that several cases of typhoid had been found and more people had been put under observation in the East End hospitals. I was thinking that I knew why the cricket team hadn't wanted to touch Tahir's cocoa. I was wishing I had picked it up. I knew that Tahir must be thinking the same thing too. It struck me that he must have thought that I had the same idea as the rest of them.

Sometimes I have funny dreams and that's when I can't sleep. That night I dreamt of the letters K B W painted up across our door, and then the letters spread out with other letters on to the whole of the estate, and the letters growing and becoming bigger and bigger till they were too heavy and had to come crashing down, falling on top of me, the K like two great legs and the W spinning round like giant compasses.

I went very tired to school. I didn't tell Mum about the dream. Tahir wasn't in the playground and he wasn't at registration. I thought he might be late, but he never came late, and then it struck me that I knew he wouldn't come to school that day.

I stayed in that night and so did Dad. He usually goes down the pub for a jar, but he didn't bother that night. He turned on the telly and I could see from the way he folded his legs, and from his eyes which were glued on the screen but not taking in the programme, that he was worried. He usually starts on at Lynn when he's like that, asks her to polish her shoes for school the next day and for her homework and everything. It felt to me too as though something was about to happen, and it did.

I heard the crash and then another thud and another crash of glass and a woman screaming. It was Tahir's mother. Dad sprang up from his chair. I felt that he had been expecting it. He rushed to the door. Mum came out of the kitchen. The crash of brick or stone sounded as though it was in our own house. Dad opened the door and went out on to the gallery.

'Bastard, cowards!' I heard. It was Mr Habib shouting his lungs out.

Dad rushed back into the flat. 'There's twenty of them out there.'

'Shall I call the police?' Mum asked.

Dad didn't answer. Everyone hates coppers on our estate, and no one ever calls them. Coppers don't need invitations. I could hear the blokes downstairs shouting. Mum pushed Lynn away from her and went out on to the gallery.

Mr Habib was still shouting, 'You are all bastards, white bastards.'

Then we heard the running steps on the stairs. The blokes were coming up, and they were shouting too: 'Paki filth,' and, 'The girl's dead.'

It was all hell. Mr Habib went in and got Tahir's cricket bat. The blokes from C Block had bottles. There was more crashing of glass and Mrs Habib kept screaming things in Indian and I could hear Tahir crying and shouting and a lot of thumping.

'Why don't you help him?' my mum shouted to Dad. 'What kind of bloody communist are you?' But Dad was pushing her into the kitchen.

'Shut your mouth,' he said to her. He never talks like that

normally, but he looked as though he'd pissed himself. 'Let the police handle this. There's twenty of them out there.'

By the time the police came, with sirens blaring, pulling into the courtyard, jumping out and slamming their car doors, the blokes were gone.

I said, 'Mum, I'm going out,' and before she could stop me I went to the door and unbolted it. Other people had come out of their flats. The galleries of all the floors were now full of people trying to see what had happened. The police called an ambulance, and they took Mr Habib, who was lying outside his door groaning, to hospital. Tahir was bending over him when the coppers came with an Indian bloke and started asking questions. Tahir looked up at me as I stepped out, and he looked away. His dad had all blood streaming down his face. The day after, the blood marks were still there, all over the gallery.

Two hours later, we were all still awake. It was still as death outside and silent.

'I'll take it up with the council,' my dad said. I knew what he felt. He had wanted to help Tahir's dad, I am sure, but he felt helpless. There were too many of the others, he couldn't have said nothing.

'I wouldn't be seen dead at that girl's funeral,' Dad said after a while.

Four Indian blokes came and took Tahir and his mum and all their stuff away that same night and we could hear the coppers who'd stayed behind arguing with them.

The next day at cricket Mr Hadley asked me where Tahir was. The other boys told him the whole story, that bricks had been thrown through their windows and that Tahir's dad was in hospital.

Mr Hadley knew our school and he turned up there the next day. The headmaster sent for Tahir and for me from class and we walked together to the office without a word. Mr Hadley was there. He said he was sorry to hear that Tahir's family had been in an unfortunate incident and that he wanted Tahir to come to cricket practice.

Tahir answered all his questions about where they were living and that. He said, 'Yes, sir,' when Mr Hadley said that he must realize that he had a lot of good friends like me and that wherever he lived he must continue to play for Devonmount. He said, 'Yes, sir,' his legs apart, his hands folded behind his back, his head bent and his lips tight together, his eyes moving from Mr Hadley's face to the floor. But he never came again.

~

6.

Good at Art

RAJU WAS SHY. HE DIDN'T say much and he hadn't any real friends amongst the other sixth formers. He couldn't play cards, didn't like ping pong, wasn't interested in the Velvet Underground or in David Bowie or any of the other crazes that periodically captured the rest of them. He couldn't even tell jokes about Irishmen and though he listened carefully, he could rarely understand them.

His usual place was in an armchair in the corner of the sixth form room, behind a copy of the *Daily Mirror* or the *Sun*, away from the radio and the record player which blared at the gossiping, coffee-drinking card-playing groups. So when Kim brought the new art teacher round the room and introduced him, as the deputy head had told her to do, she made it a point to take him to Raju's corner.

'That's Raju, he's nervous, but he's the best artist of this lot.'

The man with her smiled and said he had a right to be nervous in a mad house, and he put his hands over his ears. He was conscious that the group around the record player was sizing him up and at the same time was determined not to show any extra politeness because he was new.

'What's the matter, don't you like Genesis?' one of the boys asked over the din.

'Genesis?' he said. 'It sounds like apocalypse,' but they didn't get his joke.

'Take no notice of them. They behave so childishly, some of the time,' Kim said, a mock annoyance on her face.

When they'd gone, Raju retreated behind his paper again. He'd been taken by surprise by the new art teacher. They'd been expecting him to turn up for a week to replace Mr Cole, who'd had a heart attack.

'Cole's blacked out,' Steve had said. The headmaster had told them that the new art teacher was a very talented and qualified young man.

'Seen the new art geezer?' Lesley asked that morning. 'You mean …'

'Yeah, the Paki bloke we saw with Dunny down the hall, real freak.'

'If he's so talented and all, what's he want to come to a dump like this?'

'Because he's a Paki, and it's better than trying to get bus fares out of you.' Steve said.

'Paki-Picasso,' Lesley said.

'Very good, want to paint an elephant?' one of the others said, mimicking an Indian accent.

'He's got more A levels and degrees, and that, than you've had hot dinners,' Kim said.

'Hope he speaks English better'n my doctor.'

'The way Dunny was saying his name I thought he was Irish,' Steve said.

'That's the way she was pronouncing it. It's a very common Indian name,' Raju said, thinking that he could offer something to the conversation.

'Like Andy-Gandhy,' Lesley said.

'Oh do leave off,' Kim said, the edge of irritation in her voice telling Raju that she felt protective towards him.

Raju didn't feel he needed her protection, but was glad of it anyway. She had been, in a sense, his guardian angel in the sixth form. If the sixth were planning anything or if there was a conversation in which everybody joined, it would be Kim who, with some remark, would invite Raju to join in. She was in the upper sixth and he was in the lower.

Raju felt she was the most mature of the lot, even though she was younger than they. Raju had bothered to look up her birthday in the register when one of the teachers asked him to return it to the office.

Of course she wasn't to know that part of the reason Raju had wanted to stay on at school and not go into partnership with his uncle in the grocery business, as his father had insisted, was her. She wouldn't know that he had daydreams about her, and that when she singled him out to say something polite, he felt a thrill, a strange ticklish feeling which he was shy of calling love.

The teachers all liked Raju. He never said a rude word to anybody, and he was considered very good at art. He spent most of his free periods in the art room, drawing and sketching the models, the broken violin, the bottles and pots and table lamps, the oranges and apples that Mr Cole had left around the dark, bare room. He told himself that he would try for the A level, and the deputy head told him that he would have to wait for the new teacher to arrive and decide.

When Ravi, for that was the art teacher's name, arrived and looked through their folders of work he said, 'Good God, you'll never make A level with this rubbish. Haven't you done anything apart from these shady objects?'

'We've done lots of painting,' Raju said. 'They're behind the lockers.'

Ravi looked at the paintings, all on cardboard and sugar paper, and he bit his lower lip, and smoothed his hair self-consciously. 'Look, you can't all be landscape freaks,' he said. 'How did you land up all doing the same things? Mind you I like most of them, but they look like you did them from slides or something.'

'We did,' Kim said. 'Mr Cole believed in bringing the outside world into school.'

Ravi got down to hard work with that group. They hated him at first. They thought he was too cocky, too flash in his dress, too familiar with them. 'At least he believes in getting us the bloody A level. Old King Cole didn't have a clue,' one of the boys said.

As their folders began to swell with work and their heads with Ravi's careful praise, the group decided that they could cooperate with him.

Raju wasn't sure. Mr Cole had always dealt with kids as they should be dealt with, Raju thought. At first he even resented the fact that Ravi brought in a hundred new ideas and spent the evenings of his first week painting the walls of the art room. Mr Cole never stayed beyond bell time. His little joke was, 'If you want me, my phone number is RUShome 345,' and Raju was disturbed by the clatter of the machines and furnaces and potters' wheels that Ravi began to install, inviting the group to help him with them after school.

Raju felt that Ravi knew of this resentment but had decided to ignore it. He had thrown himself wholeheartedly into shaking their sleepy art department into a busy awakening.

Besides, Raju felt that Ravi's slightly West Indian accent was phoney and forced and cheeky for an Indian. He had to admit, nevertheless, that Ravi had some warmth, he'd talk to you as an equal and let you call him by his first name even though Raju never did. Old Cole was always telling him that these new-fangled art teachers didn't know about art and didn't know about kids and didn't know about teaching. 'They're all layabouts and communists, and the head and the governors are stacking the pack with them. Something underhand is afoot,' he would say and chuckle at his own joke.

Raju had been Mr Cole's favourite and still felt loyal to him. He was the only one out of his group who had sent him a 'get well soon' card in hospital, until the deputy head had told the rest of the sixth formers, and they agreed with her, that Raju's thoughtfulness had put them to shame.

'Let's paint him one,' Steve suggested, sorry to have been reminded of their collective ingratitude.

Ravi helped plan the card. It was to be a collage of Mr Cole's face stuck on to the bodies of Superman, Batman, a dalek and others, doing amazing feats of strength. Lesley and Steve got down to drawing the card, but when they got to drawing the heads they couldn't get the features right. They asked Ravi to do the heads, but he said he'd never seen what their wonderful Mr Cole looked like.

'Oh, you know, a sort of turnip head and a long neck and ears like Mr Spock.'

'Right. Try and imagine the Loch Ness monster in a tweed jacket and bags.'

'Don't be so mean,' Kim protested, 'and anyway get on with the card.'

'Can't do the blinkin' head.'

'Then let Raju do it,' Kim suggested.

'Come on, Leonardo,' Steve said.

'He's t'riffic on heads,' one of the others said.

Raju had in fact been waiting for the invitation. He was at his own work a little away from the group which had gathered around Lesley's desk. They made way for him and crowded round as he took the stool Lesley had vacated and began to erase the faint sketchings of malformed heads above the muscular action that Steve and Lesley had begun to colour. 'I can only do it in pencil,' Raju said.

They watched as Raju, with small strokes, as though he were writing a script, brought the face of Mr Cole from out of the sheet like a face emerging from a mist. He shaded the hollows of the cheeks. In the pupils of the eyes he captured with a shiver of highlight the inspired madness that seemed to leap out of his subject's forehead.

'You got him, spot on. Great,' Lesley said.

'Colour it in now,' Steve said.

'No. Leave it in pencil,' Ravi said, 'you can't paint over drawings.'

There were five heads in all to do, and as Raju worked, cosy in the admiration of the group, he thought of Mr Cole in his hospital bed. On the one hand he felt excited that the old man would recognize part of it as his work, and on the other hand he had an uneasy feeling that Mr Cole would hate the card. It wasn't the sort of thing he would have encouraged them to do. The card was one way of telling Mr Cole that they were happy and busy without him, that 'art' at the school had changed, that his years of broken violins and fractured pots had been swept away with the cobwebs. The rest of them couldn't have thought of that, they were just being nice, and they were also playing up to Ravi, using the styles and the freedom he'd shown them. A flush of shame at his unintended disloyalty came over Raju. He thought for a moment that he shouldn't have participated in this card lark. He shouldn't have let himself be flattered into doing the heads. But his pencil wouldn't stop. He had no words with which to say what he felt to the others, they wouldn't understand. He knew that the rest of them treated him as though he was Cole's pet and he wanted to outlive that reputation.

While Raju worked at the card Ravi made up an envelope for it.

'It won't fit in a post box, and we can't really fold it.' Steve observed.

'Go and deliver it yourself,' Ravi answered, as they passed the finished card round for signatures.

'Come on, Raju, put your handle there,' Lesley said, handing him the pen.

'I've already sent one,' Raju said. He had decided that at least he wasn't going to sign the card with the rest of them. Cole would notice that.

'It isn't a cheque.'

'I think one is enough,' Raju said, determined to be firm.

'Suit yourself, mate,' Lesley said, shrugging.

'I'd feel silly sending two cards to the same person. They'd think you're in love with them or something.'

'Can we go with it in school time?' Steve asked Ravi.

'I don't see why not,' Ravi said, 'you can say I let you out.' They were jubilant.

'Straight up?'

'We'll be back for lunch.'

'Sure, go on,' Ravi said, 'I've got to get this wheel set up. Not much I can do with you.'

They were gone and Raju dipped his head into his work. He didn't acknowledge Ravi's presence.

'Have you ever done a portrait in oils?' Ravi asked after a while.

Raju shook his head.

'Why don't you try it? Not straight on canvas, but after you mess around a bit I can stretch the skins for you.'

Raju was quite excited with the idea, but he didn't want Ravi to know that. He just lifted his head to say yes, he'd try it after he'd finished what he was doing.

'How long have you been in Britain?' Ravi asked.

'Since I was eight.'

'And your parents, where do they come from?'

'India.'

'Yes I know, but it's a big place as you'll remember.'

'From Jalandhar.'

'Never been there. You know I'm from Bombay.'

Raju didn't acknowledge the remark.

'Have you ever been back to India?'

Raju shook his head.

'I can't go back there, though I'd like to. Get away from London and the cold.'

'Why can't you go back?' Raju asked, his interest faintly aroused.

'Oh, all sorts of things. Running away from it, you know, women and politics and so on. I got involved with an anti-government movement. I used to teach at the university, and they put a couple of my friends in jail.'

'Are you a communist?'

'Yes, I am, sort of, but it's very complicated. Do you know anything about Indian politics?'

'My father gets the newspaper. He knows everything, but I don't bother. Still, I'm very interested, my uncle was a communist.'

'I suppose you feel quite British. You've decided to stay in England?'

Raju hadn't decided anything. That sort of question hadn't crossed his mind. 'I want to do art. Can you do art in India?' For a year or two now he'd made up his mind that he'd be an art teacher, like Mr Cole, but it hadn't struck him that it would mean giving up the possibility of working in India.

'You can do lots of art in India, but you have to do a bit of fighting too.'

As the weeks passed Ravi became the group's favourite teacher. Raju found that Ravi was constantly telling him things about India and the college where he used to teach, and forcing him to think about things he hadn't considered before. Ravi showed him how to work on metal and make bangles and bands out of wire and out of copper plates. Slowly his ambition shifted from wanting to be like Mr Cole to wanting to be at least a bit like Ravi. He talked about his new teacher at home and brought Ravi's arguments and sayings back to try them on his dad. At school he spent more and more time in the art room and found that he wasn't alone, that the rest of the sixth form had taken up the gadgets in the art room as their latest craze. Steve was always there, and Lesley and Kim.

While they worked, they talked to Ravi. He'd go down to the pub with them at lunch and play darts with the boys and he'd give them lifts home in his van after school. When some teachers in the staff room complained that he was getting too familiar with the sixth formers, Ravi came down and told them about the row he'd had.

'He can talk,' Lesley said, referring to a senior member of the staff, 'the second year's call him Pinching Tom, he's always up the girls' skirts.'

'Bent,' Steve said, 'a cross between Hitler and Danny La Rue.'

Raju found himself drawn into the class circle. He began to say things, and at first the rest of them were amazed. He even bought himself a pair of jeans and an embroidered denim shirt because he had overheard Kim talking to another girl about them, and he stopped wearing school uniform as the rest of them had done a year before.

Everyone in the sixth knew who fancied whom. Some of the boys and girls paired off and went out with each other and acquired reputations for being loose, or for being tight, or for being nice or flash or oversexed. Raju heard it all and was glad in a way that he had nothing to do with it. And yet he longed to have the confidence to ask a girl out. There were all sorts of things that stopped him. He would have to keep it a secret from his parents, who wouldn't approve. Still, that wasn't what kept him from trying. He had the feeling that he wasn't capable of it. He had no words with which to approach a girl. He knew the games the rest of them played, or at least he thought he could imagine them, because in spite of all the pairing off that went on, you could never actually hear the boys asking the important question. That seemed to go on in secret. Or maybe nobody asked, they just understood that they were in love, Raju thought.

He longed to be able to steer Kim round to a conversation about a film, or about records, and wait for a sign from her, test her out. If the sign came and the way was clear, he could ask her if she wanted to meet that evening at the Elephant and go to the pictures. Or he could get her phone number after talking to her and phone her in the evening to continue the conversation and ask her then. That way he wouldn't have to ask face-to-face and if she said 'no', he could pretend it never happened.

So Raju's secret passion stayed a secret, but it grew. He watched Kim with an uncanny interest. When they were left alone in the art room, even for a moment while Ravi went to the stock cupboard or something, a strange feeling came over him, a sort of thrill in the chest. She would talk to him about the work they were doing. She began to work very hard at art towards the end of the term, and he overheard the boys saying that there was something wrong with her, she'd turned weird with overwork and overenthusiasm.

Raju didn't think there was anything wrong with her. He felt, but hardly admitted even to himself, that her work was in some way connected with him, that she stayed behind in the art room day after day because of him. He felt she was returning his attention and she began asking him strange questions, about whether he remembered India.

'I've only heard of Delhi and Bombay, but you're not from there, are you, Raju?'

'I'm from Camberwell,' he said, smiling.

'I wish I wasn't. They're such a pig-headed lot.'

She would ask him to criticize her work and Raju discovered a new language in himself. He began to talk about pictures and design. Ravi would join in and usually take over the conversation, bringing out prints and art books to show them the work of strange artists like Escher and Dadd and Kitaj.

Raju felt that Kim was the first person in school who wanted to know what he was like before and after the starting and finishing buzzer of the school day. 'Do you eat Indian food at home?' she once asked, and she inquired about his family, his mother, and what language they spoke at home and even about him getting married.

'Will you let your mum choose your wife, then?'

'No chance,' Raju said. 'This is England and my parents can't bully me about. My cousin ran away and married whomever he wanted. An Irish girl.'

He saw her smile at this. He loved the way her broad mouth opened into a narrow smile, her one buck tooth flashing the mischief in her face. He thought he'd managed to tell her indirectly, ever so indirectly, that his thoughts about girls and about getting married had something to do with her. And she had smiled. He thought of her expression ten times in the next few days, and he wished that Ravi hadn't come in and interrupted their conversation.

Kim seemed quite willing to carry it on later.

'Ask your mum, please, how to cook a real Indian curry and tell me about it, would you do that for me?' she asked, and Raju thought if she only knew how willing he'd be to do anything for her. Get her the recipe? He'd get her the Golden Fleece if she asked for it.

He spent that evening pestering his mother for a recipe and writing it out for Kim, changing 'ghee' to margarine and making a trip to his uncle's grocery shop to ask him what the English names for 'dhania' and 'jeera' were.

'I'm going to try it tonight or tomorrow,' Kim said when he gave her the neat sheet of paper.

For the next few days Raju waited for a sign from her. He was certain that she wanted to pass some message to him, some mysterious token. She was telling him, by the way she looked at him, that she understood the transparent silence that he'd wrapped himself in. She had put a value on his shyness and wasn't going to crash through it, but she was going to ask him, in careful steps, for access through that armour. He saw himself, in a daydream, walking down a long street and she coming towards him and taking his hand, hesitantly, and turning and walking with him and getting him to talk as he had never talked before, explaining how his silence and his modesty were a cover for a feeling as deep as a well.

She would also understand that he had respect for girls, and being Indian, he wouldn't expect to kiss her and feel her and fondle her just because she had agreed to walk down the street with him. She would give herself willingly to him and he would only take what was given. But he knew that nothing would be given without asking.

Two days after Kim took the recipe from him, they were working together in the art room. Kim asked him which way he was walking home, and he looked into her face to reply and felt his tongue thicken with excitement and his words coming out in a jumble. He packed his stuff and they left together.

Ravi had gone home early, so they shut the art room behind them and walked together to Oval tube station. When she left him, she didn't say 'See yuh', she said, 'Goodnight Raju, you'll be in school early tomorrow as always, won't you?'

Raju felt that the blue of her eyes had suddenly turned to silver, and in that mirror was reflected the map of his hopes and maybe of hers. Even though there was some satisfaction in that, he felt his courage had failed him. As they walked together, his folder of drawings under his arm, and her skirt swinging very carefully around her hips, he had made the effort to turn the conversation to a subject which would enable him to ask her what she did with her evenings.

'I want to try some oil portraits,' he said, 'but I'll need a model, you know, who'll sit without fidgeting right through.'

'Oh, can I have my picture taken please?' she said. 'I'd love to do it for you, but I suppose I can't, because I can't really keep still.'

'I'll make a film instead, then,' Raju said.

'Why don't you ask Ravi? He gets paid to teach you, doesn't he? He'll be a good model, with all that thick black hair and funny browny-greeny eyes.'

'No, he won't do.'

'Not your sort, huh? Not handsome enough for you.'

'Not that, he has too much work.'

'Him? He's a lazy sod,' Kim said, looking up quickly at Raju's face and looking away.

'I must practise portraits for A level,' Raju said.

'You'll easy make it and go to art school. Ravi says he thinks you'll be a great illustrator.'

Raju was flattered. He scanned her face and distinctly saw in it something unexpected. She was shy too, she wanted to make some move, to tell him something, but she too found herself incapable.

The next day at school he started on his project. He asked Ravi for a canvas and began sketching a face in pencil. He didn't tell Ravi what he was working at, and he waited till Kim came into the room and looked at her face in a new way. His eyes were not watching, but measuring. He was looking at the pores of her skin, the pinkness, so patchy and running into light, even yellowish skin, her eyes separated by a stubby bridge. He was looking for every twist and shadow of this face that he'd looked at so many times before, and he felt that he was beginning to know it afresh, to know it like an object, coolly.

As soon as he felt that the picture he was working on was faintly identifiable, he took it home. When the sketch was finished, he turned the canvas over and began the portrait in oils. He propped it up against the wall of his room and knelt before it to work on it every day after school. Working for hours on one little piece of Kim's face, and working from his sketch and from his memory, he felt a possessiveness begin to come over him. Slowly, brush stroke by brush stroke, he was bringing her into his room.

Then it was finished, the schoolgirl face which seemed to say that it knew more about life's uncertainties than a schoolgirl should know. When it was done he felt a bit exhausted, and possessive of it more than proud. He had struggled with the hundreds of images and expressions that he could imagine when he thought of her, to distil just one, the one that had all the others in it. When he took it to school, he had a plan. He'd take the first opportunity to ask her out, and he'd give her the canvas. He would return the little piece of possessiveness he had earned; he would give it back to her.

Ravi was the first to see the canvas. 'So that's what you've been doing, you sly bugger,' he said, and then, 'Raju, it's really beautiful. You've caught her as she is, half old lady and half Lolita. Listen, baby, it's fantastic.'

He held the portrait and looked at it in the light.

Then he placed it against the blackboard and ran, taking the steps two at a time, to call the rest of the sixth to see it.

Raju's heart sank as he heard them approaching down

the corridor. He felt suddenly naked. That canvas was a confession. They would all know, they would take the piss out of him. For an instant he felt like grabbing the canvas and running out with it, or even tearing it up. But a pride in his work and the knowledge that he'd done something truthful and had spoken openly for the first time kept him sitting where he was.

They came straight to the canvas. The sight of it struck them as they walked in. Kim was at the back of the crowd. Without a word they let her follow her fixed stare to the front.

'Should've been down to here, in 3D,' Steve said, indicating with his hand below the canvas that Raju should have painted her down to the waist. The moment of dumb wonder had passed. They gathered round Raju and thumped him on his back, as though he'd scored a goal for the school team. Kim stood in front of the painting.

'Raju, it's very good, like a twin,' she said. Raju saw that she was embarrassed. His shyness had flown to her and her boldness to him. He understood, sensing her excitement, that it was not only himself he had exposed in painting her picture.

'I'll show it to the staff room,' Ravi said.

'Not to old Bodger, he'll get overexcited, not good for him.'

'Don't you like it, Kim?' Ravi asked.

'You should have posed in the nude!' Lesley said. 'Blimey, how many hours were you cloistered with our Kim, Raju?'

Of course, something changed in the sixth form from that day. There was evidently a new respect for Raju, both for his skill and for his daring in choosing Kim as a subject. In Kim herself, Raju detected a coolness. She was pulling away from him, as if she feared, ever so slightly, that Raju had declared with that picture that he wanted to work some spell on her. She was there just as regularly, working away in the art room, but she did it now with a total absorption in her work. She only turned to talk if she had something definite to say, not just to chatter. Raju thought she was getting worried about her exams, and it confirmed for him the maturity that made her different from the others.

He had to move fast to stop this new silence from solidifying, from becoming an accepted treaty of distance between them. After all, he'd made his confession and if there was going to be any embarrassment, he had been through it. He thought he should ask her outright, just as the white boys would. The first time would be the only difficult time. He was sure she wouldn't expect it from him. How could he say to her, 'Doing anything later, Kim? Would you like to meet me round the King's Head for a drink?' They would be the wrong words to come out of him. She would laugh. But so what if she laughed, as long as no one heard her. Or him. And if she said yes, then he could see a new kind of existence beginning for him. He would tell her she could take the portrait of herself away from school, as a present. They would go together to all the places she talked about, and they would be together in school in the common room and at work in the art room and she would watch him as he became a struggling but successful painter and when he was earning some money from his first job....

Another pressure bore down on his thoughts. If she did accept, how would he take her out? It would mean getting hold of some money and he could do that easily enough by asking his mum and telling her to keep her mouth shut, but what about the next time? Maybe she'd understand and offer to pay for herself. Or maybe he could get a weekend or evening job like Steve and Lesley did and get a few bob to spend on her. If his father found out, or saw them walking down the street together, he wouldn't approve. They would have to meet secretly and keep themselves from all the prying eyes and gossips of the Indian community.

For days he couldn't muster the courage. There were moments when he felt like swallowing the stone that came to his throat when he thought of it, and asking her outright. Then his opportunity came.

Towards the end of the term, Ravi got the group together and, before the lesson ended, told them that there was an exhibition of Cuban paintings at a gallery in town and that they had better go and see it, because the poster technique was perfect and because he'd like to discuss it with them after. 'Better spend your time sussing it, than getting drugged out of your minds at the King's Head.' The class could never tell if Ravi was serious or half-joking, but they promised to take in the posters in the next week.

When they had gone, Raju continued his work. As he worked he felt the presence of someone else in the room, though he had assumed he was alone, and turning round saw Kim. She was sitting on one of the tall stools, her brow wrinkled, silent and uncertain.

'Still here? I'd thought you'd buzzed off.'

'No,' she said. 'I'm just thinking.'

'You'll get cross eyes if you do it too hard.'

She didn't seem to hear him. 'Are your parents very, kind of prejudiced, Raju?'

The question took him by surprise. 'My father don't like Jamaicans,' Raju said.

'I had an argument with my dad last night,' Kim said, 'about Indians. He's really stupid and he was saying they're all jungle bunnies, not as bad as the coons, but still from villages and that.'

'Some are,' Raju said.

'I was telling him about you and how you were the best artist in the class, and you'd be better than the stuff in the galleries, which is half rubbish and a con anyway.'

Raju felt she was steering the conversation in the direction he had watched for.

'He just said that didn't matter, even cavemen could do drawings. He makes me so mad, and he's so thick, he always argues and he knows he's wrong.'

'Why were you talking about Indians?'

He thought he knew what the answer would be. Surely she was looking in his face in that particular way to see what expectation she had stirred in him.

'I don't care. I couldn't give a monkey's what he says, I'll go out with whichever blokes I choose, black or blue or green with horns and bells on.'

To Raju it felt as though the silence was begging to be shattered. 'Would you go out with me?' he asked, 'I mean to the exhibition. To the posters, the Cuban ones.'

She didn't answer immediately and Raju seemed to hear the question echo like a crashing tray of crockery. He had blundered.

'I've seen it,' she said eventually, 'and I couldn't today anyway. You know I'm really getting into my books and exams. I have to leave this dump.'

It was like being slapped in the face. Or it was like jumping and the parachute not opening. He'd snapped the cord by pulling it too soon.

'I don't much care for posters, really,' he said.

'No, you *must* go.' She sensed she had hurt him. 'It's excellent. It gives you a whole new idea of what art can be used for.'

Raju tried to finish his copying, feeling now as though the air was still foggy with his disappointment. What should he do?

Just then Ravi came in. 'Still here?' he said, cheerily. 'I've got to clear out now because I've got to change and come back to school for the third-year parents.'

'I'm coming out too, I've finished,' Kim said.

Out in the street, Raju couldn't allow himself to think about that moment. He had built himself up, prepared himself for the right moment, and now the moment had failed him. He got home, his head still fixed on the scene, and his mother asked him if he was feeling all right and touched his forehead with the back of her hand. Raju shook it off impatiently. He sat in front of the telly all evening, and he wondered how he'd face her the next day. Kim might tell the others that he'd tried to take her out, but that she'd tactfully refused and given him an excuse because she couldn't bring herself to tell him outright that she didn't fancy him. She probably hadn't even heard of the exhibition. She should have made up some other excuse, told him the truth, that she was afraid her father would see her with a black. That too came as a shock to him. He had thought about whites and blacks and discussed it in class and at home but he had always presumed that he wouldn't ever have a severe problem with being black, not with the kids he'd grown up with, or at least not with some of them.

He went up early to bed and lay awake. He couldn't sleep till the early hours of the morning and, when his alarm rang, he shouted downstairs to his mother that he didn't feel well and he wasn't going to school.

Raju lay on his back through the morning. He thought he'd been cowardly, but he couldn't bear to enter that sixth-form room. He moped around the house and refused to go to school for the two remaining days of that week. He read his texts and his notes at home and told himself that since the mock exams were so close, there'd be hardly anyone from his class going in.

For exam weeks the desks were set out in the hall, and the school changed completely. The younger kids were moved into the lower school and there was no buzzer for periods and no lessons and people came and went as they had to or chose to. Raju went in and did his exams and avoided seeing Kim or any of the seniors who were all engrossed in their A levels. He wasn't allowed in the art room because the art exams were on, and so Raju never got to see Ravi except once when he was on exam duty during maths, giving out blotting paper and graph books.

After the exams Raju didn't go back to school, as some of the others did, to join in the lounging and card playing and football and cricket sessions that always followed upper school exams. His studies had put Kim to the back of his mind. He had resolved to himself that he'd never ask a white girl out again. She had led him on, he was sure of that. It was her way of breaking that bond of possession that he felt he had built towards her. She had proved to herself that she could humiliate him. And the portrait of her was still his, she hadn't accepted it, hadn't given him the cue to offer it to her. When he thought of the portrait he felt it was a wound he'd inflicted on himself. He wanted to get hold of that portrait now and destroy it, burn it. But he couldn't. Any theatrical action would only give him away. Suppose she hadn't told anyone. She might really have seen the exhibition and really needed her time for study. Then it would be best to act as though nothing had been said, nothing had happened. He could go back to school and continue to be 'nervous', and continue as he had always done and work in the art room for the rest of the term because she would have gone and probably got herself a summer job.

The day Raju went back to school, Ravi was putting up an exhibition of students' work in the hall. 'Hey, we've been trying to get hold of you,' Ravi said. 'You've been away … are you OK now? … and we've had an idea. Head's idea really. We're going to have the usual exhibition for inspectors and parents and bods and pick the best work, pottery and jewellery and even paintings, and offer them for sale, flog 'em and give the artists the money minus something for charity. What do you think? Head thinks it'll give you lot a sense of being at work, and time means money, and all that shit.'

Raju agreed it was a good idea. Ravi asked him to sort out all his work and decide what he wanted to sell. The other sixth formers had already put out their best work to flog. The game did make them feel like professionals and for once they were giving a hand with the arrangement of the exhibits.

In the afternoon, Ravi approached him again. Had he decided? Raju had. He handed Ravi the drawings he'd chosen and two canvases.

'You don't want to flog this?' Ravi said when he came to the portrait of Kim.

'Why not? It might get me some money,' Raju said, and Ravi looked at him, surprised at the unfamiliar, strong tone.

Raju didn't go to the exhibition that evening. He had told Ravi that he didn't know about prices and that, so Ravi should do it. He wanted to go to watch the people react to his painting, but he felt he couldn't. If someone wanted to buy it, and he was actually there, he wouldn't want to part with it. If he stayed away they might get rid of it, and he could forget he'd ever painted it.

'I've got almost twenty quid for you,' Ravi told Raju the next day, 'and the head asked all the artists to contribute what they wanted to the Children's Fund.'

'I'll give half,' Raju said.

'Now hold on, you don't want to go promising. This isn't a con, you know. We'll get everyone together and discuss this whole charity thing and how much you're all willing to part with and so on. After all, it's your work. I tell you, I asked a couple of friends from the Royal College and they said your paintings were really nice. I'd told them about you.'

Raju didn't ask Ravi who'd bought the paintings.

In the sixth-form room later, as Raju was stirring himself a cup of coffee, the deputy head, all miniskirt and efficiency, bounced in and said, 'I see Kim liked her portrait enough to put her money on it.'

Raju, while acknowledging her compliment with a smile, felt as though her words had only pulled to the front of his mind what he had known deep down. So she had bought it. It must mean that she had lived with the idea of it too. Some of the money he would get would be hers. He would ask how much it sold for and keep that much and give the rest away. She must want him to know that she'd bought it. She'd take it home and treat it like a twin, and she could say to anyone who asked, that the painter was some Indian bloke in her school, and she thought it was quite a good likeness. She would know different, she would remember him differently, he was sure.

At the start of the holidays Raju began working in his uncle's grocery store. He thought of spending Kim's payment and buying himself some clothes, but changed his mind and bought some books instead, on China and India and on art that Ravi had recommended. School went out of his mind, and after a few weeks so did Kim.

Then one day his mum called him to the phone and said it was his art teacher.

'Raju, you're a hard man to locate. The head thought I should let you know. Very sad news. Mr Cole died in hospital yesterday, he had another attack. I'm just phoning round and letting all his pupils know, at least your lot, about the funeral and so on.'

'Yes.' It struck Raju that he had forgotten old Cole, and the news shocked him, but he was also somehow glad that Ravi had called him.

'Do you want to go to the funeral?'

'Yes … I … I don't know what to wear.'

'Oh anything, it's not like India. The dead don't care anyway. Will you come over to our place at ten tomorrow then? I could take you in the van, it's at Streatham. And later we can come back and chat if you feel like it. I've been meaning to ask you round for some time, after all you're my star pupil now.'

'I'll come at ten o'clock,' he said and Ravi gave him the address.

The next morning, wearing his school jacket and tie, Raju went to Ravi's flat. He rang the bell and Ravi came down, buttoning his shirt. 'Yeah, come in, I've called Steve and Lesley too and they should be here but as usual they'll be late,' Ravi said, taking the stairs two at a time. 'I'll just have a shave if we're going to a funeral,' he said motioning Raju into a room. 'Kim will make you some tea.'

It was a large room, with a thick carpet and floor cushions and a single settee. There were rows of books and a stereo set. On the wall, between two paintings of what looked to Raju like terribly distorted, agonized human shapes, was his portrait of Kim.

As Kim herself came round the door to the kitchen, Raju was standing in front of the picture. As soon as he saw her he made an effort to pull himself together and went and sat on the settee.

'Do you like it there? Ravi hung it between two of his own pictures. I kept telling him to bring them to school but he ...' The voice seemed to ramble on, Raju wasn't catching the words. '... so I said it doesn't matter what you say ... she was saying and Raju turned his face towards her. '... so I thought I'd buy it for him, and then he can have something to remind him of the time when we were all pupils and he put us in touch with ...'

'Raju?' she said, or at any rate he thought she said.

She was asking him, with a housewifely expression on her face if he'd like some tea.

'Yes, of course I want some tea,' he said.

Ravi came back from his shaving and when Lesley and Steve turned up he said, 'You lads can cram into the back of the van, we'd better go.'

It began to drizzle as they laid Mr Cole to rest. The head was there and several of the teachers and a few pupils. They nodded as Ravi joined the teachers and Kim stood with the other girls. Raju nodded back solemnly. Raju looked at Kim just once as they stood in silence and saw her looking back, hard, at him. Her eyes were asking him to understand, he thought. It seemed to him that he knew that expression intimately, and he wished he hadn't tried to paint it.

THE SIEGE OF BABYLON

For the *Race Today* Collective

1.

HURLY STANDS BEHIND THE HALF-DRAWN curtain so that he can look into the street but can't be seen from it. The police have mounted three huge searchlights on tripods, and they light up the ground outside with the artificial daylight of a football field. The glare from two of them is directly in Hurly's eyes. The third is out of sight, mounted outside one of the adjoining buildings. If he pushes his head back, right up against the frame of the window, he can see wire barriers that have been thrown up thirty yards down the street. Beyond the encircling barriers, just outside the circle of light, he can sense the presence of an unnumbered crowd. Their audience. Now and again he fancies that the flash of a camera has burst above the heads of those people, but he can't be sure; it may be some other kind of flare.

Within the circle of light nobody moves. At the edge of the circle, just under the window out of which he is looking, Hurly can see a blue-uniformed policeman standing casually, his arms behind his back, his head perpetually sideways like the face on a coin. Below his blue starred helmet the clean-cut features are unrecognizable.

'Bully still stand up out there?' Hurly hears Kwate's voice behind him.

'Can't see nothing. They've place a man under here.'

Hurly has been at the window for hours. 'I tired of looking,' he says.

He draws his body into the shelter of the wall and glances at Kwate who is sitting with his back straight, his head tilted and resting, looking cool and collected on a chair in the centre of the room. Beyond him, between the door to the corridor and the door to the kitchen, Rupert has drawn up a stool. Against the mantelpiece, next to the tattered divan, their faces to the wall, their backs bent like question marks, arms raised and palms spread flat, resting, their weight shifting from haunch to haunch on the three-legged stools, sit their four hostages.

From time to time the Greek man with the face like the fiddler on the roof and a droopy moustache turns around and tries to plead with Kwate.

'I am poor man, working hard. You is like my son. We come on your side now, we come on your side.'

Kwate's forearm is outstretched, steady. In his hand, pointing at the two men and at the young boy and the girl, is the Smith and Wesson automatic. On Rupert's spread thighs rests the shotgun.

Hurly transfers the Browning from his left to his right hand and wipes the sweat off its butt. He is not sure where to point it, so he holds it drooping down by his side.

'They go cut the electricity,' he says.

'How do you know?'

'They've brought up a whole heap of searchlight and thing outside.'

'I want sight it,' Kwate says, and rising from the chair, backs slowly, cautiously, to change places with Hurly. Hurly gets to the chair and imitates Kwate's sitting position. Once again there is silence in the room. They seem to be waiting for Kwate. Hurly can now hear the breath of the big man, regular as a clock. Occasionally a stool creaks as the weight of a weary body shifts on it. The noise of traffic comes in through the window behind the hum of some machine that has begun throbbing in the street below.

'I goin' call out,' Kwate says, casually, as though announcing to the others that he is going for a leak.

Hurly's eyes dart towards him and then back to the watchers at the wall.

'Burgess!' Kwate shouts, and then again, stretching the two syllables, 'Bur – gess!'

Hurly can hear the buzz of the crowd outside. The sound seems to come through the still air. They have heard Kwate's shout. Then there is the voice on a loudhailer telling the people to get away from the railings.

There is a stamp of boots, and a voice, tinny but amplified through the hailer, calls back, 'We're still here.'

Kwate doesn't reply.

Then the voice again:

'Kwate.'

The name rings out like a clap in an empty courtyard. Hurly sees Kwate's eyes leap to the hostages to see if the sound of his name has any effect on them. The police haven't used any names before. As Kwate raised the double-glazed window when the police moved in, Chief Superintendent Burgess introduced himself to them.

Now they know our names, Hurly thinks, and it makes him feel that somehow the police are getting closer. He backs towards the kitchen door.

'Stop your dancing,' Kwate says. 'Snipers. Babylon will mount snipers in them room across the street. Keep down if you want to come out of here on your feet instead of *after* them.'

'They wouldn't shoot; they might get one of these lot,' Hurly says.

'No, boy, them snipers trained. They could make out a black face from a whitey nose from three thousand yards.'

'They would shoot us, them, anybody,' Rupert says, more to the prisoners than to Kwate.

Hurly watches the hostages carefully. All through the night he has watched them, admitting to himself that he is afraid, actually frightened of these four helpless people they are holding.

'Kwate,' Burgess calls out again.

How do they know his name? Hurly thinks. If they got it out of police records, it wouldn't say *Kwate,* it would say: *Aloysius* Brown, *b.* 1948, *Kingston, Jamaica. Colour* of *eyes: dark brown, negroid hair. Identifying marks: scar* on *left side* of *neck. Three years juvenile detention, nine months for causing actual bodily harm. Involved with black extremist political groups.*

They'd been picked up. Hurly remembers, one night walking home from a blues party.

'Your name?' the sergeant on duty at Kennington police station asked.

'Kwate.'

Slap. He hit Kwate with the heel of his palm straight in the face. 'I want your name, Sunshine, not your boogey-boogey.'

'Aloysius Brown.'

'That's more like it.'

'Kwate, you can't hope to gain anything.' Burgess's voice is eerily clear. 'Have you thought it over? You don't have much time.'

'Don't cut the light,' Kwate shouts back. His voice echoes round the room.

'Say that again!'

'Don't mess with the electricity. If you blow the light we gonna blast one of them hostages and throw them out the window at you.'

For a few moments there is silence outside the window, then the sound of voices consulting.

'We have no intention of cutting off the electricity. Our men can see all of you in the room. Do you want to cooperate with us and tell us your names?'

'Rest it,' Kwate says, and sliding along the wall he thumbs off the light switch.

'What are you doing?' Hurly asks. The darkness is soft to his eyes at first, but soon he begins to pick out the shapes he is guarding. The kitchen light is still on and throws long shadows in the room.

The girl breaks the silence. 'I can't sit like this any more.'

'Shut your mouth, woman,' Kwate snaps.

'I really can't. My arms ache. I feel itchy.'

'Hold them where we could see them. You ought to have more bath, filthy bitch.'

'Where does it itch?' Rupert asks.

'Don't talk to them, man, this ain't no Butlin's. They ain't here for their health. They here because of our health.'

'I asked where it itched,' Rupert repeats deliberately, ignoring Kwate's bark.

'You are something else,' Kwate says.

'All right, tell me,' Rupert insists to the girl.

'Down my back. Oh, please let me put my arms down.'

'I said shut up!' Kwate kicks the divan, but it doesn't make the noise he expects.

'Let her put her arms down,' Hurly says.

'We don't want no argument. I'm going to scratch your back for yuh,' Rupert says, and getting up he walks up to the girl. He sticks the gun in her back and moves it up and down against her flesh.

'Where you say it itches?'

'Please,' she says. 'Please.' There are circles of dried sweat on her white blouse under her armpits, and the small muscles of her neck look fragile under the light down of her blonde hair.

'All right, your arms down.'

'Not you all, just she,' Kwate says, trying to remain in charge.

'Let them sit like that they can't do us nothing,' Hurly says.

'All right, ten minutes' recess,' Kwate says, and his voice is weary. Sleeplessness is beginning to wrinkle his smooth, shiny skin. The sweat stands out in clear beads on his upper lip.

Again the voice from the loudhailer floats up.

'You all must be hungry, Kwate. How much food have you got?'

No answer.

There is the sound of consultation once more and a voice, this time in clear cockney, asks: 'Oi, Quatty, do you agree to accept some food? We've brought up some steaming hot soup, and some snout. Let the hostages have 'em if you don't want 'em.'

'Tell them no, to blood clot. It's Bully, innit?'

'We should give them something, I feel,' Hurly says.

'Aw, come on, we eat nothing from when we come up here,' the Greek man says, turning round on his stool now, his eyes making sure that none of the gunmen will be goaded into using their hardware. 'Police say want food, we take it, yes?'

Rupert has earlier brought out all there was in the kitchen and laid it on the floor for Kwate's inspection: a packet of damp biscuits, four eggs, a couple of slices of mildewed bread and a pat of rancid butter. They are still in a corner of the room where Rupert left them.

'If we take the soup we can make them drink it first to see if it's poison,' Hurly says.

'What do you say, boys?' PC Bully shouts up again. 'Friend and benefactor of wayward boys, the man Bully,' Rupert says.

'All right, send it up,' Kwate shouts back. 'Don't forget the fags, and if you try some trick you could send one food less for the hostages. You try anything and one of them won't be needing food at all, at all.'

In the next ten minutes the tray of soup is in the room with four packs of cigarettes. The police leave the soup in the corridor. They hear the man come up to the top of the stairs and descend again. Hurly counts his footsteps. He counts twenty eight. He says to himself that he'll store the information in his head. He remembers that his father once said to him, 'Don't forget nothing. Count the inches a man made of, then you know his size.'

Rupert goes to fetch the tray when Kwate indicates with a jerk of his head that he can. Hurly, watching Kwate and keeping his revolver trained on the white man, gets to his feet and moves to the door behind Rupert, trying to give Kwate the impression that he is going to cover Rupert's return down the corridor. He sticks his head out. He wants to see if the corridor has a skylight. He wants to look around every crevice of their cage.

He watches Rupert moving cautiously, almost on tiptoe. The corridor looks strange, as though Hurly has never seen it before. There's no skylight, but there's a little window at the top of the stairs. It looks much shorter than it did earlier, Hurly thinks, when they rushed up the stairs, pushing the hostages in front of them. Kwate had paused at the top of the stairs, holding the Greek man while Rupert and Hurly had run the girl and the younger man through into this room. Hurly had left them with Rupert and gone down the corridor again to grab the child who was struggling with Kwate, trying to get his father loose from Kwate's grip. Hurly remembers the panic, the feeling of being up against the wall, as Kwate screamed at the police who were below the turn of the stairs. He was ordering them down and his threats, in spite of his screams, were cool and clear.

'We is armed. We all got gun. I'm going to blast you to blood if you don't back up.'

Hurly heard them scrambling down the stairs, the two PCs who had got out of their car just as the three of them had tried to make a break out of the door with the bag of money. They must have radioed for help, Hurly thought.

It's all gone wrong, the whole bloody thing. But the police will have to give in in the end, Hurly tells himself. The desperate scramble up the stairs seems like a nightmare now, the pushing and pulling and clutching the arms of the white man who had refused to turn round and have the gun conveniently in his back. Hurly had made him walk backwards up the stairs as soon as the heat of the wrestle had turned into the cold fear of the shining black pistol, of its compact but gaping authority. The fat Greek man had held onto Kwate's neck like a man scrambling onto a lifeboat in a choppy sea. They had made the hostages lie down on the floor, and the girl had started crying, long, slow, almost inaudible gasps and sobs. Hurly was still not sure that the hostages understood what had happened. It was a mistake. He could see Rupert, the exhaustion of the first moments gone, blinking his long eyelashes, looking from Kwate to the four figures lying on their bellies in the centre of the room. He could see that even Rupert wanted to say something to the hostages, but neither of them dared in front of Kwate. Kwate couldn't stop himself barking threats at the hostages.

'Hush up,' Hurly said to him, but accepted Kwate's command to stand by the door, to look into the kitchen, to take particular positions around the hostages.

Hurly hands out the soup, watching the hostages as they turn on their stools, as instructed, to eat, clutching the metal mugs with both hands to restore some of the warmth that sitting still has drained out of them. The Greek man begins to speak to his son for the first time now.

'What's your names?' Hurly asks.

'Photopoulos,' the Greek man answers. 'Is my son here, Panos.'

'Cut that nonsense,' Kwate says, rising.

'It's best we know their names,' Hurly protests.

'Rest it. This ain't social security, asking people them private business.'

Kwate's tone tells Hurly that he is determined to give orders. He is the oldest; he has masterminded the whole mess. Hurly thinks he knows how to handle Kwate. They have to keep him cool. I know Kwate as Rupert don't know him, he thinks. There's always a reason for Kwate's temper. OK, he's right. We shouldn't get friendly with these people. It's us or them, after all, Hurly thinks.

Then as though Kwate has been reading his mind, he says, 'It's not us and these here, it's us and the whole Babylon. Them out there. You got a piece of Babylon in here and you hold it the distance of a bullet, boy, don't go asking names and stupidness.'

'The queen versus the queen's niggers,' Rupert says. As the night wears on, Hurly can feel the sleep crawling from the back of his skull. The words of a reggae tune keep going round in his head. 'The righteous shall stand and the weak heart drop,' he says, staring at the ceiling and rocking on the back legs of his chair.

'If it's the Bible you're after quoting,' Rupert says, parodying his mum, 'you'd best remember your strongest prayers.'

~

2.

'WHY AIN'T THERE NO FOOD here?' Kwate asks the Greek man.

'Nobody want work weekends. Only for plenty money. So nobody stay here. I was waiting till all the money come in on Friday night; all drivers come for money Friday. Is pay day.'

'All right leave it,' Kwate says.

The Greek man won't leave it. A direct question gives him the chance to reach out with words to his captors. All day his eyes have been trying to search their faces for some point of contact with them.

'If they want work overtime, then they tells me Friday night. If they don't, then too bad.' He shrugs his shoulders and smiles. 'No white man want to work Saturday. Only Greek, Jamaican, Paki drivers work Saturday.'

'What were you doing here?' Hurly asks the white man.

The man looks at the girl. 'She's my girlfriend.' Only for an instant does he take his eyes off the guns.

'So, did we ask you for a marriage certificate?' Rupert says. 'My spa here asked a simple question.'

'I work here. I was sitting playing cards with Photo when you came to pay us a call,' the man says, with an edge of insolence in his voice.

'So what's she doing here?' Rupert asks.

'Search me. You brought her up here.'

Hurly sees that the white man is tense and the tension makes him talk faster, speeding up his drawl. He looks into the man's blue eyes which refuse to look back. His Adam's apple jumps under the unshaved stubble on his neck.

'So you were going to have a little bap-de-bap with the lady here?' Rupert says.

'I stay the night sometimes. I live down Bromley, and if it's late I hole up here. It's a kind of waiting room.'

'So you make him wait?' Rupert asks, turning to the girl.

Hurly feels that Rupert is pushing them too far. He watches Rupert and can see that there's an uncertainty about his smart talk. He's putting on this bullying to prove to himself that he's not afraid of these people. Especially the white man. He's the sort of white man who would lick you down first and then ask questions. Hurly can sense that the white man is uneasy. He too can see that these three pairs of eyes have singled him out as potential danger.

The girl looks nervously at the white man. She looks uncertain, as though she doesn't know whether to reply to Rupert or not.

'I wish I hadn't stayed for that game with Photo now,' the white man says.

'I wish I was Mao Tse-tung,' Rupert replies. 'No, not him, I wish I was, what's that daft millionaire's name in the States? The guy who locks himself up in one room with his friends, and his friends turned out to be enemies? Howard somethin.'

'Howard Hughes,' the white man says.

'Yeah, him. We coulda be rich today if you didn't shoot your mouth off. What you had to lose? It's your money.'

'I should be so lucky. It's the company's money.'

'So you guard it like Judas's treasure?'

'I wasn't to know what you was up to, was I?'

'Stop mess with them. No talk,' Kwate interrupts.

'No names, no talk, what is this? You figure how we going out? Them should talk a bit to us, you know, like pay their way, do a like drama or something,' Rupert says.

'Who drop the money?' Kwate now asks.

Rupert had been carrying the bag as they started to make their way out of the little office downstairs. They had made too much noise smashing the lock, forcing the doors of the cupboard in which Slingo said the money was kept. The money was there all right. If they had been half a minute faster, they could have got away with it. So enters the white man. He had come running down the stairs followed by the Greek man, the girl and the child who all began to shout when they realized that Rupert had gone out of the door with the money. For an instant, Kwate had attempted to bluff. He caught the man at the bottom of the stairs.

'We have to bang all night to get a cab in this place?' he had asked. And then, 'If you've closed up you shouldn't leave the light on.'

The white man hadn't hesitated for a moment. He looked past Kwate, and pushing him with his elbow in his neck, he ran after Rupert into the street. Kwate was thrown off balance and the Greek man saw the shotgun which Kwate was holding behind his back. He threw himself on Kwate and tried to wrestle him for it.

Then Rupert came rushing back into the shop, still trying to fight off the white man. The next thing Hurly knew was that Kwate had jerked free with a shout and rushed to the door, pushing Rupert and the white man. Hurly had taken two steps to follow when the police car screeched to a halt at the kerb and the two policemen jumped out. Hurly had taken the initiative. 'Back up the stairs,' he shouted to the girl and the child, and Rupert and Kwate had dashed past him, herding the white man and the Greek at gunpoint.

Rupert can't remember dropping the money. He knows that Kwate's question is directed at him to make him shut up. He goes back to his station now, the chair between the two doors. They have boarded up the kitchen window by pushing the rickety kitchen cupboard up against it and piling the table on top of the cupboard. The kitchen leads to a miserable hole of a toilet, a little boxed-in square without a window.

The faces of the hostages are not very clear from where Rupert is sitting. His ear is on the corridor and the stairs beyond. The child has said nothing. He looks at his father who pats his hand periodically, and says to them, 'You look fine boys to me. Nothing against black myself, everybody is same. Lots of Jamaican drivers work for me, but I not the boss, eh? Is not my money. I'm a worker. Pay rent, pay tax, gas, electricity, nothing left, eh?' He turns the cloth lining of his jacket pockets out. Rupert can see that though he is trying to make them feel at ease with him, the man is terrified, not of him, but of Kwate.

Kwate has decided that a message must be sent out demanding a deal with the police. They will go to Algeria. They will ask for safe conduct to Heathrow airport and carry their hostages with them. Hurly doesn't know where Algeria is, but Kwate says that they are on the side of terrorists, revolutionaries, anyone who strikes a blow for the oppressed of the world.

'What you for and what you against?' Kwate demands.

'Isn't Algeria communist?' Rupert asks.

'Communist wouldn't have an ambassador in Babylon. Them countries is dread, and they wouldn't send nobody here or they get the chop as spies,' Hurly says.

'Leave the politics to I,' Kwate says. 'Just write the note.'

'We have to write two notes. One to the Algerian ambassador, one to the po-lis,' Rupert says.

'We could go to Africa from there,' Hurly ventures.

'It is in Africa.' Rupert looks at Hurly as though he is a schoolmate giving stupid answers in class.

'No. I mean to our own people,' Hurly explains.

'You mean Brockley,' Rupert says.

'Don't jester,' Hurly says. Kwate looks around the room for something to write with.

'We should call the Jamaican ambassador,' Hurly tries hopefully.

'He's called the high commissioner,' Rupert says. 'We want to send it to the high commission.'

'There would be a whole heap of pressure on those dogs from the people. Jack them up. They'd have to think before refusing us. I never buy a passport for nothing,' Kwate says.

'What people?' Rupert asks.

'The masses,' Hurly replies, thinking he's gauged Kwate's meaning.

It seems to Rupert as though nothing has been decided. They've written the note. It says: *We demand a plane at Heathrow airport with a black pilot and crew to take us to Algeria without refuelling stops. We demand to see the Algeria representative and the Jamaican high commissioner, who is empowered to negotiate with us. We are going to shoot one of the hostages if you don't agree. This deadline expires at noon.*

Now there's an argument about how to sign it. Rupert wants to leave it unsigned, and Hurly wants to sign it *The Freedom Fighters*. Kwate decides. It will be left unsigned. Kwate gets Rupert to read the note to the hostages.

'You doing a wrong thing there,' the Greek man says.

'Can we write notes out to our relatives? We can say you're treating us well. It'll be good for your propaganda, you know,' the white man offers.

'Eh-eh, I ain't allowing no code and thing to pass this window. Next we know they'll come crashing through the door.'

'The world will end with bang bang and not with whisper,' Hurly pronounces, opening his revolver, pulling the bullet out of the chamber and blowing through the barrel. He feels the weight of the bullet for the first time.

'What's that?' Rupert asks.

'That's what the poet say. They tell us that in school.'

As dawn breaks it begins to drizzle. The hostages are allowed to go to the toilet, one by one. The note is thrown out of the window. Kwate has Hurly guard the hostages as they pass through the kitchen, the child first, the girl, the white man and then the Greek man. A silent procession. They have heard the death warrant that these boys have pronounced on them, and alone in the kitchen with each of them, Hurly feels awkward. The girl tries to smile, a weak, unsure smile. Hurly doesn't want to smile back. Kwate is right. We shouldn't get friendly with these people. If they're in dead trouble, so are we, Hurly thinks. For all he knows, one of them is going to have to shoot one of these people tomorrow. And yet he wants to convince them, the girl, the Greek man, even the child, that he is not being mean, that he's doing what he has to do, he's just trying to remain private, to keep his anxieties to himself.

The white man throws a glance at him as the girl leaves. He has singled me out as the soft one of us three, Hurly thinks. Rupert plays tough but he isn't really tough. He's keeping himself going with all his smart talk, but he'll crack sooner than me. It's funny watching this white man going to the toilet, forcing him to leave the door slightly ajar as Kwate has instructed. The man don't show any fear, he hides it like all white men do, Hurly thinks, with a twinge of admiration. And yet he can smell the anxiety off him, and off the Greek man.

Years ago, his mother told him that cats never die in the house. They go out and choose their resting place because they don't want to bother the people who've kept them alive, with the inconvenience and terror of death. He remembers hearing also, somewhere, maybe in school, that elephants bury themselves before they die. If they killed one of these hostages, what would they do with the body? Blood and stink and horror. Hurly thinks, people have to bear each other's blood and stink and fear. Maybe you can bear that in your family, with people you love, you can take on the idea of their death, but the smell of anxiety that comes off these people, the hostages, even off Kwate and Rupert, it's the stink of strangers. Any moment those fears might break out into panic. What could he do, or Kwate do with his cool and his calculation? They were messing with something that was beyond calculation here. They were caught up in a drama without a plot. They would each have to learn how to be completely private, to prevent trapping the others in fear, like the fear of soldiers in a trench war, your own side and the other side, all those Germans stumbling in the mud with barbed wire in their guts, bleeding, sweaty shirts and gaping mouths.

It was stupid wanting to sign the note *Freedom Fighters*. What sort of freedom were they fighting for now? We have to find a way of living with these people and not being bothered by their stink, and that's freedom, Hurly thinks.

Over the loudhailer comes Burgess's voice: 'Boys, we've got your note.'

～

3.

BEFORE THEY WILL GIVE ANY reply to the demands, the police want confirmation of the names of the hostages.

'I don't want to give my name,' the girl says.

'I ain't want your name,' Kwate says. 'You are the Greek man and that's your chile, and we have here a beast-man and his piece. No names.' He has been careful to call 'oi' when he wants Rupert or Hurly. 'I the only person with a name. Just call me Kwate.'

'You hear now, don't call us all John, either,' Rupert says.

'Write it down on a piece of paper, your names and addresses,' Kwate commands.

'My dad don't know I'm here,' the girl says. The circles of half-sleep have begun to mark her eyes.

'You just write it,' Kwate says handing her a sheet of paper. 'Can you write?' he asks the white man, and then for the first time grins.

One after the other the hostages sign. The child gets hold of the paper and puts it on the floor. His father looks over his shoulder. Kwate glances at the sheet, folds it up carelessly, winds it around the handle of one of the police mugs and throws it, clattering, to the street below.

Rupert walks around the room and opens the drawers of the writing desk. 'Where you put the pack of cards?' he asks Hurly who tidied up the room the previous day.

Out of the drawer comes a pack of cards, a box overflowing with cigarette coupons, some account books and a thick text bound in yellow.

'What's this book?' Rupert asks the white man.

'It's my book,' the man replies.

'So, I ain't stealing it,' Rupert says. 'You want to call me a thief?' He leafs through the book. It's called *I Ching*.

'You interested in kung fu?' he asks the white man.

'Nothing to do with kung fu, mate,' the man replies.

'It's a Chiney book, isn't it?' Rupert thumbs through it. 'What you do with this book?'

'Read it.'

Rupert turns to look at the man. This is too cheeky, he feels.

'Is for fortunes,' the Greek man says, 'he tell fortunes with it. Your luck for the days.'

Rupert nods, accepting that as a satisfactory answer. He opens the book at random and reads:

> The best man in his dwelling loves the earth
> In his heart he loves what is profound
> In his associations he loves humanity
> In his words he loves faithfulness
> In government he loves order
> In handling affairs he loves competence
> In his activities he loves timelessness.
> It is because he does not compete that
>   he is without reproach.

'This is a true book,' Rupert says. He scratches the back of his head ritualistically. *Competence, timelessness, faithfulness:* he tries to absorb the ideas. Little bags under his eyes bunch up as he squints at the paper. Edwina always says that he looks like a child when he's reading, amazed that the print can trap his mind.

'What did your fortunes say?' he asks the white man.

'It said I'd be in deep trouble,' the white man answers. Rupert looks at him, stares into his startlingly light-blue eyes, lets his eyes roam slowly over his tartan lumbershirt and tight jeans. The man dresses younger than he is, he thinks.

'Your stars must be the same to mine. I'm in dead trouble and all.'

'Not when you're still holding the gun, mate,' the man says. It reminds Rupert of what the white kids in the drama group used to say: 'What do you call a nigger with a gun? You calls him Bwana.'

'This thing,' he says, picking up the pistol which rests on the table next to him. 'It's a passport to Algeria, eh Hurly?'

But although he speaks of it, Rupert doesn't want to think about Algeria. If only the white man understood how desperate he is to disown that gun. He hadn't been told about the guns when they were planning the robbery. Only about the money, only about the simplicity of it all. 'Liberate' the money, Kwate had said, not steal it. A thousand pounds in his pocket, and that would be a passport to a future, a way of looking forward to the next day. You could measure days by the ways in which you could spend money through them.

Rupert had seen it as a way of getting Edwina back. Not that she'd be attracted by the money. She never thought about that sort of thing. Her kind of whites took money for granted. Ever since she'd gone, he had thought the only way to get her back was to give her the idea that he was going places, give her some vision of the future with him.

He would do this one job, he thought, and then he would get out of Kwate's way, out of Hurly's way. He would do it and forget them.

Kwate had called the robbery 'an act of survival'. You couldn't grudge people the things they had to do for 'survival'. Everything Rupert had done, his whole life up to the time he'd met Edwina, could be looked at like that – 'hustle' and 'survival'. Kwate had the knack of truth; he found words to make experience fall into line.

Six months ago, Rupert would have been down on the Portobello Road selling second-hand macs and coats. That was his last successful hustle. A white boy, Nick, a boy he'd been at school with, had taught him the trick. Nick had dreamt it up. They would dress up politely and go to Hampstead or to Dulwich, to the doors of town houses, the houses of the rich, and spin a yarn to the ladies who answered the doorbells. They'd put on a sober face and tell them that they were collecting clothes for a jumble sale in Brixton to finance a nursery school for young blacks. They would be back the next day if 'Miss' wanted to contribute anything, any old thing, like raincoats which nobody used and so on.

Rupert collected stacks of stuff; the people they tapped were suckers for the line. Then chuck all the Burberries and Gannexes into the laundromat dry cleaner, iron them out, and take them, round to the 'Bello to flog.

That was the real work, the sweat for which money was exchanged. The regular market-stall people down the Portobello had canvasses to keep the rain out and estate cars and vans in which to stash their loot. Rupert made do with an old suitcase which he'd taken from his mother and a set of piled packing cases to display his wares.

The blacks who floated down the 'Bello would look contemptuously at him. 'What you selling there?'

At first Rupert had been terrified of them. Then, after Slingo had moved in on him, and he got used to Slingo's cat-and-mouse manner, his game of constantly threatening the people he was talking with, he became more comfortable with these swaggerers. He had begun to learn, through being with Slingo and his friends, just how much of their swagger was a manner. 'You can see what I'm selling, Jah,' he would reply.

One Saturday a 'Power boy', a man with dark glasses and a beret and an imitation military jacket sauntered up to him. 'Why you want to keep the white man dry when a hard rain's gonna fall?' he said.

Rupert felt that he'd made up the line and crossed the street with the sole intention of delivering it.

'Talk to me if you've got fourteen pounds, otherwise move on,' he said to the man.

'A tough brother,' the Power boy said, in what he fancied was an American accent, 'a rough mother. I'll be seeing you when the home fires begin to burn.'

'Yeah,' Rupert said, 'and bring your fourteen pounds.'

He did his business on the right side of the tracks. Beyond the antique stalls and the throng of Saturday tourists on the Portobello Road, beyond the concrete feet of the elevated highway that seemed planted there to make a separation between rich and poor, black and white, sprawled the ghetto. There were West Indian restaurants, reggae shops, second-hand clothing stalls, stalls selling black revolutionary literature and an endless line of junk shops. At first, Rupert would do his business and go home. After Slingo moved in on him and came down occasionally to the stall where he was selling on Saturday mornings, he would venture, under Slingo's protection, into the black cafés beyond the divide. Sometimes they would meet Kwate. Slingo would talk about the hundred schemes he had of doing really good business, but Rupert knew, Kwate knew, everyone who sat around them knew, that Slingo would stop short of effort. He regarded work as subhuman activity, he wouldn't dream of doing it.

Rupert kept his own business and his plans and hustles from Slingo and from the others who hung around the squat. He didn't trust Slingo. He slept with his money under his pillow as a precaution, even though he knew that Slingo wouldn't do anything as crude as rob him. Yet it was better to be safe than sorry.

Until he met Slingo and Kwate and Hurly, he hadn't any black friends. Brixton had been a mystery to him. He would go into the market for his mother, and he would see the black gangs hanging around the record shops. He knew their reputations, and some of them he knew from school, but he kept himself aloof. Once he saw a black girl pick a woman's handbag and the girl saw him seeing her, and she smiled. He couldn't get himself to do that, he thought, he'd have to be more inventive, he'd have to be safer.

When he lost a job his mother would moan at him and she would get her husband, who wasn't Rupert's father, to 'reason with the boy', which years ago meant a belting, but now that he was older, a shouting match and a punch in the face if he was unlucky.

Since he'd quit school, Rupert had had twenty jobs. At one time he'd been a jewel polisher in an East End firm. He'd only taken the job, out of all the others the careers' officer had suggested to him, because it sounded as if one could take advantage of other people's carelessness in such a job, pocket a diamond or two. But the guys who ran that racket knew what they were doing. They'd give you a chance to slip something under your overalls and then they'd have you. Set up and send down, that's how the world is kept honest.

He'd lost that job because the guy on the bench next to him had tried to steal an uncut stone. The man in the office said, 'We tried to teach you a skill, here, Mr Dowling, but we believe you abused our trust in abetting Andrew in his dishonest ways.'

'I never troubled the stones, Mr Conchy.'

'No, but you left your register unmarked until Andrew could fill it in. We'll leave the police out of this because no damage has been done. But please remember, after you get your cards from Tony, that wherever you work you'll be handling other people's wealth. You have to learn to distinguish what's yours from ...'

After that came the job of salesman at the posh leather merchant in Bond Street. One day Nick had come in, dressed in a pin-striped suit and carrying a huge paper bag of clothes he'd bought. Rupert had stuffed an identical bag with watch straps, handbags, belts and wallets and swapped it for the 'customer's' bag of clothing. He had stayed in that job for a few more days, then told the manager that he wanted to leave as he was going to Palestine to train as a guerilla, but that he'd very much like to work in the same capacity when he returned in two months' time.

'Have a nice holiday,' the manager said. 'But since you're not eligible for leave till you've worked for at least six months, we may find that we need somebody permanent ...'

It was Nick who told him that he could squat a place, that it was possible to set oneself up like the hippies did by smashing through the glass of an empty house, getting oneself inside and claiming squatters' rights. Nick had gone with him one afternoon and helped him move into the empty, four-bedroomed, damp, stinking domain. He had moved in a mattress and lived like a ghost in one of the rooms, the rest of them echoing with emptiness.

That's when he met Slingo and Kwate and the rest. He had returned from the Portobello Road one Saturday to find them already in his house. He put his key in the door and found that it didn't work. A sort of panic seized him. He thought the police had moved in and changed the lock or something. He peered through the letter box and voices floated out of the house. A figure came down the stairs.

'What you want?' Slingo had asked.

'I live here.'

'Who it is?' a voice shouted down the stairs.

'Some lickle half-caste boy say he live here,' Slingo shouted.

'I got the key,' Rupert said, lamely.

'So that's all your stuff, upstairs?'

'Yeah, it's my stuff.'

'Well, you better get it shifted, because you don't live in this here yard no more.'

Rupert didn't know how to react. 'I got this place first.'

'I got it second,' Slingo said.

Then Kwate had come down the stairs.

'Let the boy in,' he said to Slingo, and Slingo moved aside, withdrawing his arm that barred Rupert from the door.

'I pay rent for this place,' Rupert lied.

As soon as he saw Slingo's face in that doorway, he knew that this was what he had feared from the beginning. Someone else would move in on him. In a flash Rupert had decided that he would fight to keep his place. He couldn't turn tail and remove his things. He had nowhere to go.

Kwate had resolved it. He asked him to come upstairs.

'Let's go into your room,' Kwate had said and Rupert led them up. There were two other people in the empty room upstairs. Slingo had brought his own stuff into the house. He had changed the lock on the door. He was talking about bringing in a cooker. 'You better ask this brother,' Kwate said to Slingo. 'We didn't know the place was already squat.'

There was no hope of getting them out, Rupert thought. He addressed his remarks to Kwate whom he could see was in charge. He explained how he had moved in and lived there for six weeks.

'Now you have to share,' Kwate said. 'If this is your room, this is your room. Slingo here has the next door.'

That's how it was settled. Rupert heard Kwate tell Slingo to give the boy a key and to treat him nice, because the boy could call the police on them if he wanted. 'Don't ever call nobody half-caste,' Kwate had said, 'one grain does make the whole sea salt.'

Kwate gave him confidence. He was the only person Rupert had ever met who seemed to understand the whole jigsaw of the world and place the pieces to make an already conceived picture. Rupert learnt that Hurly was his disciple, and that Slingo, though not impressed with Kwate's advertised wisdom, hung around him because he felt he could put Kwate to use.

'The man have theory,' Hurly would say. It never became clear to Rupert what Kwate did for a living, but it seemed to him that everybody owed him favours. He would use his authority to make one person do something for another. He was a contact man.

But he was more than that. Kwate it was who had explained to Rupert, sitting in Slingo's room, and later in the cafés of Brixton or Notting Hill, why things happened the way they did. He said that slavery hadn't been abolished, that working on the buses or cleaning up white man's dirt in the hospitals was a new kind of slavery. He had some startling opinions. He told Rupert that blacks weren't hated by 'the man'. In Kwate's world picture it was 'the man' who was the power that made the world run. 'The man' loved blacks really, he loved their hands and their cotton-picking fingers and their strong muscles, because they made money for him, and you have to love your instruments. The world was made up of love and hate, and most of all it was made up of power, and people who had power, or wanted it, must know how to manipulate the love and hate of other people. When Hurly said the police were racists, Kwate argued that they weren't. They just had some misdirected hate, because really 'the man' wanted the police to treat blacks like everyone else, he wanted Babylon to do its job, which was to keep the rich that way and the poor any way they could.

Kwate declared that he didn't talk politics. Rupert had watched him argue with a white man who walked into the Portobello café one day and tried to sell them a newspaper of some sort. Kwate was telling him that his newspaper was no good because it didn't know who hated what and why.

The white man listened to Kwate for a bit and then said, 'The mistake you make is you don't see the classes in society, you don't see it as a class problem. The exploitation of black people is a class problem.'

Kwate didn't hesitate. 'It's not a class problem,' he replied, 'it's an arse problem. Too much arseholes like you try to tell black people how and when to fight.'

They had laughed. The white man had shrugged and gone away.

One Saturday, sales had been slack. A short stout Japanese man had come up to Rupert and grinned. He looked through the coats and picked out the two with the Burberry labels.

'They're nearly new.'

'What is nearly, please?'

'It's when you get close,' Rupert said, and gave the Japanese what he took to be a definition of 'nearly' with one hand almost touching the other.

'And seeing as you are an honoured guest in our country,' he continued, trying to put on his best posh accent, 'I'll give them both to you for twenty pounds.'

'Only American dollars,' the man said, smiling apologetically. He pulled out a fat wallet and began to shrug and show Rupert a wad of foreign money.

'No Anglaisy?' Rupert asked, and smiled back.

The man shook his head.

'All right, give me dollars,' Rupert said. 'How much dollars for a pound? Wait a minute.' He went over to the next stall where an Indian man was selling Japanese transistor radios.

'You know about foreign money?'

'A little.'

'How much is twenty quid in dollars?'

'From Japanese you could get forty dollars,' the Indian whispered turning suddenly conspiratorial.

'OK. All right. I'll see you right next time, old man.'

'Forty dollars,' Rupert said to the Japanese, and the man, still smiling, adjusted his camera strap on his shoulder and counted out eight notes.

On Monday, Rupert took the five-dollar bills down to the bank in Brixton. The assistant came back with the manager.

'We're very sorry, sir, but these aren't valid currency.'

'You mean bank don't change American money?'

'I mean this isn't American money. It's counterfeit. These notes are as good as Monopoly money. We've had a lot of it recently. I'm sure the police would be interested in where you acquired them. You see it's my duty to...'

Rupert grabbed the notes and walked out. Play money!

Hustle and be hustled. He didn't expect it of the Japanese. He wouldn't have trusted a white man with this foreign money racket. How stupid, how bloody stupid. You look clean, you act dirty. How to pass these notes off on someone else? He wasn't going to the police. They'd have him for printing the money. No, he wasn't going to no police....

Rupert went up to Slingo's room, the dud notes ashamedly deep in his pocket. He wouldn't tell Slingo about the Japanese man. He knew that Slingo was of the opinion that God made suckers to preserve a holy balance in the world. Slingo had theories about the smartness of different races, and the Chinese and Japanese ranked low on his scale. Once Slingo had said to him that yellow people had to invent unarmed combat like kung fu and karate because they didn't have the science to put machine guns together. 'What's one better than black belt?' was Slingo's question to the young blacks who were in love with Bruce Lee and kicked and posed in imaginary victories over fabulous foes. 'Gun belt.'

'Wha' go on?' Slingo asked, reclining on his bed, the record player booming out its endless combination of *Natty* and *dread* and *Babylon* and *Jah-Jah* and *Rasta don't do this or Rasta do that.*

'Nothing much, I there,' Rupert replied, with studied laziness. With Slingo he talked as Slingo would. At first Rupert had felt a bit awkward adopting Slingo's phrases and his slurring speech, but surrounded by lads who belted it out and competed with each other for the possession of the latest phrase, he had accepted it. It helped him dramatize himself when he wanted to. In arguments with

Edwina he'd begin to 'talk black'. She liked him to do it. 'Tcha, I cyan't deal with that, don't mess with my head,' he'd say. He didn't feel false talking like that any more. He'd talk like that at home when he wanted to be difficult and his mother would tolerate it as she had tolerated long years of her husband's moods.

And yet Rupert knew that even Slingo, even the most far-out hustlers who hung around their squat, could talk straight English when they wanted to. Only Slingo never did. To him the very obscurity of his language, the trickiness of his accent, were sources of power. Rupert knew that Slingo enjoyed forcing him to listen carefully and concentrate on catching the drift of what he was saying. Language was identity, Rupert had learnt, even for him, a half-caste with an Irish mother and Nigerian father. Identity was power.

~

4.

THE DRAMA WORKSHOP HAD BEEN a real 'period of development' for Rupert. More words he'd picked up, this time from Michael who ran the group. They were all right words, they made sense of the tumble of his existence. One of the youths he hung around with at the jeweller's shop had taken him to the workshop. Rupert had never taken part in anything the school had asked him to do. After the third year, when he began wearing Rasta caps and going around predominantly with the blacks who lounged around the school corridors, carrying pre-release records for prestige rather than to play, treating school as a meeting place, teaching each other the rude-boy idiom of the ghetto and doing as little work as possible, he had given up running in the athletics team or bouncing a ball for the basketball teacher.

The only thing he'd ever done for the school play was sit at the back of the audience and laugh uproariously at the wrong moments till the lights were switched on and he and his mob were marched off to the head's office, protesting that blacks weren't even allowed to enjoy Shakespeare in that school. But his friend told him that there were lots of black girls in the drama group, and that induced him to give it a try.

His notions of it changed with the first visit. He found he liked Michael, and Edwina, his wife, who ran the group with him. Edwina was a teacher at a school near the workshop, which was held in a youth centre called the Rampant Project. She was the mastermind of Tuesday evenings, even though it was Michael who got them all round in a circle to begin each session and help them to discuss different things with as much freedom and complication as they could muster. It wasn't like school. The seriousness of the old members of the group was contagious. They would act out the little skits and improvisations on a theme which followed, with all the vanity of footballers entering the arena, eye on object, ear on approval.

After a few Tuesdays Rupert felt easy with the group, even though there was a lingering feeling that those who asked you to put your anxieties or hang-ups into words were in some way trying to control you. Yet Edwina and Michael were pretty straightforward themselves, or at least Michael was. Behind his gold-rimmed glasses, his sincere eyes seemed always wide open in utter frankness. And when they all talked in the pub afterwards, Rupert discovered that the talk continued, that most of the group saw each other and knew each other outside the circle of chairs and props that formed their Tuesday evenings.

The group had sat back with a sort of embarrassed expectancy the day Michael began a session by stating flatly that he and Edwina had 'decided to split'. They had talked it over – what else could they do? – and they had decided that it was their duty to tell the drama group. All right, he had to admit that they had treated some of the group's confessions as kids' stuff, he was willing to say that now, but they both felt that they had grown up together over a year or more – yes, I've got grey hairs but you never stop growing – but they would like to tell the group exactly, or as best they could, what conclusions they had come to.

A hush fell over the fourteen people assembled there. Usually when one of them was struggling to say something difficult, the rest of them encouraged him or her, bantering and making jokes to steer the atmosphere away from that of a psychiatrist's couch or of a priest's confessional. Michael gulped several times during his monologue.

One of the girls asked if that meant an end to the drama group.

'No, we've decided to carry on with the group. I hope you want us to, I mean all of you. I don't want anyone to misunderstand. We aren't parading private miseries in front of you. We've known each other – how long, Edwina? – five years, and we're not getting a divorce or anything hasty like that; we just feel we haven't put our energies into exploring other people. It's a wide world, and we live in London and the city may be a dark satanic mill, but it's also a possibility of souls. Something has made us stale, I wish I knew what. So we've decided to try and live our own ....'

The group was waiting for Edwina's interruption. Some of them knew that Michael had a neat way of imposing explanations on people. Edwina was warmer. 'Michael's right, there's no need to split from the group, even though we're both sure you can carry it on on your own.

There was a chorus of 'Naw'.

'Thank you, fans,' Edwina said, waving her arms. 'We've always insisted that you dig into yourselves like mines, and it's our turn to put the cards on the table, see?'

They saw. Michael said, 'So shall we work out today why exactly people get stale for each other?'

One of the girls began to giggle.

'OK, so we're funny,' Michael said. 'And if we are, you're entitled to laugh.'

'It's not that,' the girl said. 'It's my mum and dad. Mum's always saying to him, "You smell bad, bad, man, and you don't leave no cash for the children, as though I don't have to put up with your rubber smell all me life." Dad works in the rubber place up Harlesden.'

'That's a pretty straightforward reason for splitting. I ought to say Ed stinks of kids, at least her mentality does.'

They took it as a feeble joke.

'Marriage is a convenience,' Rupert contributed, looking at Edwina. It was what she had said to him the last time she was at his place.

'A public convenience,' Michael said, and there was a pause before someone suggested that they should talk in groups about how you get bored with people you've known for a long time.

Both Michael and Edwina avoided being in the same group as Rupert that session. When they were going to the pub, Edwina said quickly to Rupert that she'd see him later, at his place. She had never openly been there. She told him that Michael didn't ask her where she went.

Rupert had never wanted to deceive Michael. At first, soon after he begun to go to the drama group, he and Edwina became friends, but there was always something in their relationship which made Michael react with contempt. Rupert would go to their place and listen to records, and smoke with Edwina while Michael sat in his room and pretended to work, figuring out school syllabuses and writing for the journals to which he contributed. Then Rupert began to meet Edwina after her work. They would mostly talk about the people in the drama group, but often they would talk black politics. Edwina assumed instantly that Rupert would have something to say about them. For her he began to make up complications about his life which didn't exist. He would talk to her about the tragedy of being a half-caste, and she would listen. He learnt through her and Michael that even sincerity was a weapon, a hustle. He was flattered by her attention and turned his mind to anything that would get it.

She, in turn, would talk about herself, about how her mother who never even told her who her real father was, was ashamed of having a bastard child. She told him that she was called Edwina because her mother had 'middle-class hang-ups'. She said ever since she'd read some book or the other she wanted to be called 'George', but then decided that 'Ed' would do, and now women's liberation had taught her to be proud of her own name.

He had never met anyone like her. Once or twice, when he sat up late at their flat, she drove him home. Rupert had kept her a secret from the daily round of people he met, but in his thoughts he lived for her. He was nineteen. She was five years older. He knew she had fancy friends who had nothing to do with the drama group, with the kids she met at school. Rupert sensed also that she was fascinated by the fact that he lived in the squat. She'd asked him how he'd broken in. She questioned him about Slingo, and when Rupert threw bits of Slingo's phrases into the conversation she would ask him to explain the words. He took her reggae LPs from Slingo's battered and scratched and ever-renewed collection, and he told her stories that he'd picked up from Slingo and his mates and put himself into them.

Edwina had made the first move. She had dropped him home after the group session one Tuesday. She'd seemed preoccupied. He went to bed and two hours later heard the thud of pebbles against his window. She was back.

'Can I come in, Rupert?' she asked, looking up from the pavement, standing next to her car. She'd left the engine running.

'What's the problem?' he said, putting on his jeans and shirt before going down.

'Plenty.'

'I thought you said nothing bothered you.'

'Well, I'll have to think again, won't I ?'

She came up to his room and settled herself on the mattress. She took in its complete disorder, the absence of furniture, the clothes piled in corners and the bed with threadbare blankets.

She asked for some coffee and he made her some, muttering an excuse for having only condensed milk.

'I've had a terrible argument with Michael. He's got a girl in the flat.'

'I thought that sort of thing didn't bother you.'

'Yeah, that's easy to say, isn't it. That sort of thing spoils my sleep. I don't want to go back to separate bedrooms and him sneaking off to Croydon in the morning. I can't stand the look in his eyes in the morning. It almost hurts him more than it hurts me.'

'I like to be hurt like that,' Rupert said.

'Can I stay here, though? I won't if you can't handle it.'

Her face was partly covered by the strands of her thick wavy brown hair. Rupert didn't know if she was telling the truth, but he knew she had come to him.

'Do you have an alarm clock?'

'No.'

'Oh well, we'll have to stay awake all night and talk, so I can be on time for work.' She said that and smiled. There was a kind of mock sadness in her smile. He watched her as she took her clothes off and threw them in a pile, and, striding nimbly, climbed under his blankets. It was as though she had done this little act in a hundred unfamiliar rooms before, Rupert thought.

'Sorry to have woken you up with my troubles. Stop frowning and come to sleep. Too late to throw me out now.'

He was about to say that he didn't want to throw her out, that it would be like refusing a winning ticket on the pools, but his words stuck in his throat. She was thinner than he had imagined her and her breasts hung lower than he had thought they would. His heart thumped furiously.

'Shall I switch the light off?' he asked huskily, and then, trying to cover his embarrassment, 'So that you can sleep if you're tired.'

She laughed, her arms behind her head on the unclothed pillow. 'No. Let's have a look at you.'

When he thought of that first time she had slept with him, Rupert could remember the furious thumping of his heart, the shiveriness that came over him, and the hunger of his eyes, wanting to take her in and imprint the images of her on his brain. Yet he didn't want her to do the same. He was ashamed of his bony, hairy legs that stilted out under his shirt, his sweaty hands, his pounding chest. They were confessions of inexperience.

Edwina was so different from the black girls he had known. She declared who she was and what she wanted, like a man, whereas the girls he had known had to be worked on and worked at. There was no coyness about Edwina. Rupert decided she had the kind of maturity he liked.

It was the first time that he had a woman in the squat. He had known girls in school. One or two of the girls at the drama group fancied him, or so the rest of them said, but they were the sort of girls who would challenge him to ask them out and then refuse to go, or make fun of him and his choice of film or Wimpy bar afterwards. Edwina had ideas about the world. These other girls only had a bitchiness about the people immediately around them.

It had been beautiful in the beginning. Edwina would come to his place once or twice a week. He would stay in and wait for her. He had wondered whether any of the others in the drama group suspected, when Michael came out with all that confession about breaking up, that he was involved in it.

Up until that day, Edwina would spend the night with him and would disappear in the mornings, carrying a change of clothes with her in a canvas bag like a waif. Sometimes she'd come in the evenings and take him for a drive. They'd go to the pubs by the river out in the west of London, a London he didn't know existed. She knew all sorts of places to eat and to drink and to go and watch plays in.

Rupert had a sense of inadequacy with her. She would tease him: treat him like her baby, like her eldest son with whom she had a 'talking relationship' as she called it, when she was with him alone, and like her tiger on a leash when they were in public. She would talk about the books she'd read and about the architecture of the houses she stopped to stare at. He hated to bring her back to the dirty squat at night.

Although he hardly admitted it to himself, he felt possessive about her. She seemed hungry for the world of noises and arguments beyond the wall of his room, but if Slingo's friends, who went with black girls and brought them up to the house to make noisy love in Slingo's room, found out about Edwina, Rupert felt his position with them would become shaky. He kept her hidden like a weakness, and daydreamed about being able to take her away from it all one day. He would buy a house, like the one beside the river, and keep her amidst his sound system and his Lamborghini, like white people kept white, long-haired Persian cats.

When she found out that Rupert was out of a job, Edwina talked him into going to sign on at the Social Security. He didn't know anything about it and she had patiently explained it all. He went one morning and sat for three hours in the queue and answered the questions the girl put to him.

When he got back home, Slingo shouted out to him. 'Where you been?'

Rupert didn't want to tell Slingo that he'd been down to draw dole. That would be an admission of defeat.

'Why your girlfriend never speak to me?' Slingo asked.

'You ask her.' Rupert shrugged.

'She nice, you know. She's a fit daughter.' Slingo always referred to women as 'daughters'. 'Does she wan' make some breads?'

'Not with you, Slingo. I doubt it,' Rupert said, trying to turn and walk off. 'If you're giving it away, I'm starting a pension fund for old-age bag snatchers.'

'Come here, nuh, jus' make me sight you.'

Rupert went back. Something in Slingo's tone told him that Slingo was engaged in thinking, a rare occurrence, and he wanted to witness it.

'Listen. You know Kwate, yeah? He's a photographer, and he and you and the chick could work some scene.'

'No, no scenes for her, boy, just keep her out of anything you plan, all right?'

'Just hear the plan one time. Is a lot of donzai in it.'

'How much?'

'Hold on there. Kwate, he's cool, you know, a political Joe, and we need a white chick who understands things, like.'

'What things? She hasn't got any credit cards or chequebooks or nothing, I tell you.'

'One day's work. Black man, white woman, tiger skin, have a little scene, mix business with pleasure, sell the film and split the donz.'

'I don't think she'd do it.'

Slingo propped himself up on his elbow and showed his black tooth in an evil smile. 'You mean you couldn't control she?' There was a sort of sympathy in Slingo's voice, but Rupert knew it was blackmail, gently applied. 'She give you a lot of horrors, I hear.'

'Naw, she's a decent girl, straight. She wouldn't fancy making no sex films.'

'You don't ask she what she fancy, man, you tell her. It's your woman isn't it? Give her little soft talks. You is a man always popping it on white woman.'

'Maybe, but I don't treat her like that. She used to be my teacher, man. That's using people.'

Slingo sucked the air through his teeth, making his spit screech in derision. He sank back on the bed.

'I will ask she,' he announced to the room.

Slingo's proposition worried Rupert. It added a disturbing sediment to his already cloudy mind. It made him wish he didn't live there any longer. Undoubtedly Slingo would carry out his threat and ask Edwina if she'd perform in his proposed film. He was sure it was Slingo's idea. Kwate, he thought, wouldn't get involved in that sort of scene.

Edwina didn't turn up that evening. Just before midnight Rupert heard Slingo leave the house, a cat on the night prowl. Perhaps by the next day he would have forgotten his plan. He would only remember it when he wanted to taunt Rupert with being a white man, with having an incoherent morality beneath the skin.

They were all like that, Slingo's mob. Except, perhaps, Kwate, who was more thoughtful. Kwate was the only one out of the dozens of boys who visited the house, lounged and slept and ate there, with whom Rupert felt he could talk. Kwate didn't throw words around; he was much more deliberate. And yet he knew that Kwate too was capable of wild action. Not of small-time hustles. Kwate was distinctly big-time.

5.

THERE IS NO REPLY FROM the police through the second night of the siege, and hostages and gunmen sit through the next morning, waiting.

'My watch stop,' Hurly declares. 'When I don't sleep I forget to wind it.'

'What's the time? Give me the time,' Kwate says to the hostages who are sitting on the settee now, bleary-eyed but alert. Kwate faces them with the shotgun.

'Eleven,' the white man says. He looks more bored than terrified now, as though he feels that his captors and the police are handling the whole thing in too tedious a fashion and he could have planned the moves of either side much better.

'So they don't care for the deadline,' Rupert says.

'The embassies will have just opened, they'll need time,' the girl says. 'Oh God, I wish I'd never …'

'The old bill are up to no good as usual. Give them time,' the white man interjects. 'They couldn't organize a piss-up in a brewery.'

'We'll do our own countdown,' Kwate snaps. 'The po-lis working on your time.'

The white man shrugs and looks away from Kwate towards the window.

The deadline of noon approaches. None of them has had more than a few minutes of sleep at a time, and yet they are all as alert as jockeys in a race. Rupert and Hurly hold their pistols indifferently, as though these are no longer part of the dialogue between them and the hostages. I'm not doing any shooting, Hurly thinks. He knows that despite Kwate's unflinching stare and hardened, determined features, he isn't either.

The next time Kwate demands the time, it's ten to one.

The Greek man licks his lips and asks for water. Kwate

says he can go to the kitchen and get some, and he motions to Rupert to stay where he is, even though Rupert springs up to follow the Greek.

The girl begins to say something to the white man. She whispers, but they can all hear what she says.

'How long it take to send a telegram to Algeria?' Kwate asks, forestalling her.

'It might take a whole day,' the white man replies.

Kwate lifts the shotgun in both hands when he throws his arms up theatrically in a yawn. Rupert watches him and thinks he looks like the guerrilla in the poster and wants to look like him.

At four o'clock the police break their silence.

'Kwate, we've received your demands and want to install a phone so you can talk to us direct. There are some difficulties about your demands.'

They think we're not serious, Hurly thinks. We didn't shoot anybody, we couldn't shoot anybody. Maybe they'll come for us. It's like waiting on death row. He recalls all those telly films about guys going to the electric chair or the gas chamber or the gallows, with the good guys outside, the lawyers and reporters who valiantly spend sleepless nights looking for last-minute evidence, and the careful preparations inside, the death hoods, the glass jar of the gas chamber, the straps on the chair, and the echoes of steel doors, the echoes, of bunches of keys and the echoes of the boots of dutiful screws.

When they watched these programmes in Slingo's room, Kwate would say, 'The wolf will lie down with the lamb – in the belly.' He'd say that about almost any programme, but now suddenly it seemed to make sense.

Those death row movies, with their horrid fascination, were a preparation for all the waiting games one had to play. Time has come, Hurly thinks, only there'll be no reprieves and no last-minute pardons; it's a game of chess in which black starts second and always loses.

'Go talk to them,' Kwate says to Rupert.

Rupert looks out of the window as Kwate shouts, 'We coming to the window. If you try something, someone going to dead.'

Rupert sees police cars and vans at either end of the street. The camera crews are standing around with electronic headgear, smoking and drinking from paper cups. The spectators throng behind a scanty line of uniformed bobbies. There are black faces in the crowd. The curtains of most of the flats in the white stuccoed terrace opposite are drawn. On the morning of the first day of the siege, the police took charge of these rooms and ordered the inhabitants out of them, but there's no way Rupert can know that. As soon as his face appears at the window there's a cry from the crowd, and Rupert ducks back in.

'Tell them we want newspapers,' Kwate says. Rupert shouts out the message.

'Will you accept the phone?' is the police reply.

'How you go set it up?' Kwate shouts back.

Burgess doesn't understand the question. Rupert can't see Burgess who's standing almost immediately below at the door of the minicab shopfront, and shouting up. Rupert repeats the question several times and hears Burgess asking for help from the other police.

'All right,' Kwate shouts in the end, replacing Rupert at the window.

Burgess's voice again: 'PC Bully is going to bring you the telephone set on a ladder outside this window.'

'We trust him without his coat,' Kwate shouts back.

The next day in the papers one headline says GUNMEN TRUST PC BUT NOT HIS COAT. Another says UNIFORM TERRIFIES SIEGE GUNMEN.

Bully comes into view at the top of the ladder looking extremely self-conscious.

Everyone in the black community knows PC Bully.

He is notorious for being crooked and fearless. He leans out of his squad car to shout at blacks he's arrested, 'Glad to see you walking straight, Sunshine.'

Bully goes down into the clubs and dives alone. He swears in a pseudo-Jamaican accent and puts on an ironic act of being one of the boys. The youths know him as one policeman who can come up behind them and say, 'Shift your raas clot.' Kwate has heard that the other coppers don't like Bully; they say he is angling for promotion, and they disapprove of his idea that jovial brutality is the way to handle blacks. Or perhaps they know, as blacks know, that Bully is said to be involved in big-time drug peddling, that he uses his knowledge of small-time weed dealers to track the big-timers and make deals with them. There are hundreds of rumours about Bully: that he blew up a German bunker in the war, that he was demoted in the force for bigamy, that he has been a sailor and married a woman in Anguilla. His seniors know him as a man who can spot blacks who've been in trouble previously. Burgess has asked that Bully be assigned to the siege.

Kwate puts one arm out to him. Rupert and Hurly stand beyond the kitchen doorway because Kwate says he can see through the trick of getting Bully to identify the two unknown members of their gang. Next to him, beyond the window frame, Kwate holds the white girl at gunpoint.

The phone is handed over without a word, the wire running out over the window sill. For once, Kwate thinks, Bully isn't cocky. His bosses are watching him.

As Bully descends the ladder, Hurly and Rupert come back into the room. Kwate picks up the phone. There is an immediate reply; it's already connected. 'We want an answer to our demands and also newspapers,' Kwate says.

The crackling reply says they'll get both. Kwate puts down the phone.

'What happens if they don't give us a plane?' says Hurly.

'One by one,' Kwate says.

'We got to show we serious. Look at the paddy-men: them, they don't mess about. If IRA say they'll shoot somebody, then they spend some bullets and fetch a body.'

'The Irish have the support of their whole country,' Rupert says, echoing something he's heard Michael say.

'If a hundred po-lis rush this place, they could kill we all,' Hurly observes.

'The po-lis want them alive and us alive.'

'They can't have us for murder. Not yet,' Rupert says.

'If you get out of here, the police, the international police and all going to chase your arse right round this ungodly world,' Hurly replies.

'If we shoot somebody, they'll think we're shooting the lot and rush the place, firing.'

Late in the evening the phone rings. Hurly picks it up. It's Burgess with the answer to their demands.

'We haven't been able to get a reply from any Algerian representative. The Jamaican government will not give you asylum. There's nowhere for you to go. We urge you to give yourselves up and free the hostages.'

He goes on to say that public opinion is building up against them. He will send them the national newspapers, and, as well, newspapers from certain black groups who have all denounced them as thieves and criminals not worthy of support. If they give up the hostages now, he will personally see to it 'that all the facts are taken into account in any proceedings that might be taken against them'.

Burgess's voice can be heard in the room, straight from the ear-piece. He pauses for a reply but doesn't directly ask for one.

Wrinkles appear on Kwate's brow. He grabs the phone from Hurly's hand and bangs the receiver with his fist. 'They bug this blood-cleet thing,' he shouts.

'How can you tell?'

'I don't know how them work, but I tell you it's bugged.'

'Let's have a look: the white man says. Kwate hands tile set over to him. The man unscrews the earpiece. He asks for a penknife and Kwate gets one from the pocket of his jacket. The man digs under the diaphragm, then unscrews the receiver set. All the others watch.

'It's got an extra wire, it bypasses the switch. Yeah, it's bugged all right.'

'Stand back,' Kwate says theatrically. He grabs the set

from the man's hand and with tremendous venom projects it through the glass of the window.

There's a terrific crash as the glass and the set fall to the pavement. The sound of running feet. Captors and captives sink to the floor without a signal. They all instinctively expect something to come through the window in return. In fifteen seconds it does: the voice of Bully.

'What's going on in there, Kwate? You all OK?' He sounds almost anxious.

Kwate motions to Rupert to cover the hostages with his pistol. They are all still crouching on the floor. Kwate and Hurly upend the table, knocking the unwashed cups, the statuette of a smiling Buddha and the pack of cards onto the floor. They push the table up against the broken window, covering half of it.

Kwate stands up. 'Now they know who's serious and who's not.'

'You can't blame me,' Hurly protests. 'I don't want to kill nobody. You said it was cool to have the phone.'

'Shut up,' Kwate commands. He is now in charge completely.

'Kwate,' the white man says. They all look at him. It's the first time one of the hostages has addressed Kwate by name. The white man puts his finger on his lips for silence. He points to the window sill, and touches his hand to his ear.

Kwate nods. The white man goes over to the window and opens it slightly. Crouching below the window frame, he runs his hand along the ledge outside.

He is right. His hand comes away with a little disc as big as a watch. He hands it to Kwate, who looks at it curiously and then, putting it on the floor, smashes it with the butt of the shotgun.

Kwate smiles at the white man.

'Who wants coffee?' Hurly asks.

'Let me and the girl go.' the white man says.

'You just wait where you are,' is Kwate's contemptuous reply.

The Greek man passes the photograph he's pulled out of his wallet to the other hostages.

'He looks so much younger,' the girl says, taking the measure of the boy who looks sick and miserable.

'Because he was, dumbo,' her man says.

Rupert takes the photograph from the white man's hand. The Greek comes and, leaning over his shoulder, points out who is who. In the snap the young boy is wearing a tie and a jacket and has had his hair slicked down for the occasion.

'She will be worried. Worried for nothing,' the Greek man says, indicating his fat matron of a wife. 'She will get so thin,' and he holds out his forefinger and shakes it. 'That's my big son, Costas, Panos' brother. Play very good football, school team, Cypriot team, all team. Costas nineteen now; Panos twelve.'

'Hang on, I know this geezer; Hurly says. 'Oi, was your son a footballer?'

'Don't be so Irish, he just said he was,' Rupert says.

'Hold on there, hold on. Archway school?'

The Greek nods and his features open up, his face beaming. 'You know my son?'

'Not 'arf,' Hurly says, turning to Rupert, and adopting now his cockney voice. 'That bloke nearly kicked my ammunition off when we was playing them for the North London cup.'

'He got a big car now,' the Greek man says proudly. 'Work for this business. Minicabs.'

'Lucky it's not him we got here: a real nasty bruiser.'

'Costas very good boy,' the Greek man insists, not quite catching Hurly's drift.

'Yeah. Good as a nutcracker.'

'Most night Costas he stay with me till drivers paid off. This night he go boxing, so Panos bring my supper and you boys catch us.'

'Could do with some supper now,' Rupert says.

'Call room service,' the white man says.

By the fourth day they have given up discussing killing anyone. Kwate is conscious that Rupert and Hurly are waiting for him to suggest a further plan but neither of them asks him for it. He has to be given his time.

Talking to these people Rupert has to make an effort to feel again that their lives are the only cards they hold now. He dislikes the white man. Much too flash. He wonders how a nice girl like that could go with a lout like him. He is sure that if the man had the gun and he was at the end of it, the man wouldn't hesitate to shoot.

Hurly tells the Greek man what their plan of robbery was. They have a friend, he won't say his name, who set the job up for them; it wasn't really their idea. They were told that all they had to do was go in and get the cash. It wasn't even in a safe. At the most they would find one man there and they could deal with him.

Kwate shuts Hurly up. He has established in the minds of the hostages that he is the boss, that he'll do the thinking for all three. The other two, and the hostages, behave now as though they are waiting for something to happen, but Kwate gives off the air that events are taking the turn of some carefully mapped-out route which he holds in his head.

'If it had been white people involved, the po-lis would have given them a plane and let them loose in Australia or someplace,' he asserts.

If Hurly had said it, the white man might have said 'Don't talk daft,' but with Kwate he lets these remarks pass. Kwate rarely speaks to the hostages except through the others.

I have to trust Kwate, Rupert thinks, because there's no one else to trust. It's grudging, but it's still a convinced acceptance of Kwate's authority.

6.

RUPERT HAD NOTICED THAT SLINGO had been watching Edwina. He had mentioned the film again, to Rupert, but Rupert had fended him off.

Maybe it was just the way Slingo insinuated himself into Edwina's attention. Rupert was sure Slingo didn't know any white women apart from the girls who hung around the blues and passed from man to man, turning from unarmed amateurs into hardened professionals who knew that there was no such thing as the best bet. Slingo was fascinated by Edwina. To him she represented the conscious surrender of those who had enslaved his ancestors, or at least Rupert felt that that was how Slingo saw her. It annoyed Rupert. He was conscious that Slingo knew very well that there were at least two types of white women, and yet he persisted in treating the eagle as of the same feather as the crow.

Slingo didn't knock. He just walked into Rupert's room, hearing Edwina's voice there.

'You ask the daughter yet?'

'Ask me what?'

'You the actress, ain't yuh?'

'Well, I wouldn't exactly say … I'm a drama teacher.'

Her response hurt Rupert. She seemed glad of Slingo's interruption of their intimacies.

'This boy tell me a lot about you. I'm very pleased to meet you.'

'You're Slingo, aren't you. I've passed you ten times, but you don't seem to look at the ghosts who pass you in this house.'

'Yeah, my mind have a lot of worries,' Slingo said. 'It's a shame this boy never tell you about some little job you could do for I.'

'Oh? What's that, Rupert? You didn't …'

'Slingo, leave it, man.'

'I'm making a film. I asked him if you'll play in this lickle film. It's educational.'

'How interesting. I've always wanted to make a film. In fact, you know the drama group that Rupert comes to, we're thinking of doing a film out of the sort of work we've done. We just haven't had the money. It costs an awful lot, doesn't it?'

'My spa, my friend is a producer, you know, and it have a film and breads and all. We wanted an actress so I tell Rupy to check you because he always tell me how good you was with drama.'

'Is it a black film?'

'It's black and white,' Slingo said, grinning, aware that he was making Rupert uncomfortable, aware also that Rupert would never challenge his right to say anything to any white woman in that house. 'I'm very bad at explanations. Rupert is better at explanations. Or the guy who's making this here film, Mr Brown.'

'I'd like to talk about it sometime. It sounds a smashing idea.'

'You want to talk to Kwate?' Slingo said.

'Yes, I'd like that. Is he coming here sometime?' Edwina sensed Rupert's shiftiness. 'Don't you think it's a great idea, Rupert? Especially if they've got film and camera and everything.'

'You may not like the script.'

'Well, I'll meet this chap, won't I. D'you know him?'

'I'm going to check him out tonight at a blues,' Slingo said, still grinning.

Rupert saw what Slingo was about. Edwina reacted to his sly invitation by sitting up on the bed.

'Kenny playing some boss sounds tonight. You want to go, Rupert?'

'I'm tired,' Rupert said, sinking back on the mattress, as Edwina sat up.

'Come on,' she cried, 'don't be such a drag. It's lovely of Slingo – I do hope that's your real name; you don't mind being called Slingo, do you – to tell us about it.'

She was showing real enthusiasm. Several times she had asked him to take her where the black youths hung out. A 'reggae party' she called it. She was constantly pushing for just those things he wanted to shield her from. He could see that Slingo had sensed that and was playing on it.

'Cool, cool sound,' Slingo said.

Rupert didn't like the blues. They were carnivals of bewilderment for him. The black girls who went there were unapproachable. He felt he'd make a fool of himself if he asked a sister to dance and she ignored him and turned away. He couldn't comfort himself there – as he had done when he'd gone to the Mecca dancing halls with his white friends – with the thought that these potential partners were demonstrating their innate racism, that they wouldn't dance with him because he was black.

'If the boy tired, you'll have to come with me,' Slingo said.

'I'd really like to meet this guy,' Edwina said, turning to Rupert.

'If you want to see blues, I'll take you to blues,' Rupert said.

They went by cab. Slingo always travelled in style when there were other people who could pay. As they walked in, Edwina felt the eyes of the scattered crowd outside the church hall, upon them. Slingo seemed to know a lot of people. He had put on a red velvet jacket and wore rings on every finger. He greeted the people to-ing and fro-ing from the hall with 'All right' or 'Sights'. As they reached the door, he turned to Rupert and said, 'You have money?'

Edwina paid the white man who stood at the door in an assembly of intimidating faces. He was a vicar. He smiled at them. The sound of the party floated out into the sharp night air. Beyond the reception party, in the foyer, were a lot of young blacks with caps and totally sullen expressions, leaning against the wall and moving rhythmically to the beat at the same time. It was incredible and menacing to Edwina, and exciting at the same time. She took Rupert's arm and felt him pull away from her, a slow determined move which told her that he would keep close to her but didn't want her to claim him before that audience.

Red bulbs hung naked in the room they entered. The music seemed to quake the creaky floorboards. The place was absolutely packed out. The young men wore fancy suits, sported silk handkerchiefs, danced in a slow pounding rhythm with their coats on. A row of watchers, gazing into some deep distance, lined the walls, shuffling their feet to the music, their fists raised in gestures of loose, confident combat. The air was thick with smoke and a vaguely nauseating sweet smell.

Kill Pope Paul
And hold the seventh seal thereof
Kill Pope Paul
And -a- Babylon fall.

The loudspeakers blared. Rupert stood in front of Edwina, not acknowledging her, yet sensing her dependent presence just behind him. She looked round, uncertain, but keeping her chin high. The voice on the record was almost speaking, not singing, and yet the swaying shoulders made it sound like the most danceable melody in the world. There was an agony and threat in the sound which drowned everything.

Slingo wound his way through the dancers and Rupert followed him closely. Edwina noticed that the crowd appeared to part for them, but blocked her way as she followed, and she was wary of saying 'excuse me' for fear of being laughed at. Nobody excused anybody in this crowd.

She would brave it, she thought, go in breast first, when a voice behind her said, 'But wait.'

Edwina turned to see a young man standing behind her, the mouth that had spoken the words almost at her ear. He was shuffling about, moving to the rhythm with his hands drawn up to his chest in loose fists. He met her eye as she turned, as if to identify himself as the man who had ventured to give her orders.

'I'm with my friends.' Edwina gestured.

'You can't go in there so,' the boy said and carried on moving his body. 'You have no friends,' he added, smiling.

Edwina stood transfixed. There was no going forward through the thicket of dancers, and this boy had blocked off her retreat. Then she noticed that no one around them was paying the least bit of attention to what the boy had said or to her response. The boy looked as though he was going to push his body up against her, but he just finished his dance before he attended to the business he'd begun.

Edwina turned and tried to force herself through the dancers who closed into a wall before her.

'I said, *rest,*' the voice commanded again.

Edwina pretended she didn't hear him. To the others it must seem that she was dancing with him. She tried to concentrate on the lyrics of the song:

Run Cap-it-al-ist
I and I want So-shyal-ist.

Suddenly it was menacing. The man was upon her, she could smell his sweat.

They take an oath upon them own-a mother
Then them use a Bun to kill them own-a son
That's why them crime canna done.
It dread in a Jamdown, dread in a Jamdown …

People were pushing past her now. The song was coming to an end. As they squeezed past she saw Slingo's head above the rest. Rupert and Slingo had made their way back and with them was Kwate.

'What's happening?' Slingo said.

From behind her, the voice of the young man, no longer throaty and secret but public and matey said, 'I there.'

Kwate was introduced to Edwina and he in turn introduced them all to the boy behind her. 'Is my friend Hurlington. Wha' go on, Hurly?'

Hurly nodded. They stood around in a little circle, and a man who passed handed Kwate a lit joint without comment. Kwate puffed at it and passed it to Hurly.

'This killer weed,' Hurly commented, looking at the thing he'd puffed, but Edwina saw a shadow of uncertainty pass across his face and she was ashamed of herself for having allowed this boy to intimidate her.

'I taken some tablet this evening,' Hurly said.

'You charged like a battery,' Slingo said, smiling, his black tooth showing through like a breach in a defence.

'Doctor's pills, boy. He told me don't smoke no weed.'

'Weed is a natural thing.'

Hurly nodded vigorously and puffed away at the spliff. Then he passed it back to Kwate.

Edwina was looking at him, waiting for him to pass it to her in some acknowledgement of their earlier encounter. As she looked, she saw the pupils of his eyes make a slow motion upwards and his shoulders droop under their own weight and she watched his knees give way, twisting around each other.

Hurly collapsed to the floor in a heap. Suddenly there was a clearing. 'Give the man air,' someone said.

'Man drop this day here with Kenny sounds,' a fan said.

'Whose weed kill this man?' a genuinely curious voice asked above the chorus of laughter and concern.

Edwina watched Kwate lean over Hurly and touch his forehead. Kwate took charge of the situation and shifted the people who had crowded round, craning their necks for a look. He ordered somebody to move Hurly, and hands lifted the boy and spaces cleared before his curt commands.

'Call a cab,' Kwate said to the vicar at the door.

'I'm afraid there's no phone here. Take him out to the main road, there's bound to be something there.'

They dragged Hurly, still unconscious, to the main road two streets down. Edwina counted four cabs that passed them without stopping.

'Poison reach the boy.' Slingo said.

The taxi dropped Edwina and Rupert first. In the dark of the cab, with Hurly still almost unconscious, lying with his head on Kwate's lap, Edwina reached out to hold Rupert's hand. He refused her hand but turned his face to her. He wanted to convey that he had simply followed her through her wilful adventure, he hadn't taken any part in it. He had watched her at the blues. She seemed electrified to be stepping on what she took to be new ground but he knew to be quicksand.

He could see her eyes shining. There was something about white features, about the expressions on white people's faces, Rupert thought, that was a shadow of the decrepitude of age. In the very boldness of her cheekbones, in the very health of her pink-veined skin, he felt he could see the metalled wrinkles of her old age. In one way *she* was like his mother: a girl with abandon and adventure who must have taken his father for what he was – whatever he was; Rupert didn't know. In another sense, she wasn't. His mother was an Irish woman who still believed that God, if not the Pope, would one day redeem the wickedness that life had taught Rupert. His mother was a woman of hope and optimism, whereas Edwina was not. Edwina, he felt, was content to live for the moment, and would trade whatever attractions she had for the intensity of that moment. That was why she loved, or had loved, Michael. There was no denying, Rupert thought, that Michael must, at one time, have fascinated Edwina completely, held her attention to the exclusion of all else. He could see Michael's appeal. Michael could hypnotize people into believing that their rotten little problems with their mums and dads and their quarrels on Thursday night, or their wrangles with the officials of the tenant's association, were the most important issues in the life and vitality of the country. Michael was a man for people with problems.

Just now Edwina seemed to be all attention to Slingo. Rupert could see that Slingo had been throwing words her way, and she was listening.

As they went up to his room, he was sullen.

'What's the matter, baby?' she said.

'Don't try and imitate the black girls; you'll never make it,' Rupert replied.

'You don't like mixing your friends, do you ... Rupert?'

'You want to see the blues, you see it.

'You haven't answered my question, darling.'

'They ain't my friends,' Rupert said, and they walked through his door to his bed.

~

7.

KWATE AND SLINGO DUMPED HURLY on the doorstep of his mother's house.

'You got space, boy, space. I need a lickle space,' Hurly said, as they stood him upright. 'Boy, I feel bad.' He didn't want to face his mother in her tattered nightgown, shouting after him as he pulled the blanket over his head. He knew that Kwate and Slingo were 'big boys'; they would probably go back to the blues or move on to some other scene, talking and smoking the night out while he, with his unseasoned head, had to bear the giddiness and the sickness and the sharp tongue of a mother who understood only too well, but had too many worries of her own to sympathize. She didn't approve of Kwate, even though he made an effort to sympathize with her load. Slingo was banned from the house.

'You is still a boy, and you thinks you is man,' his mother would say.

'Man walk in righteousness, because I and I is the king of kings, lord of lords, conquering lion of the tribe of Judah,' he would answer, pouring the milk onto his cornflakes as she watched, knowing that it would succeed in teasing her.

'Go away with that stupidness,' she would say, knowing that he was not going to go away with it. He was her boy, and the sweat of her brow had given him a shelter he was forced to accept and be grateful for.

They fought over money.

'Tcha, I want my pocket money, Mum.'

'Every week you come for pocket money. Every single week, like you was a living calendar. Sometime it have two Fridays in the week. Is you workin' for it, or me?'

'Ah, tcha, Mum, throw me a two poun'.'

'And don't bother come back for no more.'

Off to club and spend it.

Saturday now. No *money. Knock-knock-knock-knock. Saturday heating up.*

'Hey, Hurlington dread. Shaka down the bottom of the road. Fifty pence to go in.'

'Hah, hmmmm. Hey, Mum, forward a fifty pence, nuh?'

'No. Go to bed, it pay you better. I give you two pound yesterday, no have no more. Progeny is God's leech.' She learn a lot o' rubbish in church from white preacher.

'All right. All right, Mum. You see what I can do. I make to steal it. Jus' knock over this man, take his money, ain't it?'

Whop, tish, gone.

Heavy panting.

'Thief, thief, thief!'

Fifty pence to hand over. *Tooph do do do do do do do; Tooph* do do do do *do. Eeeeeeeeeeee ....on; eeeeee...... on; eeeeeeee ... on.*

'All right, you. We saw you. Is this the man who mugged you?'

'Yes, it's him, it's him.'

'Right, get him, lads.' *OOOOOOOOOOOOOOOOH – ffffffff ...... Ring ring. Ring ring. Ring ring.* 'Hello?'

'Your son is down Kennington Police Station. He mugged a man. Could you come down and retrieve him?'

'*What?*'

'Your son mugged this man, he'll be going to court.'

'I give my son all the money he need! He has never needed to come and ask for money I don't give him. He had no need to steal.'

Never any need to steal.

She will swear to lies before the magistrate, Hurly thinks. He can smile. On his face a plastered grin, the eternal golliwog. 'Jam jar coon,' the kids at school used to say.

'Sit up, young man, you are not a gentleman of leisure. You are on trial here and this is an extremely grave offence. I have the deepest sympathy for your mother who has, unaided, attempted to bring you up. I believe every word of this honest lady. She has apparently stood by you. You have given your mother endless trouble, young man. The social report clearly shows that you were unenthusiastic at your school, and unenthusiastic about finding suitable employment.'

'He keep bad company, the boy. Rasta man, bad. Kwate, Black Power trouble. Slingo, which ain't the name his respectable parents give the boy, is thief.'

Mum you must forward into new kind of views. This is backward thinking. To you my friends are wrong men. Doesn't matter what, they are wrong. They're nasty. They don't wash their hair ... no matter if they do, they are Rasta and they're wrong. We're not supposed to associate with them. We're not supposed to go to sound system because a whole heap of black people together is bound to cause trouble. It's bad company we keeping up.

'You read *Daily Mirror,* it makes your brain soft.'

'Black people is bad company.'

One or two friends come round my *house.* 'Mind them don't thief up me something, you know.'

'Mother, they wouldn't do that.'

Next morning. 'Hurlington, where me ten pound … what! … me rent money gone.'

'There it is for you. I never stole it, Mum.'

'Don't bring in them friend again, them too thief.'

'All right, Mother, I'll dissociate myself from them, I'm going to turn white.'

'Don't do that, you can't do that. If you come in house with white woman, you nah come in here again. Kick out.'

A man who is *by himself will pay better.*

'Mum, I don't know what to do. Can't go with white people, can't go with black people, what am I supposed to do, Mum?'

Them say, 'the sweet nanny goat go bitter'. 'What you want out in them world with black people, you going get it.'

'Yeh, Mum, I want a whole heap of money.'

'And you goin' thief it.'

'All right, Mum, leave it, jus' leave it.'

8.

A<small>FTER</small> <small>THE</small> <small>NIGHT</small> <small>AT</small> <small>THE</small> blues, Edwina established herself at Rupert's. That contact with a forbidden world, forbidden by her upbringing and by Rupert, had excited her. She referred to her own place as 'Michael's flat', going back there only to pick up a pair of curtains or a bedcover or an LP that she remembered and said she didn't want to live without. Slowly she was taking over. She painted the walls of Rupert's room, she bought a desk and sanded it and varnished it and piled it with her books and her school-work.

Rupert would wait for her to return from school. He liked having her clothes hanging up in the wall cupboard, he liked the smell of her, her natural perfume reminding him of the charm that he had won. He hadn't returned to the drama group after the night of Michael's confession. He knew he couldn't face Michael. It would be like facing a man who deserved what you had taken from him. He felt confused. Sure, he'd won Edwina away, he wanted her, but he didn't want her now in the way she gave herself. He wanted her to belong to him and yet to not be there. It seemed to him that she had stopped giving him her seriousness now that she had given him herself. She didn't talk to him in the way she used to.

He was proud that the rest of them, Hurly and all, looked upon her as 'his woman'. He wouldn't say that in her presence. She objected to that sort of phrase; she was no one's woman, no one's wife, no one's girl, she said. She said that what mattered to her was the feeling of not being tied down. She said that women were just like blacks, and though Rupert thought she was wrong, he didn't say so. It would cause her to argue and she always won arguments, she was better at words than he was, but she was still wrong. It made him smile when she compared herself to his mother. 'Your mum has put up a struggle all her life. It's difficult enough for a white woman who takes up with blacks now, but think of what it was like twenty years ago.' She would talk to him about the prejudice that his mother must have had to put up with, and Rupert would listen. In his heart of hearts he knew that his mother was not like that.

She never thought like Edwina. She had just done what she had to, what she wanted to, she wasn't on no crusade.

On Tuesday nights Edwina still went to the drama club. Rupert knew that it was where her seriousness would be given free rein. She knew about drama, she knew about young people, she would pose, posture, make them want to imitate her. He didn't want her to go. 'Rupert, you aren't jealous of Michael?' she would say. She'd smile and then frown and immediately reassure him.

'It's all kid stuff,' he would say.

'You're kid stuff,' she would reply. 'It's my work. I've known Michael so many years. We can do things together without the feeling of doing them together, you know what I mean?'

But Rupert would sulk.

Edwina didn't like Rupert's possessive moods. She didn't like the way he glared at her when she talked to Slingo or to Kwate or the other boys that came there. Kwate fascinated her. All of them, even Rupert in a strange way, gave off an air of challenge. They were not like white men, Edwina thought. They wouldn't make it clear in any way that they fancied you, and yet they'd set themselves up as targets of attraction.

In Kwate, she felt, there was an extreme self-consciousness about every move, every gesture that he made in front of her. He had a way of summing up the faces and people before him, just as Michael had the knack of adding up facts that made an argument. Both Michael and Kwate were wary of being cheated, but Michael was wary of opinions and arguments and people's mentalities and interests. Kwate seemed to be wary of people as they presented themselves, of the pretences that people put forward for other people to see. And yet he was a pretender himself.

He flattered her. After the night at the blues she met him again in the house. He didn't give her the attention she wanted as they sat around Slingo's room, but he turned to her when Rupert had gone out of the room to make some coffee and suddenly said, 'You must have done some modelling.'

'No,' she said.

'Naw, I just thought from the way you sit. You look like you was one of the gel I saw in the TV ads.'

When Rupert came back into the room, Kwate abruptly stopped talking to her. There was a recognition in this circle, she thought, that she belonged to him, and Edwina felt instinctively that she wanted to defy it.

Being around that house, she picked up phrases from Slingo and Kwate, and used them with her drama classes in school, to the delight of all the black kids. She would refer to money as 'breads' or 'donzai'; she would use the words of reggae lyrics as though they were proverbs. 'Who the cap fit, let them wear it,' she would say, or, 'Those who deal in violence shall go in silence,' and the black boys in her fifth form would say, 'Where you get that from, miss?' She knew that it was whispered around the class that she went with a lot of black men. She liked conveying that impression. It gave her a sense of power.

Rupert didn't like her adopting the phrases and language of the ghetto.

'You do it yourself. It's just as much a bluff for you as for me,' she would argue.

'You make yourself out like white trash. Like the girls who hang around black clubs looking for a bit of black.'

'Don't ever talk to *me* in that way!' She was terrified that there might be some truth in Rupert's accusation. She knew that in speech she insisted on talking about black people, white people, anybody, as though they were the same, knowing that in reality there was a world of difference between them. She had learnt, especially through Kwate, that she must not try to deny or abandon her 'whiteness'. Before him or Slingo, she was always careful to preserve her accent and the cast of mind that contact with them seemed to be warping.

But by degrees she discovered that Rupert wasn't what she had wanted him to be. She hadn't bothered to disguise her affair with him in the drama group, because she thought she saw in him a kind of wildness which she wanted, needed like a medicine. She could now see, after virtually living with him for a month, that he was confused and frightened and directionless.

One Tuesday night she got to Rupert's room from work and found that he wasn't waiting for her. She had decided she would go to the drama workshop that night and had spoken to Michael on the phone from school. He had been distinctly cool, giving her the impression that she wasn't welcome there, and it worried her. She had expected him to want to see her. When Rupert came in, she told him that she was leaving at seven.

He didn't reply.

'What's the matter? Why are you being childish again?'

'Why don't you go back to Michael if it's him you want to see all the time.'

'Don't exaggerate. I haven't seen him for weeks, and I want to see the girls at the drama club.'

'You think I'm too stupid for you, don't you, just because I can't read you all that poetry and talk about Shakespeare.'

'I only think you're stupid when you throw these jealous fits.'

Rupert stormed out, 'Go where you want,' he shouted, 'and don't bother to come back!'

She had felt the edge of his temper. Too sharp, she thought. When he'd gone, she tidied up his room, folding his clothes. She'd have to wait for him to come back, she decided. She wouldn't go to the drama club. She'd be there when he got back and tell him so.

That evening Kwate knocked on the door and came into Rupert's room. It was obvious that Slingo had told him that there had been a row.

'The boy leave you?' he asked.

'Rupert's just gone out for a bit, he should be back.' She smiled. She was lying on the bed reading.

'Is you I want to talk to,' Kwate said.

'Oh?'

'Slingo must have told you about the film?'

'He said something weeks ago, but I'm not going to drama any more and I don't suppose we can do it.'

'I want to talk to you about being photographed,' Kwate said.

'What do you mean photographed?'

'You know in m'camera a click and "say cheese"?'

Kwate was so easy with her. It was a new side to him. Edwina wanted to talk to him, had wanted the opportunity before, but now Rupert might be coming back any moment.

Kwate sensed her discomfort. 'You got a car, ain't you?' he asked.

'Why?'

'I thought me and you could go out and have a drink and maybe talk about it?'

'You mean now?'

'Why not?' He said it with supreme self-assurance, knowing she'd agree.

He asked her to drive out of Brixton, south towards Blackheath.

'Why don't we go somewhere closer?' She knew the answer. He was taking her where he wouldn't be seen with her by people he knew.

'I don't like drink in Brixton.' he said.

He drank about six barley wines and seemed unaffected by them. Edwina tried to keep up with his drinking and with the quick conversation he made. She drove Kwate home, a few streets down from Rupert's place, and he asked her up. She parked the car in a dark little side street without explaining to Kwate why. She followed him up the unlit stairs, three storeys up to his room.

On the wall there were posters, one about freedom fighters in Angola and another depicting a black man chained to a Nazi cross, fighting a fist loose from his chains and holding it up in a salute, with a tremendous strain of Promethean muscle. There were drawings on the wall that Kwate had done himself, of Rasta men with their hair in waterfalls, their beards fanning out into mountain ranges.

Edwina stood before the pictures.

'What do you do apart from painting and photography?'

'I'm a poet.'

She smiled, but checked herself when she saw that he was quite serious and that his bony cheeks and slightly slanting Chinese eyes were imposing that seriousness on her.

'Can I see what you've written?'

'Man could be a poet and not write nothing.'

'I think these drawings are beautiful,' she said.

'You could see them better if you lie back on the bed', he said.

She found herself willing to play this game. He sat in the middle of the floor and rolled a spliff. He put on a Marvin Gaye LP on the record player. His head looked defiant in the dim light. It was flattering the way he strutted about just for her. He hadn't talked about his and Slingo's films or his photography all evening. He'd talked about white people and black people and his contempt for people who didn't know where they were, like hippies and like the girls who hung around blacks. He was talking to her about it so he must exclude her from that category, she thought.

She stayed the night in Kwate's room.

The next day Rupert asked her how the drama club had gone. He was sorry for having walked out on her, he said.

'It was all right, just the usual, and you don't have to apologize, I should be sorry. I push you too much. You were right: Michael plods on with his drama and his group, but he doesn't really know where it's at.'

'Man must feel the pain,' Rupert said.

Edwina was used to men looking at her possessively. Michael looked at her as though he'd lost a battle but would win the war. Rupert had the look of a young boy with his first mechanical toy. When Kwate glanced at her his glance said that he could command what he didn't care to possess, and when he stared at her, he seemed to be saying that he could shape and mould anything that was uncertain and unformed when he took it in his hands.

9.

THE SECOND DEADLINE COMES AND goes. Chief Superintendent Burgess is almost certain that the gunmen he has on his hands are not willing to shoot anyone of their hostages. The metropolitan police commissioner has taken charge of the overall strategy of the siege and the home secretary calls a conference of psychiatrists, the social workers who will give evidence to the police, and the actual men who are to implement the tactical assault on what the papers have begun to call 'The Minicab Siege'.

Burgess and other senior officers are of the opinion that the gunmen should be given assurances that they will be allowed onto a plane and out of the country, and they argue for trapping the three on the open tarmac of the airport. If they can be brought out into the open, they can be shot. They submit a detailed plan for such an operation.

The plan is vetoed, as PC Bully tells his colleagues, 'by the big boy himself'. There is little doubt that the plan would work, a very low probability that the hostages would get shot into the bargain, but the home office says that it prefers the lawbreakers to be brought to justice alive. Burgess argues for a speedy conclusion. The commissioner, having heard the arguments, decrees that the alternative strategy be tried.

Outside the siege, unbeknown to the seven people inside, there have been certain incidents. Three hundred police with horses, vans and batons, have stopped a crowd of about a hundred young black people marching towards the scene of the siege. The incident goes unreported in the national press, but the small newspapers were there and have plastered the black ghettoes of the country with posters demanding 'An End to the Frustration of the Black Masses'. This propaganda, tied as it is to current gossip in the pubs and marketplaces of London, has something to do with the commissioner's decision. 'He's in a dead funk about the niggers,' PC Bully says, and one of the young officers at his station says, 'I think the guv's right, we'd have a bloody riot if the coons were shot.'

'Kwate's a sly one,' Bully says, enjoying the notoriety which his professional acquaintance with one of the gunmen gives him. 'He hasn't the liquid gumption to do the hostages.'

The hostages have all been sent their own clothes, a way of telling them that the police are in close contact with their relatives. The three black men are sent jeans and T-shirts and three pairs of pants and socks. Hurly notices that the police have sent two size thirties and one size thirty-four, the first two presumably for Kwate and Rupert and the last for him. They fit perfectly, uncannily well, as though the police have identikit descriptions of each of them.

Inside the musty room, the change of clothes comes as an occasion. They have spent the last night and day playing cards, all except Kwate who sits sullenly outside the circle. With the change of clothes, Kwate allows each of the hostages to have a thorough wash, leaving the door to the kitchen open and supervising them himself. The girl goes in last. Kwate jerks his head to indicate to Hurly that he wants him to take charge of her.

Kwate goes over and sits by the window and begins unloading the bullets from the pockets of his leather jacket. The Greek man and the child stare at the bullets and look away, as though embarrassed.

When Kwate sleeps, and they are left in the hands of Rupert and Hurly, the hostages carry on conversations

with them. The guns are put away, left lying around.
Rupert is convinced that none of the four will try to make
a dash for the door. He can see that neither the boy nor his
father will try anything without the other, and that the girl
seems to do only what the white man approves. He keeps
his eye on the man, certain that he can tackle him, even
without a gun, almost wishing that he'd make some move
and turn this waiting relationship into a physical scrap.

The girl washes her hair.

'Your hair look nice now, eh?' Hurly says as they come
into the room.

'You use up all the Fairy?' Kwate demands, looking up
from his fiddling with the shotgun.

She looks startled. 'I used some. I think there's some
left.'

'You let her use it?' Kwate asks Hurly. There is a hint
of frustration in his voice.

'Tcha, leave me alone,' Hurly says.

'And you want gamble with this man here because you
think I don't know?'

The previous night, as Kwate slept, Hurly played flush
with the white man for money.

There is a tense, dispirited silence in the room.

'Just passing time,' Hurly says.

'You'll be doing time, not passing it,' Kwate says.

'You can't see this man here taking you for a slow ride
and you too fool to have any understanding of it.'

'Leave it,' Hurly says.

'I feel like leaving all you,' Kwate says.

'Why don't you go then? Nobody holding a gun in
your mouth.'

'I didn't want to start this,' the girl says. 'He couldn't see what I was doing; I needed to wash my hair.'

'I was checking her careful,' Hurly protests.

Kwate thrusts a bullet into the chamber of the shotgun. 'Teach me not to play with little boys.'

'You is a big boy, you should play with the police.'

'You're like a couple of clowns,' Rupert interrupts. Kwate and Hurly are instantly silent. Hurly pretends that he is tidying up the room and busies himself with picking up the clothes that they've thrown all round the room. Nobody speaks for half an hour. It is obvious to Rupert that the hostages are frightened every time an argument breaks out between one of them and Kwate.

'How much money you take off him in the poker?' Kwate asks, not looking at Hurly.

'Two thousand pound.'

'You ain't going to get a chance to spend it in a wooden box.'

'You'll be wearing some plank yourself,' Hurly replies.

'You two should go on the box, better than the Fosters,' says Rupert.

'We *going* to be on telly,' Kwate says.

Hurly doesn't pick up the remark, but Rupert can see that Kwate is anxious to end the bickering.

'How you mean?'

Kwate isn't going to explain straightaway. He waits till their consignment of food arrives. He does not allow anyone to touch anything.

'Get a pen,' he says to Rupert. Then he goes over to the Greek man. 'You could write English, couldn't yuh?'

The man nods.

'Write this note.'

The man takes up the pen.

'*Calling Burgess,*' Kwate dictates. '*We are taking no food until you give* us *a proper television set.* Write that down.'

'Why you don't just ask Burgess straight?' Hurly asks, unable to contain his curiosity. Kwate does not answer.

The Greek writes the note. Kwate puts it on the tray full of sandwiches and hands the tray to Rupert.

'Put it out in the corridor.'

'I want eat,' Rupert says.

'Put it in the corridor.'

Rupert does as he is told.

Kwate goes to the window and, standing behind the curtain, shouts to the street below: 'Burgess! Come and get your tray and your sandwich!'

Kwate has taken charge once again, but Hurly is still smouldering.

No food is sent up the whole of the next day. Hurly sleeps and Rupert follows him. When Rupert wakes up, Kwate and Hurly seem to be on speaking terms. Kwate is lecturing. He is aware that the hostages are listening to each word, weighing it up for the force of personality behind it rather than for the meaning.

'If we are free, we have to be free together. We have pose a problem for your mother and others like her, boy. They now have to stand up and be counted. I sure the government count them, and when they see that we are all in numbers, black people of the whole world, then it terrorize their mind. We have to rely on the community and know what they are doing. It doesn't matter what happens to us, the fight have to go on ….'

It is Kwate's turn to sleep after Rupert. Rupert makes sure that he is asleep before he motions to Hurly and walks to the kitchen to fetch the biscuits that have been put back there. He hands the hostages a fair share of the packet and he and Hurly begin to eat, casting an eye from time to time on Kwate's form, covered over with a blanket.

'How much days you think we got?' Hurly asks.

Rupert raises his hand to his lips to tell him to shut up. 'I want some coffee.'

When Rupert comes back from the kitchen with the mugs he can see that there is something wrong with the Greek man. He is slouched against the wall behind the settee and his face has gone grey. His moustaches hang down, looking sad, and his large eyes seem full of involuntary pleading.

They sit drinking the coffee in silence. The Greek man begins panting like a dog after a chase, and the sound of his breath, pulled through his open mouth, turns everyone's eyes to him. His eyes roll back and his lungs seem to strain for air.

The boy rushes to his father and starts clawing at his shirt and undoing the belt on his trousers.

'Attack,' he says to Hurly, not caring if he wakes Kwate. 'Must get a doctor, right away, please.'

'He's having a fit,' the girl says, and her voice awakens Kwate who throws the blanket off his head and sits bolt upright, holding the shotgun.

The Greek man has now sunk onto the settee, his legs sprawled out. He is holding his chest with both hands. Tears trickle out of his eyes and he holds out one of his palms to motion Hurly away. Hurly dashes to the window and draws the curtains back.

'Get him to some fresh air,' the white man shouts, following Hurly's cue, and he rushes to the Greek man and begins pulling the settee towards the window.

Kwate leaps up and switches off the light, plunging the room in darkness.

'What go on?' he shouts.

This man dying.'

'What you done to him?'

'Is *you* stop his food.'

Kwate pushes the white man and Hurly aside. By the light of the street lamp which comes through the window, he examines his eyes.

'He's had a heart attack,' the white man says.

'You a doctor?' Kwate turns on him.

The Greek man's body lies like a machine, gasping for air.

'It's true, his heart faint,' Hurly says putting his head to the man's chest.

'Call the bloody ambulance. Call the police, they'll get him out of here,' the white man says.

Kwate turns on him and pushes the gun into his chest. The man backs away.

'Oh no,' the white girl begins to scream.

Rupert throws himself in between Kwate and the white man. Even in the dark he can see Kwate's eyes flashing, and for an instant Rupert believes that Kwate is capable of killing a man.

Hurly pushes his head outside the window and shouts for Burgess. The policemen in the street rush into the doorway of the building, and Bully's voice comes faintly down the corridor.

'Put that down, man, put it down,' Rupert begs Kwate. The white man stands with his hands in the air against the wall.

'I'll blast your head off,' Kwate says over Rupert's shoulder. 'You think you're smart, but I'll carry you with me.'

Once again camera bulbs begin flashing in the dark outside.

Kwate reaches for Rupert's shoulder and pulls him down, the shotgun still trained on the white man.

'We want to get a man out! Man dying!' Hurly is screaming through the window. Kwate makes a deft movement towards him and pulls him down by the leg.

'What's going on?' says Burgess's level voice.

'The Greek man, you could take him, get him out of here,' Hurly shouts desperately over the sill. 'He's sick or something, he need doctor.'

Burgess takes a second to consider the implication in the statement.

'We'll send a stretcher up.'

Kwate relaxes slightly and nods. Rupert can see that Kwate didn't quite know what to do, but has regained his calculating balance.

In the street there is an ambulance standing by. In a moment two men come up the stairs and down the corridor.

'We're coming through, we're ambulance men.'

'Is all right, Rupert?' Kwate asks. His voice betrays anxiety. He crawls over to the boy who has thrown himself across his father, fanning him ineffectively and crying. He pulls the boy off with a tremendous struggle and drags him across the floor to the kitchen.

'You killed him!' the boy shouts.

'I'm letting them through,' Rupert says, his voice raised unnecessarily.

The men bearing the stretcher don't look in the least intimidated. They go straight over to the Greek man and pile his unconscious body on the stretcher.

'Can we call through the window, mate? Who's in charge here?' one of them asks, looking round the darkened room as he kneels by the Greek.

'Just get him out,' Hurly says, training his pistol on the white man who is still standing with his hands absurdly aloft.

'Get him downstairs,' Rupert commands, standing at the door.

From the kitchen the boy screams and Rupert can hear Kwate slapping him. The boy shouts in a combination of Greek and English and Kwate growls at him. The boy begins to sob. None of the others move. The stretcher-bearers behave all through as though it is not their business, or at least that's what the routine movements of their bodies imply. They hurry through the door, taking small mincing steps, loaded with the weight of the Greek man.

Kwate pokes his head through the kitchen door and the rest of them can see that he is holding down the boy with his left hand. For the first time his expression is one of genuine uncertainty. 'Keep your eye on the boy,' he says to Rupert and his accent is amazingly English.

He goes up to the window and peers out. The ambulance has driven up to the door. Kwate turns and trains his shotgun on the door to the corridor. He is desperate to show the others that everything is under control.

'Sit against the wall,' he says to the white man and motions the girl to sit next to him.

Burgess's voice comes over the loudhailer after the ambulance has gone. 'You'd better send the young boy down now. We want you to surrender one of the hostages.'

'Send us a telly and we'll send him down,' Kwate shouts back. The police want him to repeat it. Kwate does.

'All right, we'll send you a telly; send the boy down.'

'We can wait.'

'Kwate, are you listening? So can we!'

Kwate turns to Rupert and asks him to bring the boy to the window. The boy is silent now, shepherded under escort. He licks his lips like a whipped puppy and he looks at Kwate with hatred. Kwate seems to change his mind and motions to Rupert to send the boy to sit next to the others.

'You could go soon,' Hurly says to the boy, who refuses to sit, but stands defiantly against the wall.

An hour later the television set arrives. It is placed, according to Kwate's instructions, at the end of the corridor. Rupert drags it in while Kwate stands over him with a weapon to cover his return.

'So let the boy go,' Hurly says.

'You gone mad or something?' Kwate asks. 'The boy ain't going nowhere.'

~

10.

THE TELEVISION SET IS ON all day. Kwate has turned the sound down. He doesn't look at the box. The others sit, glancing now and then at the silently moving image. The boy sits with his elbows between his knees and the girl talks to him in whispers. He nods or shakes his head every now and then. Hurly resumes his card game with the white man.

Rupert is despondent. He is thinking: We'll never get out of here. All of them, three hostages, three captors, are aware that the television set gives them a possibility of one-sided speech with an organized world outside.

At five forty-five, Kwate twists his body on the floor and turns up the sound.

The siege of the minicab office enters its sixth day. Police report that they have supplied the three gunmen with a television set. The condition of the hostage released yesterday, fifty-three-year-old Georgias Photopoulos, manager of the car firm, remains critical. In what is referred to as a major breakthrough, the fourth man in the robbery and ransom plan was apprehended in a flat in South London earlier today and has been charged.

The names of the three gunmen are now known to be Rupert Dowling, aged nineteen, Aloysius Brown, aged twenty-eight, and Hurlington Macaulay, aged twenty-two, all of South London. Chief Superintendent Burgess, in charge of operations at the scene of the siege in Corbett Street in London's West End, said that several people are helping police with their enquiries. Earlier the gunmen agreed to release a second hostage, twelve-year-old Panos Photopoulos, but they failed to deliver him when negotiations between them and the police broke down. Several MPs have welcomed the home secretary's statement that there will be no surrender in this country to terrorism of any sort.

Kwate turns the set off and paces the room.

'They lie,' he says through his clenched teeth.

The boy knew the names of the white kids, and the name of the dog. They would parade it around on its leash even in the central square where it wouldn't be killed in the traffic. When they let it off the leash the black kids would gather round it and stroke it and throw sticks for it to fetch, until the dog had to go home when their daddy called the kids in.

Hurly remembers how the boy longed to own a dog himself and train it to ferocity, to protect him from his enemies. His yellow dog, he was sure from the first, couldn't be taught to do any of that. It was a ridiculous dog. He couldn't even stop it from straining at the string, rushing nose first to the garbage cans when he took it into the street. In a week the puppy grew thinner and began to lose its hair. His dad, when he came home, would spank it off the chairs and kick it into the corner. His mum fed it, now and then, with scraps from their own meals.

The boy tried taking it for walks as the white kids took their dog, and found that Tiger had to be dragged most of the way. He learnt that the cur had a mind of its own, living on a wavelength of smells, poking its head through the parapet bars of basements on the way, magnetized by all the filth it encountered, blandly unaware of the commands that the boy barked when other people were looking.

One day, on one of these dragging walks, an old white lady crossed the road and called out to the boy, 'Where are you dragging that dog?'

'It's my dog,' the boy said.

'We are all God's creatures,' she said, 'and it's not your dog at all.'

'My dad bought it.'

The old white lady bent down and stroked the dog's head firmly, stretching the circles of its eyes. 'They don't feed you too well, do they, my lovely? They've starved my little thing. Oh, look at the state of you, poor doggy.'

The boy dragged the dog away from under her hand, and holding the string tight, began to run. She shouted out something after him, but he didn't hear. There were tears in his eyes. He knew that they didn't feed it enough. He hadn't wanted it to live as a tottering skeleton.

He went home and told his mother, 'The dog must have the tins we see on the telly.'

'You speaking to the dog now?'

'I tell you he's very sick.'

'I never want the beast in my house. I go tell the man take it away before it fill its belly with my everything.'

When his dad came that night, the boy saw he was drunk. There was a terrible row, and the boy knew it was over the dog, because he heard his mum say that one beast was too many for the house, and his dad struck her. The boy knew that some blows were going to reach him too. As his dad came for the dog in a rage and carried it out, staggering with the struggling pup under his arm, the boy tried to hold him back and joined in the general shouting. His mother was crying.

His dad banged the door behind him with a curse and his mum clung to the boy, partly to pacify him, partly to console herself.

The next morning the children gathered in the square around the pile of old furniture, gutted mattresses and eviscerated TV sets, staring at the fly-infested body of the yellow puppy. The boy had taken one horrified look and dashed back into the house calling his mum. His mother saw the terror in his face and came out with him into the square and stood before all the willing stares of the neighbours, shouting, 'The filthy dog break the boy's heart,' which they all knew referred not to the yellow dog, but to the boy's father.

The children in the square were too amazed to laugh. Days later they told the boy that the puppy had been battered to death with a brick from the building rubble outside the posh houses. The boy wouldn't go out and play. The shame had cut him; he felt the derision and pity of the other children and their mothers. They knew. Life had so many open windows without curtains. That was the beginning of his wish to be away from there, to go and live in a house such as the old white lady must have had, and buy the proper dog food from the supermarket.

His dad had committed murder, but didn't act like a man who had. He came home a few days after and without the least exchange of words, his mother settled down to cooking him a meal and to drinking rum with him. His dad brought the boy some comics, Hurly remembers, and he spent the next few days staring at them, turning their pages, lounging on the carpet or sitting at the kitchen table. 'The boy fond of reading,' his mum said.

Hurly remembers the school and Mr McSweeney with the thick curly hair and the sticking-out ears. The other kids called him 'Big Ears'. He taught them English and paced up and down the class while he talked, like a clockwork lion in the cartoons.

He would sometimes say to the boy, 'The Queen's English is not the English of the jungle, and it can't be wrote that way.' The class had been trained to laugh dutifully at his jokes, and they did it with a mixture of delight and contempt. He used to call kids to his desk, seat them next to him and go through their books with a thick red pencil making sarcastic remarks. Big Ears was funny: jovial on the outside, but when the boy stood next to him, able to smell his heavy breath, he knew there was more to Mr McSweeney's sarcasm than the desire to be funny.

He filled the boy with a kind of fear. Hurly remembers that he hated him.

He gave a lesson once on 'Negro English'. 'What is a young black baby called?' he asked the class.

'*A little nigger.*'

'*A jam jar label.*'

'*We can only be sure if we are sensitive.*'

'It's called a piccaninny,' he announced when no one answered.

That's mustard stuff sir,' a girl said.

The class laughed and McSweeney seemed well pleased.

'What does your mother refer to you as, Hurly? Not as her little blue-eyed boy, hmm?'

'She calls me Hurly, sir.'

'The word is piccaninny. Come on, you must have heard it, hmmm ?'

'No, sir.'

'What is it, what's the word, Janice?'

'Piccadilly, sir.'

He told his mother about the lesson. She didn't take any notice, but when his dad next appeared she said, 'They teaching this child all kind of rubbish in that school you put him.'

'Mr McSweeney taught us some Negro English today. He said all black boys were called Piccadilly.'

'Who tell you that thing?'

'Mr McSweeney.'

'What he is? Is he Irish?'

'That headmaster too fool, calling on paddy man to teach English. He says we speak like the jungle.'

'Kick him on his knee,' his dad said, visibly annoyed. Hurly was glad of it.

'Send him back to Dublin and tell him take his nasty potato back with him,' his dad said. He rose from the table and picked up a potato from the vegetable bucket and gave it to Hurly.

His mum laughed. 'Say your dad give him his wages.'

The next morning, on the way to school, Hurly remembered the potato. He slipped it into a paper bag, excited by the idea of getting a laugh out of the others.

He gave it to Mr McSweeney as soon as the lesson began and the class was coming into the English room and taking their places. Big Ears pulled the potato out of the paper bag.

'My dad sent you extra wages,' Hurly ventured.

The kids tittered but stopped when they saw the face between the ears turned red. It was as Hurly had suspected. Big Ears could dish it out, but he couldn't take it.

McSweeney threw the potato into the bin without a word and after class called Hurly over to his desk, ordering the rest of the children to clear out of his room.

Thirty-five-year-old McSweeney confronted twelve-year-old Hurly across the desk. His eyes glinted and his mouth was turned ever so slightly down at the corners.

'Never play those games with me, little boy. Never again make any jokes about anyone's race. You can't make a fool of me, the Almighty has done that already. But I, my lad, I could make a cripple of you.'

The edge in his voice told Hurly that these words he should not remember or repeat. Not to his dad, not to the others who would definitely ask what Big Ears had said and done.

The threat made Hurly swallow hard. 'No, sir.'

Some days later McSweeney, his jovial mood restored, asked the class, 'Why do you think the Irishman put a lock on his trouser zip? To stop people taking the piss.'

The class laughed. Hurly didn't. He looked away from the teacher when he saw his eyes turn to him in the third row. After class McSweeney turned to Hurly on his way out.

'I see we understand each other perfectly,' he said.

Hurly remembers the boy, confused at the ripe age of sixteen, wanting to imitate the limp that the 'rude boys', the 'Johnny-too-bads' of Brixton affected. They called him the 'lame-dance boy'.'

He remembers the boy learning from his associates to give off confidence like a body smell. He remembers his first encounter with Kwate.

He went now where the other black boys went. He heard of a gang called the Rebels, and in his dreams he wanted to join them, but the Rebels were nowhere to be found. Everyone talked about them. They struck here, they attacked there. There were many stories, but no people, no faces to fit into the stories. The Rebels were bad! Badder! Baddest! They'd robbed a whole supermarket, they'd gone into Brixton nick and rescued a boy belonging to their gang, they'd set fire to a police van and still they were free and unfettered. Some of the boys he knew by name and face were reputed to be Rebels, but they weren't the people in the stories at all: they were the same rude boys, the same lame-dance men who were no smarter than he was, and as poor as he was.

'There ain't no Rebels, boy, *you* is the Rebels,' Kwate told him.

'You don't know what the Rebels do,' Hurly said.

'I know what they do. They get on bus and don't pay ticket, that's what they do,' Kwate said.

He met Kwate at the fair. He had gone to Brockwell Park with a crowd of boys from the youth club. It was summer. The sun was shining so that you could wear your shirt open as they do in Jamaican films, sweating, shining. They had come down to the park to listen to the music at the festival. But the music at the festival was no good. The sound, amplified and pumped through twenty boxes, faded away into the clear sky. It was not a sound of freedom, it was a sound that needed to be enclosed in four walls, tightly packed with bodies to be effective, to deliver its mysteries. In the clear open air, it hung above the heads of the crowd and vanished. There were clowns on the platform, hundreds of boys and girls clambering on, dying to be seen. The park was thick with policemen. In front of the platform stood an indifferent crowd. A few hundred people, mostly white people, the sort of hippy whites who live in Birxton, squatted on the grass. Hurly's gang was fed up with the sounds, fed up with the clowns who tried to make funny speeches before they tuned their guitars.

They wandered down to the stalls at the back of the mob. A white man was selling ice creams from a painted van. He was doing hard business. One of Hurly's crowd suggested that they go and get themselves some ice creams. There was a crowd of young blacks around the van. Hands reached out for the cones which hung above their heads. The white man wanted money in his hand before he loosed his tight grip on the ice creams.

Suddenly there was a shout. Hurly looked up to see that several hands had grabbed the cones from the man's hand and the man was shouting for help. Two policemen rushed up and began to push their way through the crowd. Some youths shoved Hurly forward while others, retreating from the confusion, tried to push away. The white man had climbed down from his van and grabbed hold of a black youth by the collar. Hands reached for his white coat to pull him down. The policemen were in the thick of it. Helmets began to fly.

Some of Hurly's gang were now at the base of the van. It began to shudder. Hurly saw that it was being lifted and overturned. More police arrived from nowhere. Hurly wanted to get out. A blue-sleeved arm grabbed him and began to wrench him away from the crowd. He protested that he wasn't in it: it had nothing to do with him. 'I've got you,' the voice said. 'I've got you. Come here!' He was in the grip of the law.

Then just as he was being yanked to the edge of the crowd, into what he saw was a group of waiting policemen, a black palm fell like an axe on the hand that gripped his sleeve. The hand let go. Hurly was free. He looked up to see Kwate.

'Keep going,' Kwate said.

Ten youths were arrested. The police van took them away. Hurly was standing on the edge of the audience which was still digging the sounds, lazily, ignoring the occurrence round the ice-cream van, when Kwate's face loomed up again.

'Why you want to steal the man ice cream? You so hungry?'

'I wasn't in that,' Hurly protested. Kwate smiled.

'You don't like ice cream?' he asked.

There was no need to thank Kwate. Hurly felt that that was understood.

He met Kwate again at the youth club. Someone was trying to sell Hurly a gold watch for two pounds. Kwate sauntered up from nowhere and handled the watch. 'That's not worth two pound, it's worth two years,' he said.

Hurly recognized him. He hung around, back to the wall, talking to Kwate. A man of purpose, he felt.

Hurly remembers that the boy had wanted to be like every man who frightened him. His mother used to tell him to love his enemy, and he found he wanted to love him because it was a way of keeping 'in' with him. *Love thine enemy's power,* he used to think each time he looked at the ornate Christian motto hung on the wall of his mum's house.

Kwate changed all that. You have to be smart enough for the world, Kwate told him, not only violent enough for it. Hurly recalls striving to wrap that sense of dread about him, that cloak of mastery, a way of holding your head and speaking in the deepest tones, censoring your voice before it came out of your mouth. He had been slightly frightened by the men who hung around the corners in the marketplace, passing comment on the girls going by. Now he himself loitered on the very same corners; he had become one of them, preoccupied with the records one could buy from the booming shop on a Saturday if only one had the money.

From Kwate he learned that a man must have one soul in his body, that he has to choose his corner and defend it, that two styles don't live easily in the same body. But from so many around him, he did not know which style to adopt.

He remembers his first political meeting. Kwate advised him to go, but didn't go with him. He went with Slingo. It took some persuasion to get Slingo to agree to come along, but Slingo wanted to try to raise some bread.

'There'll be a whole heap of black people at the meeting,' offered Hurly.

'Where is it?'

'Down the youth club in Railton Road.'

They went. Slingo from the beginning began to look around the room to see which of the crowd might buy little packets for a pound from him after the business was done. Hurly had dressed for the occasion. He was wearing a hat and a green satin shirt with a jacket he had bought from Cecil Gee.

There were about fifty people in the room, mostly young but with a sprinkling of long-haired white men who worked in the social services in the area and were generally known but not acknowledged by the crowd.

At the front of the small hall in which the chairs were laid out as though for a church gathering, the politicos were assembled, talking to each other, and ignoring the crowd which sat in clusters, avoiding the front rows.

A half-bald man called the meeting to order. He said he was from the Black Revolutionary Action Group (BRAG) and he'd like to welcome the brothers and sisters to the meeting on the problems of black youth. He was wearing a tatty olive-green jacket, and Hurly thought he must have bought it from the army surplus. He had startlingly wide eyes.

'Good to see so many of my brothers and sisters here tonight,' the man from BRAG said. 'Black people beginning to take the struggle seriously, boy.' His remark raised a laugh from the members of his organization in the front row.

'Tramp,' Slingo said, refusing to sit down and leaning up against the wall with the air of having wandered in because he had five minutes to spare.

The first speaker of the evening was introduced. She was a fat young woman in her late twenties with short, close-cropped hair, wearing what Hurly called an African shirt above a pair of baggy khaki trousers. She stood up with a show of seriousness and then, without warning, gave the audience a really charming smile. She began to speak. 'Brothers and Sisters,' she said, stressing every word, 'we call this meeting because we want to speak to our own people and especially the youth who are at the forefront of the struggle today.' The front row cheered and some people further back joined in. 'The youth are fighting terrific odds in this country which some people call Great Britain. I can't see what's so great about it [cheer] when the sun don't shine half the time and a mango cost you ten bob in Brixton market [cheer of recognition].'

Hurly didn't like that kind of girl. Too much mouth to make up for lack of face, he thought. Yet he listened carefully, as did the majority of the audience. The girl talked eloquently about the suffering of black people in the cane fields. Hurly learned something new. She talked about why the police fought black youth and said – as far as Hurly could understand – that the government of this place was no different from the government of the islands of the West Indies.

'We are organizing,' she continued, 'but I don't intend

to tell you all how we organizing, because there are a lot of black people who are dangerous. They get a little money so they work for the Special Branch. We serious in this business, you know. We must criticize ourselves for all the loose talk that we do, because black people talk loose, you know, their tongues loose like a donkey tail.'

She finished by saying that she didn't want to talk too long because the youth themselves had to be given a chance to speak.

Next to her sat a young man in a beret, worn not in the French style, pulled over one ear, but at the back of his head like a relaxed chef. He got to his feet as the girl sat down modestly to applause, and delivered a piece he seemed to have learnt by heart.

Hurly saw at once that his attention was not on telling them anything, but on winning the approval of the girl who had spoken before. He adopted the posture of a teacher, the voice of a preacher, and spoke words of bitterness, not only against the police who he said arrested black people for nothing, but against the people in the audience who had not done anything about it. He finished to scant applause and asked for questions. There were none. The audience had been stunned, and were partly shy, partly ashamed in case these political people began to point fingers at them and ask them what they'd been doing and tell them what they should have been doing.

Kwate had referred to these politicos as 'Shapesters'. Hurly tried to give this word some meaning, looking at the people behind the chairman's table and the people standing up around the hall looking as though they were in charge.

'So you're satisfied with the sort of lives that capitalism imposes on you?' the man in the beret said, looking sideways at the girl for approval. She frowned.

'Yeah,' Hurly said and the crowd laughed.

A flicker of uncertainty crossed the speaker's face. He scanned the audience, and then shook his head in exaggerated sorrow. 'The brother over there says "yeah". An American "yeah". You see, some people want to admit it. That's where they will remain, where black people have always been, smoking weed and jumping up in carnival and at the blues and snatching bags and behaving like lumpen elements without consciousness.'

'Oi, don't talk loose, there might be Special Branch!' a voice shouted from the audience. Again there was laughter.

The speaker had lost the audience. He struggled to regain it. 'Some people don't want to see what the white man doing to us. They just like to dress up sharp-sharp and go betting shop and wear all kind of hat and satin shirt...'

'I thief your mother money to buy it?' Hurly said, and found that his voice was louder than he had intended.

'Only time will tell,' the speaker persisted, raising his voice in turn. 'Everything is "real cool" until the blood start flow and fire begin to burn.'

The girl got to her feet and the man sat down. She resumed lecturing the audience. Hurly looked around for Slingo who had spotted a potential customer and had gone to sit next to him. He was speaking to this man who was wearing a fur coat with dark glasses and, abruptly, he got up and went to the door. The man in the fur coat followed him out.

'... calling on the youth to give up hustling and be conscious of what sort of reputation they are getting black people ...' the girl was saying urgently.

Hurly waited for two minutes and when Slingo didn't come back, he got up and followed him out of the hall. Slingo was at the door looking very pleased with himself.

As they walked home, Hurly wondered about whether he should try and be what the girl said he should be. He decided it wasn't possible. 'Good meeting,' he said to Slingo, because he felt guilty for having brought him there, wasted his evening perhaps.

'Yeah , nice, nice, nice,' Slingo agreed, his fist tightening around the wad of pound notes he had acquired from the man with the fur.

~

11.

To RUPERT, EDWINA PRETENDED THAT she didn't know Kwate. She never mentioned him, and when he was in the house, he understood that he was to give Rupert no indication that she went to him from time to time. She would disappear for a day or two and come back as though she had never been away. Rupert assumed that she was going to see Michael, that he was failing her by not being able to take her out and spend money on her. He was ashamed of asking her for money, but she gave it to him tactfully and paid for him wherever they went. She bought him clothes; she tried to buy him books.

Edwina allowed him to believe that she was with Michael. She felt that it kept him from treating her as he had told her that his stepfather treated his mum. She cleaned and cooked for him, but even though he didn't like it, she would leave food in the kitchen for Slingo when she cooked, not suspecting that Rupert imagined that she had a secret scene with Slingo. He hated it when she went to Slingo's room at night, attracted by the sounds and the promise of a smoke.

She was making a fool of herself and of him, Rupert thought.

Slingo could feel this tension too, and he amused himself with it. He would say, 'Woman leave you and gone,' when Edwina stayed away. Or he would say, 'Her father must be an MP or something, the way she talk. Why you don't go visit their house and rip them off?'

Rupert couldn't afford to show Slingo that he was jealous. With him he always behaved as though Edwina was somebody he was using as a convenience for the moment. He had to give out that women were no bother to him, they would come and they would go, and he could treat them just as casually as Slingo did.

With Edwina, he let his jealousy loose. If he had to stop what he suspected, he had to stop *her*.

'Do you lend Slingo any money?' he asked her.

'Don't be mad, I'd never get it back,' she said, but Rupert was sure that Slingo was hustling off her.

One Saturday Slingo returned home in the afternoon with a load of stuff he said he'd acquired: a couple of pairs of boots, a new amplifier, a pin-striped three-piece suit, a leather coat and stuff like that. When Edwina got home Rupert asked her if she'd pulled any deal with Slingo.

'With whom? What deal?'

'Where's your chequebook and your credit cards?'

'In my bag. I don't know what you're getting at,' she protested and groped in the bottom of her bag. Too deliberately, Rupert thought, she squatted down and emptied the contents of the bag onto the carpet and looked through it. 'I must have left it at Michael's,' she said. 'I thought I had it; I can't understand it.'

A week later Rupert noted to himself that she had a new chequebook but he didn't mention it to her. She must have given it to Slingo to forge cheques.

When he was with Rupert, Slingo would needle him as if to see how far he could push the boy. It was a sadistic game.

'Your wife teach you to make your bed and cook your tea?'

Rupert wouldn't react.

'Is her husband a butty-man?'

Or if Slingo was surrounded by his friends he'd say, 'Rupert keep a nice little thing in the back room there. She have the boy working hard, hard, but the woman tell me she need a man, not a pickney boy.'

One day Slingo brought in a cardboard carton and left it in the hallway downstairs. Rupert checked it and saw that it had several reels of movie film in it. That night, in his room he confronted Edwina.

'Has Slingo asked you to make this film?'

'He asked me months ago, in front of you. I think they've abandoned the whole project.'

'Who's they?'

'Slingo and the people he was going to make it with. You know how scatty they are. I never thought they'd be able to organize it anyway.'

Rupert suspected that she wasn't telling the truth.

'You know what film they want you to make?'

'Some youth thing, isn't it?'

'You don't know what that man's getting you into.'

'Don't start that again. I'm perfectly capable of looking after myself.'

'I doubt it. You think Slingo's a big superstar hustler, but he's just a bag-snatching small-time crook.'

'You're beginning to sound like Michael.'

Rupert caught the distinct tone of dishonesty in her voice.

'And you're trying to cover up something, ain't you?'

'Look, let's stop this squabbling. You're getting paranoid.'

'Slingo is a pimp, and you behave in front of everyone here like one of the women he's running.'

'I don't know what you're talking about.'

'You know what I'm talking about, you just come to this ghetto looking for a bit of black, didn't you, and you don't care who you get it off of.'

'Don't talk filth to me. Anyway, there's not much chance of getting much off you, is there?'

Rupert grabbed her by the arm and tried to turn her round to look into his face. She jerked loose of him. 'Don't try that rough stuff on me.'

'You going to make the film with Slingo, aren't you! That's where you were gone yesterday. You think I'm stupid.' Rupert was shouting now.

'All right, I am, and you can't stop me. I'm fed up of being pushed around by you. I've also told Slingo that it's no good asking you to co-star in this great film because you can't get it up. Wouldn't make a very hot skin flick, would it.'

Rupert felt a red flash of anger fall across his vision. He doubled his leg and kicked her in the stomach. It was a satisfying blow.

'Don't hit me!' Edwina screamed, and Rupert, totally consumed now by confusing rage, struck her with his flat hand across her face. Then he doubled his fist and hit her again. He felt his knuckle connect with the bone of her eye socket.

'I won't hit you, I'll kill you, you bitch!'

'I'm going, I'm going,' she shouted.

Rupert ran to the kitchen as Edwina dashed out of the room and down the stairs. He caught her on the landing and she saw that he'd grabbed up a kitchen knife. Terror clutched her ribs. She'd never seen him with his face contorted and his eyes blank with anger that made him almost shiver.

He held the knife close to his body and kicked out at her again, catching her in the back as she ran out of the front door.

Tell Slingo he's going to get it, too!' Rupert shouted after her. He heard her footsteps running down the pavement, and turned back into his room in torment.

He had only one thought. He would catch Slingo and confront him. Already Slingo must have made him the laughing stock of the town. Suddenly his suspicion became a certainty. Kwate's remark, Hurly's smirk, Slingo's blatant hints – he should have done something about it before.

There were tears in his eyes as he left the house, but in the cold night air, his rage cooled to calculation. He couldn't let Slingo get away with it. Perhaps all his friends knew that Slingo was 'keeping his breakfast warm for him', as he'd heard Slingo put it when talking about seducing someone's wife or boasting about taking women from other men.

He walked down the 'front line', the row of cafés and liquor shops in which he knew Slingo hung out. He couldn't find him. He walked one way and then the other with some vague idea that he might come across Slingo in the street. Finally he decided to go home, not back to the squat, but to his mother's house.

'You come in here all hours, Rupert! You're after thinking this is a hotel.'

'I got chuck out of my house, Mum. I want to sleep,' he said. He went to his little sister's bedroom and threw himself on the bed.

'You come here in your troubles. I have my troubles too,' his mum said as she went back to bed. 'Mind, don't wake the girl.'

Rupert couldn't sleep. The idea of Edwina conspiring against him, the image of her and Slingo, kept him awake and restless. Before dawn he got up again and let himself silently out of the door. He walked briskly back to the squat which was at the other end of Brixton. The car was still parked outside. Even though it was four in the morning, Slingo's light was still on.

Rupert opened the door, not certain how he'd react. He still had the knife in the pocket of his jacket. He'd have to say something to Slingo. Maybe he'd allowed his imagination to run riot, and the sight of Slingo would prove that his jealousy had made his reason dizzy, that Edwina would never sink so low as to give herself to this gangling ape of a man.

As he opened the door there was a movement on the upstairs landing. The house always felt damp. The rooms on the bottom floor had plaster peeling off and broken floorboards and smashed window frames. He and Slingo had left them empty, hollow enough to reflect the sound of footsteps in the hall.

'Don't bother come up here,' Slingo's voice said.

Rupert stood still in the light of the half-closed door.

The voice, deep and serious, came round the bend of the staircase. 'Boy. I'm not messing about. You get your arse away from this house, 'cos I got a couple of guns here and I'll shoot you in your big mouth if I see your face in this place.'

Slingo spoke slowly and deliberately. He's trying to scare me, Rupert thought, and his hand tightened round the handle of the kitchen knife. Behind him was the light of the street lamp and ahead of him the darkness to which he was just getting accustomed.

'Is Edwina here?'

'I said to split.'

He hesitated for a moment. 'All right. I'm going,' he called out, and his voice which he had steeled with defiance came out as a long whisper. He backed away through the door and slammed it, and walked back to his mother's house.

∼

12.

'RUPERT'S GOING TO KILL SLINGO, he's gone mad,' Edwina said when Kwate answered the bell.

'I've been up and down these stairs six times this evening. Town going crazy,' Kwate said, letting her into the bulbless hall. He saw that her hair was bushed wildly round her face, that she looked frightened. She'd been running.

'He's serious. Rupert. He went mad on me.'

'The boy beat you?' Kwate grinned. 'He growing up, putting lash on he woman.'

'Don't come that machismo stuff, Kwate, this is serious.'

'Serious for you. Where he beat yuh?'

That doesn't matter. He's got a knife and he's looking for Slingo. I think he'll do something stupid.'

'You come to sort out the world again. Leave it. Slingo could look after himself.'

'Rupert can't. I think he'll listen to you.'

'What you expect me to do ? Go in the night and hold the boy's hand?' Kwate turned and ushered her upstairs. 'If he has a knife, Slingo have a gun,' he said.

'What are you talking about?'

'Slingo is getting a bit desperate now. So why is the punk worked up ?'

'About this damn film of Slingo's. He got all prickly and suspicious. Rupert has a lot of problems.' She had learnt the phrase from Kwate. 'He have a lot of problems,' he would say in dismissing anybody.

She didn't like Kwate's amused tolerance of her state of near-panic which she had to fight herself to control. She had told him about how Rupert had behaved in the past few days. When she told him, she had felt it was part of her exploratory adventure. She watched his reaction, which was sympathetic. He had spoken to her about Rupert and Hurly and how they were the great black hope of the future.

'Except white women, they always mess up the youth's head. I've seen too much fight over white pussy in this town.'

She hated him when he put on this arrogant mood and tone. She felt with all of them, except Rupert perhaps, that they lived on the edge of an unspoken violence. Kwate was capable of doing anything, even though he never seemed to lose his temper.

Kwate had given her no indication downstairs in the hallway, or while climbing the long flight of stairs, that they'd find Slingo sitting in his room. He greeted her with an obscene grin as she walked through.

'Boy lost his cool and put a beating on Ed here,' Kwate said.

'So you ain't going home now. No place to go, judgement and mercy gone,' Kwate said as Edwina settled into the only chair in the room.

'He might come up here,' Edwina said.

'Don't worry about him, I'll deal with him.'

'We were going to start shooting tomorrow,' Slingo said. 'You've gone and screw it up now.'

'I never said I'd do your bloody film. What do you think I am?'

'You asking me your price? I ain't your ponce,' Slingo said.

Edwina looked at Kwate and he took the hint in her expression. She couldn't take Slingo's nonsense tonight. 'Leave it for tonight,' he said authoritatively to Slingo.

Slingo rose slowly from the bed and put his leather coat on. 'You keep the machinery,' he said to Kwate, and, 'All right, I'll check you up my house,' to Edwina. Kwate went onto the landing and walked part of the way down the stairs with him.

'You backed out of the film too?' Kwate asked, coming back into the room and putting some music on the player.

'Kwate, you know very well I never consented to do anything of the sort.'

'What's the difference between one thing and another? If you're a go-go dancer, you could be a stripper. There was good breads in it.'

She knew what he was alluding to. 'I thought that was something personal between you and me.'

'There's no personal thing with me and anybody.'

There was a sinking feeling in Edwina's stomach. The ghost of a suspicion she had had as she ran to Kwate's place had taken full body.

'What have you done with those snaps?'

'What snaps?'

The ones I let you take of me. I want the whole reel.'

'It's still in the camera.'

'Where is it?'

She felt foolish, looking at the deliberate remoteness, the distance in his face. Kwate sat on the edge of the bed with a little mirror in his hand, his tongue stretching the skin on his cheek as though he were examining his face for pimples. 'Skin dry up in your climate,' he said.

'You've given them to Slingo, haven't you?'

'Your photo ain't worth nothing. Slingo took the reel to develop it. There's plenty girls will pose for anybody. You can't sell them pictures, nobody want to buy them. So relax, nobody's hustling you.'

'Maybe Rupert found the photographs in Slingo's room or something.'

'I'm a photographer. I could take what picture I like. What it got to do with the boy?'

'You want to explain that to him?'

'They're not developed yet, anyway. I just gave them to him today. You want them back, you can have them back. I don't want to sell pin-ups of your ugly white body anyway.'

She hadn't seen Kwate like this before. She knew that when he was annoyed he used the word 'white' to sting and insult her, but she had always taken this as a game, a battle of wits that was a test of her self-assurance. Edwina pressed the small of her back where Rupert had kicked her. She told herself that she didn't care if Kwate was contemptuous, he couldn't rule her with his contempt. He pushed around the black boys who hero-worshipped him, but he treated even them with more respect. She should never have consented to allowing him to take photographs of her. Kwate had set up two spot lamps and a camera on a tripod and had said to her he wanted to take pictures of her. It had flattered her, even though he asked her in a totally businesslike tone. He had induced her to take bits of clothing off, and after an evening of making love, he had sat her on a stool in the nude and snapped her relaxed body and sullen but spirited expression.

Perhaps she was being paranoid about the pictures, she thought. Maybe he *had* given them to Slingo just to develop and add to the folders he had in the corner of his room. Rupert didn't know anything; he couldn't. There was nothing much to know in any case. It wasn't his business. She had the right to do as she pleased; she wasn't going to step out of one relationship and move into another repressed 'scene', as they called it. A sense of failure struck her.

'You really treat me like white trash, don't you? I don't mean a thing to you, your hustles and your ego are all that ever matter to you.'

'You used the word,' Kwate replied. 'Far as I know there are only two kinds of white people: those who afraid of blacks and those who aren't. You white girls who hang around Brixton is scared of we. You come looking to put a little collar round Rupert's neck. It's him need protection from you, not you from him. In the end you'll go back to your butty-man husband who'll become headmaster and lick little boys with a stick. You like to eat good and live good and drive your car, and you want a bit of black under your control because it something that frightens your mind.'

'That's a lot of shit. Racist shit. I treated Rupert like a friend.'

'That's why you come sleep with me and hide it from him?'

'He wouldn't understand. I have my own needs too. He's just a boy.'

'He's your boy, but I'm not your man.'

'You better get that film back.'

'Or you'll call your husband and ask him to beat me?' Kwate laughed.

'All right, play it that way,' Edwina said, rising from the bed, her hands in her pockets. 'Be seeing you.'

He is a vulture, she thought as she walked out into the night. He lives off the dead feelings of those around him. Maybe he was right, though. She had had enough of Rupert and of Kwate too. Yes, she had been afraid of something, a quality of ambition it was, that threatened to burst out from them. She remembered thinking they were men in a hurry with nowhere to go, and she began to wonder now, listening to her own footsteps on the deserted street, where it was she was going.

~

13.

EDWINA GROPED IN HER POCKET for a twopenny piece. She'd left all her stuff at Rupert's. There was some change in her denim pockets, but no tuppence. It took ages for the operator to pick up the call. She wanted a reverse charge call. She gave the number and waited tensely for Michael to pick up the receiver. He would know it was her.

His voice was sleepy. 'It's rather late isn't it?'

'Michael. I want to come over.'

'This is all very sudden,' he said, sarcastically.

'I'll explain when I get there, all right?'

'What's wrong, no room at the bordello tonight?'

'Please, Michael, I have a right to the place, you know that. I just want to come and sleep. I'd like to talk to you too, of course, but you don't sound as though you want to talk to me. I'm sorry about this evening, about some other things too.'

'We won't argue your rights over the phone. I'll leave the door on the latch.'

'Michael. I haven't got any money. I'll hop a cab, will you lend me some?'

'What happened to the car?'

She hesitated. 'It broke down, I've left it in a side street.'

'Where?'

'Look, I'll talk when I get there, right?' She could tell from his last questions that though he was annoyed, he'd be awake to pay for the cab. He wanted her to return.

She hadn't seen him for weeks. He hadn't tried to contact her at school. In the cab it struck her that he might have another woman there. She'd have to be very careful.

'You've just dropped in for a visit, have you?' Michael said pretending to be more annoyed than he really was. When he put the phone down, he'd gone and brushed his hair and gargled with toothpaste to get rid of the stink of stale sleep.

'Can I make coffee?'

'Do as you like. You have rights to the place, exercise them.'

'I didn't mean that in a bullying way.'

He was looking at her eye. He could see that she'd been hit, but he suppressed his instinct to ask her how it had happened. He could see she was uncertain, and while it made him feel slightly triumphant to have her sitting in the kitchen at one in the morning, he also felt sorry for her. She had suffered some defeat. If he wanted he could make her earn her passage back to him. That's what he'd been longing for, that was how he saw her little adventure with Rupert ending, and it gave him some satisfaction to see his prediction taking shape.

'You haven't been in an accident, have you?'

'No, nothing like that.'

'Trouble with the boys, huh?'

'Oh, please don't be frivolous, I'll explain in the morning. I need some time to think.'

'The bed in my study's still there. I'll go and sleep there. You can sleep in my bed.'

She noticed that he called it 'his' bed. 'So it's "my" bed now?'

'Has been for some time, Edwina.' She caught a low note of regret in his sentence.

'I'd like to sleep in our room, there's no need for you to move into the study.'

'We should let the cosiness take its own shape instead of forcing it, don't you think?'

'I don't want to force anything, I just didn't mean to put you out. It's my fault that things haven't worked out

recently, for you and me, and for a long time I suppose. I
didn't want to walk in and take over.'

'Not much chance of that. I have my rights too.'

'Sure.'

As he pretended to be asleep beside her, Edwina lay
awake and her mind turned over vivid images of Rupert's
angry face. What would she tell Michael? She wanted to tell
him the truth but she constantly told herself that the truth
wasn't merely the facts. It was her excuse for not being
truthful about facts. The bed felt warm, and as she looked
at Michael's naked back, getting slightly fatty, Kwate's
insult about her 'ugly white body' came back to her.

14.

RUPERT GOT OFF THE TUBE at Victoria, waited patiently in
the queue at the top of the escalator, and then with a quick
dash, overtook it and ran past the ticket collector and up
the stairs into the street.

'Bastard,' the ticket collector shouted at him, his tone
admitting that Rupert had got away, that he couldn't be
bothered to chase him.

Rupert was still nervous of pulling this stunt, but he
had no option. His mother, who had accepted his return
reluctantly, wouldn't give him a penny. 'Go look for
work,' she had said to him on his second day of lounging
around the flat. He didn't even have a spare change of

clothes with him. On the third day he went to Kwate's and told him that he'd decided to leave the place he shared with Slingo, omitting to mention why. He talked about Nick, the boy he used to work the Portobello with. Kwate listened. Rupert had been hoping to find Hurly there, so that he could ask Hurly to fetch his things from the house. He had to ask Kwate to go with him. Slingo wasn't there. Edwina's car had been moved. Rupert made a quick dash upstairs and picked up as much as he could, stuffing it into paper bags.

At the corner of Victoria Street, Rupert pulled out Nick's neatly written-up diary. He had told his mother he was going to find himself a job, but had gone out to Nick's place. Under the heading VICTORIA, Nick had written in ten addresses. Next to the address, written in a different pen, were ten names, randomly invented. Nick had told him that there was absolutely nothing to worry about. All he had to do was get an *A to* Z, go to those addresses during office hours when the front doors to the hallways would be open, and if there was no one about, pick up the parcels with those names on them and bring them to him. He said he'd give him fifty pounds for every district he covered. He'd been to Jermyn Street in the West End the day before and it had been easy enough. In two of the buildings he met hall porters on the stairs, and then he just went up the lift, waited a few minutes on one of the landings and came down again, marking the address with a cross for Nick to return to.

He knew that the parcels could have almost anything, from electric typewriters to chest-expanding machines, fancy barometers, clothes, hundreds of other things. Nick had perfected a new deal, he told Rupert. He went down to a place in Fleet Street on a certain day of the week when they sold off large bundles of old papers with mail-order coupons in them. He simply filled these out in different names and addresses of flats and offices with open front doors to which parcels would be delivered. He or Rupert could pick up the goods and flog them.

If the parcels got too heavy, he could take a taxi, Nick told him. He would pay. Rupert tried to look decent on this job. He had cleaned up and wore a shirt and one of his stepfather's ties.

He hadn't told Kwate or Hurly the details of the racket. He knew they were desperate for a bit of easy money, but the closer he kept Nick's business to himself, the more unlikely it was that other hustlers would muscle in on it.

Rupert came to the first address. There were nameplates on the door. They announced the occupancy of six different firms. To the left of the hallway there were lockers for the post, no enquiry window, no hall porter, nothing. On top of the lockers fifty letters were scattered, along with three parcels.

Harold Jay. Yes!

He picked it up and walked out. Easy as telling margarine from butter.

As he was walking out, a man passed him in the hallway. 'Which floor for Dempster's?'

'I think the top. I'm just passing messages.'

The man moved on. 'Should have picked a nicer day.'

It was a long, light parcel, and looked as though it could have been a pair of skis in it.

The next address. A yellow door, again with office nameplates on it. A much larger, modernized hallway with the mail laid out on a table at the bottom of the stairs. Another parcel. He read the name on it. He smiled when he recognized the name as that of a boy who had been in school with him and Nick, a tall gangling boy who was called Timothy Satchell, though all the kids called him 'Timmy Handbag', because he had a certain reputation.

The parcel was fairly large. He piled it on the other and walked out. He put the diary in his pocket and began to peel the label off the parcel in the street. He would pick up one more, and then, depending on whether it was light or heavy, he would call a taxi or move on to the next one and try to finish the district that afternoon.

He walked down the street, balancing the parcels. A white car, parked on the opposite side, started and drove up alongside him. A man leapt out of the driver's seat and another came out from the far side.

'Come here, you.'

Rupert turned at the sound of the voice and froze. He thought his best ploy would be to pretend they weren't talking to him and he began to walk faster. The man dressed in a dark tweed jacket ran up to him and caught him by the shoulder.

'I said come here!'

'I'm waiting for a taxi,' Rupert stammered.

'Let's look at that shopping,' the man said producing a card from his pocket with the cinematic gesture of a detective inspector.

15.

RUPERT PHONED MICHAEL TO SIGN his bail papers. As he had expected, Michael turned up. The police refused to let Rupert go until they got a lead on Nick, but Rupert held out. He told them that he had picked up a few parcels the week before but that he had disposed of the goods in Portobello market, a few things, not very much. The police brought a pile of three hundred written out mail-order coupons and threw it on the table in the interrogation room. 'You'll go down for ten years on this lot,' the detective said. 'If you help us and give the names of the real people behind this racket, we'll let you off.'

Rupert said he wanted to see a lawyer.

'You ain't got a lawyer, Sunshine,' the detective replied, 'and you won't be having mummy's dumplings for dinner tonight if you don't tell us who you flog the stuff to.'

Rupert phoned Michael's school from the court the next day. The magistrate agreed to let him out on bail after Michael said he'd known Rupert for six years. He agreed, as Rupert had known he would, to stand as his surety.

'Thanks, man,' was all Rupert said to him.

'I've got to get back to school,' Michael said. He had not mentioned the matter to Edwina.

'We are to bring three hundred more charges,' the police said to the magistrate who leaned over and looked as though his specs were going to fall off.

'*How* many?'

Rupert went home and that evening he went to Kwate's. For a few hours they talked about how the police had treated him and what he could do to get himself a lawyer who would get him off the charge.

'They going to send you down, boy,' Kwate said. 'You're going to get some heavy pieces for this job. You should have told them you was working for the white man and fingered him.'

Rupert disagreed. Nick had given him money in the past when he was broke.

'You'll need some money to get out of the country. Go to the Caribbean for a few years and if you come back they'll have forgotten that you was on a charge.'

'What about the bail?'

'Not your problem, is it?'

The idea of leaving the country had taken root in Rupert's head. He attached a fantasy to it. If he could get the money together, he would take Edwina with him. He wouldn't go to the Caribbean, he would go to the States or to Canada where he could get a flat with her. She had murdered his ego, but she could bring it back to life again. He'd forgive her.

The robbery of the minicab firm was Kwate's idea, or so it seemed to Rupert. Kwate proposed it to him and to Hurly with the air of a general who had hand-picked the volunteers for a special operation.

'We could make two pieces, two thousand pounds each,' he said. Neither Rupert nor Hurly doubted that there'd be that much money in the minicab firm.

Kwate said only enough to arouse Rupert's curiosity.

He couldn't understand why Kwate didn't do it alone, if it was so easy, but he didn't want to ask. Kwate would speak generally about the way in which black people couldn't keep secrets and couldn't work together, but sometime somewhere they were going to have to.

Kwate outlined the plan to him and Hurly one night in his room and said they could do it if they wanted next week.

Neither Kwate nor Hurly had told Rupert that Slingo would be involved, that he was going to be their driver. Rupert didn't even know exactly where they were going. He was afraid to ask lest his curiosity be mistaken for nervousness. Kwate asked them to meet him outside a particular club on the Friday evening. Rupert turned up separately from Hurly and they both waited on the pavement for almost an hour and then walked round the block to see if there were other entrances to that particular club.

An hour later, Kwate drove up in a Ford Cortina with Slingo wearing a hat low over his forehead. Slingo was driving, slouched in the driver's seat.

'I ain't going with him,' Rupert said.

Kwate came out onto the pavement. 'Come on, boy, business is business. Don't mix your woman trouble with your work.'

He gripped Rupert's shoulder. 'If you terrorized now, you could go home.'

Rupert climbed in the back of the car and Hurly went round to the outside.

'Why are we going by car?'

'You want to hop a bus after?'

Slingo turned into Oxford Street and again down Regent Street, heading for the lower side of Soho. In one of the side streets he parked the car, and leaving the three of them sitting there, he went down some steps into a basement and re-emerged with two guitar cases. Hurly opened the back door and took them from him. Rupert felt that he had been left out of all this prearrangement because Slingo was involved. For some reason, Kwate wanted him on this job and had been very careful about what he said to him about Slingo.

'Sweet, sweet music,' Slingo said. 'Sweet soul music. Rebel music, taking over.'

They drove off.

'We're two hours late.' Rupert said. 'Is it still all right?'

'Later the better.' Hurly said, when the other two didn't answer.

'Open the case and take one each,' Kwate said to Hurly.

Hurly opened the cases at his feet. Kwate leaned across the front seat, picked up a revolver and held it out, below the level of the car windows, to Rupert.

'What for?'

'It's not loaded, just to scare someone if we meet them,' Kwate replied.

He passed the revolver to Hurly who slipped it into the pocket of his denim jacket.

Rupert was thinking that Slingo didn't have a licence to

drive a car. 'You don't have licence, do you? Suppose we get picked up on a check with all this stuff here?'

'Shut up, boy, lysuns never improved people driving. More people killed by people with lysuns than without.'

Rupert felt Slingo had been drinking. It gave him some comfort to feel that the hard hustler had to strengthen himself for this ride. 'Too many people involved,' he said.

'Look, you want to get out?' Kwate asked turning round in his seat. Kwate was on edge.

'He must tell he girlfriend. How is she?' Slingo said. Kwate put his arm out and gripped Rupert by the knee. He looked almost pleadingly at Rupert to avoid replying to Slingo. It was the first time, Rupert thought, that he had shown that there was some understanding between them. He had felt that to Kwate it didn't matter if you remained a stranger because he wasn't interested in what he could do for you or you for him. The job was a partnership, pure in its definition of self-interests.

'Give me one,' Rupert said to Hurly. 'You sure it's not loaded. I mean I don't want to fool around with that thing.'

Hurly handed Rupert a pistol from the floor of the car. Rupert worked his backside off the seat and with a quick crouching motion hefted the gun and thrust it inside his pocket. It stuck out. He pulled it out and put it down the front of his shirt, tucking it into his trousers.

'You take an iron, boy,' Slingo teased. 'Those irons good for holding off lickle boys who come after men with a knife.'

'Stop your fockries,' Kwate snapped at Slingo, and turning to Rupert, 'It's all right, he's terrified out of his mind. Man's had too much Special Brew.'

16.

KWATE SWITCHES THE TELEVISION ON. For two days he has forbidden anyone to turn the knob, and he pulls the plug out of the socket and sleeps with the lead under his body when it is his turn to rest, to make sure that the others don't turn on the news. He wears the gun over his shoulder now, with the white man's discarded shirt tied in a sash to its barrel and trigger guard. Kwate has been thinking hard. He is morose, but apart from the ban on TV, he allows the others to relax.

The police have sent up the ingredients of a recipe which Hurly sent down to them. He says he wants to do some cooking and, after a day, two saucepans arrive with a plastic laundry basket containing vegetables and groceries. Hurly has already cooked them one meal and now the girl is in the kitchen cooking another with him. Rupert plays cards with the white man, and the boy sulks all day, behaving sullenly with them all. The only person who can get through to him is the girl, and she coaxes him to eat the fried plantains that Hurly has cooked. He refuses at first, but hunger gets the better of him.

'This flour no good,' says Hurly, 'and they didn't send suet for dumplings. Tcha.'

'Make an Irish stew instead,' the girl says.

The kitchen now smells lived-in, with the stink of spices. The girl helps Hurly with the dishes and they chat pleasantly, like colleagues at a dirty job rather than captor and hostage. Kwate makes the white man tidy up, and he does it without a word but with daggers of unspoken resentment in his eyes. The man is sure that he is going to come out of here alive, Rupert thinks. He is the kind of white man who pretends he knows how to repair aeroplanes and would have a damn good try if they'd hijacked him in a plane and something had gone wrong with the controls.

'I just eat and I hungry again,' Hurly says to the girl.

'You didn't sleep much.'

'I couldn't.'

She looks up from where she's slicing onions and catches Hurly's eye for a moment. He averts his eyes. She keeps looking at me as though I could let her go if I want, he thinks. It makes him uncomfortable. Yet today in her gaze there is also the recognition of something else. It is as though she's telling herself that this one is just an ordinary boy, no gangster, no monster.

'I get hungry dreams,' he says.

'You mean greedy dreams.'

'You are a man-watcher,' he comments.

He feels easy with her when he isn't under the eyes of the others. He wears the Smith and Wesson tucked into his trousers. He has been to the lavatory and pulled the bullet out of the chamber and put it into the flush tank. He is wearing a dummy gun because he says to himself that he doesn't want it blowing up in his trousers while he's asleep, and he doesn't want Kwate to know that he's unloaded it.

On the TV screen, Big Ben strikes.

'Oi, in here,' Rupert shouts to Hurly, who grabs the butt of his revolver and dashes to the kitchen door, his head turning quickly to make sure of the girl. Hurly behaves like a man on drugs, making sudden movements. He is letting the girl know that he is determined not to be thought of as harmless. At a pinch, he would kill to survive.

'The bells of Babylon,' Rupert says, turning his head to see if Kwate has caught the remark.

The siege is the first headline.

Newsreader: In London the minicab siege enters its seventh day. We bring you, in Part One, a remarkable piece of film, shot as the news came through of the siege's first victim. Police have formally charged the fourth member of the ransom gang. Derek Obute interviews the mother of one of the gunmen of Corbett Street. In Libya, President Gaddafi has accused the United States of ...

(Scene: Outside the siege. Shot of police cars and the entrance to 37 Corbett Street.)

Newsreader: Senior police officers today admitted that they can make no prediction about the outcome of the Corbett Street siege. Earlier today, they confirmed reports that the fourth man in the siege, the man who is said to have driven the getaway car, has turned state's witness and will testify against the gunmen in the siege when they are brought to trial. From the press release of his testimony, it seems that the siege was not part of a robbery plan that went wrong. Notes have been exchanged between the police and the gunmen who still refuse to release the twelve-year-old son of Mr Photopoulos who died in hospital yesterday after being released as a hostage from Corbett Street. In another part of the city, police have cordoned off the house of Hurlington Macaulay, one of the gunmen.

(Scene: Street corner in Brixton. Derek Obute stands, microphone in hand.)

Derek Obute: Here in this street in Brixton, people have gathered outside the home of one of the gunmen of the minicab siege. Police have cordoned off the street after violent incidents involving the mother and stepfather of the gunman known as 'Hurly'. We spoke with Mrs Violet Macaulay, Hurly's mother, earlier this morning.

(Scene: The interior of the Macaulay home. Mrs Macaulay sits on a chair before a tiled mantelpiece. Family photographs are ranged behind her.)

Derek Obute: Mrs Macaulay, you told the police earlier that you were making an appeal to your son and to all the gunmen, boys with whom you are acquainted, to give themselves up.

Mrs Macaulay: Yes, that is what I have said. They must realize what it is his mother having to live with daily here. I said that the police must let my son go because I pray like a mother for the speedy return of my son.

Derek Obute: Well, yes. You know that the men who are holding the hostages have been given a television set. Do you hope your son is watching this programme and have you …

Mrs Macaulay: Well, he had better hear his mother, and I hope so. And I been to the Jamaican embassy and to other people, friends of ours who helping with this problem, you know, and they say the police lie about that embassy because they tell me personally that they have not banned my son.

Derek Obute (a bit flustered): The embassy did make a statement in the early days of the siege, saying they would not accept the … er … the gunmen.

Mrs Macaulay: My Hurly is a good boy. My boy is not a boy of violence unless he pushed into it and the police they …

Derek Obute: You have actually applied to the police for protection. Obviously you feel that there is strong feeling …

Mrs Macaulay: Yes, I feel very strong about it, Mr Derek, because a lot of reporters and television people and everyone been coming daily to my house and I fed up of answering their stupid question. What do they want a mother to say when they call she son all sort of name? Eh?

Derek Obute: Thank you very much, Mrs Macaulay. This is Derek Obute, reporting from Brixton.

Newsreader: Yesterday the siege claimed its fifth victim indirectly when we learned that Mr Photopoulos, father of twelve-year-old Panos still being held by the gunmen, had died in hospital. News that he had had another stroke came when our interviewer, Tony Green, was with the family of Mr Photopoulos. Mrs Photopoulos, mother of Panos, was making an appeal to the gunmen to release her son.

(Interviewer sits before a large Greek lady leaning forward in an armchair. Behind her, standing at the edge of the chair is her eldest son who keeps a hand on her shoulder throughout the interview.)

Mrs Photopoulos: Of course we hope for his release. Your heart cannot be in two place. I am relief and I am worry also, both same time. My son never harm nobody. He go to school with a lot of coloured people. My husband always work with coloured people. Why should men do this to my poor family?

(Her eyes are swollen with crying; she lifts a handkerchief to them. She is about to go on when a girl dashes onto the screen. Viewers can see only her back and she shouts in Greek to her mother. Mrs Photopoulos gets up from the chair and holding her palms out, gives a cry. Her son rushes to support her. The voice of the interviewer announces that Mr Photopoulos has just suffered another stroke in hospital. End of film clip.) Newsreader: With that tragic news we end Part One of the news. We will bring you, in Part Two, film of a speech which President ...

Kwate rises and switches the set off.

The boy, on his knees now in front of the TV set, is aware that all eyes are on him. His mouth twitches and he lets out a sniff. The hot tears begin to roll down his cheeks.

'Ai,' Kwate says to him, 'that not for you, that for us. Your father ain't dead. Nobody dead. The police playing games with us. They lie about Slingo, and they lie about having names. They want to terrorize us and demoralize us.'

The rest are aware that Kwate is talking to them, not to the boy.

'I want to go home. Let me go home,' the boy wails.

'You bloody well killed him, didn't you,' the white man now says, staring at Kwate.

'Just everybody keep cool,' Kwate says and his arm goes uncertainly to the shotgun.

'We have to let the boy go,' Hurly says, answering the appeal which he sees in the girl's eyes and watching the boy sobbing now and looking up at him.

'What's the matter with you? You giving orders here?' Kwate demands.

'We've got to do something,' Rupert says lamely. 'They can have us now for …' He hesitates to say the word.

'They can have you. They ain't having me and they ain't having the boy. You see what Hurly's mother say? The police haven't been to no embassy. They give us this thing here to freak us out. And the raas clot cooking.' Now there's an edge of confidence, menace, even accusation in Kwate's voice and the other two acknowledge its authority. 'Psychology!' he barks, looking at Hurly.

'This thing needs discussion. We ought to ask the police to see some people, someone we can trust.' Rupert is only half-convinced by Kwate's argument.

Kwate feels he is losing the initiative. There is a nasty look on the white man's face, as though he would leap at them, force them to shoot him. Kwate goes to the window and shouts to Burgess.

'Oi, we want to talk to you.'

There's no reply. He tries again and then again. It is as though there are no listeners among the police or the crowd outside. The silence, almost total outside, is puzzling. Kwate doesn't pull the curtains back as he usually does.

Each one of them is thinking that if the police have moved the crowd, cordoned off the place perhaps, they are getting ready to make some serious move, perhaps to rush them.

'Games, games, games,' Kwate says.

~

17.

THE EARLY MORNING LIGHT HITS Rupert's eyelids, and its soft heat coaxes them open. It is strange, because in that room they have been used to waking in shadow. In his dream he has seen Hurly's mother and confused her with his own. Her voice calls him from somewhere outside a darkened room, and his mind struggles awake from this hypnotic call as though he is swimming out of some dark depths of water, his lungs bottled and bursting for the surface.

He sits up and the blanket falls away from his shoulder. He looks around the room. Kwate is asleep when he should be sitting on the stool by the door. He is curled up beside the stool and looks fierce in his sleep, even though his arms are tucked between his drawn-up knees like those of a sleeping baby. The white man is snoring. The girl sleeps beside him. Only Hurly is awake.

The strange light in the room makes it seem smaller than it usually appears. Hurly is sitting by the open window. He has obviously moved the table that was supposed to block off the window and has drawn the curtains fully back.

'Hey! What's happening?' Rupert whispers.

His impulse is to grab Hurly and pull him down. He's cracked under the strain, Rupert thinks, seeing his mum on telly and realizing that there's no way out of this place. Hurly sits impassive. He is wearing Kwate's tam on his head and leaning on the window sill.

Rupert remembers that Kwate tied up the young boy the night before and left him in the kitchen on some blankets. They couldn't stop the boy sobbing and Kwate said he didn't like to do it, but it had to be done. The others didn't stop him.

Now Hurly turns his head slowly. His eyes look distant, but they call Rupert to the window.

'They ain't going to shoot us. There's no one there,' he says.

Rupert goes up to the window and looks out. The street below is completely deserted. It looks as though it has been washed. The police barriers are still there, but there isn't a person in sight. The windows on the houses opposite are curtained and blank. It's like looking at a picture, the silence of it.

'Somethin's goin' on. Police pull out,' Rupert says and looks questioningly at Hurly. Should they wake Kwate? he is thinking. He pushes his nose right up against the window but can't see beyond the ledge if there are policemen or anyone else in the doorway or along the wall of their own building.

'The Trojan thing,' Hurly says. 'You know that story.' It strikes Rupert that Hurly has gone mad and he looks carefully at his face.

'Beware the Greeks bearing gifts,' Hurly says slowly, recollecting.

'Are you all right?'

'I hear this story in school, boy. The Greek army leave the shores and them Trojans wake up one morning and find all the ships and soldiers gone, and on the beach they leave a wooden horse.'

'There's no horse,' Rupert says. He's heard the story too. 'Look, close the curtains, there might be spiders. They're up to some tricks.'

'They want to tempt us to come out and then lightning strike and the valiant shall taste of death.'

'Just draw the curtains,' Rupert says and pulls at Hurly's shoulder. He draws Hurly into the room and drapes the curtains back into place.

Kwate begins to stir. He sits bolt upright.

'It's all right, they're asleep,' Rupert says to him, and goes to the kitchen. The boy is also asleep, breathing deeply, rhythmically.

'The street empty, the police gone,' he tells Kwate. 'Gone nowhere,' Kwate says, rubbing his eyes. He goes into the kitchen and washes his face.

The hostages wake up, hearing the bustle in the room.

It is very mysterious, Rupert thinks. They don't make coffee or get themselves anything to eat. A mood of immobility and hopelessness seems to have settled on all of them.

'Without the help of the community, we going to be stuck here till your hair turn white,' Kwate says.

There have been black people watching in the street throughout the siege. I know West Indians, Rupert thinks: they'll talk endlessly about the siege, but they'll do nothing. In a few days the novelty, the gossip value will wear out.

He wishes they could start all over again. Not the robbery, not this business of the hostages. These people are no good as hostages. Maybe the police think that their lives aren't precious enough to trade for other lives. They should have taken them into the street instead of rushing up the stairs into this trap, taken them at gunpoint in a cab straight to the airport. They may have stood a chance then. Or they could have threatened and released them, and maybe even got away with the money once they were a few miles from the site of the robbery. How would the police know who pulled the job? There are thousands of young blacks and to these people we all look alike anyway. Like the Chinese and Japanese look alike to me, Rupert thinks.

For the first few days he felt as though the world was looking on. Now this room is stale with the smell of the people in it. He wants to get away from them. But how? And where to go? They'd have to find a place in which the laws of life and of people having to pull guns and hustles on other people don't operate. There's no such place. There's no place where you can start life each day as though the last hasn't happened. People just aren't willing to give you that chance.

He thinks of Edwina constantly now. If he ever gets out of this, he'll give her a chance, and she'll give him another short lease on her life.

At about eleven in the morning, after the noise of traffic begins to pervade the room again, the occupants of the siege hear a tramp of feet in the street outside. Hurly doesn't move from where he is sitting on the settee, but Rupert jumps up and looks out from behind the edge of the curtain.

'A demo coming down the road,' he says.

There must be fifty people. They are carrying placards. 'Black people wake up,' Kwate says with a flicker of triumph in his eyes.

'They're white people.'

Kwate rushes to the window. The police are back.

They are all over the street, more than he has ever seen before. In front, at the edge of the barrier, stands the line of demonstrators, and behind them a looser crowd, all scrambling for a look.

The demonstrators are chanting something, but Rupert can't make out what it is.

'What the placards say?' Kwate asks.

Rupert reads them aloud: 'KILL THE MURDERERS. END THE SIEGE. POLICE ACTION NOW.'

'The pigs brought them here,' Kwate snaps. 'We could stop them.'

He runs the heel of his hand over the butt of the shotgun and lifts it as though to aim through the window. The chanting breaks into confused shouts.

Kwate puts the shotgun down. The girl comes to the window and looks out.

'The police should send them away,' she says.

'Are they Greeks?' the white man asks her.

The girl doesn't reply. She is watching the effect that the shouting is having on Kwate. He rushes to the kitchen and looks in to see what the boy is doing. He slams the kitchen door.

'The police bring them people here,' he shouts. 'Burgess too damn smart. Burgess is a master, he pull a whole demo on us. Psychology, boy, psychology is a devil.'

~

18.

SEVEN DAYS AFTER THE SIEGE began the police called on Edwina: two men in plain clothes. She had been dreading their visit, had known it would come.

On the third day she had driven down into the West End and stood amongst the crowd outside. She wanted to forget it all, forget Rupert, put Kwate into the closet in her mind reserved for the things she had bought by mistake, things which wouldn't fit outside the seductive atmosphere of fashion and vanity in a boutique. She couldn't escape the feeling that she had something to do with Rupert being where he was; she had been irresponsible, pushed him to edge of desperation. She hadn't wanted to taunt him. She was surprised, though it had flattered her, that he had taken her offer of intimacy as a promise of something lasting. He had begged for all the strength she could give him and hadn't been able to see her as what she was. Kwate was different. She had never mentioned Kwate to Michael. He was the sort of man that made you feel that anyone was entitled to do anything to anyone else. She could understand how he'd hold hostages. She feared that he'd shoot them too. If Kwate was besieged, he had chosen to be. Rupert – she had been accused by Michael of using Rupert to alleviate her failing sense of herself.

'There's no reason why we can't still be friends,' she had said to Michael. She wanted Rupert to trust her again. It would have been possible. She imagined meeting Rupert with a black girl pushing a pram some day down the streets of Stockwell or Brixton; she'd stop and be introduced. But now this period of coming to terms with herself was transformed into a wound she would carry with her. The words of a song that Slingo used to play came back to her, and his rhythm beat in her head: *The tables gwyne turn and the fire gwyne burn.*

Michael had so many good phrases, 'If I don't give you a promise of growth,' he said, 'you can't live your tomorrows through me.' He had wanted to talk about what exactly she meant by 'love'. She had wanted to put these abstracts away. She felt she had been taught – no, that she had paid the price of – a lesson.

Edwina first heard of the siege on her radio as she was brushing her hair for school. Michael didn't seem to pay it any attention. The news bulletin didn't give the names of any of those involved. Three men had held up a minicab firm; they were holding hostages.

In the staff room, the other teachers were talking about it. All blacks, they said; it was getting serious. Some of the pupils in her fifth-year group came up to her in the corridor. She was the one to discuss these things with. They said she knew the boy who done it, didn't she?

Edwina left work early. She drove the car to the squat. There was nobody there. She had a sinking feeling in her stomach. The evening papers were full of it. She went home, waited a couple of hours and drove back. There was no one home. There was no other answer. Slingo didn't work, Rupert wouldn't have found himself a job yet. She went home.

Michael knew what the matter was as soon as he walked in that evening. 'So your lover turned out to be more than a petty mugger. I suppose you think he's a great political hero. Did you help them plan this piece of black consciousness?'

'Michael, stop it. I haven't seen Rupert for … I swear I haven't seen him. I don't know why …'

'People are difficult, aren't they? They do all sorts of things.'

'You're so bloody smug.'

She stopped him as he was putting his clothes into a case in the bedroom. 'Michael, don't be silly. What are you trying to do? Punish me for your hang-ups?'

'I'm not being silly,' he replied, 'I just want to leave you with your deep and honest concerns for the great black hope. Don't you want to think it over?'

'I have, Michael,' she said. 'I have!'

The inspectors came and sat in the kitchen.

'You know what we want, Mrs Cross,' they announced. 'You are acquainted with Rupert Dowling, and, we have reason to believe, with Aloysius Brown as well.'

'Do you mind if I sit in on this?' Michael enquired.

'We'll require your cooperation, Mr Cross,' said the detective inspector, and to Edwina, 'You're not denying that you know these characters?'

Edwina shook her head.

'Very good. Our chief superintendent, you must have heard over the news, he's running this operation, he'd like a word with you.'

'What about?'

'I want to make clear to you and to your husband that this is a kind of social call. We want to make a request. There are no charges against you or anything like that. We want you to help the police.'

'I've got nothing to do with it.'

'No. Not directly of course; we don't believe you have. But we have reason to believe that you have some influence over the lads, over this boy Rupert. Your husband stood bail for him, didn't you? He was your student or something.'

Edwina was frightened. Half-formed questions flashed through her mind.

'There are lives at stake, Mrs Cross, and we believe you can be very helpful.'

'How?'

'We'd like you to come down to the station now and Mr Burgess will explain.'

Chief Superintendent Burgess was very polite. He sent for cups of coffee and sat Edwina down.

'Now please don't misunderstand. I've asked for your help because lives are obviously involved here....'

He began to talk about the drama club and about blacks in South London and how one of their chief concerns was community relations. 'And I'd like to assure you that your name and your husband's name will be left out of this affair entirely. We are looking for a peaceful end to the siege.'

Burgess was sitting across the table from Edwina. He twiddled his thumbs, and looked steadily and seriously at her.

'We want somebody to put the arguments to them.'

'How ... ?'

'By approaching them.'

'What do you mean? Go into the siege?'

'You know these boys, Mrs Cross. We know them too, we feel. Brown has a long record. We know they are not desperate criminals. They've been foolish boys and we intend to treat them as such, but of course you realize that our prime duty is to the hostages. Other people have volunteered to negotiate. Mostly Black Power maniacs and we don't want to put them in touch with anybody who'll make the situation worse.'

There was a silence and Burgess drew a long breath. 'I must be honest with you, Mrs Cross, and admit we've made a mistake in the way we've handled this siege.'

'I don't know what I can do.'

'I'll tell you. We've let it be known that the Greek man whom the boys released is dead. In fact he's not.'

'But I saw it in the papers! You're going to charge them with murder or manslaughter or whatever it is.'

'I'm letting you into a secret. I miscalculated. I take the blame. We hoped they would let the boy go, but they haven't. Let me be frank with you. We wanted to create the atmosphere for the release of the second hostage. We stand more of a chance against the three if they're holding only two adults.'

'You mean you're going to shoot them?'

'I'm afraid if they don't surrender very soon, we're going to have to take some strong steps. But before that, we want you to approach them. We want you to ask them to surrender and say that we'll see that it's taken into account at any trial that may follow.'

'What do I tell them about the man, about Mr Photopoulos ?'

'Tell them the truth, tell them that the police have lied about him. They should be relieved. God knows what they've done to the little boy, his voice isn't coming through any of the devices.'

'You've bugged the place?'

'It'll contribute to your safety. We'll know exactly what's being said in the room and we'll intervene if necessary. 'We've considered it all before asking you, Mrs Cross,' he added, 'and we've come to the conclusion that you'll be in no personal danger. The gunmen expect to have a pow-wow with someone. They've been asking us for one.'

'I don't think they'll listen to me at all,' faltered Edwina. 'You don't know Kwate ... I mean Aloysius Brown.'

'We perhaps know him better than you think.'

❧

19.

'IT HAS NOTHING TO DO with you,' Michael said when Edwina got back to the flat. 'Unless you think it has.'

'They just want me to pass a message.'

'I met the guy from BRAG – you know, the Black Revolutionary whatever-they-call-it. He's convinced that the police want a shoot-out. I don't think you ought to venture into that. Look what they did to the IRA thing, just walked in and killed two people.'

'It's not like that. I know these boys,' Edwina said. 'Those BRAG people are just maniacs. I think the police are playing it straight.'

'I never thought I'd hear you say *that*,' Michael said. 'They don't set a thief to catch a thief any more, it's all sociologists.'

Edwina wasn't concentrating on his words. She was thinking of the song that had gone round and round in her head in Kwate's room. Yes, she had smoked too much, she had had the drink he gave her, but everything, all the thrill she had felt, was not the product of wantonness. That's what Michael would have her feel. He was slowly, ever so gently, making her apologize. She should never have loved Rupert. Yes, loved him. She should try and live in a more sensible world. The song came back to her:

Come away, Miranda, day is done
Night spreads its wings to follow the sun
Come away, come away, come away
Time and the bell have buried the day.

Edwina phoned Burgess. 'I'll do it,' she said.

'Wear a tight-fitting sweater or shirt and come down to the siege headquarters,' was the reply.

It was a small room on the ground floor of a building fifty yards from the scene of the siege. Edwina was fetched from her flat by PC Bully and a police driver.

'We saw your photographs,' Bully said. 'Very nice. Mrs Cross. Very nice.'

His remark startled her.

'You've got Slingo?' she asked.

'Oh yes, we've got him. It was funny. He crashed into a lamp post a couple of miles from the place on the first day. We didn't know what we'd got hold of till the next day.'

'He gave you my name, did he?'

'As a matter of fact, he didn't. He wouldn't give us anything. He pretended to be a drunken driver without a licence. The constables at West Central took him for just that. We found you through your photographs, Mrs Cross. We looked all over the Brixton brothels, and wasted about three days doing that. You schoolteachers shouldn't get involved in things like this, you know.'

At the siege headquarters Edwina was shown six newspaper cuttings clipped onto a board. Burgess came in as she studied them.

'I'm very glad you've agreed to cooperate, Mrs Cross. We want you to absorb these facts. Here they are in black and white.'

'I don't trust black or white.'

Burgess smiled. 'In print, I mean. Read this statement from the Black Revolutionary Action Group; I believe you know of them.'

Edwina read the clipping. *The misguided youth are doing untold harm to community relations in this country. We must tell them that this isn't Trench Town. It's London. They are in the heart of the capitalist metropolis …*

'You see, they don't want to know,' Burgess said. Then there's this,' he added, turning' the page. 'See for yourself.'

Edwina read: We *call on the home secretary to take into account the repressive police action which has led to these tragic events.*

'That's some of our friends down in Brixton.'

'How do I know you didn't plant these?' Edwina asked. 'You've done very well with the television.'

'We have no control over these fly-by-night organizations, Mrs Cross. Also, look at this. The Cypriot community newspapers have appealed for the release of the boy Panos. We want you to tell them that.'

'But you told me his father's alive.'

That's no reason for not releasing him. Mrs Cross, you are a brave woman. Play it by ear. We'll give you about half an hour. You've come in at their request, remember.'

'They asked for me?'

'Of course they did. We believe that a difference has arisen between Aloysius Brown and the other two, perhaps you could report on that.'

'I'm not reporting on anything, Mr Burgess. I'm simply going in there because my concern for life, I'm sure, is … er … deeper than yours.'

'No doubt.' Burgess smiled his cold smile.

He escorted her to the door with two other constables. The path through the crowd and the reporters was cleared by the policemen standing around. She recalled her last words to Michael:

'Do you think they can really stop the papers from getting the story? Everyone knows we ran the drama group.'

He was watching her clean her face in the mirror and comb her wavy hair.

'Why do you insist on tarting yourself up?'

'I want to look as I normally do,' she had said, turning from the mirror.

'You'll be remembered as the girl who ended the minicab siege.'

'As the one who started it, maybe.'

'Or as the woman who sent the blacks to jail.'

Edwina wanted to tell him that if that was true, it would be because of him. She had decided to nail all this, all the events of the past six months, into a tidy coffin. He must help her. It was best that it ended this way. She could always pretend she was in charge till the end. People only blamed you for what you left unfinished and this was a way of finishing with the world she had flirted with.

Michael was strange. At the last minute, just before she left on her mission, he said, 'You're pleading with them to go to jail, you know that.'

'Maybe they deserve to go. And otherwise they'll be dead.'

'I don't understand you. Three weeks ago you'd have been singing hymns to black vitality.'

'Vitality has to make its terms with reality. Whatever you think, Michael, I don't think Rupert knows what he's got himself into.'

'Aw, poor little fellow, he just wanted to play Cowboy with the Great White Squaw.'

'You're so cynical.'

'No, I don't mean that. I say, that sweater looks quite good on you.'

She made a face at him as she left the room and went down to the waiting police car.

There are a thousand eyes watching her as she walks. Burgess says, 'No photographs, please, gentlemen.'

He has the loudhailer in his hand. He raises it to the window.

'Kwate, a friend is coming to see you. Now.'

She hears Kwate's voice call back, 'Send him in.'

Edwina wipes her sweaty hands on the hips of her jeans. She is in the building. There are men in the room downstairs and two on the stairs as she passes. They nod to her.

She can't remember what she has been asked to say.

She gets to the top of the stairs. There is no one there, just a tatty corridor leading to a door. She walks down it, her heart thumping furiously.

She doesn't know whether to knock on the door or to wait. As she hesitates, it opens. They have heard her coming. The first thing she sees is the muzzle of a pistol and she freezes. The door opens wider.

She desperately wants to go to the toilet. Her bladder is bursting, her guts rumble.

Kwate says, 'It's you.'

As she walks into the room, Edwina can see that Rupert is amazed. He is pleased that it's her.

'There are men in the corridor and in the alley at the back,' she says.

'They have gun?' Hurly asks.

Edwina expected a warmer reception. 'I think they have,' she says.

'OK, what you want?' Kwate asks. He is standing in the middle of the room, the shotgun over his shoulder. The hostages sit in a row at the edge of the settee. Rupert stands by the window, Hurly by the kitchen door. All three have their pistols and guns at the ready.

'I thought you wanted to talk to me. I haven't volunteered, you know.' She looked at the boy. 'I have something to tell you. Can I sit down?'

Rupert motions her to the stool with his gun.

'The man Photopoulos is alive. He isn't dead. The police were trying some tricks on you.'

'You come here to take us?' Kwate asks. 'How come po-lis tell you. You give some police a little bit?'

'Talk to her straight, you,' Rupert shouts. 'Don't you see she's our last chance. I think she's telling the truth.'
'Have they got Slingo?' Hurly asks.

'They got him the first day. It's true. He crashed the car into a lamp post.'

Hurly is the one who smiles.

'How did they get hold of you? They raid my house?' Rupert asks. Edwina doesn't answer the question.

'I didn't ask to see no white people,' Kwate states, and turns his back on her. 'She working for the police,' he says.

'I'm not working for anyone. They told me you wanted to say something and they wanted you to know that the murder ... the death of this boy's ...'

'Murder! We didn't touch nobody. You ask these people. You come in here and start calling ...'

Kwate is interrupted by Rupert. 'Let her talk.'

'She's your girl,' Kwate says. 'You let her talk. I don't want no white chick negotiating for me.'

'What shall I tell them?' Edwina asks Rupert.

'Don't know.'

'They want you to release the boy. I think the police are serious about shooting it out.'

'The boy ain't leaving here,' Kwate says. 'If anyone else want to leave, they could leave, but I'll deal with them.' He moves to the kitchen door and raises the shotgun.

'Listen,' Edwina says to him. 'The police showed me cuttings from the black revolutionary groups, and they don't support you.'

'You can't trust that woman, she tells too much lie,' Kwate says.

'It's you who tell the lies,' Edwina shouts back. 'I'm not scared of your little rifle, Kwate. I've come to try and help, and if it freaks you out to hear what's going on, well, you'll have to take it.'

'No, look,' Rupert says. 'There's only one way out of here. If we can get to the Jamaican embassy, we're safe aren't we? They could fly us out.'

'I don't think there's much hope of that, but I'll say what

you want me to say.' Edwina hadn't expected this sort of confusion. She'd imagined she'd give them a message, they'd put their demands, she'd be free.

'This woman working with the pigs,' Kwate says. 'She's come to freak us out.'

'Is Slingo working with the police?' Rupert asks.

'I don't know anything about that. I was talking to Bully on the way here. He said that Slingo didn't tell them anything. They didn't even know he was with you.'

'How they find you then?' Hurly asks.

Edwina avoids the question again. She shoots a glance at Rupert. 'I'll tell you what I think, if you want to know. The place is absolutely surrounded by police. I can't see that you'll ever get away.' She turns to Rupert. 'I've talked to Michael about this too. You respect his opinion, don't you? He thinks ...'

'Don't try and play games with boy, woman,' Kwate interrupts.

'It's you who are playing the games, Kwate. You've got them into this mess. Look at these people. They don't even know what you're arguing about. You'd use anybody, just to prove that you're the fastest mouth in the West. You might want to prove that you're a martyr. You're posing as a great revolutionary, but everyone outside, at least, knows what you are, a petty hustler and a small-time thief. I don't care if you don't want to use me as go-between, but these people have a say in it too. You're playing with their lives.'

'I'll use you when I want,' Kwate replies. 'I know how you play. It's kicks for you and bullets for us. It's my life you messing with.'

'It's everybody's life, Kwate,' Rupert says.

'They send in their wooden horse,' Hurly says, his eyes distant. He doesn't seem to be participating in the argument. He has slouched back on the settee, and is pointing the gun towards himself, shutting one eye and looking down the barrel.

Everyone in the room turns to him.

'What you think, Hurly,' Kwate shouts.

Hurly smiles at all of them. 'You deal with it, guv. This woman is your woman and she Rupert woman and she everybody woman, and you say she police woman, so don't ask me. I don't have no woman.'

Kwate looks alarmed. 'Look, she freak the man out. Get the bitch out of here!' He goes swiftly up to Hurly and grabs the pistol from his hand. Hurly lets go of the pistol and begins to laugh on the settee.

'They send horse into the citadel, and the horse graze in all pastures.'

'Get out of here,' Kwate commands.

Edwina gets up. The hostages sit transfixed. Hurly chuckles to himself, and looking at him, Kwate's blood seems to drain out of his face. He motions to Rupert to take Edwina out.

Rupert has his revolver in her back as she goes into the corridor. She takes four or five steps and an impulse grabs her. She turns round.

'Rupert, I may not see you again. Please listen to reason.'

'Keep moving,' Rupert says, menacingly, holding out his revolver.

She turns round again and starts towards the stairs. 'You thought it was Slingo,' she says. 'But it wasn't. It was that madman in there. I know what he's after. He got you into this, now you get yourself out of it. I've done what I can.'

Suddenly he is upon her. She feels herself grabbed by the neck of the sweater.

'All right, bitch, just keep walking. You're taking me out of here. I'm going to get out of here.' His voice falters, but she feels his breath, and his grip is firm, pushing her down the stairs.

'Don't make no move, or I'll kill her. I don't care if you kill me,' Rupert says to the two men in the downstairs room who jump aside as he forces her to the door, blindly, firmly.

'Rupert, don't! Let me go,' Edwina shouts. But she feels the determination in his grip, and the kick of his knee as he moves her on, almost lifting her off her feet.

He pushes her to the door. There is a cry from the crowd as the two figures come into sight.

'That way,' she hears him whisper, hoarsely, forcing her to the side of the door.

'*Rupert!*' There is a loud scream from the first-floor window. Edwina thinks she recognizes Hurly's voice, and then two or three or four or five shots ring out. Rupert falls against her as though he has stumbled, as though he's collided with her while running, and she sees the pavement come up and hit her face, and, in an instant of blankness and terror, there are hands all around her.

'Get her out of the way.'

She is dragged by two men along the pavement, close to the wall and the gunfire explodes, *toph, toph, toph,* all around her, seeming to her to boom in the distance.

~

20.

HURLY REMEMBERS A BOY BEWILDERED by the task of arriving at the truth, the truth that lawyers wanted to know, the truth that friends nagged him for, the truth that was to be presented to a jury and the truth that was going to come back to him again and again as a vision of something he had done, something he must remember himself as doing. What might have happened was mixed up with what actually happened.

Kwate was at the window. He told them that. Kwate was led out of the room by five men who held his arms while he himself held his own stomach, the blood crawling over his hands.

He remembers the shout that escaped him, the hope and despair that were wrung from his throat and lungs. 'Rupert!' he'd shouted. 'Rupert!' He remembers the certainty that Rupert was dead; he didn't need to be told. He was gone as certainly as his hope of vaulting the walls of Babylon; the Babylon that surrounded his body, surrounded his spirit, turned all longing into waiting.

Hurly remembers a boy who made no plans because plans were for tomorrow and today was more important.

Kwate had shed tears as he was led out of the doorway. He remembers the clear vision, the instant feeling of being able to hold for ever in his mind every little detail of what he saw, what he heard. Kwate's feet had gone limp with pain as they dragged him through the door. The girl and the white man and the boy had left before them, walking out of the room like people who were first in a queue. Hurly remembers standing up, the terror of the ten pistols that pointed at him, he remembers raising his arms and resting them behind his head. He was no longer part of Kwate's plan, now that he could look into tomorrow, into the day after.

The people crowded into the gallery of the court. They were still the audience, but he was no longer an actor. They gave him fist salutes. He made them a speech which he rehearsed with his lawyer in the grey cell below the courtroom. He remembers the feeling of being beyond judgement, beyond wanting to dodge, with evidence and cunning, the fact of what he had done, the fact of what must be done. The newspapers published his statements. A black man and a black woman came to see him in Brixton prison. They told him he should say that he didn't recognize the court. He asked them if he should say he didn't recognize the handcuffs. They brought him cuttings from the papers. He kept them for a few weeks and then flushed them down the toilet.

His cellmate, who talks of 'tie-up men' and 'bird' and 'porridge', counts the weeks as workers at the end of a working day count the minutes. He talks to his cellmate about 'survival', a word he must never forget. It's more than a day's job, this 'survival', more than the decision to be the way you want to be. It's other people, what they want of you, how you fit into their world, how they darken your rainbow by clouding your sky.

He remembers every word of the books he reads. The Greek man comes to see him on Saturdays. The girl visits him now on Saturdays and Sundays. She brings him some books; she wants the boy to forget. She talks about tomorrow and he never reminds her that tomorrow drags along its yesterday; it goes forward like a wounded animal dragging a trap. She talks of the new jobs she has, she talks to him of the trades he could learn, she tries to tell him that to make peace with Babylon he will have to forget.

But Hurly doesn't want to forget, he wants to remember.

COME TO MECCA

For Rahim, Khusru, Shafiq and Nosha

1.

Come to Mecca

WHENEVER SHAHID GOT ANGRY HIS short cropped hair seemed to stand up off his head, like the feathers on the neck of a fighting cock. He was very angry that day. When the four of us left the factory and reached the street, he said we should go straight to his uncle's house.

'He will deal with the guv'nor,' Shahid said. 'I will show that Rasul. Son of a hired woman. When he comes out of the factory I will see him.'

'We can't make trouble in the street,' I said. 'Guv'nor will call the police. Come on.'

We went to Masterji's house. We all called Shahid's uncle 'Masterji' because back in our village he was the schoolteacher. Shahid didn't want to waste any more words on us, he walked ahead.

'I don't worry about getting sack. He can keep his bloody job,' one of the others said, 'there's plenty work. My cousin has a factory. I'll ask him job for you too.'

'We're not going to work anywhere,' Shahid said, turning his head. 'We'll fix this guv'nor first. When I say I'll do a thing, I will die but I'll do it, ask Farid.'

Masterji opened the door to us.

'Salaam-aleikum,' we each muttered as he let us in.

'As-aleikum-salaam,' he said, having fun with the greeting.

Shahid began rattling away in Bengali as soon as we stepped in.

'Wait till you've had a cup of tea. You catching a train?' Masterji said, but as soon as Shahid told him we'd all got the sack and quarrelled with the 'bastard' guv'nor, he changed his tone.

'Sit down, start from the beginning, and don't use such words before your elders.'

Shahid held his tongue between his teeth in a show of repentance and lightly struck both his cheeks with his palm. He told Masterji the story.

We had all been working at 'Nu-Look Fashions'. We'd been there for nearly the whole year now, except when the season was out and there was no work. We left school together, Shahid, myself and four other very close mates. Four of us went with the elder brother of another fellow we knew to Nu-Look and he told the gaffer that he'd brought the four machinists he wanted.

The guv'nor took one look at us and knew that we were straight out of school. But that didn't mean we were inexperienced. All of us had done some tailoring for our fathers or mothers at home. Everyone knows machining in the East End. When you are ten years old you begin to forget about being a pilot on Bangladesh Airlines and start thinking of being a cutter or machinist. Of course you usually have to start with just helping out, doing some pressing, fetching Fanta and making tea. This friend of ours told us that there was so much work that this guv'nor would let us start on machines straightaway.

He paid us training wages. After a few weeks we were doing about ten garments a day. He would give us sixty pence for each job we finished, but he wanted us to work faster. The cut cloth was piling up in the corner of the factory and on the guv'nor's desk.

The older workers who sat in the same room were paid sometimes one pound twenty, double what we were getting, but they worked very fast while Hindi songs played on the cassette all day and the machines hummed with business.

The guv'nor would stand beside Shahid's machine and he would say, 'You'll get donkey rates for that, I'll cut you down to fifty pence.' First it was a joke. Then he began saying it every day and it became serious, and he'd get angry if we said we wanted to go home when the others went.

'Even a child can work faster,' the guv'nor would say.

'I'll get my little sister, then,' Shahid would say.

He was not a bad bloke, this guv'nor. He was a white man, but he understood a little Bengali and he'd joke with us all the time and leave us to go to the toilet when we wanted.

'I don't know what you blokes do in there. Where I come from, a piss doesn't take you half an hour.'

When a man has worked for sixty pence, he doesn't want to work for fifty. One day the gaffer said he'd been fined for not doing the contract on time, we were ruining his business, we were lazy Bengalis, and the old ones only thought of 'taka' (money) and the young ones only thought of 'peta' – a dirty word.

Then he said he'd give us fifty for a garment and no more.

He was in a filthy mood. Next morning when he let us in, he stopped the four of us at the door and said, 'Look lads, it's fifty pence a garment from today, unless you do more than twenty-five, then it's the old rate.'

We sat at our machines. Shahid said to us he wasn't working for one halfpenny less, not for this gaffer or for his grandfather.

'You can take your cards and clear off,' the gaffer said, 'you should clean the streets, you can take your time doing that.' At the end of that day he went to the drawer where he kept his ledger, and reaching inside his coat pocket took out his fat wallet and peeled off some notes for the four of us.

'That'll be for the last two days,' he said, 'sixty pence a garment. Not from tomorrow, though.'

The next day we turned up to work as usual. Shahid told us to wait near our machines but not to start work. We stood with our arms folded just inside the door of the one-room factory.

'Clear off, lads, I've made other arrangements. If you won't work for new rates there's others as will,' the gaffer said and carried on with his own work, walking round the other machinists and filling his ledgers with scribbles.

For two hours we just stood there. Then the gaffer went out for his sandwich and his beer, which one of us usually went down to the street and fetched for him. Shahid addressed the other workers in Bengali. One of them said they'd taken a cut in rates too and then they all dipped their heads down into their work, ashamed.

Shahid said he was only sixteen years old but he knew liars from truth-tellers. He said they were not men and should wear bangles and sarees and stay at home.

The guv'nor came back with Rasul, an old Bengali with sly eyes whom we all knew. The two of them pushed past us and the guv'nor showed Rasul to Shahid's machine. Rasul sat on the stool.

'So you've come to put your foot on my stomach, eh Rasul?' Shahid challenged.

Rasul sheepishly picked up the cloth that Shahid had been working at and started to put it through the machine.

'Don't talk so big when you're only a chit of a boy,' Rasul replied.

'I have more pride in my chin than you have in your white beard. Only orphans work for fifty pence,' Shahid said.

'I work for what I can get. When you have three children you'll stop going to the pub with your money and going with rubbish white girls,' Rasul said, still working away.

'Like your mother,' Shahid replied.

'Clear off, that's enough of you,' the guv'nor said.

If I hadn't pulled him out of the factory, Shahid would have beaten Rasul there and then.

'I'll see you outside,' he shouted, and Rasul just laughed.

Masterji listened carefully to the story.

'That Rasul is the son of a sow,' Shahid said.

Masterji put on his coat and we went together to the factory for lunchtime. When the other workers came out, Masterji spoke to them. That evening we all met at Masterji's house. He had persuaded three of the older workers to come. Masterji said we had to call a strike at the factory, otherwise this guv'nor would get away with murder. We didn't come to this country to be slaves.

'The others won't listen to us,' one of the older workers said. 'You all know what Bengalis are like.'

'Don't talk about Bengalis to me,' Masterji said. 'Don't talk about our countrymen in front of me like that.'

'Look at that Rasul,' Shahid said, 'I'll kill him.'

'You won't kill the disease, you'll kill the germs that cause the disease,' Masterji said.

There was a lot of interest in our strike. The next day we went outside the factory with Bengali placards saying 'PAY US FAIR RATES'.

One by one the other workers decided to join us, especially after a crowd gathered on the pavement and we began shouting. On the second day of the strike the guv'nor called the police because not one person went to work. The police came and then newspapers came. On the third day one of the older workers came to us with Masterji. We were still standing on the pavement and a lot of our friends had come to support us. This man said he had to go back to work. His wife was in hospital and he was heavily in debt. Masterji told us that he had a fair case, we should not stop him going back to work. He should be allowed to go back till the end of the week at least so he could be paid on Friday. Shahid was sulky but he didn't contradict Masterji. On Friday we knew what would happen. The workers would want to get their two days' pay for that week. One by one they all went back and began to work. The guv'nor came to the first-floor window of the factory and shouted at us. We didn't reply. By the afternoon there were only the four of us left.

It was that afternoon that Betty and Sylvia came to the door of the factory. We saw these two white girls coming down from Aldgate end, carrying a camera. They stopped and asked us if we were the 'comrades on strike'.

'It's not a strike,' I said. 'We've just stopped working till the guv'nor changes his mind.'

They wrote down everything we told them and then Betty took a photograph of us. We all brushed our hair and they asked us to lift up the placards even though we didn't want to be in the photograph with placards in Bengali. We put our arms round each other's shoulders and stood under the 'Nu-Look' sign. Betty went with the camera and knelt down in the street. All the traffic had to stop as she took her photographs, but she behaved as though she didn't even notice the horns and the shouts from the obstructed cars.

'Cheeky woman,' Shahid said to me in Bengali.

Some days later we were sitting in one of the cafés on Brick Lane drinking tea. All the boys who are out of work hang around the five or six cafés there and drink endless cups of tea and wait to hear of any jobs that might be going. We knew that the season was over and even experienced men couldn't get much work. Betty walked into the café and she seemed to recognize us. She came over to our table. At first we didn't recognize her. The day she took the photographs she'd been wearing jeans and a leather jacket and a sweater with a black fist on it. Now she was in a dress and her hair looked as though she'd washed it and brushed it just for us.

'I've been looking for you,' she said to Shahid. 'We've written you up magnificently.'

Then she put the pile of newspapers she was holding on to the table and began turning the pages.

Now white girls rarely come into that café, and if they come they are with their men. Only rubbish women sit in the café all day and go with men who make friends with them and pay them. Bengali girls never come to that kind of place. Some Ugandan people come, and some stylish Punjabi girls, but they are allowed to have boyfriends who bring them. They are decent girls and nobody says anything to them. Betty was a decent girl too, she had a good accent, but like other white girls she didn't know how to behave, where to go and where not to go. She went anywhere she liked and did what she liked and nobody said anything to her.

We didn't want to insult her so we asked her if she would like to have coffee and we told her to sit at a different table from us, because the boys we were with were just staring at her and grinning. They were third-class, good-for-nothing rascals, but we were sitting with them because they were telling us how to buy and sell cars for plenty money. Betty motioned to them to push up and sat at our table. There we were in the photograph. The newspaper said: 'Workers Fight Blacklegs in Sweatshops.' Shahid was not sure of what it said so he asked Betty to read it to him.

'No blacks in that factory,' Shahid said to her, 'only Bengalis.'

'It's black*legs*,' Betty explained, 'people who attack workers.'

'If anybody attacks me I will punch them,' Shahid said. The others in the café were now curious and gathered round the newspapers. The papers were passed from hand to hand.

We told Betty that the strike was finished and she said that it was a shame.

'I'm not ashamed,' Shahid replied. Then Betty told us that she worked for the newspaper and she started selling the paper to anyone who would buy it for five pence.

'Anyway,' she said to Shahid, 'I'd like to talk to you. We want a whole story on the sweatshops.'

'We don't know much stories, only Bengali stories,' I said.

'About your sweatshops, your factories, Nu-Look.' Shahid looked puzzled, so Betty said, 'We call them sweatshops because the labour is sweated labour.' She was anxious to explain.

'When I sweat I always take bath, not like English people.'

'You've got me wrong. The factories are filthy and dingy, all of this area.'

'My cousin's factory is very clean,' I said.

'You must be joking,' Betty said. 'I've seen some of them.'

'He never jokes with ladies,' Shahid said.

After leaving the café that day we went to Shahid's house. Shahid told me not to mention the paper and he screwed it up tight and put it in his shirt because he said that if his father saw it he would say that it was giving

Bengalis a bad name. We sat all evening watching telly at Shahid's house. That was the kind of mood that came over us when we were out of work. Sometimes we went to the cinema on Commercial Road and then came back and watched more telly. When we had money we went to the West End.

All the boys told lies about their adventures in the West End. A fellow would be sitting in the café and he'd tell us how he'd been to a gambling casino and won fifty pounds on the gaming tables, or how he'd gone to a dance hall in Leicester Square and picked up two beautiful white girls who were really decent girls, and they really fancied him because of his hairstyle and he could do anything with them whenever he liked. When we were still in school we believed these stories and waited for the day when we could go out, go dancing, get some girlfriends. You live and learn. When Shahid and I went to the West End we had our own fun, but no one talked to us except to pick a fight. We'd go on the bus and then we'd play the pinball machines and see some sex films and eat ice cream and take the last tube back to Aldgate or walk home if it was too late or if all our money was finished, first along the river and then through the echoing stone walls of the city streets.

We were aimless, at least Shahid was aimless until Betty discovered us. Shahid had met her on the street again, he said, and he had made an appointment with her to go to her house with me.

'You're fixed up,' I said, grinning, but he turned savagely on me.

'She's a good girl,' he said, 'she's educated, not like you.'

'Her father will take one look at both of us and kick us down the street.'

'These kind of girls don't have fathers,' he said, thoughtfully.

'Her brothers, then.'

'Just shut your mouth and come with me.'

We went the next day. We sat on the floor in her strange room. She didn't even have a settee, and her bed was just one mattress on the floor, like a villager. There were hundreds of books all over the place. Everyone who came to her room sat on the floor on cushions amongst all the books and tea mugs and papers. Even the light was hanging down from the ceiling nearly to the floor with a paper bowl on it, and there were coloured candles which had spread pools of wax on the furniture.

She told us that she was a translator and showed us some Russian books and French books and Shahid asked her to say something in French and in Russian, and she said it and we all laughed. When he asked her what that meant, she said 'It means "I love you" 'and we all laughed again, and she could see that Shahid thought she was saying it to him, so she said, 'It's the easiest thing to say in any language.'

Then I said it for her in Bengali and Shahid said it in Urdu like they say it in the pictures and she tried to learn the Urdu.

Whenever we went there, Betty talked about the strike we had been in, but after the first time there was nothing new to tell her. She told us that we were not only part of the Bengalis but also we were part of the working class and we should forget about being Bengalis only. So I said

I'd always be a Bengali and Shahid told me that I didn't understand what she was trying to say.

'Working class are third-class people,' I said. Betty tried to explain that we had learnt all that from the newspapers that were against workers.

Betty liked explaining those sorts of things. She would talk very slowly so we wouldn't have to say 'pardon'. It seemed to me that Shahid loved listening to her voice, even though I'm sure he didn't understand half the things she was saying.

I only went there because Shahid kept wanting to go back. Betty said we had told her very useful things about Asian life and then she began telling us about her political party. She was part of a political party and it wasn't secret, anybody could join.

'You are a communist?' Shahid asked.

'Well, I'm a socialist. All workers should be socialists and trade unionists. It's the only way working people can lift their heads up. Communism comes after that.'

'Communists are no good,' I said, 'they blow up railway trains in India.'

'You are ignorant,' Shahid said. 'You know Maulana Bhashani, he's a communist. Has he ever blown up a train?'

'He's a saint,' I said.

'And you are a simpleton. Masterji said he's a communist.'

Betty was very pleased when Shahid agreed to go to the meetings. He told her that I would have to come too. She had light grey eyes and Shahid said that her eyes were like a cat's, and she asked us if we thought cats were beautiful.

Shahid said he thought they were very beautiful and they also caught rats.

When she was alone with us Betty talked a lot, but she didn't say much in her group meetings. When we went to the first one with her, it was in a row of houses which had been taken over by people just like hippies. At each meeting there were about a dozen people in the room. A bearded man was their leader. He always spoke second, waiting for someone else to start him off. Shahid asked Betty if he was the president, but she said they didn't need a president, he was only very clever and very active. At the first meeting the leader asked her to tell the meeting about the Nu-Look strike and she told them and we agreed with everything she said. Then the bearded man talked straight at us and said we had to get into a union if we were going to win. Someone else explained that we could start talking to Bengalis about joining the unions and we should go back to Nu-Look and persuade everybody to join the union. Everyone in the room said that was right and Betty nodded her head and said she should have thought of it first. On the way home Shahid became very sullen and he said that he didn't trust Bengalis, they wouldn't pay any money to join anything. Then he said he didn't trust the man with the beard, the leader. I said I was never going back to Nu-Look even if they paid me a thousand pounds for each coat.

The next time we went to Betty's house the bearded man with the checked trousers was there. Betty didn't chat with us as she usually did and I could see that Shahid was disappointed. Instead, she told us that they were making plans to get all the workers into their party and we must help because we were Bengalis. Then the bearded man started giving us a lecture and walked up and down the room. Shahid didn't want to listen, so he said he had to go to Hessel Street for his mother. Betty said we should listen and after we'd finished the discussion she wanted to do some shopping too. The leader said that we weren't fighting the Nu-Look manager, but we were fighting his whole system. He said the police were on the side of the manager, and the government too, and that even the Government of Bangladesh was on the side of the manager.

'Do you like China?' Shahid asked.

'We have theoretical disagreements with the Chinese party,' the man said, impatient at being interrupted.

'So you don't like China? My uncle likes China,' Shahid persisted.

'We disagree with their theory of social imperialism. Look what they did in Chile.'

Shahid didn't know about that, he said, but added that his uncle had lots of books on China, more books than there were in that room even, but they were all in Bangladesh. If he wanted, Shahid said, his uncle would lend him some books and he could read them and maybe he'd understand a little more. He said this defiantly to the man and the man turned to Betty and said, 'It's useless, I don't know how to reply to that.'

Betty could see that I was uncomfortable because now Shahid was getting angry with the man.

There was a silence and Shahid and I got up to go. Betty walked to the door with us.

'Roger's just a bit impatient,' she said. 'He's brilliant really. You'll get used to him as you start working with us.'

Then she did something she'd not done before. She reached out and held Shahid's hand. She was looking at him and smiling to let him know that she wanted to talk to us too, and to drink coffee and laugh as we usually did, and that she was sorry it had turned serious with Roger there.

'You have to come to the next meeting,' she said. 'It's really very important. We'll get you organized then. We'll train you to understand all the theory. You must join the group properly, I really want you to.' She winked.

As he walked away, Shahid seemed suddenly happy. He lifted the hand she had held, elegantly to his nose, as though to keep the fragrance of her with him. I didn't say anything. There was nothing to say.

When we were in school together, we had known some rubbish white girls, but we never went to their homes. We'd meet them in the cafés and play Hindi love songs for them on the jukebox, '*Kabhi-Kabhi*' or any nonsense song of the time, and we'd play pinball machines with them and they might let you kiss them once or twice if you could overcome your own shyness. We hadn't known any girls like Betty before.

'Do you like that girl Sylvia, Betty's mate?' Shahid asked me. I didn't like that. It was as though he was trying to make me beg him for favours.

At the next meeting Betty didn't sit with us. She sat next to the leader because she was giving a speech. She got to her feet and talked about fighting the National Front and then something about Jews and about 'Asians'. When she talked to us she said 'Bengalis', but when she made speeches she said 'Asians'. She abused the National Front for selling newspapers. The rest laughed when she said filthy words. I could see that Shahid admired her for being able to swear in public. He said afterwards that when girls like Betty used filthy language it was all right, it wasn't lowering their family name, it just meant that she had very strong emotions against rubbish people who attacked Asians.

After that meeting he tried to ask her if he could go round to her place, but she said to him that she had to go now, but he should definitely make it a point to come round before the meeting of the group on Saturday. Shahid said that it was a signal. I shouldn't go with him this time. He said she'd asked him to go alone. I understood.

For three days I didn't see Shahid. He was working at a friend's factory, I heard, to pick up some quick money. On Saturday the meeting was supposed to start at two o'clock. I didn't want to go. I had gone to be by my brother's side, because Shahid was like a brother to me, but you don't always want to be 'kabab me haddi'; the 'bone in the kebab', someone who gets in the way.

I sat in our usual café from about ten that morning. About eleven o'clock Shahid came in, his hair looking as though it was flaring out of his head. He was wearing a new suit, blue with pin-stripes, and a new shirt with its huge collar covering the jacket lapels. I could tell from the way his mouth remained slightly opened, his thick lips parted, that things hadn't gone as he had expected. In his right arm he was carrying a whole pack of newspapers.

'Come with me,' he demanded, looking around the café to see if anyone else was staring at him.

'You getting married?' the manager asked him, mockingly.

'Why should I, when I get your wife and daughter free?' Shahid said as we walked out.

'What's the rush, where are we going?'

'They gave me these,' he said, thrusting the wad of newspapers at me.

'You've had your picture taken again?'

He was in no mood for mucking about.

'I have to sell them to "Asians",' he said.

'Wasn't she there?'

'She was there. They were all there. She called me before the meeting because she said I was ready to help the group with its work. They gather at her place before Saturday meetings to sell newspapers.'

'Where are we going to sell them?'

'Tower Bridge.'

He was angry and walking fast.

'There are none of our people on Tower Bridge, only tourists.'

'Sometimes seagulls,' Shahid replied, tight-lipped.

'Where have you been all these days?' I said trying to get him to talk to me.

'Saving money like a fool,' he said.

We walked on past the Aldgate roundabout and turned down Alie Street.

'I asked her to go to Mecca with me,' he said finally.

'So you got somewhere, what're you so furious about?'

'I followed her to the kitchen where she was making coffee for all of them. I said, "will you come to Mecca with me?" She's so stupid, she thought I meant Mecca in Arabia and said she wasn't a Muslim and asked what I believed in religion for, because religion was like drugs. So I told her I meant Mecca Dancing, this evening, later tonight. She thought I was messing about.'

'Did she say she'd go with you? Do you want her to be your girlfriend?'

Shahid didn't reply. We had reached Tower Bridge. He took the newspapers which I had been holding. The headline said: 'Fight Nazi Front'.

We walked down the bridge and when we got to halfway between the two great trunks of the bridge with the water swirling round the curved stone, he threw the whole pile of papers over the grey railings on to the fast water of the high tide.

'What the hell are you doing? Police will catch us for throwing litter about!'

We walked back to the café. We drank some coffee and talked to some of our friends about the football fixture between The Welfare Team and Navin Sangh that was to take place on the Vallance Road field that afternoon at two o'clock.

We were lost in our talk when Betty walked into the café with Sylvia. She came straight up to us, her arms draped with her own pile of newspapers.

'Where's your lot, Shahid?' she asked. 'You can't have got rid of them already!'

Shahid looked up at her, pretending to be very offhand.

'Oh yeah,' he said, 'I got rid of the lot.'

'That's great,' she said, 'fantastic. Now we can really make an impact on blacks. Start with the Asian community.'

She was smiling and she and Sylvia exchanged looks.

'You must have worked very hard and fast,' she said to Shahid.

Shahid pulled out his wallet. He held out a couple of pounds to her. 'I have to pay you off,' he said. 'That's for the papers.'

∽

2.

Two Kinda Truth

MY NAME IS IRVING, BUT they call me Clyde on account of my friend Bonny. Bonny and I used to go together from the time we knew almost nothing. You could say we grew together. We went to the same primary school and then to the same big school and we always met after, and on Saturdays we washed cars down the street together and split the breads we made from that and from anything else. We weren't like twins, because I was like Bonny's shadow. I even caught my name off him. The youth them, they started to call us Bonny and Clyde after we were accused of doing the same robbery. The name stuck, even though the charge of robbery didn't. We got off because this smart lawyer … but that's another story, yes?

Bonny, boy, he grew smarter than any of the youth we used to hang around with. The first day we moved to this dread school in Battersea, he takes one look around the place and says, 'It soft. Man could be happy here.' Now, looking back on it, I don't know how we could have made such a mistake. That school was split up in three. There was the main building, all new and still being built, where they kept the smart ones. They were all white and one or two Asian kids and a couple of blacks. We were kept in what we called the 'coal heap'. It was down in Wandsworth and we called it that because there was a whole heap of coal in the yard. The teachers, they called it the 'Annexe'. There was only a few whites up there, most of the youths on the heap was black.

We stayed in that place three years before we was moved and had to come up to the main building because it was complete and the heap was shut forever. Before that we only saw the main building when the coaches fetched us to carol services or some other jive occasion and the headmaster would stand up and do he thing.

Anyway, this story's not about that school and about blacks and whites, because it would have to be longer than the longest book anybody so far writ. This story's about Wordsy and Bonny. Wordsy was a teacher. He wasn't called 'Wordsy' at all – that was the name Bonny gave him. He was an English teacher. No, first he was a student guy, one of the people who come and waste your time because they're training to be teachers and they need guinea pigs. We met him, all those years ago, in our English class. Old man Cottage usually came in and gave us some spelling test or told us to read *The English Way Reader*, Book I, II

or III. But this day here, Wordsy come through the door.
He was carrying a handbag on his shoulder. He was a
young guy with long hair, kinda hippy. He walk in cool,
cool, and say to us that Mr Cottage was going to come
down and introduce him, but he was a man believe in his
own introduction.

Most of the youth just mucked about in that place. We
never listened to nobody. We just didn't want to know.
When we got to know Wordsy, years later, he told us
that he was nervous that first time, like really shaking.
He'd never been in a class before and he was not even
sure that he should have been teaching. And we told him
that he shouldn't have brought his handbag with him.
He should've suss the place and come with a briefcase or
something.

As soon as the youth saw the handbag they began to
shout 'butty, butty, butty man'. Of course Wordsy didn't
twig what they were calling him. He wanted some quiet,
so he tapped on the teacher's desk and stood up straight to
show that we couldn't mess with him. But nobody would
listen. It was like that; we always tested out the newcomers.
Then Wordsy tried getting hold of one of the youth in the
front and tried to reason with him.

Bonny just watched him careful. Then he said, 'Hush
your clamour and let the man speak.' That's how Bonny
talked, always a bit fancy. They called him a wordsman.
Immediately, Wordsy saw that Bonny was some kinda
leader in that mob, so he turned to him.

Then Bonny stood up and turned to the class and started
bowing and making a little speech and everyone turned to
watch him and laugh. He pretended he was mucking about,

but really he was getting everyone's attention, helping Wordsy along.

'All right, now that you're quiet, we can start,' Wordsy said but even Bonny's effect didn't last long and the others started throwing things at the man. He just sink down in the teacher's chair and say he'll sit there till it quiet.

'You'll have to be bury in that chair, sir,' Bonny said. 'It never going to be quiet, we ain't quiet for nobody.'

As the class went on Wordsy got desperate. He'd brought some papers along and me and Bonny walked up to his desk and asked him what he'd got there. He showed us. It was some poem by a man called Wordsworth and Bonny asked him if he'd writ it himself. The man say that he wish all his life he had writ it, but he hadn't.

'You got the copyright, then?' Bonny asked, just to be feisty. Then he shouted to the class that the man was called Wordsworth and he was no ordinary man here, he was a PO-YET. The class wasn't interested. Bonny looked at the sheet and said, 'Hmm, it all right,' and Wordsy smiled, but he was nearly crying before the bell went and he'd wasted the whole lesson.

Two days later, when we'd all forgotten the guy, he comes back. English was in the afternoon and it was in a classroom just by this heap of coal, looking out on the yard. The room had huge windows, like doors almost. When he come in, the whole class cheered.

Bonny nudged me with his elbow because he had a key to the doors of all the rooms in that place and he indicated to me that we should lock the door so that Wordsy wouldn't be able to get out. The man was trying to smile. In the confusion, Bonny slipped over to the door and locked it up.

'You see I haven't given up with you.' Wordsy told the class.

'What's your name?' they were asking.

'Never mind my name. Let's get down to some reading,' he said and he distributed the papers straight away. He began to read as soon as the papers had reached our desks.

'"Let us go then you and I,"' he read.

'I ain't going nowhere with you,' someone shouted.

'Are you really a butty, sir?'

'This man drunk,' one of the boys in the front row shouted.

'To tell you the truth,' Wordsy said, 'to face you lot, one has to be either drunk or superhuman or mad. And since I can't induce the oblivion of madness, and since God made me painfully mortal, I've had what we call a little nip, as weakness shall be my witness.'

'Your breath smell foul, sir,' the boy in the front said.

'Talk fancy again,' Bonny said. 'This guy's good, you's a preacher man like old Cottage.'

Bonny always appreciated that sort of style. Cottage would talk a bit like the Bible, you know, a bit of high talk. 'Do unto thy brethren as they would do unto you. Betray them. Grass them up,' he'd say, and then he'd say, 'Put your hands on your hearts, remember your Maker and confess to throwing chunks of coal through the staff-room window, or I'll flog the lot of you.'

The youth liked that. Cottage kept order with the cane, and with little tricks like that. He'd talk grand and then he'd talk cockney all of a sudden and it make everyone laugh, but it make them scared at the same time.

Wordsy read his poem after that, and he got the hiccups and some boys rushed over and started hitting him on the back saying they'd make his hiccups go away. By the time the lesson was finished, Bonny was saying to me, 'This man all right.' I could see that Bonny liked the way he was talking, using big words, laying it on when he found the class silent for a moment. Bonny was fascinated by words even then. If we went to a blues, he'd listen to the new lyrics and dub tunes and try and learn the rough bits and change them here and there and use them himself in his speech.

By the time the bell went the youth were waiting to see how Wordsy would get out of the room. They all knew the door was locked. He tried the door. Then the boys crowded round him and asked him if they could see his handbag, and if he had a boyfriend and all kind of rudeness. Wordsy was desperate to get out. He crossed over to the big windows and tried to open one. It was jammed shut. The school-keeper had nailed it down to keep kids from running out of that classroom. Wordsy didn't see the nails and he just banged on the catch harder and harder till he missed, and his fist went clean through the window, smashing the glass.

'That's school property,' someone shouted.

It wasn't a joke. The glass had cut right through Wordsy's wrist and the blood was pouring out. Wordsy fell to the floor saying, 'Oh my God,' and holding his wrist, his eyes wide with disbelief.

Bonny pushed the others aside and went up and knelt by him. There was going to be trouble now, we could all smell it. The joke had gone too far.

'Go sit down,' Bonny motioned to the rest and they did as he said.

'Mr Wordsworth,' Bonny said and the student man looked up. There were tears in his eyes and still the blood flowed. 'Shall I call Mr Cottage?'

The man shook his head. The class was dead silent now.

'Gimme hanky,' Bonny shouted.

Someone gave him a coloured hanky and he tied it round the man's wrist. Wordsy looked finished, boy, he couldn't even kneel straight, he was going to topple over.

'Go get Cottage,' Bonny said to me, holding the man upright.

'Mr Wordsworth, hang on there, guy, we fetching somebody.'

Wordsy shook his head.

'My breath,' he said, 'drink. Don't call Cottage.'

Bonny understood. He got the key out of his desk and rushed up to the staff room to call the young drama teacher. He was thinking right. She was also a bit hip, like Wordsy, and she wouldn't grass him up. She came down and took him away.

We didn't see Wordsy again till we'd nearly finished with the main school. I was in the sixth form. Bonny left at the end of the fifth, telling the head that he wanted to look a job. He didn't look a work. He just came back when he got fed up of lounging about and told the sixth-year master that he had been discriminated against and all the jobs always went to the white boys and all this, and they sympathized with him and let him back into the sixth form, even though he hadn't been bothered to take any CSE or O levels or nothing.

Bonny told the head that he was interested in maths because he could get some technical training after, but we knew that he wasn't really. He was just interested in relax. He joined the English class because I was there. I'd done my O levels and I was going on to do A level English. I was interested in it. I liked reading books. When Wordsy reappeared and started doing his kind of thing, English became more interesting. In a way even Bonny admitted that Wordsy was good.

Wordsy came back as a teacher this time. He didn't look much older to us.

'Where did I check you before?' Bonny said, strolling up to him in the sixth-form room. 'I see you before somewhere, Jah.'

'You tell me,' Wordsy said.

'You was a bouncer in the Stalawart Club up in Islington, right?' Bonny grinned, 'and you call the Babylon when things get too hot for yuh to handle, right? And the youth swore revenge as they drag him off to prison to do some heavy pieces. But now I break loose of the dread calaboose and I come for my revenge.' Bonny stretched two fingers out in a mock gun.

Wordsy caught on fast. He raised his hands and said, 'You may have shot the Sheriff, but you mustn't shoot the deputy.'

'Nice, nice, nice,' Bonny said, 'you all right?'

'Have I seen you before?' Wordsy asked, narrowing his eyes.

'You still owe me one hanky, for bandage your hand,' Bonny reminded him.

'Of course,' Wordsy said with real wonder and astonishment and respect, 'of course. You know when I came in this morning I asked some of the staff if the old three-ten were still around and they said, "Yes, some of them." What they meant really was, "God send the plagues to try us instead of these pupils." How are you?'

Bonny was never in Wordsy's class, but Wordsy would let him come and sit in on lessons.

'Not for the work,' Bonny would say, 'I like being with my *spa* Clyde.' But Wordsy could see that when we were discussing poetry or reading it in class, Bonny's attention was just there. Bonny and I had never split up really. Even during the term he was off school and I was doing exams, I'd see him a few evenings a week. He began to move with a new crowd, but I tagged along with them and we went to the 'Centre' in the evenings. A whole posse of youth hung out there. It was supposed to be a youth club, so two nights a week there were sounds, and sometimes guys hired the place and brought in Coxson and Sofrano B and the big boys. The rest of the time, the Centre was boredom and hustle. Guys would sell weed and just use it as a meeting place for play ping-pong and dominoes, and drift in and out of the judo class which was run twice a week by a Japanese man.

Though Bonny had made some kind of mark, even there, he was just a swordfish with a lot of sharks around. Maybe that was why he wanted to come back to school.

He'd got some sort of reputation as a dread man. Not that Bonny is heavy or heavy-looking. He's thin as a whip, but fast, you know, real fast. And he could talk. He'd got in with a gang of youth who ran a sound system called 'Kool Skank', and when they were playing at the Centre, Bonny would take the mike and play DJ. He'd carry on a whole rap in front of the music, imitating Big Youth and Jah Stitch and Dr Almantado. He was building himself a small reputation as a real dub artist, a man whose toasting was really hot.

That was the time Wordsy started his poetry circle. He'd done some writing himself and he always boasted that he had friends who'd written real books and poems. I said I was interested and so did Bonny. On Wednesday nights we'd stay after school, and several girls from the English set would stay behind too and Wordsy would give us some sherry to drink and we'd go up the staff room when nobody was there and start the sessions with him reading some poetry. That was his little trip. He'd read some T. S. Eliot and then some guy called Hopkins which was like Rasta poetry about God and thing. Bonny said, 'They all sound like West Indians, them poets, with names like Gerard and Wystan and Dylan.'

He'd ask Wordsy some funny questions, but really honest.

He would ask, 'How man could learn hard words?' or he'd ask, 'Could you lend me a book with all the rhyming words in English inside?'

Wordsy didn't like them kind of questions, but he'd try and answer them serious.

'Don't obsess yourself with impressing people,' he'd

say. 'A poem doesn't have to rhyme. Rhyme is a sort of escapism.'

'Rhyme is musi-kal,' Bonny would reply.

'Well, it depends,' Wordsy would argue. 'A poem has to have its own internal music, something more convincing than rhyme.' Then he'd leaf through the books piled by his chair and say, 'You hear that? It seems to have the whole rhythm of speech.'

'I ain't speak like that,' Bonny would say. 'You don't speak like that either. Find me a man who talk so. Poetry is not natural talk. If you talk like that on the street, man will think you mad.'

Wordsy would fend off the arguments. 'You have to be a little mad to write with inspiration. Poets, drunkards, madmen, you know what Shakespeare said about lovers …'

Bonny was impatient with Shakespeare. He'd ask if Wordsy had managed to sell any of his poems. The others would get shifty, and yet they enjoyed the sort of interruptions that Bonny would offer.

Wordsy would say no, he hadn't sold none, but success was a bitch goddess, it was not what a poet should be after. A poet should work like a carpenter, finding the right-sized nail, shaping the right joints between his thoughts.

'And between him fingers,' Bonny would say, 'are true, are true, are true. You sight it?'

Wordsy's stuff made some sense to me because you have to learn all that to get through A level, but Bonny said it made no sense to him, it was all failure talk. Sometimes the girls would bring their poems and read them aloud to the circle. Wordsy would sit back, biting his lip and pretending to think hard about the words. Bonny would watch him. The poems were all about high-rise flats and how depressing they were and about loneliness and old people on park benches and shit.

'Methers again,' Bonny would say and look at me.

One day Bonny brought his own poems. He'd kept them a secret. Only now and then he dropped me a hint that he was going to be a great poet.

'Hold on there,' Bonny said as the session started. 'I and I have something here I want to present to the attention of this circle.'

Wordsy was pleased. He always wanted other people to read before he dragged out his own typed stuff.

Bonny took his floppy cap off and lifted the sheets from under it. The girls laughed.

'This one come straight out of my head,' he said.

This was the poem:

All across the nation
Black man suffer aggravation
Babylon face us with iration
Man must reach some desperation.
It have to be iron, brothers y'all, it have to be iron, my sisters.

Babylon hold up the power
Black man reach the final hour
Our strength in Jah is like a tower
Bringing down a merciless shower
Of bitter rain, my brothers y' all, of bitter rain, my sisters.

He read the verses with tremendous seriousness. The others listened and, as he read, their eyes darted to Wordsy, who was sitting with his head in his hands and his elbows perched on his knees.

Bonny finished and met with absolute silence.

'What's wrong with it?' he asked aggressively.

'Oh, nothing, nothing in the least,' Wordsy said. 'It's fine, just one or two things, a couple of small points.'

The rest of us didn't say nothing. We were in Wordsy's English class and we knew that when he didn't approve of somebody's work he'd say, 'Fine, fine, a couple of points,' and then he'd launch in for the kill.

'Don't dig no horrors,' Bonny said. 'No big thing, say what you like.'

I knew that there was a certain amount of defiance in Bonny's voice. It was like an unsureness. He'd stuck his neck out and now he was going to protect it, but he had to know where the attack was coming from.

'I can, or at least I *think* I can appreciate what you're trying to say.'

'Deaf don't even hear thunder,' Bonny said, quickly.

'Quite, quite,' Wordsy said, licking his lips which had gone dry. He was pulling some determination out of himself. 'Yet it seems like you've thrown together a lot of words without much thought.'

'I think all the time, you don't need a degree to think.'

'For God's sake, I'm not saying …' Wordsy trailed off. 'Well, all right, I'll give it to you straight. I think there's a lot of rhyme there, but there's no poetry, if you see what I mean. I don't mean to be discouraging, your sound patterns certainly show you've absorbed something, but there's no personal emotion. The poem is too much of a slogan; to be poetry it has to have the sound, not of propaganda but of, well, how shall I put it, of *truth*.'

Bonny screwed up his face. He put the poem back under his maroon velvet cap.

'Yeah?' he asked. He was hurt. He kissed his teeth.

'But we can ask the others. We should get more opinions,' Wordsy said. The girls were embarrassed, either by Bonny's righteous, strong poem, or by Wordsy's reaction.

'All right' Bonny said. 'It cool. But remember,' and he got up to leave and turned round as he was leaving, 'remember, Mr Wordsworth, that there's *two* kinda truth.'

'There was no need for that,' Wordsy said after he'd gone. 'No need for anyone to take criticism so personally. If you're a writer, your work is public property, it's not your little toy ...'

There were no more poetry sessions. The circle was closed.

Bonny didn't appear in the English lessons the next day. Then he dropped away from school. Wordsy seemed tense and nervous in those days. He never mentioned Bonny to me and he stopped calling me Clyde. He started calling me 'Irving' and I stopped calling him 'Mr Wordsworth'. Bonny disappeared from school. Once, when the sixth-form master asked Wordsy in front of the rest of us whether he'd seen Bonny, Wordsy said, 'Humankind cannot bear too much reality'. And that was all.

Just before my exams I started going down the Centre again. I recognized some of the faces and began getting back into it. The poetry circle hadn't been cancelled, it had just faded away. So one Wednesday evening I was down the Centre and the poster outside said: 'The Immortal and Versatile Sounds of Kool Skank, Hosted and Toasted by the Byron of Brixton, Bonny Lee'. I smiled to myself, because I knew who Byron was, but most of them youth, them wouldn't know. It just sounded good. The sounds were in the usual hall. The lights were turned down and the amplifier turned up and a jam of bodies presented itself as I went in.

For half an hour the music played, and Bonny's voice introduced the discs with a flourish. 'The latest creation of the Jamaican nation …' etc.

The bodies undulated. There was a thick smell of ganja about the room. 'Strike while the weed is hot …' Bonny shouted over the mike and he was greeted with catcalls and approving shouts. 'Go on, boy, fire some heavy shots, dread word 'pon the waves.' Then all of a sudden the record faded with a scratching sound. Some of the sounds-men gathered round the turntables with torches and began to put it right. 'Hold on there, hold a stool and keep your cool, brothers and sisters,' Bonny's voice announced over the mike. 'The emergency disco have hit an emergency in itself.'

The crowd was restless. They waited for a few minutes and then in the darkness they began to shout. They were threatening a stampede.

'Record player bust to boomber,' someone shouted. The youth workers charged down from their office when they heard the commotion. They worked their way to the sounds table. There was an argument going on. The turntable had stopped functioning and the sounds-men were trying to figure it out, but the crowd wanted its sounds or it wanted its money back.

Then Bonny's voice came over the mike again. He was reciting some verses. They were his own verses and he read with a sort of threatening solemnity. Gradually the noise of the crowd, its protest, died down. People were listening.

'More,' they shouted when he'd finished his first poem. Bonny went through another, his voice reaching a higher pitch with excitement. Now the crowd was listening spellbound. 'Of bitter rain, my brothers y'all, of bitter rain, my sisters,' Bonny declared.

Then the record player was fixed and Bonny's debut as a real poet was over. But when the record came on, the crowd shouted for more poetry. When the first record was over, another voice introduced Bonny again and a third and fourth and fifth poem boomed out over the amplifier.

After the session, Bonny waded his way through the crowd to the door. He saw me. He was sweating and his face shone with wet elation.

'I like it,' I said.

'Wha' go on there, Clyde?' he said.

'I there,' I replied and smiled.

Bonny and I stood outside the club and we talked of school and we talked of Wordsy. Bonny laughed and gave me a message for him.

I didn't give Wordsy the message. Then the day I was leaving school a black girl in the sixth form brought in a poster and pinned it to the notice board. It said: 'BONNY "BYRON" LEE', and it announced a poetry session by the 'Poet in Residence' at the Lambeth Library. There was a paragraph explaining that 'Byron' Lee had been given a grant by the Arts Council to work at 'black poetry and literature'.

Wordsy came into the room and his eye fell on the poster.

'So our friend Bonny's a professional poet,' he said to me.

'It would seem so,' I said.

'Do you ever see him?'

I told him I had and then, because he'd brought it up, I gave him Bonny's message.

'We was talking about you as a matter of fact,' I said, 'and he told me to tell you that he was wrong. That there aren't two kinds of truth. There's only one: Truth is what the masses like.'

'Hmm, that may be, that may very well be …' Wordsy said.

'But listen, he also said to thank you very much for being his teacher and showing him the ropes of poetry, Wordsworth and Eliot and Byron and all. He said he's been reading Wordsworth.'

'He didn't, did he?' Wordsy said, his eyes lighting up.

'Yeah, that's what he said,' I lied.

∽

3.

Iqbal Café

ON WEDNESDAY AFTERNOONS THE CAFÉ served fish, Bangla-style, and Clive always found it crowded with Bengalis. There was not only the usual young crowd who hung around the café day in and day out, but crews of older Bengali workers who only came for the fish. Clive knew he could pick up leads for several stories from the café. He would have to wait for the business to subside and go in late in the afternoon. Hoshiar Miah, the proprietor, whom the boys called 'Langda Miah', 'the lame one', would always drop him the hint of a story. Some of the boys he knew would fill him in on the goings-on around Brick Lane. He'd pick up things other reporters couldn't get. He had become the *East London Herald's* Asian specialist, and half his work was done in the Iqbal Café.

When he first acquainted himself with the Iqbal Café, hardly any whites went there. Only two or three regulars. There was 'old Annie' who'd walk in with seven or eight carrier bags, place them in the corner and walk up to the counter to ask Langda Miah for a small loan to have a coffee in his café. Langda knew her, the boys knew her. They would start calling out, 'Hello, darling,' and the bolder ones would make vulgar kissing sounds on their palms and some would ask how much she was charging nowadays. It was a routine. She would turn to them and swear in Bengali. It was said that she'd been married to an

Indian once, and he'd left her and that she'd been through two world wars, and had entertained gentlemen of all the races in the world. Langda would give her a free coffee provided she didn't make an appearance more than two or three times a week.

Langda had been at pains to explain to Clive that his name wasn't Langda at all, that it was Hoshiar Miah, 'the clever one'. Clive remembered this and always called him by his correct name. The lads didn't seem to care. They called him 'bionic' sometimes, because he was lame in one foot, wore it in iron clips and in a huge padded boot which he dragged after the other leg as he walked, leaning on a stick or on the tables as he passed them.

'I like you always coming,' Langda invariably said to Clive. 'It is good to talk with intelligence people.'

His remark was directed at the two young men who were at the far table slopping up curry with a shared plate of chapattis.

'Teach him something,' one of the boys said. 'As he grows older his hair is falling out and his brain is in his hair like Samson.'

'Of course Mr Clive can teaching something. He is journalist. They knows lots things.'

'What things do they know?' Clive asked. 'You've told me everything I know, Hoshiar Sahab.'

'Don't talk with these puppies, Mr Clive,' Langda said. 'Leaves them. They don't even know to read and write. Stupid as donkeys.' One of the young men looked up, provoked.

'You are the donkey. We saw you carrying two rice sack on your back.'

When they were teasing him. Langda always addressed his remarks to them through Clive.

'You know how hard it is for business these days,' Langda said. 'I tell you, Mr Clive, why a boss man have to carry his own rice. This boy here, you see, I bought his grandfather for slave, now he sick and complain he can't work.'

'He don't want buy trolley, Mr Clive. Always carrying rice on his own back like donkey.'

'Leave them, crazy peoples,' Langda said, bringing Clive his curry and rice and a cup of tea and sitting down opposite him at the table.

'I want you to give one thing in your paper.'

'What's that?'

'It is Iqbal birthday.'

'He want to advertise his dirty restaurant,' one of the young men said. 'When you write it, tell the public that Langda was fine hundred pound for cockroach in the rice when the inspector come.'

'This is a friend of yours, this Iqbal?'

'Mr Clive, why you joke with an old man? It is Iqbal's birthday. That's why I name my restaurant Iqbal Café. The greatest poet in Persia, India, Pakistan, Bangladesh, Burma and Ceylon. I don't know about China and England.'

'How old will he be?'

'He dead.'

'A centenary?'

'Whatever you like,' Langda said, thinking Clive had agreed to run the story. 'If you like you can write that the famous restaurant is name after famous poet. When I first came Brick Lane I saw all the stupid peoples and

I'm thinking this restaurant must giving some knowledge, some beautiful.'

'You should change the name after the Bangladesh war. Iqbal is a Pakistani poet,' said the young man who'd been silent so far.

'These boys not understand poetry,' Langda confided, leaning forward, then turning to them. 'Why you doesn't only see Bengali film, why you see Indian film, Paki film? See? Now the boy can't answer. I like Urdu poet. Most sweetest language in the world, just next to Bengali and English. Iqbal, Tagore, Nazrul, Shakespeare, all artists, all brothers.'

Clive could see that he was glowing with sentiment, probably recalling some favourite verse in his head.

'He is a traitor, this Langda,' the young man said. 'He never have Bengali name or picture or anything. Look what he prefers. Naked white ladies.' He pointed to the prints that Langda Miah had recently put up on the wall to raise the tone of the place. There was a huge print of 'Déjeuner Sur l'Herbe' with a nude sitting in the midst of a lot of well-dressed nineteenth-century men.

'Too much dirty mind. You know how he lose his leg, Mr Clive? They cut it off for going with other man's wife,' 'Oi, shut your mouth and have respect for elders,' Langda said to the boy.

The two had finished eating and went in turn to the basin at the back of the long narrow room and washed their hands. They were about sixteen or seventeen years old. Under their shiny black, well-styled hair, they gave off a sense of assurance, a sense of smiling confidence. One of them, whose name Clive knew was Rafiq, was a sort of leader. He had high cheekbones and the faintest suggestion of slant eyes, some throwback to East Asian ancestry. When ten of them were gathered together, he'd set the pace, tell them when to go, when to pay, how to set the style of teasing Langda that day. And he was the best-dressed one among them. Most of them wore flared Terylene trousers, open-necked shirts and checked jackets. Rafiq wore blue suede trousers, a denim jacket and pointed boots.

Langda wore baggy trousers and a faded navy blazer. Since Clive had been there, he had heard a hundred different versions of how Langda lost his leg. Langda Miah's own version was the most heroic. Several times he had told the story in Clive's presence, sometimes in Bengali, sometimes in Urdu, sometimes in English. Each time it was somewhat different. It was always heroic, but the odds stacked against the hero, himself, changed.

The leg had been shot off by dacoits in his village when he was the only man who would stand up to them to prevent the women of the village being raped. They had raided at night with shotguns. In one version they were disguised policemen, in another version they were Indian spies, in another version they were hirelings of the landlord. In all the versions, Hoshiar Miah had stood firm against them. He had gone out with his bare hands and taken on six of them, killed two and had his leg shot off in the battle. He had driven them away from the village. The whole band had retreated before his single-handed defence, and the village was so grateful that his wife and children would never go hungry. He had left them in Bangladesh and the village would feed them in perpetuity.

Langda limped up to the picture the young man had pointed out, and pretended to adjust its position.

'He call *me* dirty mind. *I* don't go with rubbish girls,' he said.

'You saying you saw me with rubbish girls?' Rafiq asked, pausing behind Langda.' 'If you saw me then you must have apricots instead of eyes,' he added in Urdu.

'I will tell you about these boys sometimes, Mr Clive. They think they are too big now, their heads become swollen with politics.'

'So they should be,' Clive said. He wasn't getting much news this afternoon, but as it wore on, there were bound to be more young men coming in with gossip of some sort.

'Some mens come to the Bangladesh Welfare Association and call all these boys and they go like little sheeps following its mother for milk. A big Jamaican leader, he come and say everybodies must do fighting. What these boys knows about fighting? They comes from between mother's legs yesterday.'

'Ai, Bionic, don't go on mothers. You say anything about mothers and I'll break your other leg.'

'Now they all want fight, but don't know how, Mr Clive. In Bangladesh is too much fighting. First British, then Pakistani and always dacoits. This boys is cowardness, can't fight, no bottles. The white people in East End very rubbish people. If this boys makes troubles, *phuta-phut* going to finish them off. Scared inside itself.' He touched his heart and grinned at Clive.

'This same boys, Rafiq and Mushtaq and Altaf and that black-faced Hussain,' Langda said, 'the police catch them in car with iron bar, milk bottle, big wood stick. Look for trouble. No good.' He shook his head.

Clive remembered the incident. A few months earlier some of the young men who hung around Iqbal had been nabbed by the police for running what the newspapers had called 'vigilante groups'. When he interviewed them after their release from the police station, three of them had told him that the police had slapped them and roughed them up and told them to 'piss off back to Pakiland'.

'We has to defence ourself,' one of the young men had said to Clive. 'Too much white peoples coming and attack Bengali for nothing.'

'I reported the case,' Clive said, recalling the wrangle that he'd had with the editor who refused to allow him to publish anything but the bare facts of the arrests.

'You should be support for us instead of complain to Mr Clive,' Rafiq said.

'If you want to thrash Paki-bashers, you should thrash them, not going round in car and looking girls.'

'We were looking for the white gang who beat up Mushtaq Ali.'

'Now he say this! In magistrate court in Old Street, he begin beg. "I was going to evening college with friends",' Langda rose from his seat and began mimicking, putting on a whimpering voice. 'Then magistrate say "Why you carry milk bottle?" So this boy here who is too much big liar say his mother wanting some milk. So much lie. Talk politics in Iqbal, tell lie in Old Street.'

'Don't shout it all over Brick Lane,' the boy said.

'Mr Clive, this boy Rafiq. Big leader, eh? One day he sitting where you sitting now and making joke with me and a Punjabi boys comes in. Six peoples. They sit down and Rafiq start his insulting, so the Punjabi boys gives him one tight slap. So this boy bring three other boy. These Bengali boy all think they is big expert of fighting. So Punjabi boy pull out a dagger and stick it in the table and Rafiq just make shitting his pants, gone home.'

'When was this?' Clive said. He looked at Rafiq. It was obvious from his expression that Langda's story was essentially true. Rafiq looked worried.

'Don't worry. Mr Clive is a reporter, not a police,' Langda said, going behind the counter now to take the boys' money.

'These boys don't know what fighting is. When I was Bangladesh, during the war, lot of soldiers come and shoot. Then we has to fight. No one afraid, everyone like lion.'

'He telling lies, Mr Clive. When the war was going on he was in Leamington Spa, working in factory.'

Now Langda changed tack. He felt he'd pressed the lads to the point of retaliation.

'You call him "Mr Clive". Oi, boy, do you know what that name is?'

'It's the name of a reporter.'

'It's the name of your conqueror, you fool boy.'

'Is he in National Front?' Rafiq asked.

'No, I'm not in the National Front, he's just being frivolous,' Clive said.

'Didn't Clive conquering Bengal and this boy's great-grandfather?'

'*Your* great-grandfather, or whatever, too,' Clive said. The boys didn't understand.

'You see, they have no knowledge of history,' Langda said.

'Clive was the name of the first Paki-basher,' Clive said, but it didn't seem to leave the young men any wiser.

The boys paid and left, and Langda smirked.

Clive decided he wouldn't wait and gossip with Langda. He had to rush back to the office and file a housing story before the secretaries went home. He got into the office car and drove down the one-way of Brick Lane, under the brewery causeway, under the bridge and down towards Bethnal Green Road. The corner of Brick Lane and Bethnal Green Road was deserted on Wednesdays. On Sunday, in the morning, there was a market there. It was where the fascists sold their newspapers, spitting and swearing at the unwitting Asian shoppers who passed. Clive had attempted to report some of the skirmishes that took place, but the editor had dismissed them as minor incidents not worthy of notice. He'd told Clive that he'd had enough of petty assault cases. Clive hadn't had enough and he thought that the editor was a racialist and a mug.

The Iqbal was just one of Clive's haunts. Sometimes in the afternoon or in his own time in the evenings, he would walk into a pub where known members of the National Front, or other fascists, met. He knew them and they knew him, and they'd give him a lukewarm welcome. The articles which appeared under his name constantly sided with Asians in housing disputes and the like, and once or twice he'd ventured to write bitter attacks on racialists. And yet the people in The Feather or The Clock and Orange wouldn't confront him directly, wouldn't goad him into a serious argument. Someone of them would always say

'Watcha, Clive, old cock,' and buy him a pint and slip him the hint of a story.

Though Sunday was Clive's day off, he normally put in a few hours of investigation. He woke up late that Sunday and regretted it when he finally got down to Brick Lane, parking his car at Aldgate and beginning to walk the length of it. There were police cars everywhere. The street was full of constables.

'Some trouble?' he asked, going up to one he knew, putting on his reporter's manner.

'Trouble at the other end.'

'Come on, Handley, be more specific, what sort of trouble?'

The copper smiled and looked away, pretending to be bored. 'That's for me to sort out and you to find out.'

No use wasting time on this sergeant. The higher-ups would be more forthcoming. They understood about press–police relations. This fellow was a punk anyway, Clive thought. They were all racialists, these junior coppers.

He walked briskly down the street. The Bengali shops, even those that stayed open on Sundays, had closed down. There was a kind of hush in Brick Lane. Clive looked at his watch. The market must have folded by now; it was past one o'clock.

There was a crowd of young men outside the Naz cinema and further down on the left, by the mosque, a group of older men in long black coats and black caps had gathered. They all seemed to be looking down towards the other end of the lane. Clive walked to the Iqbal. Six young Asian men stood outside. They looked him up and down.

Two of them he recognized and said 'Hello' to, and they in turn said something to the others in Bengali. Clive didn't like the tension in the atmosphere. Even the ones who'd greeted him didn't have that edge of normal exaggerated politeness, the 'Hello Mr Clive, how are you' tone. They simply nodded, sullenly. Behind this group of young men, Clive saw something new. One of the big plate-glass windows of the Iqbal had been plastered over with a huge portrait of the queen, with a Jubilee announcement below it. It covered all but two feet of the six-foot-tall glass. Clive was mildly amused. As far as he could recall, there had been a small poster of some Indian actress, with her breasts bulging improbably out of her swimming costume, stuck on the inside of that window. He vaguely remembered that there had been some banter about it between the young men and Langda Miah.

The café was darker with the huge Jubilee poster shutting out the light. Clive noticed immediately, on going through the door, that the poster had been stuck outside to cover the shattered glass of the shop window. There was no evidence of mayhem, but the glass of the window had clearly been smashed and the splintered edges which remained removed hurriedly, leaving a few jagged seams in the frame.

'Hello, Mr Clive,' Langda Miah said. 'Fish only Wednesday.'

Clive pulled out his shorthand pad and pen from his sheepskin coat. He stood with his weight on one leg, holding the book, deciding to abandon the slow, chatty approach when he saw the faces in the crowded café look up at him as though he were an intruder and not wanted.

'Hoshiar Sahab, tell me what happened.'

'Sit down and have a coffee. It is nice to talk with educated peoples.'

Langda was clearing up the leftover cups, limping from the tables to the counter. The two young boys who did the waiting for him, carrying balanced plates of curry and trays of rice and chapattis from the kitchen to the tables, stood idly at the counter. Hardly anyone had ordered a meal. They were there for the shelter, it seemed.

'Tell me what's going on here. What happened to your window?'

'I'm advertising for the queen. She is good lady,' Langda said. There was a hush in the café. Normally at that hour on a Sunday there'd have been a flare of noise. Clive would have joined anyone of the groups of young men he vaguely knew. He'd listen to their talk about factions, how someone was for the pro-Bangladesh and someone for the pro-Pakistan lobby. They'd tell him stories about Langda, about how he'd tried to cheat his partner when he owned a tailoring shop, or about how he had offered to help them set up a Bengali Youth Arts Club because he desperately wanted to be elected as its president.

Taking in the scene, Clive decided that he'd address his questions to Langda. 'Who smashed your glass?' he asked. Langda was behind the counter making him a coffee.

'No one smashed the glass, I'm advertising. Not enough money in tea and coffee business. This boys is not eating curry nowadays, their stomach full with politics.'

'Mr Clive,' Rafiq called from a table at the back of the café. Clive knew from the tone that it wasn't an invitation to sit down, to have a coffee and a chat. Clive turned to

Rafiq. He looked two feet taller. He had a bleeding scar on his left cheek. His forehead had been cut open and was dabbed with toilet paper.

'Rafiq, what the hell is going on?'

Rafiq didn't seem interested in answering the question. He was looking at Langda as he spoke.

'What you say to a man who's scared of the sound of his own footstep?'

'Is this the news you came for?' Langda Miah asked.

'The hero of Bangladesh,' Rafiq said. The only sound that followed was the clump of Langda's foot as he dragged it along the floor, fetching Clive's coffee. His face was drawn, weary. He wasn't going to exchange any banter with Clive. He looked as though he was thinking about some distant event. 'We win it, Mr Clive,' Rafiq said. Clive began to understand. They were all waiting. There must have been twenty-five young men there, and as Clive looked from one face to the other, he was reminded of a scene in a film in which American GIs were waiting to be flown out to take a parachute jump into the middle of enemy territory.

'Tell me all of it,' Clive said. As he looked around he saw more scarred faces. There had been a battle. There were a few torn shirts and ruffled hair in evidence. Clive looked across at Rafiq. He leaned over Rafiq's table, placing his hands on it. The young men at the table didn't look up at him. One of them said something to the others in Bengali. They didn't reply. None of them was making an effort to make him feel comfortable, Clive thought.

'They did a lot of damage?' Clive asked Rafiq.

Rafiq said something in Bengali, raising his voice as though addressing all the young men in the café. Then he turned to Clive.

'No. We beat them good. Teddy boy or something like this. Come in twenty-five from the National Front market. They beats up one Bengali boy and send him to hospital. Ambulance come in half-hour. Afraz Miah was shouting from the street and we was in here and in the other café and then we all comes out. Lot of Bengali men, young men, coming out and then when mosque finish, they all behind and in front of the Teddy boys. We beat them good. Seven almost dead on the pavement. Ten, fifteen run away and start throw brick and then more Bengali boys come and beat them to the ground. One white boy get glass in the back of his neck. Police come and catch ten Bengali and two white and the ambulance pick up the rest of the white. They tear Rahim shirt off his back.'

As Rafiq told the tale, his chest expanded with a kind of pride. 'They will come back with more,' he said. 'They say they come back with guns.'

'My God,' Clive said. 'Look, there are cops outside, the place is lousy with them.'

There was a titter in the restaurant. Clive felt suddenly self-conscious.

'You live long time in East End, Mr Clive,' Rafiq said. It was clear to Clive that he was addressing everyone in the restaurant now through him. 'The police is joining National Front, coming on the side of anyone who is attacking Asians.'

'Yeah, yeah, I sense that,' Clive said. He looked round at the faces that were looking up at him.

'You might be knowing it,' Rafiq continued. 'You are writing story in the newspaper. You are knowing for writing. We are knowing for living.'

Some of the young men smiled. Clive felt himself shuffling from foot to foot. 'Maybe some publicity will help. It'll expose these people, get the police to move instead of brushing it under the carpet,' Clive said. As soon as he'd said it, he wished the words back in his mouth. None of them there would believe that the newspapers would do them a blind bit of good. Clive had the uncomfortable feeling that he didn't believe it himself.

'Newspaper never go against police,' one of the young men near the door said. Rafiq gave him a reply in Bengali and then turned to Clive.

'It don't matter. You writing a good story, Mr Clive.' Clive could see that Rafiq had sensed his discomfort and was patronizing him out of some Asian sense of politeness. Slowly the café came alive in talk. It was all in Bengali. Clive wanted to tell them that he was on their side, that maybe in some small way he could help, but he remained silent. He felt he couldn't leave the café either. Their eyes would follow him. It would be something of an admission, like saying to them that he understood that they were reluctant to trust any white man. It would be admitting that he had suddenly begun to feel like a scavenger, moving in for news whenever he picked up the scent of a kill.

'And some people too scared of these dacoits,' Rafiq said in English. His tone had turned challenging. 'Write one last story in your paper. All Bengalis not stay together like white peoples. Some is too much scared.'

Maybe that was Rafiq's way of saying that he'd finished with him, Clive thought. On some previous day, he would have been sitting opposite Rafiq and the statement would have been part of the testing banter, an opening gambit for an argument. The young men seemed to approve of Rafiq's words and his tone. He was rallying them. So maybe the Iqbal Café had finished with him, Clive thought. No more fish curries on Wednesdays.

'This boys always make up big, big story, Mr Clive,' Langda said, breaking the silence. 'When this Rafiq went to court, they gave him swearing to do. He hold up the card.' Langda Miah stood before Clive and self-consciously began again to act the scene out. 'They hold up card, but the boy can't read. He go to school and thinking only one thing, about dirty girls. Don't learn, read or write. Then judge say him, 'Swear by Allah', and he say he swear by Allah, but he don't know what he swearing. The boy don't know British rules and British peoples. He don't know what to say.'

'When they smash his window, Bionic didn't know what to say. He run to kitchen, phone up police: "Yes, this is your friend, Langda Miah, Inspector, you coming quick, bringing lot of police and take all fighting boys away?"' Rafiq rejoined.

'These boys' foolishness bring all trouble on whole Bengali community,' Langda said, but he sounded defeated. He turned and limped back towards the counter.

'When the National Front come up the road, he was hiding in his kitchen and begging police. He say he shot hundred dacoits. I tell you he got his leg cut off for going with women. My uncle told me.'

'Look, Mr Clive,' Langda said, turning to Clive, who was still standing in the centre of the room. 'These boys eat my bread and they coming on me. I am a poor man. I have only this one shop …'

'He come out and try and stop the fighting,' one of the boys at Rafiq's table said.

'They want a lame man to help with some kicking,' Langda said. His face was taut.

'Who is cowardness now?' Rafiq asked.

'Look, Mr Clive, look,' Langda said, and he lifted the hem of his trousers to reveal his shrivelled leg strapped into shafts of steel in the boot. 'Allah gave me this leg. These boys bring me some blame. What it is I can do?'

'Why you come into Brick Lane, then?' Rafiq asked.

'Allah gave me this leg,' Langda muttered. He turned to the counter. He walked behind it and hesitated at the door of the kitchen, turning to face his clientele again.

'If you want politics you come to Brick Lane,' Rafiq said, a sort of cruel delight in the discomfiture of the lame man overtaking his face, 'and if you want business, you go elsewhere.'

'All right, I'll go other place, is plenty place,' Langda said. Clive turned to go to the door. The Iqbal was closed to him.

'God gave me birth with such a leg, otherwise I would have fought with these boys, kick Frontwallah in the face,' Langda said, as Clive opened the door to leave.

∼

4.

Free Dinners

LORRAINE WAS IN MY FIRST-YEAR class at school and the only reason I noticed her was because she was on free dinners like me. We was the only two in that class who had to take the shame of it. We had a right nasty teacher, Mr Cobb (so you know what we used to call him). Just the way he called your name at the end of the register made you crawl and feel two feet small. He'd collect the money from the other kids and make Lorraine and me queue up separately at his table. Not that he ever said anything to us. He just finished with the regular kids and then announced 'Free Dinners' even though there was only two of us.

After the first week of that, I couldn't take it no more, so I used to go and sit in the bogs when the dinner register was taken and go down to the office after and get my mark. That was dangerous too, 'cos when some wally set fire to the bogs, I got the blame. The register never seemed to bother Lorraine. She would stand up in front of me, and even at that age she looked unconcerned with the way the world treated her. She had a look of thinking about something else all the time, and had tight little lips which showed you that she was right tough and determined – and she was skinny as barbed wire.

She was a coloured kid, or at least she was a half-caste or something like that. We always called them 'coloured' when I first went to school because we didn't think there was nothing wrong with it; but after, some of them would thump you if you called them 'coloured'. They didn't like that, they wanted to be called 'black'. I'm not really sure to this day what she was, on account of never seeing her mum or dad. All the other kids would talk about their mums and dads and the gear they had indoors, but Lorraine always kept herself to herself. She wasn't much to look at and she didn't get on with any of the other girls, because some of the white girls were right snobbish. The other coloured kids would talk black when the teachers weren't there, and they left Lorraine out because she never.

She was good at sports and she was good at drama. I wouldn't have noticed her, I tell you, because at that age I wasn't interested in girls. The other lads would talk about what they done with girls and that, but I couldn't be bothered, and because I was skint till the fourth year, I never took no girls out or even let the kids in the class know who I fancied. It was a girl in our class called Wendy. She had a nasty tongue, but I liked her. I remember the first time Lorraine and I stood in the free dinner queue, Wendy said, 'She looks like she needs them and all.' The other kids laughed, and I must have blushed all over my fat cheeks. Old Cobblers didn't tell Wendy off or have a go at her, and Lorraine just pretended she didn't hear.

I kind of hated Lorraine. I knew that the rest of the class thought that we was tramps. I knew it wasn't her fault, but she was kind of showing me up just by her existence. She wouldn't go and hide in the girls' bogs, she'd just stand there in front of Cobblers's desk and be the only one in the class on free dinners, and because she was there the other kids would know I was hiding, because Cobblers would say, 'Biggs has gone underground again,' or something.

When Lorraine started coming flash the other kids began to take notice of her. In our fifth year she was going to get the drama prize. She was good at acting, and the drama teacher had sent her to some competition which she'd won. She dressed her up as a pageboy and gave her a boy's part from Shakespeare. It made her look nice, because she had short hair and sort of squarey shoulders, even though she was as thin as a broomstick. I was the captain of the football team and had to pick up the cup for the team on prize day. The deputy head called all the kids who'd won prizes into the hall and told us that the bishop would be there to give us our prizes that evening and how we should make sure that our parents came. She went on and on about school uniform and what the boys should wear and how we should wash our hair and have clean hands for the bishop to shake. Then she turned to the girls and did a right turn, showing them how to curtsy, which made them giggle. Then she goes, 'I've told you this before, but I'll rehearse it with you again. You won't be allowed to accept any prize unless you're decently dressed, and that means school uniform. If you don't have one, you'll have to get a skirt below the knee, a clean white blouse and blue cardigan. And no blue and green tights. I want all the girls to wear flesh-coloured tights.'

'Whose flesh, miss?' Lorraine asked.

The deputy head stopped as though Lorraine had clocked her one. Some of the girls giggled.

'Go and wait outside the hall for me, will you, Lorraine? she said quietly, and Lorraine walked out, saying, 'I only asked a simple question,' and she knew that at least a few admiring eyes were following her.

It was the first time I had heard Lorraine say anything coloured, anything to show that she knew she was coloured. I'll tell you straight up, that if anyone else had said that, I would have thought it was too flash. The coloured kids in our year were a load of wankers. They didn't want to mix with the rest of us. When they had a laugh it was on their own, and they collected together in the fifth-year room at lunchtimes and after school and took over the record player and just played their dub and reggae and that. Some of them were all right, but some of them just liked to come flash with you.

When we gathered that evening in room B12, behind the stage, waiting to get the prizes, Lorraine walked in looking a real state. She had on black velvet hot pants and a black silk shirt and had made herself up to look right tarty with crimson lipstick and heavy eyeshadow. The girls sort of turned away when she came in and the boys started making remarks and whistling to take the piss and I was looking, just staring at her because she didn't half look different, dressed like that. Then the deputy came in and threw a fit. Her jaw dropped down to her tits. She rushed Lorraine out of the room and we all ran to the door to hear them arguing in the corridor.

The deputy was telling her that she could still get her prize if she'd wash her face and change into a spare skirt and blouse that she'd give her. But Lorraine wasn't having it. It was as if she'd turned beastly at sunset or something. She gave the deputy some nasty cheek and the deputy didn't turn the other one; she just tried to tell her to 'clear off the premises', and Lorraine said she'd wear what she liked out of school time because it was her culture, and the deputy said she was still in school time if she was inside the gates. When the deputy came back in our room, she was sort of blinking to hold back her tears, looking like Lorraine had really told her which stop to get off at. Lorraine didn't collect the prize of course.

It was after that prize day that Lorraine became a bit of a loud mouth. I heard her telling some of the coloured kids that the deputy head was jealous of her and prejudiced, and didn't want her to be an actress, and wanted to shove her off to work in a laundry. And Lorraine took her revenge.

We were in the maths class and the deputy came in and put her coffee mug, which she always carried around the corridors of the school, down on the teacher's desk. She asked the teacher's permission and began telling us about some fight on a bus in which our kids had duffed up the conductor or something. Everyone was listening quietly and Lorraine, pretending to talk to another girl, said, 'I bet she'll blame the blacks.' The deputy didn't pay any attention, just finished what she was saying and then asked the maths teacher if she could have a word with him outside. She was a bit put out, so she left her coffee on the desk and went out with him.

When they stepped out, Lorraine got up from her desk and went to the front of the class and looked in the coffee cup. We thought she'd take a drink and some kids said, 'Go on, dare you.' So Lorraine turns to the class and says, 'What, drink *her* coffee, and get rabies?' and she cleared her throat with a loud hawking sound and gobbed into the cup, a huge slimy gob. She stirred it with her pencil and without a smile to the rest of the class, sat down again. The two teachers came back in the room and the deputy took her coffee and split. The maths geezer said that Lorraine was to report to the head's office at 12.30. Lorraine said, 'Yes, sir,' and the maths feller said, 'You ought to be given a taste of your own rudeness.' The kids all laughed and he didn't know why.

It was at that time I think that I began to admire Lorraine. I told myself that if I got the chance I'd ask her out, but I didn't want any of the lads to know what was on my mind because, for one, they didn't ever take black girls out, not the mob I moved with in school and, for another, they thought Lorraine was some kind of looney loner. That's why I didn't ask her to the fifth-year dance, and good job I didn't, because she came to the dance with a group of black boys from Brixton and they pushed past the teachers at the door and began to act like they owned the place. I think Lorraine just brought them to show that she moved with the dread locks or whatever they liked to call themselves. It wasn't going to be a particularly good party with no booze or nothing.

These kids brought their own records and they broke up the dance when they started threatening the guy who was playing DJ for the evening. The guy stopped the music and the teachers switched all the bright lights on and suddenly the place was full of teachers and school-keepers, and when Lorraine's crowd started arguing back, they called the police. A lot of the white kids began to drift off, because a blind man could see there was going to be trouble.

I was watching Lorraine. She looked as though she knew she had gone too far. She was trying to cool it and reason with her black friends, but they shoved her aside and shaped up like they were going to duff up the DJ. Then someone said the police had arrived outside and the black kids legged it. Lorraine got into a lot of trouble on account of that scene. Some of the kids, the next day, the white kids, were talking as though they were scared of Lorraine. The blacks were laughing about it. Lorraine wasn't laughing with them; she was just pretending she hadn't been there and getting on with her classwork. That's what I liked about her. She created hell and behaved as though she was the angel of the morning.

At this time I was going out with Wendy. She was right hard, harder than a gobstopper, and she always settled arguments with her fists. I suppose I was a bit fed up of her really. She never let me touch her all the time we was going out. She was a bit of a tomboy and didn't even want to be kissed. Her dad was a copper and strict. I had to take Wendy home at eleven even if we went to a party. I was fair sick of her, even though she was a good-looker, nice face, big tits and always dressed flash.

I wanted to ask Lorraine out and I knew that Wendy would do her nut if she found out. I brought up the subject once with the lads I used to circulate with, and they figured that Lorraine was right easy, that she'd let you do anything with her. They said the black guys from Brixton whom she went out with wouldn't hang around her for nothing. They figured she wouldn't go out with a white bloke. I didn't say nothing to them, but one day after school when I knew she had drama club, I waited around in the year-room and played records till the other kids had gone home and started chatting her up.

I was quite surprised when she said she'd go to the pictures with me. We fixed it for the next time she was staying late at school. I didn't tell the lads in school about our date, but I phoned my friend Tony, who lived in his own flat and told him that I might drop in for a bit after the pictures if my bird fancied staying out. I had six quid on me that day. I met Lorraine up the Elephant in the evening and I said I wanted to go to the Swedish movies, they were really good, but she laughed at me and took me to some crummy film about some stripper girl in Germany or some place.

Lorraine didn't talk silly like Wendy. She had sort of two sides to her. She was a bit posh and she was also hard black. She'd go to the pictures that snobs would see, and she'd want to go to plays and things, and then she'd also talk rude and swear in Jamaican and that.

Until I took her out, I never knew she talked so much. She was explaining the film to me. It was nice listening to her. She wasn't thick like Wendy. When she started explaining why the stripper done what she done, it was nice. It was like I'd had six pints and all the words made sense to me, or like I didn't care if they made sense or not, there was something new and exciting about them.

Then after the pictures I asked her if she fancied going down to my friend's place, because he might be having a party and she gave me a smile and said she was hungry.

'Fancy some chips?' I asked.

'I'm going to take you out to a meal, Peter,' she said. That touched me. It fair knocked me out, to tell you the truth. We went to this Chinese joint she knew in the West End. She was putting on the style, but I didn't mind.

When we sat down they brought this tea that smelt like bad aftershave. She started pouring it out and knocking it back and I said I couldn't drink tea without milk and three teaspoons of sugar and she laughed.

'What do you want to eat, Pete?' she asked. 'Don't worry, I'll pay.'

'I'll have a plaice and chips,' I said, not looking at the menu.

'Don't be so thick, "darling",' she said, pronouncing the 'darling' like one of the girls in the film we'd just seen.

'Steak and chips, then,' I said.

'You can stop playing cockney hero now,' she said.

'I ain't eating no ying yang food,' I said.

She just grabbed the menu from my hand and went into splits. She split herself, and on my mother's life I couldn't see the joke, so I said I wasn't hungry, but to tell you the truth my stomach was growling like a waterfall.

I sat and watched as she swallowed all the spaghetti and stuff. She kept saying I ought to try some, but I wasn't going to show myself up. If I'd said one thing, then I was going to stick to it, 'I'm not hungry,' I said.

When I left her at the bus stop she asked me if I'd enjoyed my dinner. Real flippin' cheeky she was.

'Best portion of plaice and chips I've had in years, really crisp,' I said, just to show I didn't have any hard feelings, even though my feelings were harder than exams. I'd paid for the dinner. I'd insisted.

'I've always enjoyed free dinners,' she said, as she got on the 133 to Brixton from the Elephant. That's the kind of brass you don't need to polish, I thought, as I walked back home with my hands in my pockets.

I rang up Tony and told him it didn't work out. I tried to take Wendy out again, but she was going with this geezer from Scotland Yard who had a blue Cortina and she told me she didn't want to go out with schoolboys. I'd have asked Lorraine out again, but I felt she was only tolerating me and she didn't fancy me one bit. I thought about her a lot. She was a funny girl. I didn't speak to her in school after that evening. I don't know what it was, I can't quite put my finger on it, but I felt she was telling me somehow to keep my distance. When I was going with Wendy, I always got the feeling that she'd do her nut if I packed her in, but with Lorraine it was like she expected nothing, wanted nothing, she'd take what came, and wait for more to come.

Then she started taking the mick. It was in a general studies class in the sixth form, and this teacher was going on about why the Irish were thick or something. He was saying that everybody thought that everybody else was thick, that it was natural, and if the British thought the Irish were not so smart, then the Jews thought the British were not so smart and the Americans thought that the British were all snobs or all cockneys talked in rhyming slang and the like. Then Lorraine started shooting her mouth. There was only twelve of us in that class and we sat around a table in the sixth-form suite and this geezer never stopped talking about politics and racial relations and prejudice and all that crap. Lorraine always talked to him like she was the only one in the class and we was out in the playground playing marbles and she was on telly.

'That's what all white people think,' she said. 'It's just stupidness. They think Pakis are all Oxfam and niggers live in trees, and Chinese food is ying yang food.'

I knew she was getting at me. Then the geezer asked us for our views, so I said, 'I reckon that a lot of it is true, that blacks do live off social security, because there's a black feller on our estate and he drives a Benz, and polishes it up every Saturday and when you see him he's always got a new suit and he goes with white slags, a new one every two hours, and he never works. It's nothing to do with prejudice, it's just that a lot of white people pay a lot of tax and rates and that the blacks come in and take social security …'

'And eat a lot of free dinners,' Lorraine said.

She was a bitch. She never talked to me after that. Not till we left school.

I'd meet someone from school down the Walworth Road and they'd say, 'Watcha, Pete,' and we'd have a talk. I wanted to be an architect, but I had to get my city and guilds draughtsman's exams first, so I was working with this firm on an apprenticeship. We'd talk about this and that and how much lolly we was taking home and about the old teachers and the old times. All the white kids I met from school knew that Wendy had gone for an old Bill, and she was saying 'hello, hello, hello' instead of 'watcha'. We didn't talk about the black kids, except for Keith, who wasn't like the rest of them and was trying to be a draughtsman himself. If I saw any of the blacks I'd been in school with, they would raise their hands, or just blank me, and we'd pass without a word. I thought a bit about Lorraine. If I met her again, I told myself, I'd ask her out, show her that I'd learnt a thing or two, I'd planned it all out in my head. We'd go to the same cinema and see some posh movie or other, whatever was running, and then I'd take her to a Chinese and order a Won-ton soup and crab in ginger, Char Si Pong, the lot, just to show her that old Pete had learnt a thing or two with the lads at the firm who were fond of a curry or of a Chinese or pizza after a hard Friday night's drinking down the local. The lads would talk about a vindaloo and a Madras as though they was bloody veterans of the Burmese campaign.

When I actually met her, there was no chance. Well, I didn't exactly meet her. I just saw her and we exchanged a few words. It was like this. I was round Kilburn way, 'cos our office has a branch up there, and I was told to go and discuss some designs with a top geezer in our firm who worked in Kilburn. The lads from the Kilburn office sussed me out and, after, we went for a drink in a pub round their way. I didn't know them much, but I strung along.

The pub was a young scene, Friday night boppers from round the top end of the Edgware Road. There were lights popping all over the ceiling and huge mirrors on the walls which were otherwise plastered with old newspapers to give the place the look of being in the know. Up the end of the bar was this geezer doing the disco, leaning over his tube microphone and running down the soul.

'We're gonna have some dancing in a piece, Pete,' Sol told me. 'This is a nice scene, topless go-go, strippers, a pint of real ale, a real good time.'

So the spotlight came on the stage and the disco geezer introduced the dancer. We were at the bar. A few of the lads had grabbed stools and I was standing with my pint with my back to the stage and the dance floor. When the music stopped I looked around. You could have knocked me down with a feather. Just outside the circle of the spotlight, like a ghost, like a bloody shivering ghost, stood Lorraine, in a dressing gown which she was urging off her shoulders. Some black guy was waiting at the corner of the stage to catch it as it dropped. As the DJ finished his introduction, she strolled into the light in heels and gold knickers with purple tassles dangling from them and no bra. The pub had turned its attention to her, though I could see that the fellers in my mob were pretending to take it cool. They were all screwing her and giving off that they weren't interested at all.

The strobe came on and the green and blue lights began flashing. Lorraine with her haunted face and wiry body began her dance, her skinny pair of legs like those of a delicate race horse, slim, with the muscles running on the bone shifting with some hesitance.

'I heard it through the grapevine, no longer will you be mine,' sang Marvin Gaye, and the mob I was with began to hoot and clap.

'Look at the fucking state of it,' said Sol. 'Blimey, I'd rather go to Madame Tussaud's and see the Chamber of Horrors.'

In the dark she couldn't see us, she couldn't have known where the voices were coming from. Between the stage and us there were these pillars, and I felt like disappearing behind one of them. She was dancing good, mind you, but it was true that she didn't have much meat on her.

She was a mover, give her that. And she had some guts, getting up in front of that mob and doing her thing.

'Oxfam,' one of the lads shouted, and the faces in the darkness tittered.

'Spare ribs' Sol shouted, as she danced on.

'Knock it off,' I said. 'Don't show us up.

'Spare ribs,' someone else shouted from the far end of the pub. She had small breasts, flat on her sinewy body. Of course she heard the voices, heard the laughter, but her expression didn't change. She was dancing for all she was worth and her body moved gracefully through the tune, but there was no sex in it, if you know what I mean. She wasn't no topless dancer, and if she didn't realize it, the governor of the pub should've.

'Spare ribs.' They'd picked it up at the other end of the pub and were trying to give her the slow handclap. They were going at it like it was the first laugh they'd had that week.

The record finished and Lorraine stepped hastily out of the spotlight. The DJ quickly flipped turntables and started some soul sounds. I watched her as her man gave her the dressing gown and she rushed into the ladies.

'The gaffer's not going to have her again,' the barman said.

I left my pint on the bar and waited till she came out of the ladies. She was wearing a trouser suit and a band around her forehead. As I approached her I could see her mascara was smudged and she looked like she'd rather be on the Flying Scotsman to hell than right there in that pub. She was in a hurry, but she saw me and recognized me.

'Hello, Lorraine,' I said, not knowing what else to say. I felt the lads had treated her something rotten, something shameful, and on my life if I'd been able to, I would have got them publicly on their knees to her.

She was as surprised as I was.

'I didn't know you hung around my ex-beat,' she said.

'I didn't know you'd started professional dancing,' I said.

'Well, you heard what the customers thought,' she said.

'They're a load of stupid fuckers,' I said. 'Excuse the language. How're you getting on?'

I wanted to ask her for a drink, but it was the wrong place, the wrong moment. I wanted to tell her that I'd often thought of her, that now more than ever I wondered where she'd got to, what she was doing, how she kept herself. Her man come up and touched her elbow.

'I'll see you, Pete,' she said.

'Yeah,' I said.

'I'm dancing in another pub,' she said. 'Half an hour. Rough stuff, this, earning your dinners,' and she smiled and walked away. I went back to my pint.

The last time I saw her was very brief, I met her on the pavement in Soho. It was raining. I'd finished my time at the firm and I'd bought this car and dropped my mate and girlfriend off at Gerrard Street. I'd gone to park the car. I saw her coming from a few yards down. She was with an old bald geezer in a posh raincoat. She was hanging on to his arm, dressed to the hilt, made up like a wedding cake. She looked stoned too, unsteady on her feet.

'I saw you first this time,' she said.

She stopped in front of me and smiled, and her mouth opened but her eyes stayed distant, like I'd known them, like they were when she was thinking of other things when we'd been there, children in the first year of school. The old man stood a little way behind her and she behaved as though he wasn't there. She put her fingers on my tie, and said, 'How are you, Pete?'

I stepped back a bit.

'I'm just going to see some friends,' I said.

'Have you seen anyone from the old school?' she asked. 'I haven't seen any of them bastards,' she added, veering on her feet.

'No, no, I haven't,' I said.

'Oh, hang on,' she said. 'I saw your girlfriend Wendy. You know what she said to me?'

'Yes, Wendy,' I said. 'She's in the police, isn't she?'

'She too damn feisty. She catch me on my business,' Lorraine said, her accent suddenly becoming black.

'Oh, oh,' I said. 'You been nicking from Woolworth's again, Lorraine?'

I shuffled my feet. I could see it coming.

'You see this, Pete,' Lorraine said, taking one step back and pointing with a flowing hand at the pavement. 'This here is the street. Your Wendy don't want me to walk the street and she is a po-lis.' She nodded. Now I could see that she was drunk, but her eyes which stared into mine looked sober as the rising sun. 'She don't like me walk the street, our Wendy,' she said.

'Yes,' I said. 'What do you expect from Old Bill? She wasn't ever my girl, Lorraine!'

'You want to get out of the rain, Pete,' she said. She began to walk past me dragging the old geezer after her.

'Pete,' she said, and turned round as though she'd forgotten something. 'Pete, I'll see yuh.' She was facing me again and she turned to the old geezer who looked impatient to shove off. 'It's Pete, my old schoolmate. Pete, this is Mr Smith who's just going to buy me a free dinner.'

～

5.

Salt On a Snake's Tail

THERE WAS THE SHORT ROUTE home from school and the long route. Jolil took the long route because by the time he got out of school the other boys who lived in his building had gone home. Mr Morrison had kept him behind in his office and shown him some books.

'We must do something about your English,' Mr Morrison had said. 'Come up to my room at ten to four and we'll go over some things together.'

Jolil didn't want to refuse. He didn't want to tell Mr Morrison why he was impatient to get home. He usually left the school gate with five or six of the other Asian boys. It wasn't planned, but it was necessary. If they walked home together, they could pass the gangs of older white boys who gathered outside the school gates without fear. They'd take the short route home, and if they passed the cluster of hostile faces outside the white estate at the end of their street, they could quicken their steps and feel the safe warmth of being part of a crowd. If you walked past there alone, you walked along the Whitechapel Road and came round to the flats the long way.

'I got something out of the public library specially for you, Jolil,' Mr Morrison said, and he handed Jolil a book on the martial arts. He had told Mr Morrison some days before that that was what he was interested in.

'Don't just stare at the pictures, try and read some of it,' Mr Morrison said.

His father saw him clutching the thick book when he got home. 'Go wash your face and say your prayers,' Mr Miah said.

'We're not going to the mosque till later,' Jolil protested. He headed for the inside room where he and his sisters slept. His father was already wearing his white muslin prayer cap. A bad sign, Jolil thought. It meant that his dad was in a lecturing mood. He would carry on at him.

'Get down to namaz' he said sternly. 'The devout must pray as many times on Friday as they can. There is no help for us but Allah. Who did you come home with?'

Jolil didn't reply. He sat on his bed and opened the book that Mr Morrison had given him. Normally when he got home his father would be working at the machines in the front room, sewing acres of cloth together, fulfilling the 'contract'. But Friday was the sabbath. The machines would stop. The women would be in the kitchen, his mother and sister-in-law. His father would prowl about the front room and give directives which most of them ignored.

Jolil had let Mr Morrison into the secret. He had told him why he liked kung fu and Bruce Lee.

'Read anything, read comics if you must,' Mr Morrison said. He didn't really catch on, Jolil thought, it was another reading exercise to him. His friend Errol knew about kung fu; he'd take him the book when he went over to his place on Saturday.

Jolil turned the pages. Bruce Lee's muscles almost bulged out of the photographs. His hands, fingers outstretched, seemed to be clawing magical strength out of the very air. The red scars on his body were supposed to be blood wounds, but they looked deliberately cut in neat patterns. And his face, Jolil thought, his face had the authoritative power of a humble man. Jolil tried to read the writing on the opposite page. He could read each word, but the sentences didn't seem to add up. The pictures couldn't actually tell you how to put the thing into practice, but they told a story all right. Bruce Lee was a simple man, probably a poor man when he started out. He even wore the clothes of an urchin, two sizes too small for a grown man. In one picture, he was in the air, a fierce animal, falling with puma-like fists on four shocked opponents.

Jolil rose from the bed and went to the mantelshelf and looked in the mirror. His mother came into the room and took the brass box of betel nut and cloth in which the betel leaves were wrapped.

'Go and wash your face, your father will be furious,' she said. Jolil narrowed his eyes and undid three buttons on his shirt, staring into the mirror. He touched his cheekbones. Yes, they were somewhat like Bruce Lee's.

'You bring this book of idols into the house?' his father suddenly asked. Jolil lowered his arms and turned round.

His father had picked the book up off the bed and was leafing through it with an expression of severe disapproval. Mr Miah did a dry, coughing gargle in his throat, as though gathering his spit to show his contempt.

'It's from school,' Jolil said.

'Who leads young men astray with all these pictures of half-naked actors?' Jolil's father asked. 'Who is it that teaches young men this sort of disrespect?'

'Give it to me. I'll put it away,' Jolil said, trying to take the book from his father's hands.

'You should be reading the Koran. I shall still be grateful to Allah, even though he's given me an infidel son. You'd better read the books that matter, son, before you take up all these Chinaman's tricks. You don't reply when your father asks you questions anymore, eh?'

'What questions?' Jolil asked, trying to distract his father's attention while he grabbed the book and looked around for a hiding place for it.

'Who did you come home from school with?'

'Errol.'

'Errol, eh? Well, it's time you stopped running around with the darkies. You should be down in the basement learning to read Arabic with Kazi Sahab.'

'All the babies go to Kazi's class,' Jolil replied.

'You are never too old to humble yourself and learn the words of Allah.'

'Anyway, I know Arabic. I know Urdu ... aleph, be, pet, the, zaal, zin and everything.'

'The only Urdu you know is from those rubbish films. You have no respect, bringing rubbish books into the house, and dirty pictures of actors and Chinamen.'

'He's not an actor,' Jolil said. 'He's a tiger.'

'A common wrestler. Tigers are stupid creatures anyway. They live outside the grace of God; they fall into pits built with twigs and leaves to trap them.'

Jolil knew when his father was about to begin some story about Bangladesh. He'd heard this one twenty times, about the tiger who thought that every trodden path had been paved by his own paws and was surprised to find a monkey loping along the cleared track to his waterhole. Jolil didn't want to hear the end of it. He turned and went into the kitchen and asked his sister-in-law when his brother would be home.

'He's gone to the meeting.'

'They always have these useless meetings. They are becoming Godless in this wretched country; they think they can fight white men. You know how many white men there are?' his father asked, walking into the kitchen. The women made no reply.

'I wanted to go to the meeting,' Jolil said.

'They will talk. Bengalis love to talk big talk,' his father said.

There had been an incident in the previous week. A Bengali had been stabbed in the ear on his way home from work. The white gang that stabbed him had run away. Some people in the flats where Jolil's family lived had called a meeting of all the families. His elder brother, Khalil, had gone and returned with the news that they were planning some defence of their buildings. The night of the stabbing, gangs of Bengali youths had set out from the cafés on Brick Lane, determined to challenge any white gang that offered insult or violence. Then the next day someone had thrown a brick through the window of the ground-floor flat and another meeting had been called, this time of the whole building.

'If they want a war, there's going to be a war,' Khalil said when he returned.

'What can you do if God's will is not with you?'

'Leave God aside,' Khalil replied. 'We're going to store bricks and stones on the terrace, and if a gang turns up to attack, we can all go up there and deal with them.'

'If a snake stings you once, you don't turn round and chase it so it can sting you again. Leave it alone,' Mr Miah said to his eldest son.

'What do you do if it turns round to sting you again?'

'You put salt on its tail,' Mr Miah said.

He always said that sort of thing as though it were God's truth. Sometimes Jolil wanted to argue with him. He couldn't make sense of his dad's proverbs. His dad would say, each grain of rice bears the name of the person who's destined to eat it. Or he'd say, you put salt on a snake's tail and it'll never bother you again. Another day he'd shout at Jolil for spilling grains of salt on the kitchen floor while sprinkling his chips and tell him that when he appeared before God, he would be made to pick up every grain of salt he'd wasted in his lifetime with his eyelids before he'd be allowed past the gates of heaven. It was all nonsense.

But Mr Miah used a no-nonsense tone to say it in. They were the truths of life, just like going to the mosque on Fridays, and working at the machine when your father told you to.

Jolil would only assist with the sewing work when a contract had to be urgently finished. He'd skip school and help his father and sister-in-law who sat all day at the two machines in their front room. When a contract was 'urgent', the machines would spread their clatter into the night. Jolil didn't like machining, but he wouldn't tell his dad. Mr Miah said there were two types of money; sweat money and water money, and with water money you couldn't keep a family alive, you could only gamble it away or buy water with it. You had to sweat if you wanted to eat. Jolil would load the thread on to the machines, he'd wind up reels of nylon and separate sewn pieces from the piles of cut material every hour, he'd fetch the tea and he'd run down to the shop for condensed milk and cigarettes when he was asked to.

'You'll have to miss school on Monday and work at these linings,' his father said.

'Why can't we finish it over the weekend?'

'We don't work on the sabbath.' Mr Miah said, 'and on Sunday we're going to Dog Market to get some chairs. We have to get your mother some chairs.'

'I have to go to school on Monday.'

'What for? Since when have you become so fond of learning?'

'They're going to show a kung fu film to all the third years.'

'They waste your time in school,' his father said. 'What use is that to you in becoming a tailor?'

'It's not an ordinary film.' Jolil said. 'It's about the secrets of kung fu. Mr Morrison is bringing a film which will explain everything.'

'Everything can never be explained,' his father said. 'If you carry on in this useless way, I'll send you back to Bangladesh and you can learn to be a begging wrestler, go from village to village and challenge all the idiots to fight.'

'I'll work tomorrow. I can do a hundred linings in a day,' Jolil said.

He'd do it, he thought. When they'd been at the old house, there was still some joy left in this business, making the needle hum between your fingers. Tailoring made nimble but tired fingers. It turned your fingers into tools. Kung fu converted them into weapons.

These were thoughts his father wouldn't understand. In a movie called *The Black Dragon Revenges the Death of Bruce Lee,* the hero had plucked out the eyes of several villains and destroyed with similar cruelty the faces of others. There was a knack to it. You twisted your palm in the faces of the enemy. Your hurricane hands had to be trained to lay low an army of fiends. Once he was good enough, Jolil told himself, he'd allow people to photograph him. That's the kind of hero he wanted to be. Once he was good enough he'd get his photograph in the *Martial Arts* magazine, and in *Filmfare,* which his sister-in-law read. He'd be the first Bangladeshi martial arts hero, and his films would sell better than those of Rajesh Khanna, whom his sister-in-law adored, and then he could buy a big white American car. But if he ever became famous, he wouldn't go and live in Malabar Hill in Bombay like the other film stars did. He'd use his powers to do other things, to right a lot of wrongs, to be a saint of the fighting world.

His father had once told Jolil a story about a wise man being reborn in a remote village in Sylhet. He said the souls of old bandits implanted themselves in the bodies of newborn babies and returned as flesh in the families of saintly people. Wisdom passes from man to man, his father said. Strength is God-given and can't be extinguished; it's like a flame which leaves not only embers but heat behind it. And Jolil wondered whether the soul of Bruce Lee would pass into the body of an up-and-coming young hero. It was one of his father's stories that he wanted to believe.

In the past few months, Mr Miah had come up with a lot of these stories. Jolil had noticed that the more trouble there was, the more philosophical his father became. He would put on his prayer-cap and he would mutter at the rest of the family. Khalil had stopped paying any attention to him.

Khalil said there'd be more trouble. When the summer came the whites would go on the rampage, they'd maybe come with guns. Khalil's mates all said that they wanted to be ready, but Jolil knew that they didn't know how to be ready for them. The first task was to protect their building. There were fifty Bengali families there. They were all squatters. They had moved into the building amid tremendous excitement. Some young Bengalis had moved the first family in, and the news had spread through Brick Lane and its environs. Like the rest, Jolil's family had quit their little back room in their relatives' house and moved their mattresses and utensils to the new place. It wasn't new at all, of course. It was an old building that nobody else wanted. On the first day there had been a lot of coming and going. The police came and white men from the government came in vans and spoke to the two or three young men who were conducting the whole operation. They had settled in and a month later the trouble began. Some of the Bengalis were very fierce. They'd make tough speeches about fighting and about protecting their families and their own people. Jolil's father didn't make any speeches, at least not in public. He argued with Khalil at home.

Khalil would say, 'This is a jihad, a holy war. If we want to stay in this country, we have to fight.'

And yet Khalil brushed his hair to look like a film star and put on his best clothes and went out with his friends, strolling up and down Whitechapel Road and Brick Lane and making trips to the West End. Even Khalil didn't understand what it was they had to do. Strolling around Brick Lane wouldn't make you strong, wouldn't build you up and strike terror in the guts of the 'rubbish' whites. Jolil was determined to practise the arts of discipline and meditation, because Mr Morrison had told him that being an expert at anything was difficult. At the root of all strength was discipline and meditation. But how was it to be done? He'd hit the palm of his hand against the wall a hundred times and count to a hundred because the counting kept his mind off the pain.

When he was indoors, or outside in the courtyard with the younger children from their building, he'd practise his kicks. He'd try and raise his knee higher each time, flicking his foot out from under, imitating lightning. He still struggled to retain his balance. One day he'd be perfect. He'd go to kung fu classes and win himself a black belt.

Jolil knew that Errol was also training. And Errol had learnt modesty. He'd never show off in the playground at school. He wouldn't raise a fist or a leg. But Jolil knew that Errol had hardened his palms with careful persistence and he could break planks of wood at a stroke if he wanted. He showed Jolil how to twist his fist when he pushed it out to arm's length. That was one of the secrets. It was a controlled, graceful movement and you had to learn to get it just right. And fast. Speed was another secret. Silence was yet another. Strength was more terrifying if it wasn't expected. You had to look like a priest and fight like a tiger. Then there was confidence. One of the reasons Jolil didn't practise his strokes in front of Errol or any of the other boys in school was that they might laugh at him. When they laughed, your spirit got soaked up, and then no matter how fast and rough your fists were, you'd be defeated by their stares and their grins. Your confidence had to defeat those stares and grins.

'Put your cap on, we're going to prayers now,' Mr Miah said. Jolil got his jacket on and put his prayer cap in his pocket. He wasn't going into the street with it on. His father strode slightly ahead of him. It was still light when they came out of the flats and passed under the old archway. His father turned left. They were going to take the route past the white estate. The younger children were still playing in the courtyard. They wandered around the piles of debris and stalked through the deserted basements, climbing in and out through window sills with their frames ripped out. Their voices, a mixture of Bengali and sharp English exclamations, echoed round the yard. The sound of sewing machines and the odour of frying spices floated out of open doorways.

'You hear them?' Jolil's father said. 'They won't stop their machines for judgement day. They shouldn't call themselves Muslims. See what the promise of a few pence does to our people?'

He gathered his spit and fired it out of his mouth on to the pavement. They walked across the narrow cobbled street, past the boarded-up warehouses towards the mosque. Jolil knew that the kids from the white estate at the end of that street called this territory 'Paki-land'. They'd have to pass through those shabby concrete flats and then they'd be safe again. The new concrete would give way again to the half-gutted complex of old factories and houses, the smell of 'pig-lard' as his father called it in Bengali, would give way again to the richer scents of garlic and coriander from the warren of Asian dwellings which surrounded the territory of the mosque.

Jolil saw them, and saw that his father had spotted them too: a group of about a dozen white boys and girls, leaning against and sitting on the concrete parapets that surrounded their estate. They should have gone the other way round, Jolil thought. He took a couple of hurried steps to walk abreast of his father. His father's steps became shorter and faster. He was staring straight into space, as though he was unaware of the eyes of the crowd that greeted their approach. A small lump came into Jolil's throat. It wasn't too late to turn round and go the other way, even if it meant an extra half-mile to walk. But that was what they mustn't do. His father walked on as though the thought hadn't occurred to him.

As they approached, the gang stopped their chatter. They stood sultry and silent. Jolil looked at their feet as he passed, he didn't want to look up in their faces in case they took that as a provocation. They looked massive, these white youths, in their close-fitting clothes and their close-cropped hair.

'Allah will guide us,' Jolil's father muttered, as though to himself.

They walked past the gang and a voice called out from behind them, 'Oi, Pak-a-mac.'

'Keep walking,' Jolil's father said to him, pretending to be in charge of their pace which was light with the lift of fear. Jolil could see that his father was afraid. Maybe even this gang of louts could smell the stink of funk that came off him.

'Can't wait now, eh?' one of the boys said. 'Got to rush off and put in some overtime.' He was trying to imitate an Asian accent.

'Leave off, Baz,' one of the girls on the parapet said. 'One of these days these blokes are going to lay a hiding on you.'

'Don't make me laugh,' the boy said. 'The only hiding these geezers know is under their beds when there's trouble. Even that won't help them soon, though.'

Mr Miah's step had broken into a kind of run.

'You'll have to run all the way back to the jungle,' a voice from the mob shouted behind them.

'You see why the Koran forbids us to drink?' asked Jolil's father. Jolil didn't reply.

At the mosque Jolil tried to concentrate on his prayers. His heart was still beating fast. What could they have done, he was thinking. He looked round at the other men who were on their knees, bending their bodies to the intonation of the prayers. Jolil felt a sense of calm. All these people, he thought, all these people. They can't drive us anywhere. Khalil had said that the whites wanted to drive them back by scaring them, making them so afraid to walk the streets that they'd have to pack up and go back to Bangladesh.

He looked up at his father. His panic seemed to have passed away and he looked serenely absorbed in his prayers, opening and closing his eyes. A little threat, a little discomfort, that was what life offered you, he seemed to be thinking. Jolil knew his father. To him it wasn't important. Maybe it wasn't important to all this crowd on their knees. Like the snow and the early dark in winter, this threat and hatred that had been loosed all round their surrounded lives, was just part of the fact of England. Like the kites in the skies over the villages in Bangladesh, or the locusts that swept the crops, coming like the monsoon in fatal clouds, these 'rubbish whites' as they called them, were creatures with whom one had to share the landscape. For Jolil they were different. For six years he'd been to school with white kids. He knew every twist of the language they spoke. He understood the jokes they made. He knew their reasons and their unreason. To his father they were people to be ignored, their remarks were like the noise of crows in the trees towards sunset; they signified nothing.

After coming out of the mosque, Jolil noticed that his father lingered around until they were joined in the street by other men from their building.

'Never be scared of jackals,' he said to Jolil. 'If those white men had tried to attack us or anything I would have taught them a good lesson.'

'We should go round the other way,' Jolil said.

'Oh no,' his father replied. 'Streets were made to walk on.' And he spat with conviction.

'You should have spat at them when they abused us.' Jolil said.

'My mouth was dry, boy.'

The next afternoon Jolil was at Errol's place. Errol's room was plastered with kung fu posters. Jolil told Errol about the book that Mr Morrison had given him.

'Some high books on kung fu, boy, only black belts could understand them. It ain't like foo'ball where anyone can see the tricks. Kung fu is a heavy science, boy; if you don't know the meditation, then you can't do nothing,' Errol said.

They discussed the film they were going to see. Morrison had told them that it was called *The Secrets of Kung Fu.* Errol said maybe the film could teach him a couple of things, there were still one or two things he needed to know.

When Jolil got home his father and sister-in-law were at the machines. His father would normally give up his seat to Jolil and go off to the mosque on his own, leaving Jolil to work for a couple of hours. This day he didn't budge,

He turned to his daughter-in-law and said she could have a rest now that Jolil had returned. They worked in silence. His father hadn't told the others at home about the incident the previous evening.

On Sunday Jolil set out with his father to Dog Market. It was crowded. People walked between rows of junk shops on either side. The stalls sold everything from vegetables to antique gramophones. His father poked his head into several second-hand shops and looked around for a set of chairs.

'Wanting chair, good chair,' he said to the man with the huge belly who sat outside one of the shops.

'What sort of chairs?'

'For sitting down.'

'Look in there, mate, I've got plenty of chairs.'

'How much price?'

His father walked to the back of the shop which was piled with mattresses and old tables and canvas sheets and broken furniture. He lifted a well-polished chair off the top of the pile.

'Those are no good to you, mate,' the man said. 'They're antiques.'

'How much?' his father insisted.

'What's the point of telling you if you ain't gonna want them?'

'I want them,' Mr Miah said. Jolil could see that his father understood that this shopkeeper was trying to insult him.

'All right, let's say twelve pound each, all right? Satisfied?'

Mr Miah put the chair back on top of the pile.

'Come and have a dekko at these, mate, more your sort of thing. Good strong chairs, these, last till your boy has grandchildren running all over Spitalfields. They're two quid each,' the man added, handing the steel-framed, plastic-covered chairs to Mr Miah. He dusted the chairs off.

Mr Miah handed over the money.

'I know your people, mate. I know what they like,' the man said.

Jolil took one chair and his father took the other. They passed through the crowd.

'You've got to know how to get things at their proper price – these traders are very sharp,' his father said to Jolil as they emerged from the bustle of the market. Jolil knew they'd been insulted, the man had jeered at them. He walked with his eyes on the pavement. There was no way a man could swallow an insult and still look the world in the eye. One day, he thought, one day he'd be ready. He wouldn't accept walking in fear.

As they turned down Chicksand Street, on the last lap home, pausing every few yards and transferring the awkward weight of the chairs from arm to arm, Jolil saw two of the youths who had been in the gang on Friday night. They were standing on the pavement, leaning against the wall as they had done that night.

'These rubbish people are still there,' his father said.

'When they are in ones and twos they are not so bold, eh? I'll smash this chair over their heads if they say anything to me.' He was strolling with confidence now.

'Men should be as afraid of killing as they are of dying,' he said, and gathering his spit, he spat on the pavement.

'What are you spittin' outside our flats for?' one of the white boys said as they approached them.

'Leave it, leave it, leave it." Mr Miah said in English.

'I'll give you leave it,' one of the boys said, stepping forward as they passed him.

'Just keep walking, just hold the chair out if he comes,' Mr Miah said in Bengali to Jolil.

The youth was upon them. He grabbed Mr Miah's jacket collar from the back. He tried to wrench loose, dropping his chair. The boy wore a red sweater, and its tightness made his muscles look menacingly large. There was a flash of spite in his face.

'Oi, you want to go and clean up that gob you made there.'

'No, thank you,' said Jolil's father, hastily. 'Just move on, hurry on,' he added, in Bengali, to Jolil,

'Ah, no-speak-d-English, eh? You know damn well what I said, now come back here and clean it up.'

The other youth came strolling up and positioned himself in front of Jolil's father.

'You ain't bolting anywhere, curly-caps,' he said. 'You're going to do as my mate says and clean up your gob.'

He picked up the chair that Mr Miah had dropped and banged it emphatically on the pavement. Then he sat on it.

'Why you trouble an old man?' Jolil's father said. He was beginning to plead. Suddenly Jolil felt he couldn't take it any more. 'Get off, it's our chair,' he said, rushing up to the seated youth and trying to pull the chair from under him.

'You want to digest your teeth, Paki junior?' the youth said.

'It's a very young boy, little boy,' his father said, holding up his hand as if in surrender. He walked back to the place where he'd spat and began shuffling his shoes over the pavement.

'I said with your tongue, not with your Tesco bombers,' the young man said.

Jolil picked up the chair he'd been carrying, lifted it and rushed at the young man. He nimbly stepped aside, jerked the chair out of Jolil's hands and flung it a few yards off. Then he jumped on Jolil and slapped him with his open hands on both cheeks, pushing him off as Jolil rushed at him in between the resounding flat blows.

'Don't you get funny with me,' the youth said between his teeth. Jolil threw himself at him again. The youth got him by the front of his shirt, held him at arm's length and flung him to the ground. Then he pounced on him, kicking him, as Jolil tried to cover his face.

Then he heard his father's voice behind the young man.

'Very sorry, very sorry,' he was saying, and then in Urdu, 'in the name of all-seeing Allah.'

The youth who was kicking Jolil let out a little yelp.

'Aaaaah, you bastard,' Jolil heard him say, and he fell to his knees as though he had dropped something on the pavement. Jolil's father screamed to him to run, to leave the chairs. He scrambled to his feet and ran after his father. For a few seconds the other youth ran behind them and then he turned and went back to his companion who was still kneeling on the pavement, screaming as though he had looked in the face of murder. Jolil didn't turn. Neither he nor his father stopped till they reached the broken archway of their own building.

Khalil was at home when they walked in.

'What about the chairs?' his mother asked, and then, seeing the red marks on Jolil's face. 'Oh, my God, what's happened to you?'

'We couldn't find any chairs,' his father said. 'Jolil tripped and fell down as we were coming back.'

'I didn't,' Jolil shouted. 'We ran …' he started to say.

'Don't call your father a liar,' Mr Miah said. 'Go inside and wash your face.'

'Why did you run away?' Khalil demanded. 'Who chased you? I'll kill them.'

'I'm not a man of violence,' his father said, 'and the day that sons of mine can tell their father what to do is the day I want to stop living.'

'If you live like a rat you've already stopped living,' Khalil said.

'Don't answer back, boy. Nobody's been hurt. We're all right. Allah has brought us safely home.'

Khalil wasn't going to speak against Allah. He turned on his heel and walked out of the house.

Jolil's face was burning now, with the slap and with the shame he felt. He didn't venture to tell his mother what had happened. He felt they had lost more than the chairs; they had lost the right to walk on the street. They had lost face. His feet, which should have been shooting kicks at the jaws of danger, had followed each other hastily home.

That night he lay on his back awake, his mind filled with the rage of their helplessness. The house was dark, the rest of the family was asleep. Jolil heard a noise in the kitchen. He heard the tap running and the sound of feet trying to tiptoe and then the sound of creaking wood. He got up from his bed and went through the front room quietly and peered into the kitchen. His father was kneeling on the floor in the dark. He turned his head over his shoulder, startled at Jolil's approach.

'Go back to sleep,' he said, sternly.

Jolil stood in the darkened doorway, not obeying his father. The dirty lino on the floor of the kitchen had been turned up, and his father was fiddling with a hammer with one of the floorboards. 'Listen, son,' he said, getting to his feet and turning round, whispering almost. 'Don't ever tell anyone, not even your mother or Khalil, that we bought any chairs or about those men.'

'I won't,' Jolil said. They had run away; he didn't want to tell anyone that his father was a coward. 'Don't worry. I won't.'

The next morning his mother brought some white paste she'd made up and put it on Jolil's cheek. Jolil washed it off, brushed his hair, and, taking the long route, went to school.

In the darkness of the sports hall, the kids whistled and cheered as Bruce Lee appeared on the screen, leaping over walls, dodging out of the path of bullets, tackling six of his enemies at the same time and laying them flat. Then the film turned from colour to black-and-white. A man in a suit was addressing the audience. '... so we take a look at the world in which the stars of this international cult live. We look at the way in which this game is played, we look at the magic and illusion of kung fu …' There were more shots of men lopping off other men's heads with the swipe of a braced palm. The blood flowed and the third year cheered. Then the white man came on the screen again. He was going to explain, Jolil thought, he was going to give away the secret. As he talked, the picture showed the crew of a film studio setting things up in the background. Then the Chinese man, to whom the white man had been talking, jumped off a wall on which he was perched. The cameramen recorded the jump. The man threw his arms out as he leapt. The white commentator held the film up to the audience.

'So we play it backwards,' he said. The film inside the film was played backwards and it showed the same jump in reverse, looking like the Chinese man had jumped up on to the wall.

Jolil watched it in silence. The film moved to other rooms in the studio. An actor posed next to a dummy of himself.

'Ain't it good,' one of the boys next to him said.

The dummy's head was struck off, the fountains of blood began to pour from it, and its neck was held up to the camera to show how the blood was made to gush out of a pen-sized capsule. 'All this happens at twenty-four frames a second in an ordinary film, the speed of normal life. What happens when you slow the camera down?' There was another shot of the Chinese man aiming kicks to the jaws of other actors. He did it slowly, deliberately, and the director of the film posed the extras in expressions of surprise. There was another shot of the same action at what seemed to be incredible speed.

'Celluloid has created the kung fu superman, running, leaping and fighting with fists of speeded-up fury.'

The whole film was like that. When the lights were switched on and Mr Morrison came to the front of the hall and said that they'd have ten minutes extra on their lunchtime, Jolil turned to Errol. Most of the others were indifferent to what they had seen.

'In the book that Morrison gave me, it said that Bruce Lee could really jump on to a ten-foot wall.'

'Bruce Lee dead,' Errol replied.

'It's stupid, I reckon,' said another boy in their row. 'Kung fu is for mongs.'

'White man spoil everything,' Errol said.

Jolil didn't stay to school in the afternoon. He went back home. He couldn't make up his mind about how he felt about the shattered secret. Maybe the film was lying, all kung fu was not like that, it wasn't all tricks.

When he got to their building, Jolil could see three police cars parked outside. There were policemen in the courtyard and several people from the flats were outside talking to them. The women and children leaned out of the windows.

Jolil burst through the door of their flat. His father was sitting at the machine, his spectacles sliding down his nose.

'What's going on here? What're the police doing in our buildings?'

'You want to mind the world's business? You'll have to have a million lives.'

'A white boy was stabbed at the end of the street yesterday evening,' Khalil said. Khalil was looking out of their window. 'The police want to know if any of the children found a knife or anything in the street while playing.'

'Why should we get involved in white man's quarrels?' his father said, threading the machine after licking the thread.

'It wasn't a white man who stabbed him,' Khalil said. 'It was some Bengalis and they left some chairs behind on the pavement.'

'Don't talk loosely, letting your tongue wag in your head. We've got all the chairs we need in this house,' his father said, still at the machine.

Then he turned to Jolil. 'Go and take two pounds from my purse and go down to Brick Lane and buy me a pair of cutters' scissors. Take the long route.'

❧

6.

Go Play Butterfly

I'LL FIX YOU TO FLY away,' the young man said. Then he asked Esther to hold still while he pinned on her wings. It was two nights before the carnival, and Esther was aglow with the importance of it.

She hadn't wanted to do it at first. She didn't even know what carnival was, but her mother had decided for her. Josephine, her friend from school, and Carol, who lived down the road, were both Trinidadians, and their mums had decided that they would 'play' with a band. Carol had boasted about her costume in the presence of Esther's mum. It was too much of a challenge. Esther knew that her mother would pick up the gauntlet and that she would be made to 'play mas' too.

Carol's family were moving. Her mother, who came and gossiped with Esther's mother, told endless stories about the beauty of their new house in Norwood. Everything she said implied that they'd finished with Brixton, finished with living in a council flat. They were homeowners now. There were to be lace curtains and a new colour telly and a fence which was to be painted pink, and a bedroom for Carol and one for Stanley and one for the twins, and a diningroom which was separate from the kitchen. It was too much, for Esther's mother, Mistress Waters, to take. And now Carol was in a band which was going to have its photograph in the *South London Press*, her mum said.

When Manny came home, Mistress Waters questioned him closely. What was all this carnival business? Couldn't Esther take part in it if they wanted her to? Manny said he knew Soaky who was the artistic director of one of the 'mas camps'; he could get her in, even at this late date, no problem. Manny was Esther's stepfather. She liked him. He knew everyone. He took her to the mas camp the next day. Esther could see that at first he wasn't too taken by the idea, but her mum had said it must be so, and it was.

The camp was a huge disused factory in Paddington. Manny drove Esther there and left her with his friend Soaky, a man with greying temples and a long straight nose, strange on the face of a black man. Esther was uncomfortable. Soaky's real name was Mr Dix, but all the kids in the camp called him Soaky. So Esther called him Soaky too. As soon as they walked in through the factory doors, a little gate, hinged into a larger one, Esther began to feel that sense of wanting to be anywhere but there. It was a place which would challenge her. It was a hive of activity. There were young men and women, most of them much older than Esther, working away at the trestles and the nylon and the tinsel at tables all over the large and disorderly room. They didn't look up from their work when she came in with Manny, who sought Soaky out and introduced his daughter.

Soon, Manny became enthusiastic about the mas camp. He liked to take the drive to Paddington, and would volunteer to take Esther there. He began speaking about the camp as though it was his own enterprise. Esther knew that he was eager to carry her because it enabled him to get away from her mother. He would plant her in the camp and go off for a few hours, making his rounds in 'the Grove', and hanging around the betting shops of Notting Hill. He would come back to pick her up, elevated or exhausted with the tensions of placing money on a horse.

On their second visit to the camp, Soaky had asked Esther to help make the costumes. He called out to a group of youths who were busy painting the stretched fabric of the dresses that the players would wear. Their band was called 'Fantasia of the Ethereal Air'. Soaky took Esther round to the youths and said, 'Give this girl some wings; she go play butterfly.'

The young men, four of them, were sizing Esther up. One of them was called Jojo, and he smiled at her. Another of them said they were going to make her 'high, high' and asked her if a man had ever made her feel so light and airborne before. Esther was only fourteen. Men didn't speak to her like that. At least, she hadn't known them before then. She kissed her teeth and turned her head away, pretending to look at the group of girls who were kneeling round another masquerader, pinning a costume on her with safety pins and needles clasped in their teeth. Esther moved away from Jojo and Claude and the rest of them and joined the group of women who were dyeing feathers.

From the day she had come there she had sensed that they had all treated her like she had never been treated before. Jojo and his mob had made remarks about her size. Manny had told Soaky that she was only fourteen, and the boys had said that she was 'fit' and Manny had looked at them as though to say they'd gone too far. That's what they made her feel. Esther thought, older than herself. It was the first time that she'd been made self-conscious by a group of boys about her body. It was not only the way they looked it up and down, not only the way their eyes seemed to say that she had some magnetism. It was also the first time that she was going to be one of the stars. And the other stars were women much older than herself, girls who swirled in and out of the camp and were attended with the respect due to beauty, to flourish, to independence. Esther was happy to be in that team, amongst the forty women who were to play mas with Fantasia.

Twice when Esther had been there, the star of their band had walked into the mas camp. Esther thought she was gorgeous. She had an imperial look; a black beauty with a touch of disdain on her face. Esther knew that she was called Veronica. Soaky spoke of her as his leading lady. She stood at the door like someone who owned the place but still wanted to be treated like a visiting queen. The camp gathered round her when she walked in and held out her arms to be measured finally for the draperies that were to envelop them. She held back her head when Soaky and an assistant lifted the headdress, peacock feathers and nylon and gold and black antlers, like a crown.

Yes, she would be carnival queen. There couldn't be anyone in this town more regal, more befitting the honour than her, and yet Esther didn't want to pay her tribute. As she watched Jojo and his cronies, Esther saw that they didn't want to pay her tribute either. The four young men carried on with their painting and pinning as though Veronica were a passing show in which they weren't interested, while Soaky and the other designers fawned around her, adjusting this and bringing up that, layer upon layer of costume, which, when it was assembled, looked light and natural on her lithe brown body.

Now there were two reasons why Esther wanted to be in this carnival business. There was Veronica, who was to Esther an immediate rival. Esther watched her. Ten years older, she estimated. Until a few months ago she couldn't tell anyone's age, but she knew this girl was twenty-four. She must grow up like that, Esther thought, and while doing it she must avoid some of the shortcomings of this person. Her eyebrows were shaved too thin, Esther noticed, much too thin to seem at all natural. And her voice. It was wrong. There was too much girlish excitement and high-pitchedness in it. When she was that age, her voice would have more command in it. And it would lose the suggestion of giggle which came through when Veronica pronounced herself delighted with the headdress.

Veronica looked around and Esther saw her looking all the mas players up and down, as quickly and unnoticeably as she could. That was all right, Esther decided, standing on the periphery of the orbit of the queen. That was the way the sun should cast its light on the outer planets that turn a constant face or rotate in its light.

Then there was Jojo. There was something very deliberate about the way he wasn't impressed by the leading lady. He looked at Veronica as he would at any other brother or sister who came to put in a bit towards the task of getting their collective glory on the road. Not only that, he exchanged glances with Esther and smiled at her. He was working on a hundred wings and she was as important to him as the woman who was undoubtedly going to be carnival queen.

Two nights before carnival there was a party at the camp. Manny took Esther, after persuading Mistress Waters to let her go. After all, he said, she wasn't going to go to the big carnival dance, so she should at least get a Coke and some crisps at the camp. Mistress Waters had agreed reluctantly. She set out the most childish-looking, high-collared blouse for Esther to wear. But Esther had made other plans. She had persuaded Manny to buy her a blouse with a plunging neckline which would allow the brown crescents of her breasts to show. When she dressed for the party, Esther took a white cardigan and put it on to hide her blouse from her mother. In the car, she took it off and threw it on the back seat and pulled some lipstick out of her bag. Manny looked at her while he was driving but didn't say anything.

There were plenty of girls at the party. Some of the younger ones began dancing in pairs and trios. They danced as they would at school. If Carol and Josie had been there, Esther thought, or Sharon, or Nancy, she would have danced too. But alone, she felt stiff and self-conscious.

Manny was in high spirits. He walked around the crowd with a can of special brew. At one end of the hall the steel band played. When it stopped, the reggae amplifiers were switched on. At the other end of the hall, Jojo and his friends were still working away, putting the last touches to their artistry. Esther wandered over from the circle of revellers to the row of workers.

'You get away from your father?' Jojo asked, not looking up from his work.

'Mm, hmm,' Esther replied, conscious that he was going to look up at her any moment, see her in her new blouse.

'You want to go rave in the blues, or you want help me a second?' Jojo asked.

'Depends,' Esther said.

He looked up and smiled.

'I design a new wing thing here. See this triple fold with a clip?'

'Very interesting,' Esther said, mocking him.

'You want to wear it?'

'I'm all right.'

'Look, it'll make you light, take the weight off your platform shoe there.'

'I'm not heavy anyway.'

'You go be an ariel creature,' he responded, picking up the folds of cloth he had on the table before him. 'Just try it on, nuh?'

The nylon stretched between her wrists and her hips, in a huge fan.

'Hold this end from here,' he said, kneeling beside her to pin the flaps of nylon and twist them around the spar that held the wings together. His fingers curled gently round her wrist, a grip that seemed to take all the weight out of her forearm. She was alive to the brushing, firm touch. She felt the blood coming up to her shoulders, up the side of her ribs and down her spine as though it was coming up to her head and going down at the same time.

'I go pin your blouse from the back,' he said. 'I go put my hand under your skirt.'

Esther wanted to shut her eyes, gently let the lids drop, shut out the world and feel for the moment nothing but the tingle of his fingers, but she kept them wide open. The others were looking at her. They'd laugh at her.

'Mind the pin,' she said.

'You scared of a little poke?'

The other young man, who was working on a headdress, heard Jojo and he smirked.

'Get on with your business,' Esther said, knowing she'd spoiled the moment.

Jojo was behind her, pulling the back of her blouse away from her skin to get his hand under it.

'How old are you?' he asked softly in her ear.

'I'm sixteen,' Esther lied.

'You got short arms for sixteen.'

'I'm a girl not a monkey.'

'Manny told me you only fourteen. He want to warn me.'

'Manny don't know anything, only my mother knows our ages.'

'He knows the age of every horse on the course.'

'My mum says he can remember their birthdays, but not his own children's.'

'You going to the carnival dance?'

'I don't know, I might have something better to do.'

'No one have better to do on carnival night. It's constant jamming in seventy-six.'

'I'll see,' Esther said, knowing that her mother had already told her she couldn't go to any dance, even though she and Manny were going.

'You too young, eh?'

'Look, this thing comes right to my fingers.'

'Caterpillar have to get used to being a butterfly,' Jojo said.

'You too cheeky.'

'I like your cheeks too.'

'Tcha, stop your nonsense, man,' Esther said in her most grown-up voice. She was afraid now that the rest of them had seen them in some intimate talk, and she turned round to face him. His expression was sullen. She'd expected him to be smiling. He wasn't. He was flaring the nylon out with his hands and frowning with dissatisfaction at the effect.

'It'll need two inches off, both ends. I'll have to work tonight, all night.'

'It'll take you half an hour.'

'You know nothing, Cata,' he said.

Esther hated the new nickname. His tone said that she had let him down. Not because her arms were not long enough, but somehow she didn't seem to fit his expectation of her. She hadn't fitted perfectly into his creation. Suddenly she had become to him a clothes dummy, stiff, an object to size up in inches. She saw him go back to the work bench and place the wings out flat on it and stare at them, thoughtfully. Esther noticed his long, thin fingers, the way they smoothed the nylon with pride in their handiwork.

Esther felt that she couldn't control all the thoughts and feelings that ran chaotically through her at that moment. His hands had radiated their warmth, even though they hadn't touched her stockinged thighs. When she had cast her glance down towards him, his eyes had seemed to say, 'Don't be scared, don't dig nothing, this ain't a skank, this is business.' It was only when she was back in her bed at home, trying to recall the sensation of the brush of his wrist against her hip bone, that she decided that the look in his eyes meant something more. It said, 'This ain't a skank, this is business,' but it also said that if she wanted to forget the business, there was a skank awaiting her.

On the night of the carnival dance, Mistress Waters put Esther to bed and went out with Manny. Esther stayed awake. The next day, the next morning, she'd be out playing mas. She couldn't sleep, she was restless. She heard Manny and her mum return in the early hours of the morning. She got out of bed and caught Manny on the stairs.

'Your Veronica win, she take it all, she the queen,' he said.

The next morning they drove to the mas camp. All the other mas players had assembled by the time they got there. Esther looked for Jojo but he wasn't in the retinue of young men and women who helped the band on with their costumes.

Veronica looked beautiful. Esther wondered whether she had kept her costume on through the night, preening herself. Her eyes were now painted and the whites of them looked out of the tapestry of colour. Assembling the float and the players was a massive feat, or so it seemed to Esther. On this day there were ten men fussing around Veronica. Two stood by to help her carry the weight of her fantastic headdress which stood three feet high and flowered like branches to the ground on either side. A young girl held the body of her flowing costume behind her.

The men in their steel band assembled themselves with a lot of fuss on the truck and there was some argument about whether the truck should precede the young dancers or follow it. There seemed to be hundreds of supporters and helpers milling around the camp, but when the show finally got on the road, order emerged from the confusion.

Jojo hadn't turned up. Esther realized that he wasn't just late; she had a feeling that he didn't want to be there. Claude and his friends were there, in jeans and sweat shirts with the word FANTASIA signed across them, obviously wanting to be identified as the creators of the band's visual splendours.

As the Fantasia of the Ethereal Air hit the road, the vision of its creators seemed to come alive, a still picture transformed to dance and laughter. There had to be music, there had to be the assembly of bodies in lines and circles, dancing in wave formation to the beat of the pans-men, the steady clacking of the two boys who got off the truck with pipes and sticks and stood among the dancers giving them the rhythm.

The float moved out of the side streets and on to Ladbroke Grove. Their band and its crowds were joined by others from different directions, all flowing into the mainstream. As they paused at street corners, Esther watched them approaching and felt the thrill of being part of a massive plan, part of a purpose working itself out. She decided to take a moment to leave her band and try and spot Carol and Josie dancing in theirs. She said that to herself and at the same time realized that her eyes were sifting through the crowds for Jojo. Why had he stayed away? His mates had helped her on with her costume. It fitted perfectly. The wings were lighter than she had thought and Jojo had painted extra stars on them the night before. There were more mas players than she had expected. It was the biggest, the most graceful, the most soulful, their masquerade was *it*.

In the centre, thrusting to the front in a slow and dignified dance, as though she were balancing herself within the circle of dancers, went Veronica, conscious of the gasps from the crowd.

She was the slowest mover in the group. Her wings didn't flap, they gently undulated, like the great branches of a proud tree. The feathers on her head waved to the blue

August sky, while all around her, like birds who sought her shelter, were the young ones, their bodies swaying to Soaky's encouragement.

For a while Manny walked next to Esther, who was all smiles. Mistress Waters, in a blue Sunday dress, clutching her handbag, her eyes glinting with pride, walked next to him.

Esther had never seen so many people gathered together in her life. The streets were human for the day. No cars, no commerce, it seemed to her, only people and their clamour … not only the music and the shouts of encouragement, but the arguments and the comments. Everyone seemed to Esther to have fallen under the spell of the performance. There were no spectators, there seemed to be no one who stood aloof.

There were so many white faces, so many thousands of black faces. As Esther danced, she kept her eye on Manny, on her mother, walking among the crowded throng on the pavement. She herself was in the charmed circle, the space made for those who had prepared, the respectful ten square feet of empty road that moved in the wake of the truck which looked now like a boat cutting through water, pushing ripples of the crowd to the side.

Still no Jojo. The procession wound its way under the railway arch of the Grove and turned down towards Portobello Road. To Esther it was unfamiliar territory, streets she didn't know, but in the whirl of the dance it seemed to her that they were streets she possessed. Dancing was like floating above the crowd and moving like a spaceship, and yet it was also like stamping the earth, pounding the road and making it yours with your footsteps. There were delays. The band halted, the truck stopped moving. Young men, some boys she recognized from Brixton, thousands she hadn't seen before, surged forward in long lines, like human chains, across the street, through the dance and through the crowd. When their own band stopped, Esther could hear what seemed like a hundred other sounds. She turned and saw there was another band just behind them, and the sounds of reggae and the resounding insistence of beating pan came over the rooftops and down the streets. People had established themselves at the windows of the houses, with chairs on the balconies; people sat on the walls of the terraces; people everywhere, some still moving to the beat of distant sounds … the forward and backward motion of the calypso walk.

There were brief moments when Esther forgot about Jojo, stopped looking for him, paused to absorb herself in the masquerade. But somehow she couldn't keep him out of her festive head. Her eyes would turn and look at each group of young men as they passed one way and then the other. He should have been there to see what he had helped to create. He should have been with the Fantasia to see her carry her costume and herself. Last night she had thought that she would be dancing for him. He would walk and 'chip' along with them, and she would show him that he shouldn't have called her 'Cata'; she was no caterpillar, no crawling, infant thing; she was a beauty and she could float and she felt high.

The band moved off again. Soaky walked back through it and tried to keep the dispersed players together in a tight arrangement. He looked worried and he frowned. Manny got hold of his arm as Soaky passed and asked if everything was all right.

Soaky grasped him by the shoulder.

'It's a fucking police carnival,' Esther heard him say.

It was then that she saw them. How could she have missed them? Smiling bobbies all round, in the crowd but apart from it. As they moved off, they were forced to stop once more by a blue police van furrowing through, a group of six policemen walking in front of it to make way for it in the defiant crowd. Officers passed from group to group with instructions. She saw coppers in pairs talking to each other, standing like lamp posts, part of the furniture of the streets. They leaned forward, bending their heads to lend their ears to people who asked them for directions. Esther forgot about them when their float moved on and Veronica climbed on to the back of the truck and sat down to take a rest, arranging her costume about her, facing the dancers from the back of their float.

Every twenty yards the float would stop, the players would be joined by bystanders and the steel band would rise to new heights of noisy performance. At the top of the 'bello', among a crowd of young men and women on a platform, Esther saw Jojo. He was wearing a red, green and gold tam and a black shirt and suede trousers. She had never seen him look so fancy before. Behind him and his companions on the wooden platform was a battery of loudspeaker boxes. She saw he was with some girls. They looked like rude girls to Esther.

She watched him and pretended not to be looking. Then he saw her. He was fifty yards away and a sea of people divided them. Esther knew he had seen the float, identified it and had spotted her. The next time she looked he was no longer on the platform. He had disappeared. She couldn't understand it. He had worked so hard. It would have been his day. In the days through the preparation of their mas, Esther had neglected the thought that he might have some other life, other friends. He had seemed so permanent in the camp. Every time she was there, he was. He seemed so respectful of Soaky, taking instructions from him, learning this and that about the designs, listening carefully when Soaky became all artistic and philosophic about the thing they were doing, and recalling the days in Trinidad when he had beat pan and danced and fought in the Caribbean sun.

So he had rude friends. So he could get out of his sweatshirt which said 'Harlem University' and his paint-smeared jeans and his grubby beret, and become the nifty youth-man of Brixton, his own masquerade.

Soon the day would be over and she would find Manny or he would find her and they would drive back and she would keep her costume and he would forget about the care he had taken over it; her mother would boast to Carol's mother about how Esther had been part of the 'boss' band that year, and the mas camp would revert to being a hollow wooden shell without the industry and the clamour, and she wouldn't see Jojo again. The thought pinched something inside her. Esther didn't want to dance any more. She was suddenly thirsty and dry and her eyes didn't want to look up at the faces, but only down now at the patches of road in front.

She walked forward as they moved, and there he was again. He pushed through the crowd and walked confidently into the circle. Just behind him walked one of the girls. Esther had seen standing behind him on the platform. He must be coming to greet Soaky, to meet his friends. No, he was coming up to her. The girl behind him cast possessive eyes on him, her manner saying that he was walking too fast for her, pushing too far ahead through the difficult crowd. Jojo extended his arms.

'How go, how go, how go?' he said to the other dancers, who greeted him as he walked up.

'How you dancing, Cata?' he said to Esther and she pretended not to have heard him, and bent down to adjust the strap of her high-heeled shoe.

Esther watched him manoeuvre his way through the dancers, up to the float, to the side of the truck, impatiently, forcing the girl who was with him to follow. And then, a few yards further, as she lost sight of him, he appeared through the crowd again just by her side. He was smiling. He expected Esther to appreciate the dodge he had pulled on the girl who was following him. 'We are going to play all day, all night, all the carnival year round!'

Esther's eyes searched for the girl, but Jojo had lost her. If that was his girlfriend, why had he left her?

'I been looking for you all morning.'

'You knew where we started.'

'Yeah, yeah, but I had a lickle work.'

'I saw your work.'

Jojo grinned. The pans-men started beating again, a slow, lilting rhythm. Now that the lilt of the dance had gone out of her body, Esther felt low, felt abandoned by the spirit that made people jam together. She even felt a bit absurd. She had planned to say to him that she liked the new stars he'd put on the costume, she was grateful for the best costume amongst the young dancers, but all that slipped her mind. In front of that girl he had called her by that name again. That was his woman; she was only 'Cata'.

Esther blinked to push back the liquid which seemed to seep into her lower eyelids. She pushed past Jojo, who was walking backwards now, facing her. She made for the edge of the crowd to push her way through it.

'What go on?' he shouted after her.

His hand was on her shoulder and she turned to look full in his face.

'I'm very thirsty, I've been dancing hours, I need a drink.'

'Claude will get you a drink,' he said, but she was already pushing her way through the crowd.

Behind it there was an edge of pavement along which she could walk. People stared at her as she walked in her costume along the shop fronts, against the grain of the movement.

Esther turned down a side street, not quite knowing where she was going, and as she turned the corner, she moved her head ever so slightly to see if Jojo was following her. That would be the test. Did he care at all for her? His mocking and his sarcasm; she was sure that there was more feeling for her in him than that. She couldn't see him. She began to run now, down a clear street. She turned down another one. Here the crowd was thinner, but clusters of boys and girls stood in the middle of it, like teams of players in a field before a game.

At the next street corner there were three police cars and farther down the street a blue van full of policemen.

Esther saw a crowd of people outside what looked like a restaurant, a table set out in front of it under an awning, selling Cokes and other drinks. She headed for it. Then she remembered she had no money. There was no pocket in her costume in which she could keep any. She paused in front of the stall.

'What you doing away from your troupe?' an old black man said, coming up to her.

'I came for a drink, a Coke,' Esther said. 'I've danced all through and I tired now.'

'Shouldn't get tired, carnival go on forever,' the man said and he pranced on his old haunches. Then he put his arm in a grandfatherly way on her shoulders and said, 'Coke no good for yuh, rot your teeth, you want to keep them sharp, little daughter.' Esther laughed.

'Come in here' the old man said, 'the mas must have its dues, come for a drink, nuh?' He motioned her with him into the restaurant.

It was crowded with black men and a few women. The man pushed his way authoritatively through the crowd and took Esther to the counter at the far end.

'I'm exhausted now. You don't notice when you're dancing, but it's so hot.'

'Now you notice, it's right, it's right,' the old man said and cleared a bench for her and made her sit down. It was then Esther noticed that her feet ached and she was glad of the rest, and glad of the tall iced glass of pineapple juice that the old man placed before her.

He asked Esther her name, he said he knew Soaky, he said he knew it was the best band in town and said he was going to wear a sailor suit but his wife gave it away because she said he was too old to make a fool of himself. Esther said he was not too old and the man said he agreed that you were never too old.

'All are fit,' he said, 'you are never too old for each other,' and he cast a glance from his wrinkled but laughing eyes. Sometimes you're too young, Esther thought. That was probably why Jojo didn't take her seriously. That's why he'd asked Manny her age. Until then he'd made her feel so much older than she was, made her forget her impatience to grow up.

The dark shade of the restaurant was suddenly open to daylight. In the doorway stood a group of policemen. The officer asked that nobody move. The crowd pushed against the tables as the heavy men in blue moved through them and went down the stairs to the basement. As soon as the coppers had passed, the restaurant emptied. The old man went with a bunch, following the policemen down to the basement. Esther was almost alone. The people had drained out into the streets. She could hear a clamour in the road outside. She rushed out. She must get back to the mas; she must at least get back to the shelter of the swarms and crowds.

As she stepped out of the door, she took in the scene. Two lines of policemen had formed a cordon and were moving slowly down the road with dustbin lids held in front of them. Behind them a policeman in an armoured car was looking over the phalanx at the crowd of black youth who were hurling bottles and cans and anything that came to hand. From the other end of the street, behind the throng of youth came six more police cars, their sirens going, and squads of blue uniforms wedged into the crowds.

Esther was going back into the doorway, when the line of policemen charged with savage shouts. Some of the youth in the throng turned to run and others stood their ground, hurling abuse. Still the barrage of tins came at the police line. There were bottles smashing all over the street and people screaming. Hysteria. Esther felt the panic grip her stomach. Then she saw Jojo. One of the policemen at the end of the line had grabbed him and was grappling with him. The policeman kept calling to the others for help but none of them approached that scuffle because they had their hands full. The lines of confrontation broke into hand-to-hand fights. Esther felt a rush of blood behind her ears which told her she was beyond being afraid.

She rushed forward. The policeman had his arm around Jojo's throat and Jojo's legs were attempting to get round the policeman's to trip him. Together they looked like a tripod that was whirling, unbalanced. Esther didn't notice any of the other fighters. She threw herself blindly at the policeman's arm and tugged at it. She didn't know what she was doing. She opened her mouth and sank her teeth into the arm, wild to get through the thick blue fabric. The policeman shouted, but wouldn't loosen his grip and Esther glimpsed Jojo's grin beneath his grimace of suffocation.

Esther lifted her mouth and screamed at the copper and pounded her fists on his side.

Jojo seemed to be wrenching his neck loose from the lock.

'Behind,' he shouted, and Esther felt a hand grab her by the bicep and firmly fling her away from the scuffle. Two policemen had come up behind her. She stumbled on her heels, flung ten feet into the confused roadway. She got to her feet and her instinct was to rush back into the fight. As soon as she'd gathered her vision, she saw that Jojo had been subdued. He was on his knees with two policemen wrenching both his arms backwards. And yet he was smiling.

'Don't come,' he shouted at Esther and he grinned broadly. 'Take off, butterfly! Go on ... spread it ... We free!'

TRIP TRAP

1.

Herald

'In India they'll be having Dussehra now,' my dad says, just to pass the time like.

'What's that?' Kenny goes. He likes listening to my dad's stories about his village and that.

'It is one festival for machines.'

'Don't get it.'

'You dress up the machines with garland and flowers and everything. Make the god of machines happy. Even pets. I used to have one bicycle in the house and at Dussehra we dressed it up.'

'Dressed the bloomin' bicycle?' Kenny goes. 'That's bloody loopy. On our puppy's birthday my sister dressed the mong up in dad's T-shirt. Bleeder crapped in it.'

'If you look after tools, they will look after you,' my dad says. I know he's about to start, so I says I want to go round to the games section again.

'Stylish,' Kenny goes. It's his word.

That was the first night we went up to the biggest industrial exhibition in London. There's cars, machines, hoovers that walk round on their own, all sorts of gear and the computers and the games. We got in for nothing, 'cause my dad had a job there as a security guard. Three nights we went there and Kenny and I stuck in the games section. My dad was a bit nervous like because he didn't want the other guards to think he was taking liberties.

My dad thought that since Kenny and I was always messing around with chemistry sets and electronic kits and that, we'd like to check out all the gear at the exhibition. It was holidays so my mum and Kenny's mum didn't say nothing – well they didn't say much.

My dad had to sit in this cabin with white plastic walls. It had a smart fire alarm panel, a sort of map of the whole place and it could tell you the temperature in any part of the exhibition and if there was a fire like it would flash and the automatic control would come on and put the fire out. Dad was told that he didn't have to do nothing, it would see to itself. He just had to press buttons to set off the alarm and call the fire engines in case something didn't work right.

The first night we just fiddled with the position finders. They were the best thing there and everyone who came to see the exhibition could borrow one. Like a wristwatch, it had a small TV screen which would tell you where you were when you pressed a button and a picture of the nearest exit would flash on your wrist. Neat. But, nah, that wasn't the best thing. There was this computer in the games section called Herald. It was made to tell stories. It starts when you stand in front of it and a weird voice comes out, soft, like someone trying to hypnotize you. It introduces itself to you, 'cause it knows you're there and then you can introduce yourself back and it gets to know you.

Shall I tell you one of my stories? It's about a boy called Dipak. He came to this great exhibition. No? You don't want that one? Oliver Twist? A Christmas Carol? Romeo and Juliet. Wimpy stories? Slackness. Explain that word please.

It was great. It would rearrange words like they ought to be. First time I couldn't think of nothing, so I said, 'All right, LAMB, LITTLE, HAD, MARY, A. That's it.' So I says to it, pressing the rearrange button, 'Straighten that out, headbanger.'

And the computer goes: 'That's it. Mary had an all right little lamb.'

'Not an all right lamb, you div,' I says.

So he goes, 'Mary didn't have an all right little lamb.' Stroppy kid.

I called Kenny. He was on this Deadly Aquarium machine what you stood in like a tunnel and the sharks and monsters came at you out of the seaweed and from behind the rocks. They looked like real ones and you had buttons to shoot them down and it looked like actual blood come out of them when you harpooned the monsters. He likes stuff like that, Kenny. He got sixty quid last Christmas from his uncles and big brothers and on my life he spent every last penny on the blinkin' Space Invaders machines.

'Come here,' I goes. 'If you let it watch you it will tell you all sorts of thing about what it sees.'

Kenny has jeans and a red-and-yellow scarf. He smiles and his beautiful white teeth flash in an endearing expression …

'I think it fancies you,' I goes.

'Get away,' he goes and wants to get back to the Deadlies but I'd already taught Herald some slackness so I switch on the recent memory and Herald starts up in this soupy voice: 'Kenny is a flash c---'

'Takes one to know one,' Kenny goes. 'Wally machine. You're a flash c---'

What you should do is tell it a whole story or just give it jumbled-up things and it would sort them into a kind of story. I messed about with it all night. The things the people who made it had fed into it were boring. All history stories and that.

This is the story of the great fire that overtook the first exhibition of industry in London in the eighteenth century. Many stories were told about that fire. Some people believed that God was angry because the exhibition was a boast. Human beings were showing off …

It could natter on. We fetched my dad and got him to tell Herald one of his stories. We had a job getting him out of the cabin and up to the games section 'cause he was scared that they'd give him the sack if he left the fire panel thing. But in the end he came and he thought it was smart too. When we played it back it started pretending it was my dad talking.

It was in my village in India in my father's time. There was flood after the rains came and the water covered all the fields and houses. Just like the water spreads, the rumours used to spread. When I was a boy there was a superstition in the village that a creature called the crow woman was going about at night. Stupid people thought that the crow woman had the body of a crow and the head of a woman with long black hair and frightening black teeth. It would come at night and call out to a person in a voice which they would recognize. It would shout 'help' or 'emergency' and you would think it was your friend or your brother and if you answered or went outside it would get you.

'You want to rub that story out,' Kenny says. 'This place is weird enough without the Herald johnny coming with ghost stories.'

'You can't,' I says, 'Herald learns as he goes. It can't forget.'

'Tomorrow when the public come in, some geezer's going to get a shock if it repeats your dad's stories. They'll know we've been getting at the machines.'

'I think it changes the stories. Just learns new words off of us.'

So my dad says he wants to get back to the cabin and he doesn't know how to operate the position finder gizmo, so Kenny says he'll show him and I go off to find the loo on my TV dial. That's on the second night.

One person can know only so many stories. Everything that happens can be retold. With one keyboard you make an endless number of tunes. There are only two hundred and eighty seven basic plots. The queen dies, then the king dies. Those are facts. The king dies and the queen dies of heartache, that's a story. Programme X2115938K.

'So what happens if you just read it the whole dictionary. If it's so smart, it can tell all the stories, all the books ever wrote.'

'Yeah, we'll try it tomorrow.'

'You'll do writers out of a job.'

'That's good. *I* wouldn't mind a machine doing my work for me.'

'You know the tune that's on top of the charts. I heard this geezer on telly who said a computer wrote it and he's got thousands of other top tunes out of it.'

The lights in this place are automatic. They come on in front of you as you walk and switch off once you pass. When I come out of the bog now, this was on the third day, right, I get this kind of sweetish smell like you get off some shirts when the iron's too hot. And when I got on to the escalator to the upper level it wasn't working. I looked at my position reckoner and the red dot was leading me up to the household section. The lights were coming on all right, and it looked kind of misty on top. When I got up, my eyes began stinging and I felt like my breathing was getting rough. It was smoke in the corner and suddenly like in clouds. So I turned and ran down the escalator. There was smoke coming down it too, like a stream following me. I thought about what dad had said about the automatic fire business and I ran to the other escalator. It was no use shouting, though, 'cause the other security guards wouldn't have heard me as dad said they'd be up the office playing cards. I was frightened, I'll give you that. I was tapping the position reckoner to see which way out, but the smoke was getting thick down in the basement level now. Then there was a sound like a giant walking on twigs and a kind of whistling.

When he found himself in a small clearing in the basement he took a deep breath of fresh air. He could see the wax dummies in the basement operating machines by the green and red lights of the panels they were working. Dad and Kenny must still be in the games section. Inside that Deadly Aquarium you wouldn't know of any danger outside. Now the smoke was as thick as a quilt. The lights of the panels began to look hazy, like traffic signals in a fog. He looked up the escalator and he thought the smoke seemed to have cleared. It must be the automatic fire control.

The panic in him drained away and he began thinking clearly. Like the clear head you get after the first flash of red in a fight. You know what you have to do. At the top of the escalator there was a lit arch. The smoke had cleared and Dipak went through the arch into a passage between plastic walls, made out of bits which were locked together like a puzzle. He thought he knew where he was. There was a room at the end of the passage. He rushed towards it. Now he was sure that he hadn't been there before, he was thinking of the same sort of passage on another level.

He entered the room. It was like no other in the exhibition. It was just ordinary with a pool table and a fruit machine and a kitchen unit with a kettle and an urn on top and coffee cups on the three wooden tables. There were people there. Six of them. It must be the security guards' rest room. They were weird people.

'There's a fire. The place is on fire,' Dipak said. 'Mr Patel. There's a fire.'

'Don't panic, child, there's no fire. This place is fully automated, proof against all disasters.' This was an old lady in a boiler suit.

'There's human error, it might be some bloody short circuit – these fumblers …' A young man with a punk haircut and green streaks in his hair said, but he was interrupted by a youngish lady.

'What kind of work do you do, boy?'

'I'm at school,' Dipak said.

'Keeps you out of mischief,' the young woman said.

'The fire ...' Dipak began.

'Explain to the boy,' the old lady said.

No one volunteered to explain so the old woman started off herself.

'Shall we let him hang about? He could probably give us some good advice. Look, boy ...'

'You're too soft on humans,' the young lady said to the old one. 'Tell him to clear off.'

'I'm sorry, I didn't ...' Dipak said.

'No, relax,' the big man said. 'Industria might have something there. If we can't settle it amongst ourselves, the boy could give us some indication, some hints.'

'What hints?' Dipak asked.

'We don't normally ask advice from mere human beings,' the old lady said, 'but let me introduce you.'

She walked up to Dipak and with one hand gently placed on his shoulder she went round the room.

'That's Telos, Nukita, Mobo, Calcus, Balencia and I'm Industria. Some of the others couldn't come. Telos, Nukita and Calcus, as you can see, are young ones, inexperienced, I would say ...'

'Now hang about,' Telos said.

'Let her finish, for God's sake, you are always interrupting,' said Mobo, the middle-aged fat man.

'I was saying, boy,' the old lady said, 'we are having a conference.'

'Who are you? You're not the guards?' Dipak asked.

'It should become obvious,' the old lady said. 'I'm

Industria, I've lived for thousands of years. I'm a goddess.'

'Get away,' Dipak said.

'I can't,' the old lady said, 'not till we've resolved this question. You see Telos and Calcus are fed up with you lot. Telos is the god of things seen and things unseen at a distance. Calcus is the god of all logic. Calcus has this plan to do away with all human beings. He says they're not much use to us any more.'

'That's not what I said,' Calcus interrupted, 'but if you take all things to their logical end, we don't need thinking animals any more. The machines can do it.'

'We need working hands,' Industria said.

'Not even those, soon,' said the lady called Balencia. 'If you'd just get on with what you have to do, we can soon have machines making machines. No nonsense, no people to go on strike, make mistakes, demand training, spoil everything with their filth.'

'Can't you see it?' Telos said. 'A million television sets with life as it should be going on and no one to watch and think and misunderstand. Twenty-four hours a day, every day of the year, everywhere.'

'You see, they want to get rid of you,' Industria said with a sigh. 'I don't think we're ready for that yet.'

'I'm ready,' Nukita said. 'Just give me the word.'

'We're doing a good job of killing them off slowly. Do you know how many people died in car and rail and plane accidents last year?'

'We don't want to know. I don't like all this relish of death. It's all right on the screen, but in real life ... it's unnecessary,' Telos said.

'There's no relish left in it mate,' Mobo said. 'When the *Titanic* sank, slowly, people panicking, jumping overboard. Oh dear, yes, those were the days.'

'You're distracting the boy,' Industria said. 'The question we want to ask you, boy, is do you want to do any work when you ... well when you finish school and training or whatever. What do the rest of you think, your generation?'

'Kenny don't want to do no work,' Dipak said. 'He'd be quite happy watching telly and playing space invaders and new games and that.'

'You see?' Telos said. 'They've become unnecessary. Balencia will be quite happy if there are vegetables and plants and trees and non-interfering animals around. We wipe out, Nukita wipes out the human race and we pretend it hasn't happened by keeping the telly sets on. If we get lonely for human beings, we watch old films.'

'There'll be no one to drive around and ...' Mobo started.

'That's not much to lose,' Telos interrupted. 'You can get together and make rockets which fly on their own, plant computers and machines all over the universe, on other planets, on other stars. These humans are locked in by time. They don't think big. Time doesn't matter to us, we can take millions of years to populate the other planets.'

'That's the most convincing argument I've heard this evening,' Industria said, 'but I don't think we can start immediately. We have to get human beings to set it all up for us and then, bang, we can get rid of them.'

'How much time do you need?' Balencia asked.

'We're more than halfway there,' Industria replied. 'Soon everything will be automatic and then people will just become a nuisance to each other and to us. Say ten years?'

'Too long. Much too long,' Nukita said. She was thoughtful. 'I'll wait two or three years. You'll just have to get them to work faster at it.'

'That's difficult,' said Calcus. 'They might catch on to what we're up to and act up. After all, so far they've created the machines and the machines have created us. If they get wind of the master plan, they can screw it up. If they smash all the nuclear weapons, for instance, just as an example, mind you, no offence intended, Nukita would cease to exist.'

'Well they won't get wind of the plan. They're not that smart. The only way is if the boy goes out and tells them.'

And the company turned to Dipak, but he was gone.

He looked back when he'd got down the escalator. He could hear footsteps behind him. His heart was thumping and he could feel it in his throat.

'Dippy,' he heard Kenny's voice.

'Down here,' Dipak shouted.

The smoke was unbearable. He had to shut his eyes which stung worse than soap getting in them. He felt for the walls and walked towards Kenny's voice.

He felt he was about to faint because he was holding his breath and his lungs were bursting. He didn't know if he actually fainted, but he knew that he felt strong arms lifting him up. They've got hold of me, he thought, I'll be the first to go.

'I've got him,' he heard a voice shout. He thought it was Telos's voice.

Outside, Dipak opened his stinging eyes. Kenny's face and the face of two firemen were bent over him and the world spun round like he'd just come off a whirligig. Only at the hospital, when they were being tipped into their beds, did Dipak notice that his arms and legs were burnt and his clothes were torn.

'My dad …'

'Not a scratch. He's all right,' the doctor said. 'Hold still.'

That evening the television cameras and the reporters crowded into the ward and talked to Kenny and Dipak. The doctor asked Dipak and Kenny first and let them in two at a time. One of the reporters had punk hair and a green streak in it and the lady with him reminded Dipak of someone. She was an oldish lady with a wise face.

'It's a miracle how you boys got out alive,' she said. 'Will you answer one or two questions?'

'What's happened to the games section?' Kenny asked.

'The whole exhibition was gutted,' the lady replied.

'The Deadly Aquarium?' Kenny asked.

'It's was just plastic. Finished. Funnily enough the only thing the fire didn't destroy was this computer storytelling machine called Herald. When we went in, to report on the damage, it was still babbling on.'

⌒

2.

The Bride

SO YOU'RE STILL TEACHING DOWN at the old school then? Yeah, thanks, I will take a pew this time. Can I say straight up, I'm sorry about last time I came round. Three years almost to the day. Been in Morocco and Spain and India, on the trail like. I'm not rich any more. Three years old these Levis, brought the shirt out there. Have a butchers through the window, no E-Type Jag. Shanks Pony and London Transport, guv.

Must admit, came round that time to come flash, show off, because I remembered something you used to say to us kids in school. What was it? You goes, 'You don't get rich by working hard, you get rich by making other people work hard.' And I come to tell you that I'd done it on my own. Wasn't true and I knew you wouldn't like it, but I thought I'd make you feel a mug, because you had a prejudice, like, you were always going on at us about how we was working class and would never be loaded.

Nah, not any more. What happened to it? That's what I've come to tell you chief. It's a funny story, but on my mother's life it's true. How did I get poor again? You started it. When? That day three years ago when you showed me that newspaper cutting. You had me well sussed.

Where to start? With Jaswinder, of course. You won't believe this, but it was her made me rich. She gave it me, laid it on me, I'll tell you how in a minute, hang on.

Begin with when I left school. I got these dead beat jobs. Thirty, maybe forty sheets a week. Hey, you remember that half-caste geezer what used to teach us basketball? I met him in a pub down Kew, about two years after I left school. He always pulled tasty birds, didn't he? He comes up to me and he says, 'How you doing, Les?'

'Tony,' I says.

'Yeah, Tony,' he says. Now you wouldn't have made that kind of mistake, would you, as a teacher I mean.

'I'm on the sales side of IPC and Thompson Newspaper groups, ' I said.

Very impressed he was, till John, remember John, he was with me, says, 'Yeah, Tone's got a paper pitch down Camberwell. *Evening Standard*.'

That's what I was doing till I met Carrots, remember her. Turned snobbish, goes with this art school teacher guy, but I got talking to her and her old man was trying to flog jewellery what he made himself and he's looking for lads to fifty-fifty with him for taking it round. So I left the pitch and started in for him.

'Venetian chain, box chain, Boston chain, one, two three four silly money in the store.' Diddled him too. Used to go down with his stuff to the Portobello and up the Lock and that kind of market with pseuds buying junk from con artists like me. Struck it rich with Arabs outside hotels who'd give you a twenty and ask you to keep the change for a bracelet worth eighty pence. Not bad.

Slap the box, lay out the bracelets, necklaces, rings, stuff that I got from this geezer and then from my uncle, knocked-off clobber, genuine articles that were as hot as grandma's fresh-fried chips, souvenirs that had been on police five, the lot, you name it.

I was making a small whack and having a good time, until I began to realize that being happy is looking hard for what you want, not having what you've got, if you get my meaning. You do? First one. Most people don't. You may have been my English teacher, but you never got me to say things like I meant them, but you were watching me, all those years, so you know what I'm on about.

At least you know who I'm on about. Dead right, guv. I

carried a picture of her tattooed on my brain. I thought of her a lot, Jaswinder. What do you expect. I grew up with them Pakis. What else can a poor boy from Southall do? I'll admit it, I was brought up to think white. My dad's a racialist. Still, yeah. When I was young, I mean little, he was always going on about moving because the picture houses had been taken over by Indian films.

It was daft, right, because my old man never saw no films, just watched telly, and my mum used to tell him that the last thing he'd seen was when he took her to *Gone with the Wind*. And that would start him off.

I knew you used to think I was right prejudiced, but that's because you only joined our school in the fourth year and I was a skin at the time. We had to do it. I'll tell you, I don't think you teachers knew what was going on down there. We was in the minority, right, and it was our country, but you wouldn't allow us to say it. And the Asian kids, they came flash. 'Sikhs rule' and all this, and there was so many of them you only opened your mouth if you wanted a taste of knuckle sandwich.

I fancied her something rotten, guv, but in the junior years I didn't let on, because it would have shamed me up bad, guy. But then it started. You think them Asian kids are straight, but what they used to get up to mate was nobody's business. Just like kids anywhere, I suppose. But not Jaswinder. Her dad was mad strict, wouldn't even allow her on to the Broadway. I knew that on Saturdays she'd go shopping with her mum, so I used to hang about the café, the only white café going, and check her on her way there and she'd be shy or cautious or whatever, and hardly say hello when she was with her mum and give you a total blank if she was with her dad, a big turbanned geezer. Enough to frighten the daylights out of you mate. Nah? Out of me, then.

The only Asian kid who hung around with us whites after school was Junaid. He was your favourite, wasn't he? Couldn't do nothing wrong. Butter wouldn't melt in his mouth, except he only got margarine down at the social services where he lived. He only got around with us because he was brought up in care all his life and had to go in with the tough nuts, mostly white kids, down the orphan shop. I know that all of you felt sorry for him, poor kid, teacher's pet. He was nasty, you know. How? I'll tell you. The lads didn't feel sorry for him. He had more money any day of the week than all of us put together, because them kids down that centre used to pull jobs. Remember when they cleaned out the electronics shop by going in through the roof and cutting the plasterboard ceiling? That was Junaid and his mates. He didn't care that it was an Asian shop, he just came all that Asian shit because he wanted sympathy. And he got it too.

Cry? I could have laughed. The girls, they'd wet their pillows for him, if not their knickers. 'Aw poor fellow, poor Junaid,' the super-runt of Battersea Dogs' Home. Dr Barnardo was invented for him. On my life, he lived on it. And they brought him presents and food and that. He loved it. You could have exchanged my mum, dad and the budgie for half the clobber he got off his tear-jerking violins trip.

All right, that doesn't mean he was nasty, but I didn't much care for him because I knew, from the fourth year up, there was something going on between him and Jaswinder.

And I'd made a fool of myself. On parents' day I followed her around when she was with her dad and chose all the subjects for my fourth year options that she'd chosen. Ended up doing needlework and cookery and bloody Geography. And Junaid done the same, but you teachers thought he done that to be with the girls because he was a bit like that, wasn't he? Not a poof, but kind of soft and wimpish.

When I asked her, at the end of the fifth year whether she was going to the school disco, she replied that her dad was too strict. But she made it in the end and she was necking with Junaid in a dark corner till I couldn't stand it no more. You remember that night? When I smashed up the turntable and you lot had to throw me out? You never reckoned what that was all about, did you? A fair idea? Yeah, well, it was because she was kissing him in the corner and I couldn't take it no more, so I shouted, 'Lights out at the orphanage at eight, homeless mongrels should pack it in.'

He came for me and I smashed him one before going for the record he had requested three times. It was Jaswinder stopped him and came between us, and then I was thrown out. I knew I shouldn't have said that but a red haze sort of knocked me out, come in front of my eyes, I couldn't stop myself. She came after me into the winter night.

'Why did you say that to him?' she goes. 'You're not like that Tony.'

'You know why,' I goes.

'You're like my brother,' she goes.

'Some bleedin' brother, I know what you think of whites.'

'Not me,' she goes, 'I'm not ...'

'Then how come you turn up when you said you wasn't coming when I ask you?'

'My dad, he kicked up a fuss, he wouldn't let me go and I've just come, I don't know what he'll do when he finds out ...'

I tell you what I did then. I grabbed hold of her and I kissed her. I felt her pulling away and she says, 'Tony, please,' like something out of a stupid love story and I was thinking it's my only chance, the only time I'd be with her in the dark.

Anyway her dad come round, you remember it? Takes her away and abuses all the teachers.

I went home with my head singing. It was worth it. And as I walked home by the yellow sulphur light, I was that dopey with that kiss I thought 'Romeo, Romeo, where art thou,' or whatever it was. Pure Shakespeare, guy. But next morning I knew it was no good. Straight up, have you ever loved somebody, I mean fancied her, that it made you sick?

After that I used to hang about netball practice when she was there, the only boy in the gym and I used to hold her purse and her bracelets and that because she didn't want to leave them in the changing room with all the thieving kids about.

I know you knew him well, but I knew him too, guv, Junaid. Remember the time you was reading his story to the class? You'd set us some wimpy English essay on ourselves or something and hardly none of us had done it and Junaid turns up with twenty-eight pages, guy. 'My Life of Sorrow', he'd called it and even before you took it in for homework, he was handing it round and all the girls were asking him if it was all true and softness like that. She had the bloody nerve to give it to me to read.

'Junaid's story of his life. It should be on telly. You read it, Tony, maybe you'll understand how lonely he is.

I took it off her. Garbage it was. So I told the lads that you'd probably be so chuffed to get some homework back for a change that you'd read it to the class and I filled in them bits. Two pages of filth. Gave it back to Jaswinder, keeping a straight face. Yeah, you remember that, but you sussed it. When she handed it to you, you read it straight, pornography and all, till Junaid couldn't stand it no longer and he thought Jaswinder had done the trick on him or at least helped with it and he grabbed the sheets from you and tore them up in front of the class and all the kids were splitting themselves. Junaid came in the next morning blind drunk. He was pretending he'd tried to commit suicide. Bloody joke. And you and Jaswinder fell for it and walked him up and down the corridor to get him over it.

I felt bad, to tell you the truth. But I wished he'd done it. Funny, isn't it?

And he wasn't really Indian, Junaid. He was brought up like us by the social workers and that. He didn't know about their customs like. You remember the next time he began this suicide lark? You don't know what happened. I'll tell you.

I wrote Jaswinder a letter. I finally got up the courage and did it. It was stupid, confessing, but I'd tried everything else. That's why I used to come flash about getting rich one day because I reckoned girls fancy fellers who say they're going to reach the top, any top, and I wasn't good at nothing else. I waited for a reply, but she never sent me one. Instead she came to me at break time with her mates and she tied this bracelet round my wrist. It was kind of blue and red and gold tinsel, like one of them cloth badges you wear if you support a team. And she gives me a kiss on the cheek.

Then her mate says to me, 'It's an Indian custom.'

'What's it mean?'

'You got to give her a present first, anything, a bar of Kit Kat.'

'Yeah,' I said. 'I'll get J something.'

I got her a teddy bear and I put my gold sovereign round its neck.

'Now tell me,' I said to her and my heart was thumping.

'It means you're my brother now and you've sworn to protect me.'

'Yeah?' I goes. 'How?'

'Like a brother. I really like you Tony, but not in that way, you understand?'

I understood, guv. The hollow in my stomach understood. She wants me out of the running. I was a fool to think I could beat it.

But that evening I got up to mischief. I was down the café wearing this damn bracelet and Junaid turned up with his thieving mates and they were all taking the mick out of my bracelet, so I told them it was an old Indian custom and Jaswinder had given it me.

'What's it mean?' Junaid said, going serious.

'What's an engagement ring mean, mate?'

He never said nothing but that was when they found him.

She had to explain to him after they'd pumped his stomach out at the hospital and again her dad came and dragged her away and threatened Junaid for messing with his daughter. Right Indian film stuff.

Then school was over and I thought I'd never see her again because I moved down Stockwell with my brother-in-law. I was wrong, of course. I saw her.

It must have been a Thursday night, 22nd of December. I was down an antique market in North London and the lads had lit lamps on their stalls. I didn't have a stall, but I traded off of a lamp of a geezer what sold old records and that. It couldn't have been late, because it was dark early then and when the market packed up at seven or so, we used to go off for a drink. The barrows would be left out in the cold and the fog with their lamps on till the market boys came and dismantled them. I went off to the pub like I'd done enough trade in the last half-hour and the market began to empty. When I finished boozing I noticed the strap for my box was missing, so I thought I'd go back and get it.

The street was littered with cardboard boxes and junk. It was foggy. Dark too. I found my strap and was lacing it to my box when I looked down the street and I thought I saw in the fog a figure of a woman standing by a lit barrow.

'Hello,' I says to myself, rubbing my hands for cold, 'some punter's trading late.'

There was no mistaking it. It was a lit barrow piled with showcases and that and I shifted my head and couldn't see no one attending it. But there was this wrapped figure standing in front of it.

'One of the lads left his stuff,' I thought, and helpful as ever, I went down the street.

There was no one about and this figure, a lady, turns to me. I thought I'd say something cheeky, like, so I wandered up. I couldn't recall this particular barrow and I would have 'cause it was in my trade, it was loaded with cases of jewellery, a naked bulb hanging from the wire, plugged in to the junction box on the lamp post. The light was throwing shadows on her face, so I had to get close up before I saw it was Jaswinder. She was wearing a cape and when she turned to me I saw she was in a saree.

'Stap me dead, 'I said. 'What're you doing here?'

'Looking,' she said. 'Where's the man who sells these things?'

'Is that all you've got to say to me?'

'I'm in a hurry,' she goes.

Then I see she has tears rolling down her cheeks. 'I was to be married today, it's my wedding night,' she goes.

'Don't spring that on me,' I said. 'What's the matter? You don't look happy about it.'

'Same old story, Tony,' she said. 'My father arranged a marriage with my neighbour's cousin.'

'So why are you alone on a night like this?'

'Alone?' she goes. 'There's you.'

'Don't talk stupid. What're you doing about it? I thought you'd end up with Junaid.'

'He's dead,' she said and she began to howl.

'*What?*'

'And now I'm to be married to a stranger.'

'When?'

'But I can't find the jewellery I'd like to wear. He's very particular. He is a jeweller and a goldsmith himself.'

'Why are you doing it?' I said. I was pleading with her. 'This is bloody England. You don t have to marry this geezer. Your dad can't tell you what to do.'

'No, he can't,' she said, 'but I'm to meet my bridegroom and I must have something to wear. Going without jewellery is a kind of pitiable nakedness.'

'Didn't your father get you none? How did you end up here?'

'You were here,' she said. 'I tied a bracelet on your arm three years ago.'

'I know,' I said. 'And I promised. I'll do anything you want, just name it, and if I can do it, you can have it.'

'It's England and I can do what I like,' she said and her tears seemed to disappear and she laughed.

I don't know whether I was stoned or what, but it was weird. I was thinking to myself that something funny was going on.

'I've got some jewellery. I'm in the trade.' I said. 'Jaswinder, it's just trinkets, but you can have it if that's all you want.'

'It's all I want,' she said. 'An anklet of gold, a bride should have a golden anklet.'

'That's tall,' I said. 'Not my order,' but I opened up my case and dragged out the most expensive chains and that I had. 'Maybe not perfect, but it's something. Fourteen carat.'

'You were always a bit gone on me, weren't you Tony?'

'Not a bit,' I said. 'A lot.'

'I knew you'd help,' she said. 'Goodbye, Tony.'

'Wait a bit,' I said, 'let me get you a cab. I'll go with you, see you're all right.'

But she didn't wait. She didn't even raise a hand. She just turned and walked into the fog, out of the circle of light. I left my case and I ran shouting after her. I thought she must have dodged down one of the lanes but she wasn't nowhere.

I didn't go home that night. I went to the park, climbed over the railings and walked on the frozen grass and threw stones at the ice on the ponds. I didn't do any selling for the next few days. Just hung about.

Then the next time I was down the same market where I'd met her, I left my box and went for a cup of tea with one of the barrow boys. Left the box on Frank's barrow where he said he'd keep a beady on it for me. Come back and open it to set my stuff out on a mat. Started shouting already, 'See what I've got here, darling,' all the palaver. Jesus creepers, it caught me short that. You can't guess it. I opened the box and my stuff had gone. Instead there was real hard clobber in it. I couldn't believe my eyes. Solid gold bracelets, earrings with diamonds, rings with sapphires, the metal work done like old designs.

Hullo, I thought, Frank's having a giggle on the side. I looked up at him but he was doing his own trade, poker face.

'Oi, Frank,' I said. 'What's this lark then.'

He didn't know what I was on about. I was that shocked, bits of me froze.

'What're you complaining about,' Frank said, cool and wiley.

I figures to myself, he must be trying to pin something

on me, he and his mates, fit me up like. So I said I'm taking the lot down the bullring, hand the lot in and report my trinkets stolen.

'It's your life,' he said, not concerned. He swore nobody had touched that box, though he'd been selling steady and had a crowd.

I took the stuff round to my uncle's who knows gold when he tastes it. He thought they were knocked off too and they looked hot, more carrots than a rabbit's freezer, and the bill would be round eventually, but maybe I could get a reward for the lot. They were too big to keep, he said, so I went down the cop shop and I couldn't tell them the true story so I said I found them. They took my particulars, but the sergeant there he looked at me as though I'd made a run from Cain Hill.

Three months later the cops tell me, the stuff's clean. No reports of it stolen or missing. I could have it.

I couldn't believe it. My uncle takes it down with me to this collector geezer he knows and he says give him three days, he'll trace it. I come back to him and he says it's Indian jewellery, but no mark on it to show who owned it or made it. That's what set me thinking. She done it. Jaswinder. I remembered every word she said that night and it was a jeweller she was being married off to. And I was sure because in the collection there was one of them brother – sister bracelets, only this time in gold and with stones, not a cloth one. But how had she got them to me? I went back to Frank and asked him if there was any Indians hovering about his stall that day.

'Yeah,' he says, 'Tonto came by. How do you expect me to remember?'

'All right,' I said. 'No skin off my nose, I'm bleedin' rich.'

That's how, guv, that's the story. Flogged all the stuff except the bracelet to this collector and set up shop with my uncle. That's where I got the Jag and the suit you saw me in last time. Spent a year like that. Travelled a bit – Majorca, Costa, you know the circuit. Then I thought I'd find her. I'd go to India and find her even though I was scared. Putting an end to a mystery is always a bit scary for me, I don't know about you. But I made up my mind and I drove down to Southall to check her family. I'd hung about that street a thousand times, walking down past the corner in the evenings when I was still at school, hoping she'd come out. I rung the bell and this Indian lady, oldish come out. I asked for Jaswinder. I said I knew she was in India, but could I have her address?

'No Jaswinder,' she says and shakes her head. I couldn't get her to understand what I was after.

Then this little girl in the garden, an Indian girl, comes up and says, 'They've gone. That family's gone. My daddy knows them,' she says. 'That lady doesn't speak English and neither does my mum.'

'Where's your daddy?'

'Office,' she says.

That's when I come round to you. I thought maybe you'd know. And you told me Jaswinder was dead.

I couldn't live with that. I still had the bracelet. I raced back that evening to Southall and waited for the neighbour, the little girl's father, to get home and I stepped up to him out of my Jag.

I asked him about Jaswinder.

'Whole family gone. One year ago. Gone back to India.'

He didn't look as though he wanted to talk. I had to tell him some lie. I was thinking on my feet.

'You've got to tell me what you know about it,' I said. 'Listen, please, I was …' I don't know what came into me, I said, 'I was her husband.'

'Husband?' He looked stunned. 'But she was loving Muslim boy.'

'Which Muslim boy? Junaid? I know all about him. Look, we got secretly married but then she went off with this boy she knew from school. I left her alone, I don't know what happened to her then.'

He took me inside his house. He was wondering about me, but he was willing to talk after I told him that.

He brought out this newspaper cutting from the local paper. He'd kept it. 'Sad business,' he said. 'Her father was forcing her. Very rich man but too old, he found for her. Jeweller in India. Father was very broken when she kill herself with the Muslim boy.'

I looked at the date of the newspaper cutting. It was the 22nd of December. The story was dated the 21st.

'This can't be possible,' I said. 'I saw her on the 22nd.'

'You went to funeral? Very sad,' he said.

'Look, I wasn't her husband or anything, I was just lying to make you tell me about it,' I confessed.

'What does it matter,' he said. 'But you shouldn't tell these kind of lies. You look a decent gentleman.'

'I was her brother,' I said, almost to myself and I could see I confused him even more. But I couldn't spend my time sorting him out, if you know what I mean.

I got back home and looked for the bracelet. I kept it in my drawer with my underwear and that. It was gone.

As I went home, I was sure it would still be there, but it wasn't. She would have left me that, I thought, but then I hadn't acted like a brother, I'd been a bit frantic like, I'd blown it.

~

3.

Homework

THE FOLLOWING STORY IS FOR dictionary practice.

With these worksheets take a dictionary home from your form cupboard.

The most difficult words in the story are underlined. For each of these words find the correct dictionary meaning and write it in pencil above the word. Then try and read the sentence in which the words occur and try and understand the whole sentence.

Tomorrow in class there will be a spelling test on some of these hard words.

Many civilizations known to man have <u>perished.</u> Under the city of Jerusalem, for instance, there are buried nine cities. Each of these nine cities belong to an age of the human <u>habitation</u> that <u>flourished</u> at one time on that spot. We can learn about the way the people behind these civilizations lived by examining the things they left behind. At different times in human history, people spoke and wrote different languages. <u>Archaeologists</u> have set themselves the task of <u>deciphering</u> these languages, many of which are related to the languages we speak and write today. Some of them are dead languages: which means that no living person knows them. Yet we have some knowledge of how those people lived by <u>codifying</u> their scripts.

Some civilizations, however, have left no trace except that of legend. The ancient Greeks believed, for instance, that there was a civilization that had been swept under the sea by natural <u>factors</u> and had continued underwater. They called this civilization Atlantis. Modern scientists have tried to find out when and where Atlantis existed, but without much convincing success.

It is easy, however, to imagine a civilization of the past which had no written script. The people may and will have talked to each other but will have left no record of their language in written form. Today we feel that the absence of a written script would be a tragedy. We would not, without writing, be able to <u>transmit</u> everything we know to people who come after us. Our sciences would then become <u>extinct</u>.

Imagine, for instance, that twenty-five years from the day you read this story, the world is destroyed. It may be destroyed by human <u>agency</u>, such as nuclear warfare, or it may be destroyed, as perhaps was Atlantis, by natural disaster, or in fact by a combination of both.

According to one American scientist, that is not such a <u>remote</u> possibility. He says that our factories are putting out smoke in such density that our planet is under sentence of death. His <u>hypothesis</u> is that the hot smoke rises and forms a layer above the earth. This layer destroys another layer of gas that protects the earth from the full heat of the sun's rays. If the full heat of the sun were to play on the snows of the Arctic and the Antarctic, it would melt the snows of those regions. The melted snow would flow into the oceans, and the flood that would <u>ensue</u> would make the flood of Noah look like a puddle in summer rain.

After this flood there will be silence. None of the countries and land that we know will survive, except perhaps the highest peaks in the world. Today those high peaks, such as Mount Everest in the Himalayas in India, are cold and snowbound.

If you imagine a world after this terrible flood, the snow on these peaks will melt. The valleys around them will be flooded and will become part of the oceans and only people who make their way up to the high peaks will survive. They will live on a group of rugged islands surrounded by the sea.

Do these people believe in Gods? Of course they don't. They know very little of what we knew, because they could carry very little of the objects of their <u>environment</u> when they escaped the flood. They are people who have foreseen the destruction of our world. Do they want to build the same world, believe in the same things again? Of course they don't. They want to forget about the science and the industry and the factories and the manufacture that have brought about the world's watery end. So with them they take only the essentials that nature will <u>foster</u>. They take seeds and trees and a few animals.

Their civilization grows. When the trees mature and yield wood, they build boats. They make tools by striking stone against stone. Their children and their children's children believe in the sunrise and the sunset and the heat of the day and the fresh of the night and are never told about the humans that went before them.

They learn instead the arts of the <u>primitive</u> <u>maritime</u> peoples. How to skin a fish and use its bones as hooks, how to tell the regular ebb and flow of the tides. Through generations they are happy and <u>oblivious</u> of the twentieth century and our factories and our wars and our cities and our schools and our jails and our jealousies.

Amongst one generation of these new people of Everest is a boy called Zal. He goes fishing with his father and the other men of the tribe. He knows all about hooks and bait. Several times in his life he has been dragged off one of the little crafts of the islanders to fight with some monster of the deep, stab it and swim to the surface to ask the assistance of his companions in bringing up his kill from the sea. He swims like a creature with webbed feet, one that can hold its breath underwater for several minutes. He has learnt this skill from childhood, because it is necessary to jump overboard and lure the <u>carnivorous</u> fish by using yourself as human bait.

One day the men in the boat throw Zal over the side and wait for him to rise like a bubble in a bottle of pop. He waves to them, several feet away now, and they throw out the line weighted with a stone that sinks faster than the fish he has killed. It is Zal's task to tangle the body of the fish in this line. It is a great big fish, of a kind that Zal has never seen before. A magnificent catch.

They trail the fish and row back to the island once Zal is safely back in the boat. They pull it up on the beach and require six men to drag the hauling line.

It is Zal's fish. He has the first knife cut. He slits the belly of the fish, cuts its fins and breaks its jaw with a stone. He wants to keep its teeth as souvenirs. The people of his village gather round as he explores the <u>anatomy</u> of this unknown variety of sea monster. Its blood is as wine-red and watery as that of any other fish, but in its belly it contains a strange sack. It is black and thick like the skin of an animal. Zal examines this strange stomach, like an inner stomach. Down one side it has little teeth clamped together which shine like the sun on the waters at dawn. Hard teeth they are too.

'This one has two stomachs and teeth inside its belly too,' Zal says.

'Divide the meat,' says one of the elders impatiently. 'You can keep the inner teeth as a souvenir too.'

'I've seen such a monster before,' says another elder. 'My grandfather captured one. He said they live forever unless a hunter catches them. That one had no second stomach like this.'

Zal cuts the rest of the innards of the fish and offers the body to the village. The custom of their village is that they take equal shares of the day's catch.

Then an elder steps forward and says, 'Let me have a look at that inner stomach. The fish may be poisonous.'

Zal hands the rectangular sack over to the elder.

'Never seen anything like it. I would be very careful about eating the flesh of this one. I feel Zal has caught a poisonous monster. Look at this stomach lining, it's rough and black and oily.'

There is a murmur amongst the gathering. A woman speaks out saying that she will not risk taking a piece of Zal's fish home. Others agree.

The gathering moves on to the smaller catches of the day. Zal sits on the ground by his catch. This is unfortunate. It is the biggest fish he has ever caught. Now the people of the village will just leave it there, lying gutted and open like a collapsed tent, its skin resting on the sand, its eye bulgy and misty.

Zal looks down the broken jaw of his prize. The fish has a huge gullet and the inside of its mouth is ribbed like the bottom of a boat, its palate like the white and green and shady red smoothness of some seashells. He gazes long into the fish's mouth. He doesn't notice that one of the elders has come back and is looking over his shoulder. He turns round when he feels a presence.

'The biggest fish you ever caught, isn't it?' the old man says.

'I don't think it's poisonous,' Zal replies.

'Dorjay says it is an inner stomach, but it's some kind of octopus that the fish has swallowed, I think,' the old man says, and he asks Zal to pass him the black sack. The old man examines it for a few seconds and then throws it on the sand next to the guts of the fish.

'I'm sorry for you boy, but you mustn't be disappointed. You have long to live. There will be other fish and much appreciation.'

'I suppose so,' Zal says.

When the old man has gone, Zal turns to the black sack, the inner stomach, or the creature the fish has swallowed whole. He picks it up and looks at its teeth. It is made of a substance he has never before seen in a sea creature. He thinks he'll pry open the teeth. He wrenches at them and pulls them apart, but they are shut tight. He runs his finger along the ridge of the teeth and then he notices that at the end of the row of teeth is a loose one. He pulls at that and as if by magic it unlocks the row of teeth, two by two, right down the row, and the mouth of the creature lies gaping in front of him. This thing is more fascinating than the fish itself, he thinks.

Then it occurs to him that this isn't another fish creature, it is some sort of trap, some sort of net without holes. He has often wondered whether fish have any intelligence as humans do and whether they build traps for each other. But he has always put the thought aside. The shape and form of this trap seems to confirm it. He looks into the sack. If this is a creature, it has no head, no gullet, no stomach. Inside, Zal can see something. The inner skin of the trap is dry and in the bottom of it there is a creature. An animal the trap has caught, Zal thinks. He turns the trap upside down and with a jerk upsets the strange animal on to the sands.

It falls, as though on its mouth, and its jaw stretches open, biting the sands. Zal keeps his distance, wary lest the animal still be alive. He walks closer to it. It is curious, this process of <u>intussusception</u> by which the black creature has <u>ingested</u> this one and the fish has swallowed the black creature.

The creature on the sand lies still, making no move to crunch the sand or crawl away. It looks dangerous. It has a rectangular body, no fins or feet and it looks to Zal as though it is nothing but an open jaw. Zal bends over and puts his head on the sand and looks at the creature. It seems to him to have no teeth but has a thousand white tongues which stretch from its spine. It is like a flat clam. An enormous one, but dead.

Zal wants to make sure. He takes his knife from his belt and pokes the creature. It doesn't move. Now he feels bold and grasps it by its spine and lifts it up. The shell and the tongues flap shut. As Zal lifts it, six or eight of the tongues fall out and strew themselves on the sand. Zal puts the creature down and examines these. They are funny. They are smooth and white and rectangular and have a million black markings on each, markings in regular rows such as Zal has never seen.

Now he picks up the creature and flips its tongues. He runs his thumb along the edges of the tongues. They are as smooth as any skin and they too have markings on them, row upon row. The rows of black markings remind Zal of the regularity of a wheat field, or the rows of tiny fish they lay out all over the beach to dry in the sun.

It is miraculous. On every tongue there are two columns of little black markings. There is an <u>intrinsic</u> design to this creature like nothing he's ever seen. Zal tries to dig his nails into the creature's shell which he now sees is a very dark blue, nearly black, like the ocean on some dark night.

For a few hours he sits looking at the signs on the tongues of this unknown creature. Then he buries it in the sand further up the beach. He will keep his discovery a secret. But how will he find the place where he's buried it again? An idea strikes Zal. He will mark the spot with little signs. He takes his knife out and makes several signs on the spot in the sand. Then he notices that he hasn't buried the loose tongues with the creature. He picks those up. He can bend them easily. He rolls them up, as leaves of the banana tree are rolled around fish to cook them, and he takes them home.

At home he examines the signs and markings on the loose tongues. They may not be tongues, Zal thinks, they may be smaller creatures of the same sort that the bigger creature with the shell swallowed.

Zal keeps his secret and every day when he is on his own he goes and digs up the creature and gazes at it. Then slowly it comes to him. On the tongues of the creature are signs such as he himself made on the sands. The regularity of the signs amazes him. There are darker ones and lighter ones, and soon Zal discovers that they are repeated every so often in one row. It reminds him of the knots that fishermen make in thousands to <u>constitute</u> a net.

It is when he is sitting on the beach with other boys and girls of his age one day and being instructed by the elders in the songs of their forefathers, that a thought strikes Zal like a thunderclap. The thought goes round and round in his head. The boy sitting next to him nudges him.

'Zal.'

He looks up at the elder.

'I asked you a question, Zal.'

'Yes, sir. What was it? I was thinking.'

'Daydreaming, child.'

The other children laugh.

'I asked you to repeat the song you memorized yesterday.'

'Yes, sir.'

'Well?'

'I've forgotten, sir.'

'Forgotten? I don't understand, Zal. Do you forget to eat or to take your share from the day's catch?'

'Once I go away, I forget,' Zal says.

'That's no crime. But couldn't you have asked someone else? The words are easy. It's part of your homework.'

'There must be some other way of remembering, sir,' Zal says.

'What other way, child, except constant repetition and passing on what you know so that knowledge may be shared.'

'Well, sir, I was just thinking. If we had a sign for all the words we speak, one different sign for each word, then we could ...'

'Yes,' says the elder, 'and if we had a name for every fish that lived in the sea we wouldn't have to catch them, we could call them out by shouting their names.'

The rest of the children laugh.

'No fishing trips for you for a week,' the elder says. 'Now listen while I ask someone else to repeat yesterday's song. Your mind is not on your work. Or it's like a net with larger holes than the fish.'

For a week Zal isn't allowed on to the boats. He feels hurt by the punishment. He makes sure he has learnt the song by doing exactly as he had suggested to the elder. While sitting on the sands, he makes little signs for the words of the song and the next day he comes back and finds the signs in the same order.

The more Zal thinks about it, the more he is convinced. Every day he looks at his captive creature of the tongues. If by some chance, he thinks, by some design, the signs on the flat tongues of the creature have been arranged there by some creature like himself capable of making signs in the sand and each of the signs … But no, it is too improbable to even <u>contemplate</u>.

Though he puts this thought out of his head, Zal still examines the signs in the creature for their regularity. In a few months' time he finds, by carefully tracing the signs on the sand next to him as he leafs through the tongues, that there are about seventy signs. Thick ones and thin ones, slanting ones and vertical ones. Soon Zal is able to copy on the sands whole rows of the signs. But he can never know what they mean. When he copies the signs in the sand with his knife, or carves them on palm leaves, he notices that he can never get them as straight and neat as the rows of signs on the creature's tongues. No matter how hard he tries, all he can make are squiggly imitations.

That's why they couldn't have been made by creatures like me, Zal thinks. They are too regular. And yet on the loose tongues that he found, eight of them, there are squiggly signs like Zal's. They are inscribed above other signs with dark black lines under them. Slowly Zal learns to imitate all the signs on these loose tongues. They begin like this:

Homework

The following story is for dictionary practice.

With these worksheets take a dictionary home from your form cupboard.

The most difficult words in the story are underlined. For

And then at the end, on the blank part of the tongue, are these squiggly signs, definite indications that someone like Zal could have made them: *Stuff this, this is boring.*

~

4.

The Mandarin Exam

I DID IT FOR A bet. A mate of mine bet me fifty quid, his life savings. I didn't have fifty quid so I had to win. The games hall was full of desks and we had to take our shoes off when we filed in because the teachers were afraid that we'd damage the wooden floor. *They* kept their shoes on. There were a hundred and fifty of us in our year and the desks were separated into one row for the O levels and five rows for the CSEs. When the headmaster came in and took his stopwatch from his pocket, and after the teachers had handed out the paper and stuff, it all became quiet. It was English.

I knew the stories backwards. I was good at this sort of stuff and who knows, I might have done stacks of questions, but I had to win the fifty quid and there wasn't any point passing CSE English anyway. When they all got their heads down and started writing, I pulled out my snuffbox in which I kept a bit of smoke and took some RIZLA papers from my pocket and started licking them and putting them together. I must confess, I felt a bit nervous doing it, because the teachers were watching like cats surveying mice.

The English teacher comes past my desk and leans over and he says, 'What're you doing?'

'Marking time,' I says. I knew he'd understand what I was talking about.

He takes the RIZLA pack from out my hand and scoops up the snuffbox after having a look into it and then walks off.

'Get on with it,' he says.

Now I deliberately hadn't brought a pen. I picked up the question paper. I was dying to look at it, see if it was easy and what I was missing, but I sat back and tore it up. Back he rushes.

'What the hell do you think you're doing, Spiggy?'

'Tearing up the paper, sir.'

'I see. Have you got nerves or something?'

'Steel nerves,' I says.

'Don't you want to do the paper?'

'What do you reckon, pal?'

'All right,' he says and without argument goes and gets the headmaster. Now the rest of the kids are looking round. The word has spread, see, that I'm going to make my protest.

Headmaster comes up. Kids look round and there's a murmur in the hall.

'Get on with your work,' he says in a voice raised to room temperature, then he leans over and asks me if I'd like to go outside and have a quick smoke under supervision and he'd see that I could come back and do the exam in five minutes.

'I don't want to do the exam, sir, I told Mr Scott and he didn't want to know.'

'I see.' He rubs his jaw.

I thought he'd do his nut, but he just strolls about near my desk.

'No use disturbing the rest,' he says. 'You can go.'

'Thank you, sir,' I says.

'But you disappoint me lad,' he says.

'My principles,' I says.

'Does your dad know?'

'He'll soon know.'

The rest of the kids are getting on with it.

The head asks me to go to his office to explain.

I go to his office and he says, 'What do you want to do in life? You know you can't stay on in the sixth form without qualifications.'

'I want to be a writer,' I says.

'So you tear up your English paper?'

'That's right.'

'Not logical, is it?'

'More logical than what they teach us, sir.' I wanted to remain polite. He asks me to sit down and say what I mean.

'You didn't like the books you did?'

'Yeah, I liked them.'

'Then what was the problem? Didn't you know any of it?'

'I don't know, didn't look, did I?'

'Curious,' he says, biting his lip and looking like he was thinking of something else.

'But it's all lies. We was doing this story, sir, it's called "The Loneliness of the Long Distance Runner".'

'Yes, I know it.'

'In this story there's this kid what goes to borstal for thievin' and his dad's dead and he hates the people what keep the laws, like, teachers and borstal governors and that and he only finds his freedom when he's allowed to go on cross-country runs.'

'And so?'

'He's like me, except I can't run, got asthma.'

'So you identified with him. His name's Smith in the story, isn't it?'

'Yes, sir. He has to run this race for his borstal and the posh geezers are watching and he loses the race because he don't want to win for them.'

'I remember,' he says. 'And what's that got to do with your not doing the exam?'

'I'm a bit like that, sir. I got a good imagination, I reckon, and I don't see the point in doing the exam. See, Mr Scott, he loves that story, right, but if any of the kids in his class behaves like that he don't like it.'

'I get the point.'

'Exams and that, where's it going to get you? A job? I don't want a job. I just want the loot that goes with it. Nah! I don't want that trip, it's a trap.'

'A bit of a philosopher are you, Spiggy?'

'Yes,' I said, 'cause I didn't know what else to say. 'Can I go, sir?'

'Sure, when you please,' he says, rotating in his swivel chair. 'But I'd like to tell you something before you do. Do you have the time? I don't suppose we'll see you again.'

'I'll drop in,' I says.

'It may help you with your writing.'

'I want to write the truth,' I says.

'We all do. But I want to tell you a story.'

'Is it true?'

'Maybe.'

'Go on then, sir. I like stories.'

I don't know to this day why he took the time but this is what he told me.

'It's set in China,' he begins, and he walks about the room and he looks out of the window. 'We must have failed with you. This story, though, is about a man who failed exams, except that I don't know the ending.'

'What's the good of it, then?' I asks.

'You might find some good in it. It starts in the thirteenth century AD. In China they used to call all their high officials mandarins and before you became a full mandarin, you had to do this examination. It was a most curious exam. It didn't have any time limit and it didn't have any subject as such. The person doing the exam was allowed to come and go from the exam hall and take as long as he liked. There was only one question on the paper. You know what it was? It was always the same. It said, "Write what you know." Now that wouldn't suit you, would it? That's right. You wouldn't know where to start.

'One fellow, a young man much like you, but of his time, you understand, did the exam, as far as the records show, four times. The first time he took the exam was when he was sixteen, then when he was thirty-two, the third time when he was sixty-four and the last time when he was a hundred and twenty-eight years old. They lived to a ripe old age in those days.

'His name was Wu Fan'tsi. And he had a very severe tutor. The first time he was asked write all you know, he started by looking and listening. He described the pen he was writing with in great detail, the grain and shade of the paper on which he wrote, the room, the shape of his hand as it wrote. That took him eight months. Then he wandered out and described the sky as it changed from day to day, the birds that flew past, the trees and the inclination and shape of every leaf on the trees he could see. He noted the sounds that came to him, the feel of the gravel underfoot and the exact pitch of every syllable that made up the speech of the people with whom he talked. That took him eight years.

'He was determined to pass that exam, no matter how long it took him. He began describing the features of his tutor and the other disciples who came now and then into the examination room where he sat. He filled book after book with his answer. He was now thirty-one years old.

'Surfaces. That's all you really know, he thought, and he scribed on from day to day, week to week and year to year. Hard work? I should have thought so. And then at thirty-two, he gave it up and he went to his tutor and his tutor asked him if he had completed the exam. He had to admit he hadn't. Every new moment would give him new impressions to describe. His tutor smiled. Wu Fan'tsi said he was dissatisfied with the years he had spent describing things. Things were dead and surfaces were always changing. He'd now dedicate himself to describing changes. Yes, he agreed he had failed.

'Straightaway he started his second attempt on the exam. He abandoned the books he had filled and started afresh, describing his life. One book was dedicated to the days he had spent and how he had grown. The next book was dedicated to the history of China and all the known world. At that time they thought, perhaps they still do, that China was the centre of the world, and he wrote for sixteen years on the story of the Middle Kingdom – which is what they used to call their country.

'He wouldn't read any books, but he'd wander about between writing, sometimes absenting himself from the exam room for years. He got married and had children. He didn't need to work, because the mandarins all came from families whose wants were supplied. He just observed and he wrote. He has left us a very boring but very long history of China, of his own life, of the lives of the other people he came into contact with. More than that, he wrote a geography, a rather brief one, about the changes of season and vegetation in the country he knew.

'By the time he thought he'd finished, he was fifty-nine years old and he was dissatisfied with the answer he had written. So he went to his tutor and he said, "Great keeper of our ancestor's secrets, I want leave to try this examination again. I have given my life to knowing how things are and how things change," but it doesn't seem a wise course to me any more.'

'His tutor smiled.

'Wu Fan'tsi knew he had failed for the second time and began to wander in the world once more. When he was sixty-four years old, he came back. He said he was ready to try the exam again. His tutor gave him leave.

'Wu Fan'tsi sat down at the exam desk and he called for paper.

'"This time," he announced, "I'm going to write all I know and my knowledge is in the dreams of human beings."

'He was an old man now and new disciples had come in to listen to him. They had all heard of Wu Fan'tsi the exam-doer, and they thought to themselves that his brain had gone soft with all the years he had spent writing. But still he wrote.

'This time he wrote of things to come. He wrote, and this is quite remarkable, for the thirteenth century at least, that China would no longer be the Middle Kingdom, that all human beings would be equal one day, that they would fly and go to the stars and that they would put wanting things and being hungry and thirsty and diseased behind them. He dreamt some dreams and made some prophecies that few people have made to this day.

'And after twelve years of writing, he took the thesis to his tutor.

'"Dreams and visions," his tutor said. "And what will become of the gods and of the souls of our ancestors?"

'The two old men confronted each other and looked in each other's eyes. The young disciples gathered around.

'"That I don't know, so I didn't write it," said Wu Fan'tsi.

'"Dreams," the old tutor said and he was a wise one. And he proceeded in front of the crowd to ask Wu Fan'tsi a hundred questions to which he could only reply that he didn't know. Then his tutor smiled and Wu Fan'tsi kowtowed, which means bowed very low with his head on the ground and he took his book of predictions and dreams and he said to his tutor, "I have not said what I know, the question is not answered."

'It was the third time he had taken the exam. He was now seventy-six years old. He had twenty children. His wife had died, his children were grown up and had gone into the world thinking their father a dreamer and had ten children each of their own and some of those children had children.

'"I have taken the least time to write the answer on this third attempt," said Wu Fan'tsi as he left his tutor, "because life is long and prophecy is short and dreams come to an end when you wake."

'Wu Fan'tsi went away. He travelled beyond China and lived, it is said, with the Indian people and then with the Arabian people and then with the white people beyond the bounds of the civilized world. He listened to their stories. He found out that the Middle Kingdom was not the middle kingdom at all and that no one knew where the edge of the earth lay. He found out that the Indians worshipped gods with many heads and many arms and finally worshipped no gods at all, that it was all play. He found out that the Arabs had a god whom they were willing to kill for, that white people burned witches at the stake and believed in a god who was born of a woman who had never known a man.

'After many years he came back to the world of his people. Then he walked in China and worked as a farmer, as a lifter of loads, as a beggar man with a rice bowl, as a soldier sent to far lands, even though he was over a hundred years old, as a buyer and seller of things in the marketplace, as a burier of sacred eggs, as an attender of graves, as a singer who earns his living when he doesn't have a sore throat, as a catcher of fish, as a builder of houses, and many other things. Then he thought he was ready. He came back to his tutor.

'"I am ready to do the exam again."

'"You don't have the years left in you," his tutor said, "and I don't have the years left in me to see that you have reached wisdom."

'"It won't take long," Wu Fan'tsi said. "I need but a few seconds."

'The tutor called for paper and a pen and Wu Fan'tsi bowed his head to the ground again and then he wrote just one word, the answer to the question: "Write all you know."

'The tutor took the paper from his hand and he didn't smile when he read the word. He embraced Wu Fan'tsi. That was the fourth time he had taken the exam and this time he had passed.'

'No one knows what happened to him after that. That's the story. Do you like it?'

The head went to the cabinet and took out two glasses and a bottle of sherry. I reckon he was more pleased having told his story than I was hearing it.

'It's all right,' I said, 'but what's it got to do with me not doing my exam?'

'It's a true story,' he said and poured out the sherry. 'I presume you drink.'

'I don't reckon it is,' I said. 'True, I mean,' and I looked beyond the specs into the head's eyes.

'Why do you think that?'

'Because, well, I mean, he could have lived that long, but people don't act like that, they don't do what stories say they do.'

'That might be so, but they teach you something, stories.'

'Don't know,' I said.

'Think about it when you're a hundred and twenty-eight years old,' he says.

'I know what the word is already. What he wrote on the piece of paper and passed the exam, but if I'd written that, I'd have failed.'

'That's life,' said the headmaster.

5.

Batty and Winifred

MR BATT FIRST NOTICED THAT something was very wrong when, on the last double period of a Thursday afternoon, he was in the process of teaching what they called 'English' to his pet hate of a fourth-year class. Thursday afternoons were difficult for any teacher and with this particular class called 4I, even Monday morning would have been no picnic for Mr Batt for whom most mornings were beginning to be trials and most afternoons torture. It hadn't always been like this. He had taught for twenty-two years. Times had changed.

At first, in a still vivid past of order with 'incidents' (oh dear, yes, there were incidents!), St. Paul's and All Angels had been a quiet school in a subdued though working-class area of Camberwell, London. Then the Teddy boys began to come. At least that's what Mr Batt and the newspapers called them. He was young then, could cope, could hope. They called themselves rockers. They wore forbidding leather jackets, studded belts (clearly not for the purpose of holding their trousers up) and navvies' boots. His little joke was that the place should now be called Screw-balls and Hell's Angels. No one laughed at his little joke. He was an advanced one in the staffroom at the time. There were none of these young biddies out of illiterate colleges, flaunting their legs in miniskirts and unfairly taxing the boys' fantasies and good manners. Outrageous. And now they were all around him in diaphanous dresses, in T-shirts and jeans, women who wore no brassieres and knew no etiquette.

Then the blacks came. Mr Batt tried hard to keep abreast of the times. He even read the books that his girlish head of department thrust upon him when she took over from kindly Mrs Snoraway; strange books on Jamaican dialect, the religions of the coloured children and books which seemed to say that the little animals must be allowed to do as they pleased. And still Mr Batt kept his end and humour up. He learnt from the children that the rough fellows with knotted unkempt hair, the sort that would have been clapped in leg irons if they had as much as dared to take one breath of free air in his native Hartlepool some thirty or maybe even twenty years ago, were known as Rastafari. His joke about 4I, innocently named after the year and the room in which they began each fresh day, was calling them Rasta-Four-I, Oh, they laughed the first time. There was a sprinkling of troublesome coloured among them and Mr Batt knew it made them feel acknowledged.

No use, oh no use at all, trying to drum through their reluctant heads the niceties of English, the language of Keats and Chaucer. What would they make of it through their pathetic clamour? But *she,* the head of department, *she* with the long sharp nose and rat-like eyes, *she* who fawned to the head and talked nonsense with the inspectors, *she* had approached him one day.

'Mr Batt, can I call you Harry, it's time the fourths learnt similes and metaphors. Don't call them that, tell them they are comparisons, that one thing is like another, they'll have fun with that …'

Grandmothers swallow their pride and suck eggs, thought Mr Batt. He'd stopped himself from replying that he knew about the English language and teaching it when she was shitting her nappies. But oh no, that wouldn't do. *She* was authority.

Mr Batt just smiled. *She* could tell him that. *She* could impress all the beardies and weirdies who called themselves English teachers, but she (and they) would never find the two hundred and sixty-three dictionaries that Mrs Snoraway had left in his charge. He had locked them away. She had asked for them, but Mr Batt had pretended he didn't know what *she* was talking about. The only way she could get them was to dig in his pockets, trouser pockets, and get the key. What did she want, similes, metaphors …

He tried. They wouldn't listen. So, as he often did nowadays, he stepped to the blackboard, took up a position with his head raised like an operatic soprano in full flow and launched. Oh they wouldn't understand it, not in a million years, but the person in the next class would hear his voice above theirs.

'Metaphor is the chief weapon of a poet. He flashes it like a sword. The rhythm of similarity, dancing through creation … the unseeing eye is forced in a flash, an epiphany, to see lovers as compasses, lives being turned out as lights and candles are, hearts being broken like bread …' It was no good. They could shout louder. Tracey and Sharon, God help them and their ugly names, were reading some trash in a duet. The coloured boy Homer was throwing spit darts at the ceiling. Johnson was drooling out of the window and the nasties were playing cards. What if *she* walked in? So he shouted. He gave up metaphor and then it happened.

The shouting trick usually worked. They would be silent for an instant and he would have to produce the next trick.

'Rasta-Four-I!' he shouted. And the class was hushed, but hullo? For a moment, a flash, Mr Batt saw grey and when his eyes cleared he could swear that all the children, all benighted thirty of them had coloured faces, negro faces and the bushy rag-doll black hair, the locks of those … these … people!

Blinking clears the sight, resets the mind. It did. It was gone. There was the coloured girl, Winifred, grinning cheekily at him from the front row. There were the boys, white as custard, playing cards. Thank Christ it had passed. And the girl Winifred…

Bad customer. The root of it. He had had to see the head about her the previous day. And she was grinning and her friends were grinning. This girl had broken … oh no, what she had done was write the most abject filth in her essays. At first he hadn't known if it was a new style that *she* perhaps would approve of, but when she did it again and again and concealed notes to him in her English folder, he had been forced to take action. Those words! Only when he was in the RAF had he allowed himself to say or think such words. She had cost him. Out of his mind. He must put her grinning, stupid face out of his mind.

Saved by the bell Mr Batt put his chalk into his Golden Virginia tin and walked stoopingly, carefully, to the staffroom. With never a begged pardon the animals rushed past him, brushed past him. Mr Batt found his favourite chair in the staffroom and sank in it. The colour went from his face. He brushed the few strands of hair that he placed with care to conceal his baldness on to the front of his head (what did these monstrous kids call him? They had a running developing joke: What would Batt be called if he went to Germany? Herr Batt, Ha, ha, ha! Why was Batt late? He went to a bald meeting. And, what does he do after school? He goes skate-balding. All half-baked puns), but he couldn't concentrate. A voice like the hum of a top, a yo-yo-yo-yo sound, kept speaking to him from inside his skull. Then *she* was upon him.

'You don't look too hot.'

'I'm cool,' he said and the wind swept through his sweater.

'Coffee?' and she was gone.

'Who let those kids into the bloody staffroom?' Mr Batt boomed. There were a few teachers who looked around and there were some pupils whom the dramawallahs had gathered round them, damn their souls. Strictly speaking, they were not allowed beyond the foyer, but who spoke strictly nowadays? He would have said 'gone to pot' if they hadn't changed the meaning of that too.

'Kids in the bloody staffroom,' he said again and opened his eyes to glare and they were there. Five kids: baby goats with legs splayed, gathered round the drama teacher and when he looked away, the tables and walls of the staffroom, running crimson and dripping, covered.

Oh my good Jesus. Mr Batt cupped his eyes with both palms. *She* was hovering above him again, with her foolish concern and her cup of coffee.

'You don't look at all well, Harry, like you've seen a ghost.'

'They are driving me batty,' said Mr Batt, hoping to humour her. It would pass. And he stretched a black, webbed, fretted wing, oily and veined, downed with piles of ugly hair to take the coffee cup. He was up on his feet wiping the stains off her skirt with his handkerchief. She stepped back as though she thought he was trying to feel her through his handkerchief and lifted the spilt mug.

'Sorry, awfully,' he said and he thought: It's what I saw, good god have pity, it's what I saw.

'Was it hairy?' she was asking. 'Four-I? Are they getting out of hand?'

Mr Batt sank back in his chair. She sat next to him mopping her skirt.

'You're not letting that Winifred business bother you, are you? I thought after our little chat ...'

'No,' said Mr Batt. How dare she? 'Some of these coloured kids can't swallow the poetry.'

She bit her bottom lip. She was going to be tactful in her reply. And Mr Batt saw the joke. This time he expected it. He saw the pupils in the corner again. Yes, they were kids, goaty and coloured every unthought colour of the rainbow, red, pink, violet, blue, indigo, and they were vomiting reams of it, chewed up words of poetry. And behold, he had to laugh.

'You're better,' she said.

He looked at her and it came back to him. Her long nose; it was as they said.

'Blooming Concorde,' Mr Batt said. And it came to pass that the supersonic plane looming out of her face from under the glare of her ratty eyes, began to sprout flowers. A touch of spring in a mechanical world.

'It's these silly words I use. You wouldn't call people coloured,' Mr Batt said.

'Oh, right,' she said. Stupid Concorde. Silly little bitch. She looked puzzled now. His voice had drawn the attention of the other teachers. 'One must have such respect for words,' he said. He stood up and walked out of the staffroom with his briefcase. Their eyes would stare, could stare. He knew they were recalling his shame.

It had started innocently enough. He was just doing his job. He had asked 4I to write an essay on themselves. They could write about their hobbies, their families ... all that. Winifred's essay was damnable cheek. It started off well enough, with her family and her pet dog and then it suddenly said: 'If you really want to know, you dream doll, I am fourteen and that's under age for what you want to do to me. School subjects? You darling wally, I don't like them, I only come to school to see you.'

Mr Batt scratched out those lines and he gave her two out of ten and he said nothing in class, just swallowed hard when he gave her folder back to her and she stood in front of him with her hip unbalanced and gum in her mouth. The next time it was worse. He had asked them to write about their chosen future.

Winifred wrote, 'I want to be your sexy doll. I have had it in fifty different ways with ten different men. I want it with you. All of those boys were only practice for you ...' And the essay went on to describe the ways in which she had had it. Mr Batt's glasses nearly fell off. His red pencil dropped. His breathing became thick as he read twice through this terrible, terrible filth. The bloody cheek of it. He read it six times before he remembered that the liver was in the oven. It was burnt. He went to bed hungry.

Winifred didn't give him any indication the next day. He had torn the pages out of her folder. He took no action. But he watched her. She was a comely wench. Coloured, with a cheekily protruding bottom on a lithe body that rose from tattered shoes through thin calves and athlete's thighs. And the broad mouth with the smile and eyes that laughed with it. Oh God, have mercy on me, a bachelor and a sinner, but that was in my RAF days. Must I be punished now?

The next time he took their folders in there were no answers from Winifred on the poem they had done, but a letter which said that she thought he was gorgeous (how they fail to choose their words) and that she wanted it, it, it. With him The letter said what they would do. She was carrying this too far, but Mr Batt carried the letter with him to the launderette. He read it again and again as his underwear rotated and sploshed. He said nothing. A third and a fourth letter arrived. They made dirty suggestions. Suggestions that Winifred meet him, Batt, after class and that they would go away in his free periods to the caretaker's shed where the spare desks were stored.

How could he ask her to stay after class and ask her how she meant all this? Oh, yes, she was beautiful, but she was young, so young to be so brazen and mind you, they came as bold as brass these days.

Still Mr Batt said nothing and did nothing and after class a succession of Winifred's friends came and asked him if he had liked the work they had written for him the previous day.

My job, my career, thought Mr Batt. He had heard of this kind of thing. He had read in the papers about teachers being dismissed for tampering. Tampering? A fourteen-year old girl and fifty-five year old man with a bald patch? Just a patch, yes, just a patch.

The next time he saw her he thought: 'How sweet and lovely dost thou make the shame, Which like a canker in the fragrant rose, Doth spot the beauty of thy budding name.' Shakespeare. Yes. That was his business. Not this girl. His business was language. I lie in bed, he thought and thrill over the metaphors of Keats and Swinburne. I have said it so often. I even told the English department meeting, the day they were carrying on with their nonsense about broken duplicating machines, that I couldn't be expected to care, I whose fingertips tremble as they turn a page, I to whom something unmistakeable happens in the forehead when I come to a revelation in a beautiful line ... The beardies and weirdies were embarrassed and *she* coughed and changed the subject.

She can't even express herself, Mr Batt thought, wrestling to put her out of his mind. And he took up his red pen and he gathered her letters and he corrected every sentence and marked it up for spelling mistakes. No grammar. No sentences at all, but something in her stumbling, fumbling words gave me cramp in the thigh. In the thigh? Mustn't we be exact? How am I moved by this nonsense? And he knew it by heart:

'Harry, lover, I want it 'cos mmmm I betcha, you use Brut aftershave.'

Pap. It was pap. Dangerous pap.

Mr Batt resolved to see the headmaster. Lay it before him. But not the letters. He couldn't show him those. He'd have a word. So in the morning, after his three Weetabix (Weeatbices should it be? Ha, ha) he checked to see that the letters were safely in the drawer in which he kept his carefully ironed shirts and set off for school. He made an appointment with the head and laid the truth, most of it, before him. This girl had conceived a passion for him. She had written, very poorly, to him. He had to consider his job. He didn't want her parents to find out that she was thinking and writing in this way. He didn't want a court case.

The head was understanding. He asked if he had told any other teachers. He asked if any of Winifred's friends knew.

Mr Batt waited around that evening and pretended that he wanted to consult the caretaker about keys until he saw Winifred enter the head's office. Then Winifred came out and went back in with her two friends. Then the secretary came out and called someone from the staffroom. *She* came out and two boys from 4I were called in and then another teacher, their form teacher, was summoned by the head.

And when ten of them were crammed into the head's study, Mr Batt thought he heard the laughter break out. It came down the corridors at him like an overfed animal, lazy and slobbering and yet jaunty. They laughed. Winifred's shrill laugh and the boys and the form teacher and then *she* laughed. It sounded to Batt as though they were holding their guts and rolling about the flecked carpet of the head's study.

Somewhere in his mind Mr Batt had told himself that he would wait for the interview to be over and then he would go up to Winifred and his eyes would tell her that he didn't mean to tell on her. That he hadn't shown the head the letters, he still had them. Reassure her. She would know it was impossible. And she would give him a glance as the lady in the Lyons Corner House had done in 1953, a glance that could have lasted hours. And his very eyes would tell her that three times fourteen was still less than fifty-five and that her mother – he'd seen her, at parents' evenings – she was young enough to be his daughter, and couldn't they just, perhaps …

But now the laughter was no mere lazy animal, it was a stampede. He was trampled underfoot and he ran to the staffroom for his briefcase. Too late. *She* came up. She glanced at him and below the window he could hear the boys and the girls from 4I, the ones who had been in the head's study.

'He's bloody mad, old baldy.'

'It was a flippin' joke, he shouldn't get his knickers in a twist.'

'Gawd, he didn't fall for it, he bloody went for it.'

And a penny dropped through a rusty slot. How betrayed, my Jesus. And looking out of the window he saw Winifred and her friends. They weren't laughing. He thought Winifred was blinking to hold back tears. Oh lord, what have I done? But the next morning he came back to school and carried on as normal and it was a Thursday and the staff were all laughing at him behind the palms of their hands, those women in their floppiness and those men in tight jeans with their explosives all contoured and showing.

They misunderstood him. He had gone to the head to complain about the lack of literacy and grammar amongst the fourth years. Of course he had mentioned Winifred. She was probably the worst. Bad morality, bad writing. It was all the same. So he said when *she* came up talking about 'some little affair with Winifred'.

That was the afternoon it began. He thought perhaps it would go away.

'Have you got the keys to the dictionary cupboard in your pocket?' she asked as he hurried to flee.

'Bats in my belfry, more like,' he said as he slammed the staffroom door and he heard the chimes and felt the flutter in his brain, the flapping of vile creatures which made his ears hum and his eyelids vibrate.

He saw her from a distance, beyond the school gates, at the bus stop he used.

'Mr Batt,' she began.

Have you been weeping, my angel, he thought. And he said aloud: 'The lily I condemned for thy hand,' and immediately the black hand was a sliver of white and still he walked on.

'I want to talk to you,' Winifred said.

'You're a bitch,' he said and his eyes saw red and through the red came the growl and the snarl and the bared teeth. But it might have been that it was a soft red tongue and a low switching tail, a dark nose nuzzling up to his fingers. He didn't know any more. No bus. He wouldn't wait. Mr Batt ran. Yes, he ran.

I must say nothing, he thought and he said nothing as he turned the key, panting, in his door. He said nothing as he switched on the news, nothing as he cooked supper, nothing as he picked the fluff of his dressing gown off his bedroom slippers.

He should have gone in with his brother into the timber business.

'The whole thing stinks,' he said aloud, and his nostrils were drowned in the smell of dead flesh, rotting grain, gutted fish, crockery with fungus on it …

So he said aloud to whatever power of language it was, 'I don't mean this place, I mean the affair. Winifred. These people have reduced me to I don't know what. And *she*, ever since she came I saw the school going downhill …' and there he stopped.

He could see the school buildings on skids, rolling down some long slope to destruction.

'No,' he said. 'Not downhill, it's just gone to the dogs.' He wondered what would happen. It made him smile.

Conscious of his power he became frivolous. 'My love is like a red, red rose,' he said and the scent was in his chest.

'The forbidden apple,' he said and he ate it for dessert. Sweet and a tinge of sour.

'They can all piss off,' he chuckled and he could see them all somewhere, doing it, as Winifred said, in a place called 'off'.

'A pun my word,' he said.

Mr Batt knew he had the living power of metaphor. He knew he had not much else. What he thought affected nothing. What he said could shake the world. There would be hands powerful enough to shake it like a baby's rattle if he gave the word. He wouldn't. He would ask the nurse for three teaspoons of sugar in his tea, please.

He stirs the tea. With it she gives him two envelopes. One is a card from the whole of form 4I. It says: 'Get well soon, sir.' You know the latest one? What do they give him for breakfast at the hospital? Bald eggs. Hunh, innocent enough, thinks Mr Batt. Guilty.

The other card says: 'Please get well soon,' and it has some cheap sentimental nonsense, copied from a pop song no doubt.

'Listen to the whisper of the time and the tide, that's the way baby, that's the way I cried, 'cause love's a triangle with only one side.'

Mr Batt puts the tea down and reads it over and over again.

'Utter trash,' he says and he reads it aloud.

'That's the way baby, that's the way I cried, I wish you were here, right by my side?

'You see, I am. I am uttering trash.'

And there's no comparison, but he waits.

〜

6.

The Fifth Gospel

WHEN THE PROFESSOR DISAPPEARED, TWO detectives came to interview me. I was then a very poor student in a very cold room at the top of a very old house in Cambridge. My landlady knocked on my door. I was the only 'foreign' lodger she had ever had and she acted as though she knew all along that one day the police would call. The detectives asked me questions on the doorstep and she stood in the hallway and listened over my shoulder. I told them nothing beyond the fact that I had delivered a manuscript to the professor the day before.

'What was in it?'

'I have no idea.'

'You were the last person to go into his rooms.'

'I came out again, didn't I?'

They weren't satisfied, but they went away. I had promised the professor that I would say nothing to anybody. The police left me alone for a few days. The story of his disappearance broke in the newspapers. I kept my silence. I break it now for one reason only. The man to whom I gave that promise no longer exists.

He was called Professor James Jardin, archaeologist, theologian and devout Christian. I met him in my first few weeks at the university when at the age of nineteen I came to Britain for the first time from India. And that I suppose is where the story starts, except to say that my grandfather was a great collector of old books and manuscripts. I remember very little about him, but the odour of old pages still wreathes his memory.

He spent most of his day among his books. The rest of the family were not allowed into his room, but from the time I could crawl I was given the licence to explore it. He would seat me on his knee and take down some volume and read it to me. When I was three or four, I can remember him reading aloud to me obscure passages from Persian manuscripts, political tracts in German, Urdu poetry, anything that he happened to be delving into, even though it made not a whit of sense to me. Which of course didn't matter. It was the expressive drone of his shaking voice I remember.

When my grandfather died, my father sold his collection and it was packed into the chests and carried away. All that was left of him was his steel cupboard with a few pin-striped suits with twenties' lapels, a gold tiepin, an ornamental silver watch and chain, a Parsi prayer book and cap, and a medal he'd won in the First World War as a stretcher bearer in the British-Indian army. All this was kept for me by my mother till I grew up. And with it a manuscript and a note.

The manuscript was bound in brown leather. It had no title. My grandfather had sealed it by stitching it with wire and stamping the molten sealing wax with his own thumbprint. The note was addressed to my father. It said: 'Only one man in the world is to see the content of these pages. I want this manuscript conveyed by hand by trustworthy persons to Professor James Jardin of Queens' College, Cambridge University in England. He knows something of what is in it. If anybody else asks for this manuscript by description, it is not to be given to them. Deny its existence.'

His wish was not forgotten, even though the manuscript lay in the cupboard till I was on my way to England. My mother gave it to me and was glad of the opportunity to fulfil the old man's wishes after twelve years. My father treated them as excessive and eccentric and wondered aloud whether we shouldn't sell the manuscript to a museum if it was worth a few rupees.

How that document came into my grandfather's possession I did not know. I carried it with me dutifully and in my first few days in England was so preoccupied with learning how to deal with slot meters and strange people that I neglected it. I mentioned Professor Jardin to my tutor and told him that my grandfather who was a collector had carried on some sort of correspondence with him.

'Jardin?' he said, sitting at the piano and asking me if I knew any Chopin. 'Poor old boy, on his last legs. You can look him up at Queens'. Getting a bit soft now. Brilliant fellow.'

I wrapped the manuscript in a plastic bag and made my way through the fog of the university evening. I strolled through the austere, red-brick quadrangle and came to a building which looked as though it were ready to tumble into the court. Surely nobody lived in it?

The professor did. He opened the door of his suite to me. He was not at all as I had imagined him. In my mind I saw a tall man with an imperious bald head and eyes that looked down his nose at the specks of dirt known as first year students. He was in fact a crumpled little man with thick black hair, startlingly alert eyes and the thinnest neck I have ever seen, like a bundle of stems disappearing into a vase.

'I'm Farrukh Dhondy,' I said, forgetting the sentence I had prepared and had rehearsed again on the stairs.

'How very interesting,' he said.

'I mean I've got something for you,' I blurted, feeling foolish as soon as I'd said it.

'Promises,' he said and he laughed to put me at my ease. 'Stop fumbling at the doorstep, Farrukh Dhondy, and come in. You are expected.'

'Expected?'

'Yes, expected. I warrant you are the son of the old Parsi collector R. S. Dhondy of Bombay fame. I have waited years. Do you drink sherry?'

'Grandson. Sometimes,' I mumbled.

'You are his grandson sometimes?'

'No, sherry sometimes. He's dead. Long ago, twelve years back.'

'What are you doing here?' he said and strolled across the oak-panelled room to a shelf with decanters and glasses.

'Natural sciences,' I said.

'Most unnatural, you should study classics. Alas, the old man, we knew each other well and he threatened me, grandson, he threatened me. You know what it is to believe and then to be shaken in that belief? Like Christopher Columbus actually coming across the waterfall at the end of the world?'

'No, sir,' I said.

'You come from Bombay? Splendid city. Always felt like a fly in treacle there. Spent many years …'

'I have …' I began.

'I know what you have, sir,' he said as I hung on to the glass of sherry he handed me. 'The document, yes? Don't tell me, it's in a locker at Waterloo station.'

'No, sir, in this bag here.'

'I might as well have it,' he said. 'Your grandfather spoke of it to me twenty years ago, but I have hung back. You are carrying a time bomb, young man.'

'He left a note saying your name,' I ventured.

He took the document from me, looked hard at it and then dropped it on the carpet and paced to the window and back.

'Christopher Le Clerc. He existed. Your grandfather was on the right track.'

'I am afraid I don't know anything, sir,' I said.

'That is what I fear myself. Not you, but I. You know, young man, I have spent forty to fifty years studying the life of Christ. Lunatics and vain theoreticians come at me from every angle. Your grandad was different. Tell me, was he religious?'

'I didn't know him well, sir, he died before I was old enough to think about him.'

'I have wasted my life nosing around,' he said. 'To your grandfather this manuscript was curious, perhaps frightening. To me, it might be a tight little noose.' He put his fingers around his neck and squeezed. 'But I suppose I'd better look at it.'

He reached for the document, lit a lamp in the corner and undid the seal. I could see he was breathing with a pace of excitement.

'Are you a Christian?' he asked and then laughed. 'Don't answer me. Leave me with the time bomb.'

'You want I should go?'

'Not in the least. I beg you to stay. I am going to tell you an incredible story. One that will stir the world.'

The professor sat me down. He refilled my glass. He told me this:

'Your grandfather, God rest his soul, has sent me from beyond the grave the deposition, the story, of one Christopher Le Clerc. This chappy was a monk, a missionary. He went out with the East India Company to Bengal in the eighteenth century. There he found Christ.'

'I thought you said he was already …'

'No, I mean found him, actually found him.'

'How …'

'Hush. This is your grandfather's story. He, Le Clerc, I mean, was a man of high family and calling. In India, two hundred years ago, he heard of a legend of a stone in a hillside with a carving of a pair of hands with blood dripping from wounds in the palms, palms pierced with nails, you know the sort of thing. Curious, but not unusual. He was taken by the legend and claims that he went with an Indian government survey expedition into the Himalayas to research the legend. There are records of that expedition in the archives. I've looked that up in the India Office. The expedition, seven men, disappeared, they think in a blizzard. That was 1791.

'Ten years later, a man appears in a Hindu religious monastery in the north of India. Nowadays, there are hippies and religious middle class kids and all sorts hanging around India, but in those days it was extremely unusual, for a white man to turn Hindu and go around with bare feet and his head shaved, begging alms in the marketplaces. The British authorities were disturbed. They thought he was an army deserter and they arrested him and took him in leg irons to England. This man claimed to be Christopher Le Clerc. He didn't want to cooperate with the authorities. He told them only that he had been with the expedition, had been lost in a blizzard that lasted several days, had his life saved by some natives, and had ended up by living eight years amongst a tribe of people unknown to civilization who claimed to be Christians.

'So far so good. Nothing unusual in that. But this man claimed that he had discovered in India the tomb of Jesus Christ himself. The tribe he claimed to have lived with had been visited, some seventeen to eighteen hundred years before, by a man who claimed to be Jesus Christ. That was his sensation. Do you see, dear boy? Your grandfather then gets this document from the monastery. It tells the whole story. At least I hope it does. Christ didn't die upon the cross. He spent his last days in some mountain fastness in India. God help us.'

The professor's voice trailed away.

'What happened to Le Clerc?'

'Unimportant,' the professor said, pacing back to the window. Then he made a strange clucking sound with his tongue. I remember that most clearly, it comes back to me in my sleep to this day. 'We don't believe him, dear boy, but your grandfather did. Do you see why I approach this … this thing with the greatest caution? From what I have found out these last years, Le Clerc was locked away as a madman, then as an impostor, and then released. Tolerated and set free. Frightening.'

'Why frightening?'

'Because Le Clerc, this Indian monk claiming to be him, may have been a fake or he may have brought to civilization the most startling revelation that the so-called Christian world has known. What your grandfather said to me, the old heathen, was that this brown folder contains the gospel of Jesus Christ himself. A fifth gospel. Not by the disciples Matthew, Luke, Mark and John but by our saviour himself. It's a dreadful moment, dear boy, a dreadful moment for me. I am a Christian, you see. The secret destroyed Le Clerc. All these years I have kept away from it for it might destroy me.'

These things I did not understand. It was a fascinating story but not the kind to sweat over.

'I'm going to read it tonight. What time is breakfast at your college?'

I told him and he asked me to be back at eight-thirty the next morning.

I did as he asked. The cleaners were on the stairs and one of them turned to me and said that Professor Jardin was not to be disturbed.

'Sleeps on Mondays, he does.'

The professor must have heard her, because he came out on the landing in his scarlet dressing gown and ushered me into his rooms.

He looked twenty years younger than he had the

previous night, or maybe it was the morning sun picking out the wrinkles on his face and throwing clean shadows on his skin that gave it a freshness. The waxen smoothness of the night before had reminded me of impending death.

He was solemn and brushed his long hair back.

'Sit down. I've opened it and read it. The fifth gospel is obviously authentic. It's in Latin. Do you have any Latin?'

'No,' I confessed.

'Now this stays with me and you. It's in a sense your property. I'm going to read some of it to you.'

'I'd be grateful, sir,' I said.

'Le Clerc has left a map of the kingdom of Issavali, the lost Christian tribe. I've checked its coordinates in the survey of India and it's the uncharted part of the Himalayas. Shall I translate for you? A monk writing not to mother church, but for the Hindus of his monastery.'

This is, briefly, what I remember of what he said:

'This tribe of Issavali found Le Clerc in the snows. His expedition companions were dead. They found him with a cross around his neck and they revived him and restored him. He lived with them eight years. He tells the story of the tribe, a civilization that had lived isolated, hundreds of years. He describes the valley and then tells the story of the coming of Christ to that valley. What is important is what the gospel says. The fifth gospel. It is a history written by Christ himself. He arrives in Issavali after surviving crucifixion, after wandering in Iran and Asia Minor and begging a living for years. It's all there, just as it is in the other gospels, the story of John the Baptist, of Mary and Joseph, of his birth and his miracles and his assembling of disciples. That's where it gets curious. In the fifth gospel, there are only eleven disciples. Simon called Peter, Matthew, Luke, John, Thomas, Jacob, James the son of Alphaeus, Philip, Bartholomew, Simon called Zelotes, Jude the brother of James. There is no mention of Judas Iscariot. And in the story of the crucifixion, there is no betrayal, no thirty pieces of silver, no kiss in the garden, nothing.

'Naturally he asked them what became of the saviour. They took him to the tomb. On the tomb were still carved the words "Noli Me Tangere", which means "Do not touch me". Le Clerc saw the body, preserved through the ages by cold and care, of Jesus Christ, God bless us.'

It was then that the professor asked me for a promise. I was not to say what I had heard from him. I left him to get to lunch at college. Two days later the detectives called at my digs. For me it was the end of that episode. I had done what my mother had asked me to do, what my grandfather had willed before he died.

For years the mystery of the disappearance of James Jardin haunted the minds of people who had known him. The word got around that I had told the police that I had delivered an important document to him the day before he disappeared. I carried on with my studies and put the professor out of my mind. Two years after that a television company came to me and asked if I would help them with a documentary film they were making about the mystery surrounding the professor's disappearance. I had made him a promise and I turned down the invitation. The programme was made anyway and I watched it. It traced Professor Jardin's life and talked a bit about some discoveries he had made about the life of Christ through his readings of documents. Small things which made me smile. I left Cambridge and England forever when I finished my degree and went back to India. After five years I forgot the professor. Then a friend of mine in Bombay asked me to go on a trip with him to a remote ashram, a monastery of Hindu monks who practised meditation and lived away from the India I knew. I went.

That was where I discovered Jardin again. Shaved head, bare feet, the begging bowl and the strange clucking sound of the tongue, a white monk amongst the rest, a boil on a brown face.

'Professor Jardin,' I said.

'Dead,' he said.

'Unmistakeable. You remember me?'

The monk in saffron smiled.

'Tell me, is this the monastery to which Le Clerc came?' The monk nodded.

'Will you speak to me? I kept your secret. My grandfather's wish that only you should know.'

'That you did. Come with me,' he said, 'but no talk of Jardin. I am Gurusatva, the priest, the disciple of Vishnu, the creator ...'

'Yes, I understand,' I interrupted.

It was later that afternoon that he told me the rest of his story. It had been ten years. He was still learning the vocation of being a Hindu monk. He was anxious that his life in Britain, now that he was an old man and probably at the end of his years, should not touch his belief. He had been happy to have disappeared.

'The file is still open,' I said to him.

'Closed,' and he shut his eyes.

'Tell me.'

'Dear boy,' he said. 'You brought me that document and I fled with it. What I know now belongs to you. I want no part of it. I shall never say it again, so take it away with you. Le Clerc was right about almost everything. His map was an excellent guide. I left Cambridge that night after stealing a passport from an American tourist whom I sat next to in Great St. Mary's Church. I was disturbed by what I had read, I was Christian, remember. I went to church for guidance and there it struck me. I had to know for myself. I had spent years with papers, now I wanted evidence in the flesh. I stole the passport by giving the tourist some bullshit about being a professor. No doubt the police caught up with him and my misdemeanour. I came to India and took a train to the township Le Clerc mentions. It took me forty days of trekking to find the stone carving that Le Clerc refers to. There was dynamite in my pack. I dismissed my bearers and camped there for two days and then I blasted the rock. Sure enough there was a chasm in the mountain.

'It was a passageway of ice and it took me three days, to get to the valley beyond. That valley exists and the Christians exist.'

The professor clucked his tongue.

'They received me. Le Clerc had told them, it seems, that others would follow him into the valley, a prophecy that they passed down.

'It was four years that I lived with them and learnt their language. They have a group of eleven elders who speak a very rough kind of Hebrew, the language of the man they think was Christ. I told them stories from the Bible. I won their confidence and after those years they took me up to the tomb of Christ. I saw with my own eyes the body of the man preserved in the eternal snows, the man who had called himself Jesus Christ of Nazareth. The body is clearly, with its garments welded to it by cold and time, the body of a once handsome Jew. I asked to examine the body. Its arms were folded across the chest. The one question that kept nagging me was why? Why had the Nazarene abandoned his disciples and come to this godforsaken place?

'Then the revelation. There are no marks on the body. The hands bear no sign of crucifixion. The elders kept the text of the fifth gospel. When we got back to the valley I asked to see the original copy. It was as Le Clerc had transcribed it. It was then I told them of the twelfth disciple, of Judas Iscariot who had betrayed Jesus. Eleven, they said, only eleven. I repeated, perhaps foolishly, my story – Judas was the twelfth disciple, he betrayed Jesus, that's how Jesus came to die and be resurrected.

'Who was this Judas I spoke of? they asked. How could a man betray Christ and live with himself? I knew the answer. And you know the answer, dear boy.'

'I think I do,' I said.

'Then they asked me why their saviour had not written this down if I had brought knowledge of it from the outside world. I didn't know what to answer. Perhaps he roamed the world, this Judas, I said, and came to a valley where he spread the word of Jesus Christ. The traitor became the betrayed. It was the greatest act of repentance that Jesus himself preached. The man you have there in the tomb …

'They put me in a prison hut. Day and night I heard the eleven elders arguing. Now and then they would send in a messenger to ask me a question about the gospels I knew from the outer world. On the eighth day of my imprisonment the wrath of nature visited the valley. I heard the rumbling as I lay on my mat. A rumble like an earthquake, like tanks running through crowded streets, my boy.

'My jailer said, "You have brought this evil into the valley of Christ."

'The avalanches descended on the valley. The people fled their homes. They went up the mountain slopes. I was left alone in the confusion and walked out free into the sapphire dark of that night. I ran. A vast barrage of white fell into the valley, throwing back the light of the moon. Do you want to know how I got away?'

'No,' I said, 'I want to know why you are here. Why are you a Hindu, why did you choose to disappear? The police came to me, in England, I mean.'

'I am sorry, dear boy,' he said. 'You kept your silence but I didn't keep my faith. Jai Vishnu. You can see I've put Christianity and all that behind me.'

'Is that all?' I asked Jardin. 'Whom shall I tell?'

'Tell nobody. Or tell everybody,' he said. 'I no longer care and I'm sure Judas won't mind.'

7.

Lost Soul

I SUPPOSE I SHOULD HAVE, but I didn't see the transformation coming. The first I heard of it was when Mr Patel, Nakul's father, brought me his written list of complaints early one morning. What was to be done with the boy?

'You didn't have to write it down,' I said. 'He'll think you're filing it for the police.'

'Devil is inside the boy,' Mr Patel said, sadly, not ferociously.

'The devil isn't bothered if you file his sins,' I said.

Mr Patel shook his head to say that he agreed.

'This is for the pundit. Hindu priest. Exact information.'

'So you're convinced it's the devil,' I said.

'Convinced hundred per cent,' replied Mr Patel.

How could I contradict him? There was, at least for him, no other explanation. The list was long and weird. Nakul had been such a good boy. The change had turned him butterfly to caterpillar.

I first met him three years before the day he went … well, let us say three years before I filled in the form which said 'Nakul Patel is at grave risk.' I had moved into a flat three doors down from the H.N. Stores, a grocery owned by Patel senior above which his family lived. Nakul soon made friends with me. I could feel him conquering a staggering shyness to ask me if he could pat my dog, give it a bone from the shop's freezer. Later he used to walk the dog and lounge around my flat and do small errands for me. He used to ask me about social work, what I did, why I wanted to help Asians and so on. Now his dad was approaching me for professional advice.

'National health is sometimes hiring psychiatrist,' Mr Patel said. 'How much this thing costs?'

'You won't have to pay a penny,' I said.

'Not for psychiatrist, but what about a guru, they won't pay it one?'

'I'm afraid not,' I said. 'Does your guru cost money?'

'Lots money. Maybe three, five, eight hundred pound.'

'Mr Patel, that's ridiculous!'

'For chasing devil?'

'For anything. But look, Patel Sahib,' I said. (I often called him that and he accepted it.) In the S.S. we have a provision under section one for anything the child needs if it is at risk.'

'Gambling?' Mr Patel asked. 'Taking risk?'

'No, "at risk". It means if he's likely to get into trouble.'

'Get *into*? He can't get out!'

He thrust the list at me again.

I glanced at accusation number one. It said 'Calling mother name'.

'What's that?'

'Calling always.'

'What, by her Christian name?'

'She is Hindu.'

'I mean her first name? Does he get rude and call her by her first name?'

'She have one name and he call it, instead of saying "mummy".'

'And this second thing here? What do you mean "don't sit till"? Sit still?'

'No, till. In shop. Nakul don't sit till.'

'They don't look too serious to me, Patel Sahib. Those complaints. It'll pass.'

'Read on,' he said and crossed his hands behind his back waiting for some sympathy to tear itself away from me once the truth hit home.

3. Saying 'bloody' and several dirty.

4. Calling all Gujerati uncles and mens 'John'.

5. Phoning up wrong numbers and shouting 'This is meals on wheels, your goose is cooked.'

6. Taking three saris from uncle's cloth shop and distributing free of charge to slag Asian girls outside Hindi cinema which his aunt herself saw.

7. Mixing price labels in grocery. Make some English persons, customer, very disturbed.

8. It all start when Nakul cut his hair like skinhead. He takes fifteen pounds from his mother for hire of Indian musical instrument and buy Dr Martin shoe.

The first part of number eight stunned me. 'Nakul? Scalped?'

'True.'

9. Three day ago he is gone completely under power of this crazy. He gone with one other Asian boy and throw himself in the police station shouting he is illegal immigrant. Police bring him back and tell me they waste sixteen hours of their time checking to find it is lies.

10. Go to our family doctor, Dr Hussein, and say he is having sickness in morning and his chest is growing and all things like he is going to have baby. Dr Hussein ring me up and tell me to help him to see psychiatrist. I told him he is doing it for nonsense and nuisance.

11. Take telephone out of the house on to street and give it to all passers-by. He is telling me they have to getting their calls.

12. Making experiments in arrangement design with pages of Hindu holy book.

13. Drinking vodka, Ribena mixture. Ribena is 98p a bottle.

14. Mowing lawn with Hoover.

15. Sticking needles and pins in little sister's dolls for put curse on outside persons, like teacher and police.

16. Not went to mathematics exam last week, I just find out. Letter come from his headmaster. He can't go in six form like this.

17. Spoil all groceries by painting Hitler moustache on all faces, even baby faces on nappy packet. Have to put special offer with moustache.

18. Got uncle attached to toilet seat with special glue.

19. Yesterday I catch him gone to sleep when he was supposed to go in the evening to special accountancy class paid for by his uncle. When I asked him why he is asleep he keep eyes closed and answer in gruff voice. He say the ghost of some white singer is come into him.

20. Nearly worst thing: he bring two dog he is find on the pavement and bring them into the shop door to do dirty sex things and start laughing when the lady customer come. I beat all three.

21. Too bad.

'So you left it out?' I asked.

'To a Hindu I can talk it. He must understand.'

'You can't tell me? I'm very curious,' I said.

'It is all to do with left hand and right hand, sir. British don't know these things.'

I suppose I was content not to know. I got the drift of the other twenty anyway.

'Where is the lad now?' I asked.

'Locked up in a dark room. He went to sleep.'

'It seems to me all perfectly natural if a bit too lively,' I said. 'Come on, Mr Patel, it's Britain. He's bored with life, a bit fed up with his uncles' and family's advice. Wild oats, it's not serious.'

'He speak in different languages.'

'Languages?'

'Every languages.'

'Can I come and see him?' I asked.

'I have consult all my relatives, they are coming,' Mr Patel said.

'About what?'

'Beating Nakul and these things.'

'You're not beating him, surely. He's almost a grown man for Christ's sake.'

'He feel nothing. Only the demon inside feel and shout in different voices.'

'Voices.'

'Yes,' said Mr Patel, 'like Kate Bush and sometime American accent.'

I promised I would go as soon as I was dressed. It sounded serious enough. I used to visit their house and had been specifically invited on two or three occasions for religious ceremonies. It was Nakul who had explained the ceremonies to me. One for new year, one for harvest. Nakul told me the stories of the proceedings without conviction, passing on something he had learnt. And now, according to Mr Patel there had to be an exorcism.

Nakul's mother answered the door. She had her sari over her head and she'd been crying. She didn't speak much English. She ushered me into the front room at the top of the stairs. The men were having a conference.

There were about six of them including Mr Patel. As always, tea was brought by Nakul's sister. In the background there was a scream. Some of the uncles cocked an ear to it, trying to pick up in the sound the precise characteristics of the demon. Then Nakul's voice broke through and a song followed. It did sound weird. Not like a boy singing in the bath.

'See it worst,' Mr Patel said.

'It is noisy,' I said.

The fat Mr Patel spoke, Nakul's father's distant cousin, the one with the daughter whom the family hoped would marry Nakul when he finished sixth form and accountancy. The fat Mr Patel was from Uganda. Nakul's father was from Kenya. Their grandfathers had shared the same village in Gujarat; they hoped their children would share the same freehold roof in Tooting.

The fat Mr Patel knew about these things. For the past two hours he had been with Nakul. He knew the symptoms. It was a demon all right. He spoke fast in Gujerati. Then they translated for me. The fat Mr Patel had measured Nakul's arms and his waist. It was necessary. He had heard the demon speak and had held a conversation with the demon while Nakul, poor boy, lay unconscious.

'You interviewed the demon?' I asked.

'I was trying to find who is his special enemy,' the fat Mr Patel said.

Apparently that was the procedure. The demon himself would name whom he most feared. Then you hired that person to chase the demon away. Logic. The fat Mr Patel brandished some branches of a neem tree which had been imported and sold to them for the special purpose of sweeping demons.

'It shouted something chronically,' Mr Patel said.

'Did you discover its enemies?'

'It gave me a phone number.'

'Phone number?'

The fat Mr Patel produced a slip of paper on which he had written the number he had managed to wheedle out of the demon. The conference decided to call the number. They dialled it and we waited.

A secretary answered. It was the ashram of a Dr Ananda Vidya Bharati, Hindu pundit, Sanskrit scholar, scourge of all demons this side of the Ganges.

The good doctor couldn't speak to them just then. He was in meditation, but yes, he did undertake such work. The conference would wait till the doctor came out of his meditation.

The theory was floated that this particular demon that had possessed Nakul was obviously white. The white world had a lot of free souls floating about. The wickedness of the white world was such that some souls couldn't even find new bodies to inhabit. They had to turn spiritual pirate. This was obviously what had happened to poor Nakul and changed him from a nice flared-trousered, long-haired, obedient boy to a swearing skinhead.

I told Mr Patel that I wanted to be kept in touch, but that I had to go at that point.

When I came back that afternoon the uncles were still there. The good Dr Bharati had been consulted. He couldn't do a thing for less than a thousand pounds. They could go elsewhere if they wanted, but he was not a man to trifle with. He specialized in white demons. He'd lived in Canada and the USA.

'He will take only one pound for himself,' Mr Patel said. He looked impressed and gloomy. 'The rest is for modern equipment.'

'Equipment?'

'White demons don't understand Sanskrit prayers and Hindu ceremonies. They have to scare with modern equipment.'

'We are in some agreement,' Mr Patel said. Some of the uncles, according to their seniority in the family and their wealth had promised certain sums. What could he do? He was not such a rich man. Thank God he had understanding relatives. Even so, some money was short. It wasn't a big sum.

'This is first member of this generation to be catch by devil,' Mr Patel said and as he spoke there was another piercing scream from Nakul upstairs followed by a low gurgling melody that withdrew abruptly when we strained to listen.

The Patels embraced each other over the agreement. Hope was in the air again. The good doctor would restore the boy to normality and revive the family's reputation. I felt that secretly Mr Patel was somewhat proud of playing host to a demon, a British demon at that.

I wanted to say, even at this stage, even after committing section one money from the social services, that I didn't believe in demons.

'My grandfather, someone put spell on him in our village,' the fat Mr Patel said. 'That is worst when somebody does to you because they are jealous.'

'How does one do it?'

'Many different ways. In my grandfather case, they tied a string to a fish's neck and let it loose in the sea. When fish is in calm water then my grandfather heart is calm, when it is in troubled current, my grandfather also troubled and shaking like a fish.' He indicated how with his hands.

'Fish don't have necks,' I objected.

They looked at me as though I was raising irrelevant points. I felt a bit contrite. It wasn't the right thing to have said.

'And there'll be some money from section one, of course,' I said.

'How much?' the fat Mr Patel asked.

'Substantial amounts,' I replied.

Now squeezing money from section one is not like getting blood from a stone, more like juice from a rather dried up orange. It's there but there's never enough of it.

Two days after the conference I saw to it that Her Majesty's Department of Health and Social Security had made a contribution to the expulsion of a particularly nasty and multicultural demon in Balham. I went to see how the exorcism would go. It had occurred to me that perhaps Nakul had gone stark staring bonkers, but I dared not mention it to the assembled uncles. It would be seen as more obstruction. Besides demons were welcome, relatively speaking. They were familiar. Madness was not.

The house was crammed by the time Dr Ananda Vidya Bharati stepped out of a minicab. Relatives, well-wishers and friends had come to witness the battle. I was astonished when I set eyes on Dr Bharati. He looked very young. He had a shaved head with a little fountain of hair emerging in an inky squirt from the back. He wore a brown raw-silk drape which covered everything from shins to breast. It was wrapped in a failing diagonal across him and he wore slippers, what they call Jesus-creepers. He had chalk marks on his head to emphasize his holiness and he wore dark glasses. Marvellous touch.

I think the Patels were also taken aback by his youth. A white girl, disciple or secretary, fussed over him, carrying a brief case and a couple of silver trays. The good doctor was garlanded. It was too late to start objecting about his youth. He couldn't have been a day older than twenty-five and possibly he was much younger.

He said he would start work straightaway. He blessed the threshold and the waiting crowd was impressed. Children peeped from the top of the stairs and from round the counters of the grocery store which remained open for business. The younger toddlers clutched their mothers' saris.

The good doctor wanted to see Nakul straightaway. He would invoke the power of the old Hindu gods of course, but they might fail to impress this stray white soul. He might have to use modern equipment. He had ordered it.

The cardboard cartons should be sent straight up to him. They could be left in the corridor outside the patient's room. Was that possible?

All things were possible, Mr Patel said. This fellow looked a really humble exorcist.

The reports were not good. The demon had been playing up the previous day. It had demanded to eat beef and pork and other forbidden stuff. Horrible. The exorcist went up to the chamber. We waited in the front room. There were screams from upstairs, and shouts. The fat Mr Patel nodded. All this was familiar. It was the first stage. How funny, only the week before he had been describing the scene to Nakul, how the brahmin in his village had actually had to wrestle with the victim of a demon and how they had set fire to another one by burning the victim at the stake. Nothing happened to the victim, only the demon felt the flames and screamed till it couldn't take it any more.

Was Dr Bharati winning?

The front doorbell rang and a delivery van unloaded several large cardboard boxes in the name of Dr Bharati. They were paid for by Mr Patel and sent upstairs forthwith.

In an hour's time a new sound wafted downstairs. It was the heavy thump of a bass guitar, the sound of drums through an amplified system. Dr Bharati appeared at the top of the stairs. He was exhausted. It was going well, but he was tired. It was like driving on the motorway, it was best to rest as even a split-second slip, a blink at the wrong moment, could be fatal.

It was all right. The demon was at rest too. In a few hours they would resume.

I didn't stay the night though several of the Patels did. The next morning Dr Bharati ordered breakfast and said he was eating with the demon, they had achieved a pact. Then, I was told, more screams were heard. Plates of sausages came floating out of the doorway and cups of coffee were thrown from the top of the stairs. The demon was reluctant to leave. By mid-morning the amplifiers had again been turned on and several sound and wah-wah machines were going. It sounded like a really bad disco, and above all the din there was the sound of Sanskrit prayer. Dr Bharati had settled down to a real three-pronged, multicultural attack.

And then the demon began to scream. It was horrible. It was not Nakul's voice and it wasn't Dr Bharati's gentle but firm and deep chanting bass. Then everything went silent. The doctor emerged. The demon was gone. Nakul was himself again. He was asleep. In leaving, the demon had held on to his ribcage and shaken it as a prisoner does the bars of a jail. It was painful but Nakul was saved. Could the doctor have a word with Mr Patel and the other gentlemen?

They conferred. Tea was brought. Dr Ananda Vidya Bharati was sure that Nakul would eventually be restored, but he had to take him away from his immediate home for the time being. Was that all right? Nakul should go and live with him in the ashram in north London. The Patels looked at each other.

'You see,' Dr Bharati said, 'I find that Nakul is very weak on all his Gujerati and Indian culture. You haven't even taught him to meditate.'

The Patels nodded. They explained. It was pretty impossible in Britain. They led such busy lives.

'That is why I will teach him. No extra charge. Only way,' Dr Bharati said.

Again the Patels consulted. If the good doctor thought it was best. He wouldn't be able to go to the sixth form of course. He would have to suspend accountancy classes and no doubt the fat Mr Patel didn't want his daughter engaged to someone who was such fertile soil for demonic roots. Yes, Dr Bharati could take the boy away. He would visit them and show them his progress at the ashram.

Then the doctor went and fetched Nakul. He came down, dressed now in a kurta and white trousers. There was peace on his face. He touched his father's feet and humbly greeted and thanked his uncles. It was touching.

That day Nakul left with Dr Bharati. A couple of minicabs called for them. The equipment, which was now back in the cardboard boxes, was taken away too.

His mother shed a tear and his father and sisters hugged him. The son, the brother, the hope of the family had been restored.

It was six months after that restoration that I was working on another case. It was somewhat similar. It concerned a Gujerati boy who had turned skinhead and attacked some black people in a park. I spoke to him. He made very little sense to me. Something had snapped in his pattern of life. His father told me that he had been a good boy till he became suddenly possessed. I wasn't thinking of hiring an exorcist, but I thought that speaking to Nakul would help. He had been through it. I asked Mr Patel for the address of the ashram. He didn't have it. I traced it through the memory of the minicab driver from the firm down our road.

I went looking for Nakul one morning. I had to report on his progress too. And, anyway, Dr Ananda Vidya Bharati and his powers or pretensions interested me. I was deposited by the minicab man in a street in Walthamstow. I walked up and down the street looking for Dr Bharati's ashram. Frankly, it wasn't the sort of place I'd expected. In my mind I had seen Dr Bharati in a mansion-like place with marble floors and carpets on which to meditate, supported financially and spiritually by hundreds of rich middle-class disciples.

Not so. There was no sign of an ashram. I went into the fish-and-chip shop and asked if there were any Indians on that street. Religious people.

'Don't know mate,' I was told, 'but there's freaks upstairs. Make a bloody racket I can tell you.'

I stepped out. On the door to the upstairs there was a sign. It said: NAK AND ANDY SOUND SYSTEM HIRE.

I rang the bell. There was the sound of boots on the stairs and 'Andy' answered the door. He didn't recognize me, but I recognized him. His hair had grown.

'Yeah, what do you want mate?'

'Andy?' I asked.

'What about it?'

'I get it. And Nak is Nakul?'

'You want to hire a sound, mate?' the good doctor asked.

'No,' I said. 'An exorcist.'

That hit him. He looked at me through squint eyes. He shouted up the stairs to Nakul.

Nak came charging down.

'Got a joker here,' Andy said.

'That's no joker,' Nakul said and called me up.

'This geezer's cool, relax,' he said to Dr Ananda Vidya Bharati. The room at the top of the stairs into which they invited me for a drink was jammed with electronic equipment.

On the speakers were painted the words LOST SOUL.

'Neat,' I said.

Nakul didn't know why I had found him, he was a bit uncertain.

'You won't blow it, will you?'

'To your dad and the other Mr Patels?'

'Look, I had to do it,' Nakul protested. 'They wouldn't give me the money to do anything like this. We were bust and dad kept on about going back to school and marrying that fat arse and doing bloody accountancy. I had to get out.'

'I see,' I said.

'Give us a chance. In three months we'll have enough bread to hire clubs ourselves. Then we'll start rolling in it, mate. Plenty of Asian kids and black kids follow our sound. It's new. Once I get hold of some loot, dad will forgive me anything. I can give them all their investment back.'

'And the section one money?'

'That's on the house,' Nakul said. 'But, look, it worked, didn't it?'

'How do you mean?'

'Well, they used to call me Nakul. I hated the name. Now they call me "the Nak".'

He smiled. It was contagious.

~

8.

Under Gemini

IN ANCIENT INDIA, IN THE days of the coming of Alexander the Great, there lived a wise and brave king called Porus. He had two sons born as twins under the star of Gemini. He called them Gav and Talkand. They looked identical, but two such different brothers you never saw. They grew to be splendid princes.

Gav was a thoughtful boy who would turn the skies grey from wondering why they were blue. Talkand was a young man with never a thought in the world but hunting and shooting and fighting and sport.

While Talkand rode out with falcon and sparrow hawk and spent his day in the wilds of the kingdom swimming mountain streams, daring himself to climb to snow peaks and ride for a hundred miles a day, teaching himself to be the best swordsman in Porus's kingdom, the best archer in Porus's armies, the tamer of elephants and a boxer and wrestler who could challenge the pluckiest and heaviest champions of the land, Gav stayed in the palace and read manuscripts. He played musical instruments and wrote new prayers to the gods.

From their birth, King Porus had entrusted the twins to the care of an old and trusted slave of his palace called Sassa. Sassa was a teacher to the lads. When he taught them to swim the rivers, Talkand would interest himself in striking out as fast as he could to the far shore. Gav would stand in the water and wonder why the current of the river flowed one way and not the other and what made the water foam. When Sassa instructed them in archery, Talkand attempted to bend the toughest bow and shoot the arrow to the limits of the horizon; Gav plucked at the strings of the bow and heard its vibration, placed it against hollow tree trunks and made wondering play with the sounds. When Sassa took them on horseback to spear wild pigs, Talkand spurred his horse into the tusks of the cornered beast while Gav turned his eyes from the sight of blood.

Talkand brought the tusks of the beast back to his father.

'What did you bring, Gav?' King Porus asked.

Gav produced a picture he had drawn of his twin brother on horseback spearing the wild boar and you could see in the eyes of the beast, as the blood rushed out of its pierced side, a haunted begging for mercy. The picture showed the horse from the side and the rider from his back.

'Why haven't you drawn your brother's features? The pride of the hunter at the moment of the kill?' King Porus asked.

'I can't draw my own face, flushed with pride at the sight of killing,' Gav said. So much alike were they in the flesh.

When they were eighteen years old there came the invasion of Alexander the Great. In the court of King Porus the messengers from the borders of the kingdom brought the news. The Greek army was encamped two hundred miles from the city.

'What does this Alexander want?' King Porus asked. 'Doesn't he know that we are the mightiest power in the world?'

'He has overcome the kingdom of Nicaea, and he wants to be master of all India. He has promised this to his soldiers who are thirsty for the gold that they believe our land holds,' the messengers said.

'We'll talk with him. We shall talk peace and prepare for war,' King Porus said. He sent for his sons. In the court there was a lot of trepidation. The stories had reached India of how Alexander's armies were unstoppable. They had swept across from Macedonia, across Persia and Afghanistan and were knocking at the gates, stalled at the passes of the mountains through which they threatened to pour down like lava on the kingdom of King Porus.

'We shall send out an ambassador to him,' King Porus told the court in the presence of Gav and Talkand.' We shall defy the Greek to set foot beyond the Khyber Pass. Yes, land we have, we shall tell him, plenty of land, enough for graves for all his Greek and Persian hordes.'

Then Talkand spoke up. 'Let me go and threaten him, father.'

'You have other work to do, Talkand,' the king said. 'You are of age now and the best soldier in my whole army. I am getting old. I want you to start preparing for war. You shall be in charge of the army, the infantry, the elephant cavalry, the guns, the archers. You must begin within the hour to give instructions to the armourers, to appoint new officers and to pick the terrain for your battles with the Greeks.'

Then the king turned to Gav. 'And you will go to Alexander with an armed escort. You are a man of words. You will tell him that we Indians are not easy game, that King Porus will grant mercy to the boy Alexander and forgive him his fault of distracting our peace and our kingdom with his armies and rumours. Tell him he can turn back and go his way and we will not pursue him. We are generous.'

'I have heard of this Alexander,' Gav said. The court listened, hushed. 'He is not a man to be trifled with. Half the known world has been conquered by him and we can talk of peace if we ...'

'*Peace?*' King Porus demanded. 'What peace, Gav? We have the best army that India has known and the best general the world can provide in your brother Talkand. We shan't talk peace.'

Gav was silent. The king instructed him and within two hours he was sent out with fifty-one soldiers to meet with Alexander's scouts and to deliver the message.

When he had gone, the king turned to Talkand.

'I have also heard that this Greek is a treacherous bastard. Your brother may never return alive. Alexander may hold him hostage.'

'I would have gone,' Talkand said.

'That was not my wish. You are going to prove that the undefeated Greeks have met their match. We sent him a royal prince to show him we are not afraid.'

Talkand was puzzled. He was worried. He loved his twin brother, and he knew that if he issued their father's threat to Alexander, Gav would put himself in danger.

But Alexander didn't take Gav hostage. Gav returned in the space of six days. They were six days in which Talkand spent every hour instructing the armies and holding councils of war.

Gav rode back into the city, exhausted but at peace. He went straightaway to report to King Porus.

'So Alexander has accepted? He will turn back?' the King asked.

'No,' Gav replied.

'Did you give him my message?'

'No, father, I did not. I rode into his camp. He received me courteously. He asked me to rest after the long journey and showed me great hospitality. I spent some hours looking around his camp. He has a host of archers, Persian archers and Macedonian marksmen. He has battalions of cavalry and ...'

'I don't want to know what toys Alexander plays with,' the king said. 'Tell me what you said.'

'I saw the strength of his armies and I feared for our kingdom,' Gav replied. 'The Greeks are well prepared. I offered them a treaty.'

'A treaty? I didn't ask you to offer a treaty.' The king was furious. Talkand interrupted him.

'Let us hear what my brother has to say.'

Gav continued. 'I told him that war would mean bloodshed, but we could settle the war by agreeing to give him, Alexander, all the land on the other side of the Indus river if he promised on his honour to respect our kingdom beyond it …'

'Traitor!' The king was on his feet. 'Talkand. Put this traitor under arrest. Take him away, the coward. I don't want to set eyes on him.'

Then the king turned to Sassa.

'Is this how you have educated my son? To turn against me and my wishes when we are threatened with conquest?'

Gav said nothing. He looked around the court. Then Talkand stepped forward and touched his twin brother on the shoulder.

'If I am the general of the armies, I shall take charge of him,' he said and he led Gav away. Sassa followed them.

'Why don't you repent and apologize to your father. If it's war, you can join your brother.'

Gav didn't reply.

'Sassa, you look after him,' Talkand said to the old slave. 'My father will never forgive him until we have won the war. Then I shall speak to him myself. I know my brother. He will never repent.'

Talkand left Gav in a far sanctuary of the palace with only Sassa to attend to him and went about the business of preparing for Alexander.

That night Gav sent Sassa to fetch his brother.

When Talkand came, Gav said, 'I know the numbers and strengths of Alexander's troops. We must match them.'

While Talkand listened carefully, Gav told him about the opposing army's squadrons of cavalry, lines of foot soldiers, elephant brigades, archers and about their lines of command.

'What else did you learn while you were at their camp?' Talkand asked.

'That Alexander is their supreme commander, their great champion. Without him they would not have conquered half the world. If you can kill or capture their commander, you have won the war.'

It was in the thick of the rainy season that news reached Talkand that Alexander's armies had crossed the Khyber and camped on the other side of the River Indus. The Greeks had marched in the night under cover of darkness. They had made the first move. Parties of their foot soldiers had crossed the river and two battalions of Greeks had set up a V-shaped formation beyond it, with bridges built behind them to the main body of their army.

Sassa brought the news to Gav.

'And what has my brother done?'

'He has sent the cavalry after them to break their lines in the centre.'

'Is Talkand in the palace?'

'In the palace? He is leading them himself.'

'And my father?'

'Talkand has kept King Porus away from the battlefield. The king wouldn't listen to him at first, but Talkand has persuaded him.'

'Does Alexander lead his own men?'

'You seem very interested in this battle. Why don't you beg the king to let you go and fight by your brother's side?' Sassa asked.

'I want to help Talkand. But you know I am no good with a sword or a spear. I can help him from here.'

'From here?'

'Yes. What my brother needs is not a feeble soldier by his side, but a plan of action.'

'Maybe. But until you beg your father, you won't even get a glimpse of the battlefield. You are under arrest, remember?' Sassa objected.

'You can be my eyes and ears. Sassa, bring me some sticks of wood and a carving knife.'

Sassa thought the cowardly prince had lost his mind but he did as he was told.

The next day he brought him news of the battle again. As he walked into the room he saw Gav squatting on the floor. He had drawn out a field in chalk and on it he had placed several little carved figures.

'Bad news,' Sassa said.

'What's happened on the battlefield? Did the formation of Greek infantry give way?'

'Talkand made a mistake,' Sassa reported. 'He sent out the cavalry to attack the forward foot soldiers of the Greeks, but Alexander had forded the river in two more places and it looked for an hour or two as though we were going to smash their centre. But no sooner had our cavalry broken through their lines than other foot soldiers replaced them. Our horses retreated.'

'Retreated? Weren't they supported by our own foot soldiers?' Gav asked. He was now pacing the floor.

'No, Prince, they were forced to retreat. They suffered heavy casualties.'

'Doesn't Talkand realize that only foot soldiers can hold ground? He can use cavalry as raiders, but not to hold territory. Is my brother safe?'

'Yes, he's safe. Slightly wounded, but back at camp.'
'Can you fetch him to me Sassa?'

'He is very busy. He keeps a council with our officers tonight.'

'Tell him he must come. Tell him that this battle must be fought under the star of Gemini. We are twins, we are one.'

Sassa took the message to Talkand, but Talkand did not come.

Again at the end of the third and fourth day, Sassa brought news of the battle to Gav. He had observed it from the turrets of the city wall and he didn't have happy news.

'The Greek cavalry has forded the river and stands supported by the foot soldiers. They are immoveable. Slowly this cunning Greek gains ground.'

'What else?' Gav asked, and Sassa saw him return to the toys he had made on the floor and shift his pieces of carved wood.

'The Greek elephant squadrons have moved to the bridge behind the foot soldiers. It is expected that they will cross the river tomorrow. Our own elephant troops are to pass through our infantry tonight.'

'And what news of Alexander himself?'

'He has been seen. Prince Talkand spotted him at the head of the cavalry and rushed with a troop of archers towards him, but he held ground behind his own personal guard of foot.'

Again Gav moved his pieces of carving.

'You fool around with your carving while our kingdom is in danger,' Sassa protested.

'Fetch Talkand for me. I can see what the Greek is up to,' Gav said, looking up from his little field on the floor.

'He will not come, Prince,' Sassa replied.

'All right, then,' Gav said. 'Take him this prediction. Tell him I made it. Tomorrow the Greek cavalry and archers will move over open ground to their left, towards the city walls. From behind them will come supporting infantry. Alexander will not attack the lines we have drawn up to the right, in front of his bridges.'

It was at the end of the evening of the next day that Sassa came back to Gav.

'It was as you said,' he pronounced. 'What magic have you ...'

'Not magic,' Gav said. 'Logic. So far he has managed to trip Talkand's advance. Now he is setting a trap.'

As Gav was saying this to Sassa, Talkand walked into the chamber.

'Sassa gave me your message and your prediction,' he said. He looked tired. Talkand glanced at the little carvings on the floor.

'Don't venture out at the head of your troops tomorrow, brother,' Gav said.

'I think we have the Greeks on the run. They pulled back two companies of archers on the right front today,' Talkand said.

'Your place tomorrow is by King Porus. Stay in the city walls and throw your foot soldiers forward so that the elephant squadron can move to outside the city,' Gav said.

Talkand looked impatient and exasperated.

'Come here,' Gav called to him and led him to the floor where the carved pieces stood as he had arranged them.

'Look, this is Alexander. This is our side, our foot soldier battalions. I have placed them as accurately as I can according to Sassa's reports.' Gav touched a carved piece and moved it forward on the field he had drawn. 'You must give our elephant cavalry a chance to get across the field fast. At present they hold all the territory in front of them, but they must move to the side. They are obstructed by one squad of foot soldiers.'

'You've gone crazy,' Talkand said. 'If I order those soldiers to advance, they'll be slaughtered.'

'That's the price you have to pay,' Gav said.

'Seven hundred men? Why can't they retreat?'

'They have to hold ground further up, right to the banks of the river. There's no time to bother about them, Talkand. Leave them there. The cavalry is required outside the city. The Greeks have moved their whole attack towards it.'

'You play your games, leave the war to me,' Talkand said.

The brothers looked at each other. Then Talkand left.

It was the afternoon of the next day when Sassa burst into the chamber where Gav was held.

His face told the story. In the near distance, Gav could hear the clash of swords and the screams of men, the panic in the streets and the sounds of death.

'They are upon us. The Greeks.'

'Where's Talkand?'

'He didn't take your advice. He rode out at the head of his troops this morning. It was as you said. Alexander led the assault on the city himself. We've lost.'

'The Greeks chose their own battleground,' Gav said. 'What of my father?'

'He fought like a madman. When he heard of the state of the battle, he put on his armour and rushed out. Alexander gave instructions to surround him but not to kill him. There's no retreat. Their forces are inside the city and have surrounded the palace.'

Gav sat down on the floor. He moved a few of the carved pieces. He stared at them, stunned.

The news of Talkand's death was brought to King Porus in the palace by Alexander himself.

'Do what you will with me, Greek,' King Porus said.

'You have fought bravely and given your son in this battle,' Alexander the conqueror said. 'I have never met a foe as brave as this young man and if I could turn back the clock, I would he were alive. You've lost your son, but not your dignity and not your kingdom. Though it has cost me more blood than any other campaign, I give you your kingdom back. When this young man first came to negotiate with me, he talked of peace. He talked of a treaty. He seemed to me a coward. How wrong I was. I have witnessed him these last six days of our war fighting like a demon. I will leave you to your sorrow, King Porus. It is not easy to lose an only son.'

King Porus's eyes were clouded with tears.

'My only son,' he said as Alexander bowed his head and walked backwards out of his presence.

Then King Porus lifted the body of Talkand in his frail old arms and carried him through the corridors of the palace to Gav's chamber.

'You look like him, and that's strange,' King Porus said to Gav. 'He fought today as a man has never fought.

The Greek mistook you for him. He thought today that my only son had died and I did not correct him. He was my only son. You sat here, playing with your stupid toys while he gave his life.'

King Porus stepped forward and kicked the little carved pieces that Gav had placed on the floor.

'I turn my back on you,' he said to Gav, 'When they talk of our kingdom in times to come, they will remember Talkand, the warrior, the bravest man Alexander had the honour to fight, And you, you did nothing. You will be remembered for nothing.'

And so saying, the old king, filled with fury and sorrow, spat in the face of his living son and turned his back for ever on the man who will be remembered, when all the defeated heroes are forgotten, as the inventor of chess.

JANAKY AND THE GIANT

Janaky and the Giant

JANAKY WAS EIGHT YEARS OLD and she lived with her mum, dad, grandma and brother in a little village in India. Every day, together with all the other children, Janaky would set out walking to school in the big village which was two miles away. They had to walk because there was no bus. As they walked they passed a lot of fields, some of which grew rice and some of which grew grass for the cows and some of which were empty with criss-crossing paths where the children flew kites and where the cows drank water from the pools.

One day, Janaky was late for school, and by the time her mum had plaited her hair and she'd got her books, the other children had all gone. So Janaky set off on her own.

'You better hurry,' said her dad from the doorway of their house, and Janaky ran.

After she'd gone a little way and she knew her dad couldn't see her any more, she slowed down. She was in no hurry. She didn't mind being late for school. She picked up a stick she found by the wayside and swished it at the grass that grew there.

As she got near the big village where her school was, she saw something she hadn't seen before. In the field outside the village four big trucks were parked and in the centre of the field there were eight or nine round tents made of coloured canvas with flags on them. A great many people were dragging bamboo frames and cloth and ropes and poles with purposeful expressions. Janaky stopped in astonishment. Only at harvest time did the village witness such a sight, a lot of people working together like an army. As she stopped, a young man passed her.

'What's all this?' asked Janaky.

'It's a mela, a fun fair, you silly girl,' said the young man, with his nose up in the air. 'Now, mind you tell all your friends and tell your mum and dad to bring you and tell them to bring lots of money to spend. Don't forget.'

Janaky thought he was very rude, and anyway she was late for school, so she ran off.

By the time school was over and the master had rung the big brass bell, Janaky had informed all the other children that there was a fair camped outside the village. They all went off to see it. A lot of progress had been made through the day. Where in the morning there had been a few tents, there were now stalls of all sorts, tumbling boxes, a chamber of horrors, a merry-go-round, five or six fortune-tellers, and loudspeakers, mounted on poles, playing all the latest records.

The children hurried home. The fair was fascinating but it wasn't open yet, and anyway the children had no money. Janaky went straight to her mum and told her what she'd seen.

'There's a fair and a rude boy said we have to go.'

'A wandering mela,' her mum said. 'Wonderful. Go and ask your dad if we can all go tomorrow. He's down by the neem tree tea stall, watching television.'

In Janaky's village there was only one TV set and it was owned by Babu, the fat young man who ran the tea stall under the neem tree. The wires hung down from the satellite dish mounted on a nearby house. Throughout the day he would allow the people of the village to come and watch programmes for free, but after sunset he'd take it into his house and charge one rupee entrance to all comers – including his mum and brother and sister.

Janaky ran down to the tea stall. Sure enough, her dad was sitting there with five or six other men. They weren't watching television, they were discussing the fair.

Janaky sat squat-legged next to her dad.

'I'll kill him,' Babu was saying. 'I've fought a lot of these fairground strongmen. They're no match for my massive muscles and my oceanic stamina. I can pound this idiot to dust. He should have his brains examined, coming to our district with this challenge.'

'You're just burning with jealousy,' said Janaky's father, 'because people will go to the fair and won't come to your TV shows.'

'Oh yes, they will! The TV is showing three cowboy films one after the other,' said Babu. He was a well-known braggart. He pulled up his sleeve and flexed his muscles.

'Go on then, just have a feel of that,' he said, and he offered his arm for his friends to feel. When no one raised a hand to feel it, Babu came up to Janaky.

'Come on, Janaky, you tell me if that's not hard as steel.'

'Go on then,' said her dad to Janaky as Babu knelt beside her, still holding out his arm, his fist near his forehead.

Janaky stretched out her hand and felt Babu's arm.

'So what's it like?' demanded Babu.

'It's smooth and soft like the dough my grandma uses for chapattis,' said Janaky.

The other men roared with laughter. This wasn't the answer that Babu wanted. He was annoyed.

'Right then,' he said. 'Nobody gets to watch television today. I'm taking it in.' He gathered the wires and plug and, lifting the TV set, turned to go to his house.

'But you'll see,' he said as he went, 'I'll wrestle the strong man and kill him.'

'What was he talking about, Dad?' asked Janaky as they walked home.

'Don't worry about him,' said her dad.

'Babu loves to boast and show off. There's some mela arrived outside the big village and Babu says he's going to wrestle the fairground strongman. I'd like to go and see that.'

'Then we can go to the fair?' asked Janaky.

'Of course we can go the fair,' said Janaky's dad. 'Better than Babu's television which he always turns to American programmes.'

The next day, Janaky woke up excited. It was Saturday so there was no school. She washed and dressed, had her breakfast, had a fight with her younger brother and then went out to play.

In the afternoon her dad shouted for her. 'Janaky, come on, it's time to go.'

Janaky's mum was dressed in a fine saree and her brother had been cleaned up, with oiled hair and scrubbed knees.

The fair was in full swing. There were coloured lights, loud music, sweet stalls, fruit stalls, a magician, a goat which told the future with its hooves, the little giant wheel with four wooden crates with a sign which said 'Tumbling Boxes' and the merry-go-round with red and yellow horses. Janaky and all the other boys and girls who'd come had a great time. It was huge. There were tattoo artists, people who sold wigs, stalls which displayed brass saucepans and cutlery and gadgets to chop onions, the knife-sharpener's booth and a small tent with a troupe of dancing monkeys. When they had seen most of that, Janaky's dad said, 'I wonder how young Babu is getting along. He was going to fight the giant.'

'What giant?' asked Janaky's mother. 'I'd like to see the giant.'

So off they went to the end of the fair to the giant's tent. A crowd had gathered outside. They were mostly men and women from Janaky's village.

Outside the tent sat a very short man with bulging eyes like a frog. Next to him he had a sign which read: 'Fight the strong man and win a hundred rupees.'

'Babu's in there,' said one of his friends to Janaky's dad.

Not for long. There was a long and piercing scream and out came Babu through the flap of the tent, head first. He landed with a thump at the feet of the people watching.

Poor Babu was moaning and groaning and trying to hold his head, his back, his feet, his stomach and his knuckles all at the same time. And he only had two hands to do it.

'Yaoooooöouchhhhhhhow,' he howled. 'It's a demon, he's killed me, it's not a strongman, it's a demon, get the doctor, take me to hospital, he's broken my head, he's crushed my bones, he's burnt my cheek, he's stepped on my new shoes, help me, he cheated, yowlwawlchooooooo!'

Nobody laughed. Poor old Babu. They picked him up and took him away to be bandaged.

'Serves him right for showing off,' said Janaky's dad. 'I wonder what kind of monster that strongman is to make such awful mincemeat of our Babu. He must be very very strong.'

The next day, Babu was all bandaged up and walking around on crutches.

'Why did you allow him to beat you?' asked Janaky's dad.

'Allow him!' said Babu. 'It wasn't a fair fight. That dwarf person has got a giant in that tent with ten heads and twenty-five arms and he breathes fire and he crushes bones in his fist. He eats six goats a day and he sleeps with his own beard as a blanket.'

The people of the village were astonished at this description.

'Why do you think the dwarf didn't allow you to see the fight?' Babu added.

Janaky and some other children were listening to Babu's story of his escapade.

The story spread. In all the villages nearby the children and the grown-ups heard Babu's description of the giant. The terrible, horrible giant.

Now, Janaky wasn't scared of anything. For one thing, she didn't believe in giants. When she heard that this one had ten heads, she wanted to see for herself.

The next day after school, as she was coming home with the rest of the village children, she dropped behind, saying she wanted to pick wild flowers. Really, of course, she wanted to see Babu's giant with her own eyes.

When the other children had gone some distance, Janaky ran to the fairground. She found the giant's tent with the sign outside it. 'Fight the strongman and win five hundred rupees.'

Janaky noticed that the sign had been changed.

The word 'a' had been scratched out and the word 'five' had been added.

Janaky looked around her. No sign of anyone, not even the small man. She went round the back of the tent and lifted the edge of the tent cloth. She lay down on the ground and slowly crawled forward with the cloth covering most of her head. Soon her eyes grew accustomed to the darkness in the tent. Janaky could see an empty wrestling mat and two stools in two corners of the square. On one stool sat a man. A huge man. She could make out his outline and soon she could make out his face. There was silence in the tent except for one sound, the sound of sniffing and breathing. Yes, it was a giant, Janaky saw, but he hadn't got ten heads or twenty-five arms and his eyes weren't like burning coals. He was like everyone else, just larger all round. He wore a pair of leather shorts and round his neck there was an iron collar which was linked to a chain which went to the ground and then continued out of the flap of the tent.

When Janaky heard this sniffling, she looked more closely at the giant and saw that he was crying.

'You're just an ordinary giant,' she said loudly, before she could stop herself.

'Who're you?' the giant demanded, jumping up as though he was frightened.

'Don't be afraid, it's only me, I'm just a little girl.'

'What do you want? Did ... he ... did ... er ... he send you?'

'Who? No one sent me. I came because I heard you had ... because I heard funny things from Babu about you.'

'So you're not working for Chhotu?'

'I'm not working for anybody. But what are you crying about?'

'It's your Babu, he's put an end to me,' said the giant.

'You see, I don't like fighting, but ever since Chhotu captured me, fifty years ago, he has taken me round from fair to fair and made me fight people. I hate it, but that's the way I earn my bread. Now Babu has spread all these strange stories, people don't think I'm a giant any more, they think I'm a demon and no one comes to fight, so we don't get any money.'

'Yes, Babu did tell a lot of lies. What did you do to him?'

'I didn't do anything much. He came in here swinging his fists and he pulled a cricket bat out of his trousers and started to hit me so I caught him with my bare hands and gave him a big hug and a kiss and tickled his feet and then threw him out.'

'I see,' said Janaky. She pulled herself right into the tent now and stood in front of the giant. 'So no one will come to fight you any more?'

'They won't. And that doesn't bother me,' said the giant, 'but when I don't earn any money, Chhotu doesn't give me anything to eat and I haven't eaten now for two days.'

'You don't know your own strength,' said Janaky. 'When you hugged Babu, you broke his bones and when you tickled his toes, you sprained his ankles and when you kissed him, your hot breath burnt his cheeks and hair.'

'Oh dear, I didn't mean to,' said the giant.

'I'd really like to help,' said Janaky, 'but I don't know anyone who wants to fight a giant.' She paused. The giant was thinking it over and drying his tears on his great big arms. 'And I don't like to help people I don't know. Will you tell me your name?'

'My name is Jungly the Giant, but you can't really help me. The mela moves on tomorrow and I think Chhotu is going to change my act.'

'Why don't you run away from him, this Chhotu?' asked Janaky.

'You think I haven't tried, miss? I know I'm strong enough to break this chain and fast enough to beat any truck or car when I really want to run, but Chhotu has a spell. He has eyes that stare into mine and then my head feels like a little iron filing pulled to a big magnet. It has to obey. You know this chain? It's tied to Chhotu's toe so if I try and pull it he immediately wakes up.'

'That's horrible,' said Janaky. 'A big fellow like you should be able to do something about it.'

'I can't, it's the spell, it's magic … shhhh, you'd better go. I can hear the clanking of the other end of the chain, Chhotu's coming.'

As soon as Janaky heard this, she dived back under the flap of the tent and, lying in the grass at the edge of it, she listened as the clanking got closer. Yes, it was the dwarf. He walked into the tent and he rubbed his hands as he walked.

'Now listen, Jungly,' said Chhotu. 'Nobody wants to fight you and our fighting days are over. I've got another good idea. I've been thinking it over. You deserve a rest from all this fisticuff stuff. You are going to be the chief horror attraction of the fair. I suppose if that man Babu thought you had ten heads and a tail and red glowing eyes like charcoal, you must look pretty dreadful to people who are not used to you. You can just sit on your stool and make faces at the children and we'll charge them one rupee each to get in. We'll be rich, boy.'

'But I don't want to be known as a monster,' said Jungly, and while Janaky secretly looked on he stood up and began tearing at his chain.

'Now, now, now, now, now, now, now. Steady steady steady,' said Chhotu as he started walking round the giant reciting this verse:

By Aflatoon and Aristotle
I found you living in a bottle
I gave you life, now pay the bill –
Bend your strength to my iron will.

The dwarf said this over and over again and he stared into Jungly's eyes. After he had said it the third time, Jungly sat down on his stool and little tears came to his eyes.

'OK,' he said, 'Master Chhotu, anything you say. Tomorrow I shall be Mr Boghulbumpulboochyboochy, The Ugly One, and horrify the children that come to look at me.'

'Good lad,' said Chhotu and he pulled two biscuits out of his shirt.

'You can have these dog biscuits,' he said.

Janaky didn't want to see or hear any more. The giant was under the spell of this little man. She waited till Chhotu had gone, and then got up and ran all the way to her village and home.

That night Janaky thought up a plan. She must get the poor giant away from the horrid little Chhotu.

The next day when the children passed the fairground there was a huge notice right out in front. It said:

LAST TWO SHOWS IN THIS DISTRICT.
NEW ATTRACTION: KING OF HORROR,
THE MOST FRIGHTENING, THE TERROR
OF TERROR, HIS MAJESTY
SON OF FRANKENSTEIN.
MR BOGHULBUMPHULBOOCHYBOOCHY.
WORST THAN HORRIBLE FILMS.

Next to this silly notice, in Chhotu's own brand of English, sat Chhotu himself, and as the children passed by he shouted, 'Come and get scared, tell your mammas and pappas.'

Some of the children were excited. It was the last day of the fair. Janaky told everyone that she was going to see the new king of horror.

Janaky's dad was keen to see the show. That evening they set out. The word had spread and children from all the nearby villages came. All her friends who were in on her plan were there. They filed into the tent and sat on the mats provided by Chhotu, who was wearing a red suit and carrying a whip in his hand. Janaky noticed that he still had the chain tied to his ankle, and the other end of the chain went out of the tent, most probably all the way to poor Jungly's collar.

Chhotu was in great form. He rubbed his hands and raised his voice.

'Ladies and gentlemen, boys and girls …' he began, after he'd collected all their admission money … 'You will not be disappointed. I, Chhotu, the master of ceremonies, bring to you the King of Horror, Son of Frankenstein, Mr Boghulbumphulboochyboochy. Never have you seen such ugliness. Never have you been so terrified. I promise you'll be scared out of your wits or you can have your money back. You will go from here shaken with fright or you will go away no poorer than you came. I shall return every rupee if the horror is not horrible enough. Ladies and gentlemen, the king himself!'

And, so saying, Chhotu stepped off the wooden boxes which were the stage and with a flourish began to pull the chain like a fisherman pulling in a catch.

'Snarling, biting and scratching, he will come,' announced Chhotu. 'Be prepared for marvellous petrification. Who can tell, who knows, perhaps the beast will get out of control.'

With that he began to haul on the chain again.

He pulled a yard of it, two yards, three, four. Chhotu looked a bit puzzled. There was no snarling, no growling, no howling, no clanking of chains. A few seconds later, through the back flap of the tent, in came Jungly and stood before them. It was true he was not very nice-looking, thought Janaky, and it was clear he was sad. He might even be very hungry still and she could see he had been crying because his eyes were red.

'That's not horrifying,' said Janaky. 'Poor old man – he's not horrifying, he's quite funny.'

Janaky began to laugh. She laughed loudly. 'Ha, ha, ha, ha ha, ha ha!wooooooooowha, ha, ha, hooowheyoo!'

Suddenly ten of the girls and boys in the room were laughing with Janaky and then, because they were laughing, everyone began to laugh.

'He's not horrible, he's funny,' shouted Janaky's dad.

'Yes, he's not horrible at all, give us our money back, you,' the people all shouted at Chhotu.

Chhotu didn't know what to do. This was the last thing he had expected.

'All right. Money back. No problem!' he said, pulling out his leather money bag and rattling it to show willingness.

'Son of Frankenstein, indeed. We agree he's a big feller, but there's nothing frightening about big fellers or small fellers, come to that,' said one or two people.

Janaky was the last to claim her money back. Chhotu was nearly in tears.

'Here's your rupee, miss. Now you were the first to laugh. Tell me, didn't he terrify you?'

'That poor old bald giant? It takes more than that to frighten me,' said Janaky.

'What can I do?' said Chhotu. 'I've tried wrestling him, but he's too strong. I try him on as a horror show and he's a flop.' Chhotu shook his head.

'I'll tell you what you can do. Go to the wig maker and get your giant a terrifying big wig,' said Janaky. 'And have you looked in his eyes? They are like big dark sad pools. You can't be terrified by those eyes! Get him some of those scary mirror dark glasses.'

'Do you think it'll work?' asked Chhotu, quite desperately.

'You asked for my advice and that's it,' said Janaky, 'and you're lucky there's a wig maker and a dark-glasswallah in this very fairground.'

'So there is, or so there are,' said Chhotu, 'Thank you, miss.'

'Shall I tell you what, Mr Chhotu? Since you've lost all your money I'll go and get you the wig and the glasses,' said Janaky.

'Are you sure?' said Chhotu and he was very glad because he didn't really want to separate himself from Jungly's chain.

'I'll see you in a minute,' said Janaky.

Now what Chhotu did not know was that Janaky had already been to the wig maker and the dark-glasswallah and ordered an extra large one of each for the giant.

She went and fetched the wig, which was five feet tall and spiky and coloured and looked like every hedgehog in the world had bunched together to make it. The secret of the wig was that under the hair there was a pair of earphones, and tucked into the hair was an MP3 player.

Janaky went and fetched the glasses. They were enormous glasses, shiny as a mirror. The secret of the glasses was that you could look out of them but not into them.

Janaky carried both to Chhotu who was waiting next to the giant for her to return.

'Splendid!' he said when he saw the wig.

'Splendidlydiddlydid!' he said when he saw the dark glasses.

Janaky handed them to Chhotu who put them on Jungly, pulling the wig tight on his bald head and thrusting the dark glasses onto the bridge of his nose.

'Oh horrors, horrors, Mummy, help!' said Janaky as soon as Jungly put the wig and glasses on.

'So it works,' said Chhotu and he rubbed his hands as Janaky pretended to run away in terror.

Then something funny happened. The giant opened his huge mouth and began to laugh.

'Shut your mouth,' said Chhotu.

But the giant couldn't hear him because he was listening to music on the earphones under the huge wig, and he could see Chhotu stamping and cursing but Chhotu couldn't look into his eyes.

'Stop laughing!' shouted Chhotu.

The giant reached for the chain that connected him to the dwarf and he ripped it apart like a man tearing a paper Christmas decoration.

The dwarf jumped up. The spell, he must use the spell! He began running round the giant, screaming:

By Aflatoon and Aristotle
I found you living in a bottle.
I gave you life, now pay the bill –
Bend your strength to my iron will.

It was no good. The giant couldn't hear anything. He didn't hear the spell so it didn't mesmerize him. Chhotu tried staring into the giant's eyes, but he couldn't penetrate the mirrored dark glasses.

Suddenly the giant, having broken the chain and the spell, reached out and picked Chhotu up in both hands. He frowned. Just then, Janaky rushed in and grabbed the dwarf by the legs.

'That's enough, Jungly! We've won! Let him go.

The giant didn't need to hear what she was saying. He knew. He put the dwarf down and, picking Janaky up, he ran.

He ran to Janaky's village, where all the village people were waiting.

'Take that wig off,' said Janaky. 'It really is horrible.' Off came the wig.

'Thank you,' said the giant. 'Thank you to Janaky and to all the other children who rescued me from the fair and from Chhotu. But what will I do now? Where can I live?'

'You can live in our village,' said Janaky.

'And, and … and … earn money for you by wearing the wig and dark glasses and putting on a horror show?'

'Don't be so silly,' said Janaky. 'As if!'

'But otherwise I'll be useless. What can a giant do?'

'For a start,' said Janaky, 'you brought me from the fair to our village in one minute flat.'

'So?' asked the giant.

'Well, I've always thought we need a school bus in these villages. If you can carry us up and down in a few strides ...'

The children cheered.

And to this day the giant works as a school bus in Janaky's village. The rest of the time he wears his dark glasses and listens to his personal tape recorder. Now and then he wanders down to the neem tree tea stall to watch Babu's TV.

Pally Ali and His Camels

ONCE UPON A TIME, IN Arabia, there was a merchant called Pally Ali. He mainly dealt in gold and he owned thirty-five tents and six camels.

One day, Ali decided to take his gold across the desert and sell it in the market in town.

The town was five days' walk across the desert, but Ali didn't mind. It wouldn't be he who was walking. Neither would he have to carry all that heavy gold. He would saddle up his six camels and fill five of their saddlebags with the shiny stuff and he'd get on the back of the sixth camel and ride across the desert in great style.

Ali went and spoke to his camels and told them to be ready for the long journey the next morning. The camels were quite excited. Ali was going to ride on the youngest one, Kamal, who was also the smallest.

In the morning, Ali took the gold bags and bars out of his safe and loaded them onto the camels' backs. He led the camels to their water trough and said, 'Have a nice deep drink now, because you won't get any water for five days.'

The camels drank, gulping down as much as they could. Then Ali lined them up and, one behind the other, they set off across the desert.

At the end of the fourth day all the camels were very tired and thirsty. They had trudged through the sand steadily. The sun was hot. The gold was heavy. Only once did they pass some camels who were walking the other way. It was thirsty work.

Then just as it began to get dark, Ali shouted:

'Can you see it, camels, the oasis! At last!' Sure enough, when the camels looked up, there it was in the distance. An oasis with palm trees round it, and one shop.

Pally Ali kept urging Kamal to go faster until he broke into a slow trot. Ali was dying for a drink, and so were the camels.

Finally they reached the edge of the oasis, but just as the camels were crouching down and bending their necks for a sip of the water, Ali shouted 'Stop!'

The camels looked up and saw that Ali was pointing to a notice in the oasis. 'WATER POLLUTED, NOT FIT FOR DRINKING, SORRY' said the sign. Under the writing there was a drawing of a skull and two crossed bones.

'Sorry, camels,' Ali said. 'You'll have to do without,' and off he went on his own to the shops. The camels watched as Ali emerged from the shops a few moments later with a bottle of orange juice.

He arranged his pillow under a palm tree and lay down.

'Camels are supposed to go a long time without water,' he said, 'and anyway, we'll reach the town tomorrow and there'll be plenty of water there.'

The camels looked on as Ali drank his big bottle of juice. Ali knew they were staring at him.

Then Ali remembered what his mum used to say to him when he began to demand things.

> You know the secret of the sphinx
> Is that the creature never drinks
> Although the sun is very hot
> The men who made the sphinx forgot
>
> To supply him with a glass and straw
> So he'll be thirsty evermore.
> The moral of this tale, no doubt,
> Is some of us have to go without.

The camels heard him repeating this. Ali grinned and then he turned over and fell asleep.

'That's the most unfair thing I've ever heard,' said Kamal. 'He could have at least offered to share the juice.'

'Let's go to the shop too,' said another of the camels.

The rest agreed it was a good idea. They were all so thirsty they couldn't think of anything else and thought that maybe the shopkeeper would feel sorry for them.

The shop looked very alluring. It had a huge glass front and a neon sign in joined-up handwriting saying 'Just Desserts' which blinked in the night. All the shelves were clean and shiny and the owner sat at a till with hundreds of biscuit packets behind him. The store sold everything from socks to video cameras.

The shopkeeper was not very pleased to see six camels trooping into his shop, messing up the floor with the sand they dragged in on their feet. He also knew that camels never had any money to spend.

'What do you want?' he asked, not very politely.

'A drink,' said the camels.

'Well, I've only got bottled water, and it comes from the springs of Arabia and costs money, so buzz off.'

'How much have you got?' asked the oldest camel. 'We can get quite thirsty, you know.'

'I've got cases and cases of it,' said the shopkeeper, 'but I'm sure you don't have any money.'

'We haven't got any money, but we've got gold,' said Kamal.

'Gold? That'll do nicely,' said the shopkeeper. 'Let's have a look.'

'In the saddlebags,' said the camels.

The shopkeeper could hardly wait. He wasn't a very honest man, and he knew that the camels wouldn't know the value of the gold. He dipped his hand into the saddlebags and emptied each one of all the gold.

'Well, gentlemen,' he said to the camels. 'You know water in the desert is like gold dust. I reckon you've got enough gold here to buy yourselves two crates of spring water each.'

'You mean all the gold for a few crates of water? That's outrageous,' said the oldest camel, who was called Youyouzdme. 'We could buy a hundred times that in town. You can't charge us that much.'

'Take it or leave it,' said the shopkeeper. 'This isn't the town and I can charge what I like. Or of course, there's another solution. You can do without.'

'What do you think?' asked Youyouzdme.

'Water, I want water, or I'll die,' said Kamal.

'OK then, we'll pay,' said Youyouzdme.

So the shopkeeper went into the back room and brought out the twelve crates of water.

The camels knew it was robbery, but they were very thirsty. Each of the camels drank one whole crate. Then they took the bottles from the second crate and loaded the saddlebags very carefully so none of the bottle-tops stuck out.

They all trooped out of the shop and went to the edge of the pool where it was cool and guzzled the bottles of water from the saddlebags there. Then they lay down to sleep.

In the morning Pally Ali woke up, brushed his teeth and ordered the camels to move.

The empty bottles which were now in the saddlebags were much lighter than the wretched gold, so the camels were more than happy to obey.

Youyouzdme called them to put their heads together. Pally Ali mustn't find out that they had lighter loads and so they were all to pretend that the loads were still heavy.

'Pretend the gold is really weighing you down and that you are still thirsty and suffering.'

'But I will be suffering,' objected Kamal, 'because that fat fool hasn't been transformed into a load of empty bottles and he'll get on my back again. It's OK for some.' The other camels hadn't thought of that, but there was nothing they could do to help.

Sure enough, Pally Ali had his morning swig of orange juice, climbed onto Kamal's back, and off they went.

All day they walked and in the evening they reached the town. They reached the marketplace and Ali led his camels to the gold trader's shop. Then he asked all the camels to sit down, which they obediently did.

There were a few urchins passing by in the noisy and dusty marketplace.

'Oi,' Ali shouted. 'Do you want to earn some money?'

The urchins gathered round in a crowd with smiles and eager faces.

'Come on, let me feel your muscles. My bags have heavy stuff in them. Stones, really.'

Ali didn't want to tell the urchins what he thought was really in the bags because they might run away with his gold and he was too fat to waddle after them.

'Stones, yes, ordinary, horrible, grey, worthless stones! Now stretch out your arms.'

Twenty of the urchins stretched out their arms and flexed their pathetic little muscles. Ali went from one to the other, feeling muscles.

'Hmmm. You and you and you,' he said. 'Pick up the saddlebags from the camels and take them into that shop.'

The three boys did as they were told with huge grins on their faces. The rest just stood around, disappointed that they hadn't been chosen.

Ali followed them into the gold shop. The boys put the saddlebags down and waited. Ali pulled out his leather pouch of money and, finding the three smallest coins, gave them one each. The boys stared at the little brass coins he had put into their hands.

'What are you staring at? Say thank you and get out or I'll kick you all the way to the sands of the desert,' said Ali.

'That's a very mingey wingey teeny little money,' said one boy.

'Be grateful, lazy bumpkin,' said Ali. 'Take it and go or I'll take it away and give you an injury in your hearing hole instead!'

The urchins left the shop.

'I want you to count that gold for me,' said Pally Ali to the gold trader.

The trader looked in the saddlebags. Out came empty bottles and then some which the camels hadn't drained.

'Very funny gold, this,' said the trader, who thought Ali was playing some kind of joke on him.

When Ali saw the bottles coming out instead of the gold, he was struck dumb.

He couldn't think how all his gold had disappeared and bottles with designer water labels had appeared in its place.

'Take your bottles and please go,' said the gold trader.

Very sadly, Ali put the few bottles with water still in them into his saddlebags and went into the street.

He didn't tell the camels what had happened, but of course when he reloaded the saddlebags onto their backs, they knew. They could hear the few glass bottles he'd brought back rattling against one another.

'We're going home,' Ali said.

They tramped again through the desert and a day later they came to the same oasis. Again, Ali sat on Kamal's back, even though this time he knew that the other camels were carrying a couple of water bottles each. He'd just got used to Kamal being his mount, like some people have favourite chairs.

The sun was hot and the camels and Ali were thirsty. The sign saying 'Polluted Water' was still standing in the oasis. 'Well, at least I won't be thirsty,' said Ali and he took out a bottle of water and swigged it. The camels stared back. If you've ever looked into the eye of a camel you'll know the hard, stony, pleading stare that came back at Ali.

It made Ali feel uncomfortable. This time Ali felt sorry for them. 'Have a drink, fellows,' he said, and, taking the bottles out of the saddlebags, he gave each of them a little drink. Kamal drank his bottle of water and then he looked at Ali, who was still sad and puzzled about his gold. Kamal felt sorry for Ali. Maybe they shouldn't have taken all his gold and bought water with it. He thought he'd go and see if the shopkeeper would give some of the gold back.

As Ali began dozing off under the palm tree, Kamal made his way to the shop. To his surprise, there was no one in the shop. No one he could see, anyway.

'Hello, anyone here?' shouted Kamal.

From behind the counter came a feeble voice.

'Thank God you've come, I'm here,' said the voice, and as Kamal peered over the counter he saw it was the shopkeeper sitting on a stool, leaning against the wall with his tongue hanging out.

'What's the matter with you?' asked Kamal.

'I'm dying of thirst,' said the shopkeeper. 'I was so greedy for your gold that I sold you every bottle of water I had. I didn't leave any for myself and the oasis is poisoned and I feel too thirsty and weak to walk. Can you please give me a drink?'

Kamal thought of how the shopkeeper had told them to buzz off when he thought they had no money.

'I can sell you a drink of bottled Arabian spring water, or two or three even,' said Kamal.

'Yes, yes, I'll pay anything,' said the shopkeeper.

'Well, how about giving back all the gold and only keeping back the cost of the bottles we brought?' asked Kamal.

'What! All the gold back? Are you crazy?' asked the shopkeeper.

'I suppose I am, but as you said yourself, you can take it or leave it.' So saying, Kamal turned on all four heels and started out of the shop.

'No, wait!' shouted the shopkeeper. 'Anything,

anything, just give me a drink. Here's the key to my safe. Take it all. Just give me the water.'

Kamal went out to one of the saddlebags. He winked at Youyouzdme who was sitting comfortably in the sand. He took a bottle of water to the shop and the shopkeeper drank.

'I've learnt my lesson. You can have the gold back,' he said.

Then Kamal brought in the saddlebags and loaded them with gold, making sure he paid the shopkeeper a fair price for the bottles of water they had taken.

The camels gathered round Ali and woke him up and told him to look in the saddlebags. Ali did. There was his gold! He rubbed his eyes. Gosh! It must have all been a dream.

Had he really dreamt that he had been to the gold trader and all his gold had turned to bottled water?

Ali looked at the camels.

'Shall we go home then?' he asked.

'Home? We are on our way to sell your gold, aren't we?' said Kamal. 'We are only one day away from town.'

I must have dreamt it all, thought Ali. This hot sun plays tricks on your mind.

As they were going back to town with Ali perched on Kamal's back, he could hear the camel muttering a rhyme he'd heard somewhere before to himself.

> You know the secret of the sphinx
> Is that the creature never drinks
> Although the sun is very hot
> The men who made the sphinx forgot

To supply him with a glass and straw
So he'll be thirsty evermore.
The moral of this tale, no doubt,
Is some of us have to go without.

When they got to the market, Ali again ordered the
camels to crouch down in the dusty road. The same urchins
gathered, even though they knew that Ali was a stingy old
merchant and they would only get a measly small brass
coin for their work. What could' they do? They needed
even that!

They all held out their arms for Ali to feel the muscles.
This time Ali counted the boys.

'Put your muscles away,' he said and the urchins
lowered their arms.

'This time all of you are hired. Take the saddlebags into
the shop.'

The urchins were delighted. There were now two or
three boys to each saddle bag, and even though they were
heavier than the last time, they carried them in happily.
When they put the bags down, Ali unlaced one of them and
gave the boys one gold lump each. They were delighted.
They ran from the shop shouting his praises, and dashed
into the street to kiss and stroke his camels.

Now Ali felt right and light. He had turned his money
into bank notes and traveller's cheques, and he kept them
all in his pockets.

The camels had nothing to carry except Ali himself and
all the bottles of water he had filled into the saddlebags for
the journey back.

When they got to the same oasis, Kamal took ten bottles of water and gave them to the shopkeeper. When he emerged from the shop, Ali and the camels were having a picnic under the palms.

'You know, fellows,' said Ali, 'I've had such strange dreams these last few days. It must have been this poisoned water from the oasis.'

'But you didn't drink it,' said Youyouzdme.

'I gargled with it when I brushed my teeth,' said Ali. 'And it must have affected my brain because I thought all the gold was gone and some bottles of water, even empty ones, had appeared in its place.'

The camels didn't say anything.

On the way home, as they left the oasis, Ali heard Kamal muttering over and over:

> You know the secret of the sphinx
> Is that the creature never drinks ...

And so on. Now where did he learn that? Ali thought, and wiped the sweat off his happy face.

D-10, The Two-Boy Machine

A LONG TIME AGO, IN a city called Delhi in India, there ruled a king called Tughluq. Some people said he was very smart and a very great king, but others, to this day, think he was a mad, bad, crazy dictator.

We know that he did some splendid things. He built mosques and houses and halls, and he paved the streets and paid painters to paint pictures and poets to write poetry and musicians to compose and perform. He got hundreds of people together and put them to work to build a great wall round the city.

This wall was made of stone and went round the palace and the houses. On the lower side of the wall ran the River Yamuna, a broad, brown lazy snake of a river. The people of the city drank water from the river and lower down the stream they washed their clothes in it and even further down, on the banks, they burned the bodies of dead people and threw the ashes in. It cost nothing to bathe or to wash or to drink, so the poorest citizens would use the riverbank as a meeting place in the evenings.

These poor people lived in the very worst part of Delhi in tumbledown, patched-up huts or even without any homes at all. In the daytime they worked or begged for money and food from other people, and at night they slept on torn blankets under the stars.

One of the boys who lived like this was called Lula. He had no mother and no father, no one to look after him, and what was worse, he had no legs. He couldn't remember why or how, but when he was very young, just a baby in fact, both his legs had been crushed in an accident. So Lula had learnt to move by pulling himself along on his hands. Every morning he used to go out from the stone ruin under which he lived by night and pull himself along on his hands to the marketplace just outside the great mosque and wait for people to come. People who passed by might give him a coin or two, and the people who owned the market stalls, people who sold vegetables and chickens and slippers and saddles and cloth would also give him a coin or two as he passed them. They all knew him by name.

Lula's real job, what he thought of as his job, was looking after the camels and carriages of the traders and rich people who came to pray at the mosque. He would hang about outside the mosque and, when a caravan of weary travellers arrived on camels and stopped to pray, he would say:

'Hold your camel for you, sahib?'

Or if it was the carriage of a rich family he would approach the coachman and offer to polish the wheels. If they accepted, he would get to work while they were in the mosque.

First he would clean the wheels with a wicker brush and take off all the mud and cow dung which was inevitably there, because in those days herds of cows would be driven through the city. Then Lula would polish the wooden spars of the carriages with the cloth he carried on his shoulder, washing the spars with water or spit to make them shine. In this way he earned enough money to stay alive and buy himself hot food sometimes, kababs and rotis from the vendors of the market.

A little way from the mosque where Lula looked after the camels and carriages, on the banks of the river, there was a temple. The people who came to worship at the temple had to take off their shoes or slippers in order to enter. That was the rule and ritual of the Hindu religion. The pilgrims went in, said their prayers and collected their shoes from the door of the temple as they left. Every day, at the door of this temple, there sat another boy called Bhim.

Now, I want to tell you something about this boy Bhim, who was the same age as Lula. Over the years he had collected a vast number of seashells by asking the fishermen and sailors who passed through to bring him a few the next time they came. He kept these with him at the door of the temple. There must have been in his collection two or three hundred different shapes and sizes of shells. Some were like cones, some like horns and some like fans with wavy edges or smooth round edges. Some were circles, some were long thin conches, others were tiny and flat, shaped like spades. He had rough shells, smooth ones, grainy ones, triangular ones, knobbly ones and speckled ones.

What Bhim had done over the years was to separate this vast collection into pairs of shells which he could feel were exactly or so nearly the same that you couldn't tell them apart at first glance or touch. Twin shells.

You see, Bhim was blind. He used the shells as cloakroom attendants use tickets. He was the minder of shoes at the door of the temple and, when a devotee who entered the temple left a pair, he would give him or her one shell and put the other onto the pair of slippers or shoes. Then, when the person returned, Bhim would feel the shape of the shell that the person handed him and he would know exactly in which row and where the person's shoes were. Everyone who came to the temple trusted him with their shoes. He was never wrong.

At night Bhim lived in caves that poor people had carved out of the riverbank. He bought his food with the money that his temple-door occupation brought him. He didn't really need many things.

Bhim and Lula didn't know each other. Both had heard of King Muhammad Bin Tughluq, because every now and again, when the king had a bright idea and wanted the people to know, he sent criers around to stand at the doors of temples and mosques and on the walls of the city and in the marketplace and shout their heads off, delivering the message of the king: 'The king, His Imperial Majesty, Sultan Muhammad Bin Tughluq, monarch of all Hindustan by the grace of Allah, thanks be to him, this day requires all citizens to pay an extra tax of three damri per household, which money when raised will go to the digging of wells inside and outside the city. The sultan thinks that drinking from and washing in the same river is unhygienic ...'

The criers would repeat their announcements all day and the people couldn't help but listen.

Lula and Bhim rarely paid any attention to these announcements. They drank from the river when they wanted and from the wells when they so chose and weren't ever bothered by the tax collectors.

The king liked sending out these announcements and orders. His greatest joy was for the people in his kingdom to be happy and his greatest fear was that people in his kingdom would on some pretext or the next begin fighting each other. They very rarely did, but when Tughluq himself was a boy, his father, the king before him, had told him that there was one thing he had to be very careful of. He must not allow the Muslims and the Hindus in his kingdom to be rude to each other, to insult each other or to fight. Everyone must respect everyone else's religion.

One year, when Lula and Bhim were both eight years old, the River Yamuna dried up. It was a very hot season and the rains didn't come on time. All the wells inside and outside the city walls were dry. The people got thirsty. The buffaloes, cows and goats got even thirstier. Everyone suffered. The king ordered the army to take all their donkeys and travel across the country to find places where there was still some water and fill up leather bags and bring them back for the people to drink.

The army brought back a little water, and people had to queue for hours to get a metal tumblerful for drinking and cooking. It was very hard. The city grew tense. Rumours started in the marketplace. Some wicked whispers began among the Hindus that it was all the fault of the Muslims and the same sort of whispers began amongst the Muslims that it was all the fault of the Hindus. Soon King Tughluq heard of these rumours and he sent his criers out with a declaration:

'Hear ye, hear ye, hear ye. The king of all Hindustan, Muhammad Bin Tughluq, wishes it announced that some very silly rumours have come to his attention. Some wicked people are spreading the story that the drought and the drying up of the river are the fault of either Hindus or Muslims. This is obviously nonsense. The river dried up because of a hot summer and the late rains and not because of the wickedness of any people. We must live in peace with each other and so anyone who breaks this peace and talks rubbish will be mercilessly whipped and their mouths will be stuffed, publicly, with mud.'

When the people heard this announcement the rumours stopped.

Then finally the rains came, the River Yamuna filled up and there was water for everyone. However, the next year, when Bhim and Lula were nine years old, there was no rain again. The hot season was again very hot and the river dried up. This time the king ordered all the donkeys, horses and camels in the city to go and fetch water from far-off wells. Again the rumours between Hindus and Muslims started. Even though most of them were the greatest of friends with each other, some people began to circulate silly stories. The rain hadn't come because God was angry with the Hindus, said some Muslims and some Hindus said that the heavens were angry with the Muslims and so the rivers had dried up. The troublemakers gathered outside the temple and outside the mosque and muttered and stirred. Bhim and Lula both heard these nasty whispers, but they didn't know what they meant.

Again the brewing troubles came to the notice of the king. This thing between the Muslims and the Hindus was becoming a bother. Once more the criers went into the city and threatened the troublemakers. This time they said, 'If anyone is caught talking nonsense about another religion, they will be hung up by their ears.' The rumours promptly stopped. Then the rains came and people were happy again.

The king knew that he must do something about the drying up of the river in especially hot years. Of course he also knew that he couldn't make the sun cooler or the rains come on time, but he did have an idea. He would build a city high up in the hills where the rivers were fed by the melting snows of the mountains and never dried up. It would be his capital city, a beautifully planned place with streets and marketplaces and houses and gardens and rivers that had water all year round. Then he would command all the people from Delhi to move there.

He was so pleased with this idea that he ordered a million workmen to start work on it straightaway. His engineers found a site and the building began. First they built the palace in the centre of the town and they built sixteen roads coming away from the palace. At the end of each of these roads was a roundabout and sixteen more roads went out from each of these roundabouts. At the end of the street in front of the palace was the bazaar, the marketplace. Then there were the theatres, sports stadiums, shops and streets and streets of houses. Right in the middle of the city there were parks with large lawns and trees and pools and fountains.

By the time the hot season began, the city was ready. King Tughluq waited till the River Yamuna dried up and then he sent his criers out.

'Everyone must pack up their bags, if they have any, and move off to the new city by order of His Majesty King Muhammad Bin Tughluq,' the criers cried all day, but no one took any notice.

It wasn't as though the people hadn't heard of the new city or as if they hadn't heard the king's command. They just didn't want to leave their homes and lives and start out afresh in a strange place. Besides, the new city was at least a four-week walk away, and no one fancied walking that long and that far carrying their bundles and bags.

Tughluq looked out of his palace window and saw that life carried on as usual in Delhi despite his commands. He was a bit annoyed. The new city was still empty and the people of Delhi were just waiting for him to give up this nonsense and send out the horses and donkeys again to fetch water. The next day the criers came out again.

'King Tughluq wants everyone to pack up their stuff and move off to the new city immediately. Go on, shoo, get moving! Please!' is what the criers now said, but again no one took any notice.

The next day posters appeared by order of His Majesty all over Delhi advertising the new city, saying how beautiful it all was with a big painting of the central park and swans floating on the rivers. Even this did no good. A rumour spread through Delhi that in the new city the houses for ordinary citizens had very small rooms and low ceilings and thin walls so you could hear the neighbours through them. People said the new city was badly planned and the market was far away from the houses and the roads were all paved so they wore out your shoes.

When Tughluq heard that the people refused to move, he was very angry. He sent out his criers with a final message. 'The king says that the city of Delhi has to be emptied by sunset this evening. Anyone caught in the city after sunset will be trampled by elephants or shot into the air from a giant catapult.'

Now, all the people knew that these were the cruellest punishments the king had at his disposal. The trampling elephants were terrifying because they trumpeted and panicked before they stomped you to death. The human catapult was even worse. The branch of a huge tree was pulled back with a rope attached to eight horses with the victim tied to the topmost branch. Then the rope would be released and the person would go flying through the air like a stone from a slingshot and fall to his or her death.

Horrible, horrible, horrible.

When the people heard this threat, they began obeying the king's wishes. There was general panic. Each and every person packed their bags and a sad procession began to walk and run and ride out of the city gates. There were people with their beds on their heads and bundles under their arms, driving herds of goats, cows and buffaloes, determined to get out of town in a hurry.

When the sun was about to set, a terrible silence descended on the city. There was no sound of human voices. Everyone had departed. Everyone, that is, except two people. One was Lula, who had loaded the few things he had on his back. Because he was lame, he was very very slow and he had moved only a little way towards the city gates by sunset and his arms had become very, very tired. He had cried for help to the crowds moving past him in panic, but the other people were all thinking about saving themselves, and no one had stopped to offer him a ride on a donkey or a ride in the carriages that he had so carefully cleaned outside the mosque.

The other person left behind was Bhim. He had heard the criers and he had heard the rush of people, some of whom left their shoes outside the temple and ran for the city gates. Of course, being blind, Bhim could only tell whether it was day or night by the warmth or coolness of the sun, by the sounds of crickets and birds. He shouted at passers-by to help him find the city gates, but on the banks of the dry river by the temple there was no one left to help. He decided to try and get out of the city by himself but he didn't know the way, and when he began beating the path with his stick, he knew he was going round and round in circles.

He listened for voices to ask for help but it was too late. As he wandered the streets he could hear only his own footsteps and the sound of his stick feeling the walls of the houses and clacking against the pavements. The air grew colder. Bhim knew it was nearly sunset and he remembered what the criers had said: 'By order of His Majesty the King, those who are caught inside the walls of the city after sunset will be punished for their disobedience and treason by being trampled underfoot by elephants or shot from a catapult.'

Bhim shivered and hurried along. Every now and then he paused and held his stick still. The city was silent and he could hear the sound of his own anxious breath.

Perhaps the gate was only a few yards away, he would tell himself. Perhaps if he kept very quiet, the soldiers who would come out now looking for people who had disobeyed the king would not hear him or see him. They wouldn't know he was there if he crouched in a doorway or hid in a dark alley. If they were on horseback they might not even hear the sound of his running footsteps. He listened for the sound of horses, and as he did so he heard a voice:

'Can anyone hear me? I need some help. Anyone?'

Someone else was stuck in the city too. He walked towards the voice.

It was Lula. He was sitting in the middle of the road, exhausted from moving on his hands, which were cut and bleeding. He was also very thirsty. Bhim called out to his voice.

'Are you one of the king's soldiers? Listen, boss, I've been trying to leave, but I'm blind and I can't find the way. I don't mean to defy His Majesty, I'm very sorry in fact.'

'I'm not a soldier, blind boy,' said Lula. 'I'm just a boy like you, but I've got no legs and I too have tried to get out but I move on my hands and all the skin on them is all torn with scraping.'

'I don't suppose you have any water?' asked Bhim.

'No,' replied Lula. 'I'm really thirsty myself.'

There was a silence. Then Lula said, 'I wonder which one you'll get, the elephants or the catapult. I know which one I prefer.'

'Look, don't talk about that. I've got an idea,' said Bhim. 'We're no good on our own for getting out of this mess, but if we act together, I can be your legs and you can be my eyes and maybe we can escape.'

'That's wonderful,' said Lula. 'You mean you'll carry me?'

'I'm nor tired and I'm quite strong,' replied Bhim.

'But let me warn you. The sun has already set and it's twilight and the soldiers will be at the gate.'

'Let's hope they're late. We can't just wait to be captured. Come on,' said Bhim,

Lula clambered on to Bhim's back.

'OK, turn left, then right, I can find the way from the marketplace,' he said.

The two of them set off. They turned right at the marketplace and went down several side streets. But Lula was right. When they got there, he could see a company of soldiers at the gate, guarding it, and sharing out water from their leather flasks.

'Too late,' he said to Bhim. 'As I thought. They're already there. Shall we turn back and hide?'

'No,' said Bhim. 'Let's go and talk to them. They may let us through if we explain. After all, they are human.'

The double-decker of Lula and Bhim approached the soldiers.

'By the way, if this is the end, I'd better know your name,' Lula said, 'so I can pray to Allah for your soul.'

'It's Bhim, and yours? I shall pray to Ram to preserve us.'

'Lula.'

'OK, Lula. Are we close?'

'We're nearly there. They've seen us.'

'Look what's coming,' said one soldier as the pair approached.

'You're ten minutes too late. We've got you now,' said another.

'Well, sir,' said Bhim, 'you can see that my friend here is lame and that I'm blind. Even though we wanted to, we couldn't get out fast enough. Won't you spare our lives?'

'Hold on,' said the sergeant, 'aren't you the boy who looks after shoes at the temple?'

'I am,' said Bhim.

'And aren't you the boy who cleans carriages outside the mosque?' asked another soldier.

'I am,' said Lula.

'Oh dear, that's very sad,' said the sergeant. 'Orders are orders, I'm afraid. We were told by the king that any man, woman or child passing this gate has to be punished as prescribed.'

'Well, that's perfect,' said Bhim. 'We aren't a man or a woman or a child. Have you ever seen a man, woman or child with two heads, four arms, two legs, two noses, four ears and two working eyes?'

'I can't say I have,' said the sergeant. But you're still a man or a woman or a child, so there's no escape. Sorry.'

'No, we're not,' said Lula, who was beginning to see what Bhim was getting at. 'Of course we're not. We are the first double-decker-distance-devouring-direction-divining-danger-defying-desperate-diabolical-diped. Or the D-10 for short.'

'Are you really?' asked the soldiers. Both heads of the D-10 nodded.

The sergeant put his head together with two of the corporals.

'I can see your point, but I don't know if the king will accept that,' he said. 'We'll have to let the king decide what you are. But look, we want to help. If you want to pass yourself off as a special monster we'll give you one of our extra large shirts and you can wrap it around the pair of you and the one on the back can put his arms through the sleeves.'

Lula and Bhim agreed that this would be good as a sort of disguise and one of the soldiers brought his large shirt and buttoned it up in front. Bhim held Lula with his hands behind his back and both their heads stuck out of the collar.

'We are a real D-10 now,' said Lula.

'Shall we go to the palace now?' asked the sergeant.

'Very well,' said both heads of the D-10.

The soldiers gave both heads a drink of water and immediately put the whole D-10 on a spare donkey and took it off to the palace.

The king was standing on the terrace of the palace, looking at the empty city below him. He was playing his sitar. 'So, sergeant, was anyone stupid enough to defy me and not leave town by sundown?' asked the king.

'Well, we did find something,' said the sergeant, bowing very low, 'but it's not man, woman or child. It's a kind of double boy, a monster, a double-decker-distance-devouring-direction-divining-danger-defying-desperate-diabolical-diped. Or the D-10 for short.'

'Is that so?' asked the king. 'Well, don't just grovel there, you low-down creature, ant of the earth, puppy of the mole – bring this monster forward.'

The sergeant withdrew and pushed the D-10 forward.

'If that's a D-10, Sergeant, I'm the Emperor of China. It looks devilishly like two boys, one blind and the other lame in a shirt that's too long for them, with one perched on the other's back like a tomtit. If that's a D-10, I'm a pork kabab. Speak, D-10! Aren't you a fraud?'

'Er ... I'm sorry, Your Majesty, but yes, it's true. I mean, you're right. We are what you say, a fraud,' said Lula.

'And what's wrong with the other chappie? Is he dumb too?' thundered King Tughluq.

'Oh no, no,' replied Bhim. 'You got it right first time, sire. No D-10. Just two boys who didn't want to be ... er ... found out. We had some difficulty leaving the city like you ordered sire... for... er... obvious reasons.'

'Of course,' said King Tughluq, 'just boys. Hmm. Now, I know all boys love elephants and catapults. Here's the choice. Decide amongst yourselves which likes elephants and which chooses catapults.'

The boys withdrew three steps and whispered to each other.

'What shall we say? It doesn't look good, old pal,' said Lula.

'Just play for time, I think,' said Bhim. Then he turned to the king. 'I think we've gone off both,' he said. 'We actually hate elephants and catapults.'

'So I was mistaken when I said all boys love elephants and catapults?' demanded the king.

'Oh no, no, no, Your Majesty. You were right. Quite right. It's only that we've just gone off them today. Most boys adore them,' protested Lula.

'So you're very old friends?' asked the king.

'No, sire,' replied Bhim. 'We just met today.'

'Just today?' asked the king. Then he turned to the attendants around him. 'Can't you see these boys are hungry? Get them some fruit and rice and tandoori chicken legs and lots of fruit juice. This is a civilized country . We don't do catapultings and tramplings without first giving the poor devils something to eat. Come on, boys, sit down and tell me how you met.'

So the boys sat, trembling, on the carpet on the terrace of the palace and the food was brought. They told the king the whole story of what they did for a living and how they were really trying to get to the new city and were not wilfully disobeying the king's commands.

'But if you're blind, how do you know one slipper from another?' asked the king.

Bhim told him about his collection of shells and how he used pairs of them to identify shoes.

The king was impressed.

'Now that is very clever,' he said. Then he turned to Lula. 'And for cleaning carriage wheels and brushing down camels' legs, how much do people pay you?'

'It depends on whether they are in a good mood or not,' said Lula. 'But usually when they emerge from the mosque they are feeling quite charitable.'

'That's what I want,' said the king, 'a bit of charity.'

'And the people who come out of the temple after a festival are very generous too,' added Bhim.

'That's good. That's very good,' said the king, and he stroked his own beard. Lula and Bhim noticed that he was silent and thoughtful. He began to frown.

Both Lula and Bhim were thinking the same thought. The time must have come for the trampling and the catapulting. After a minute of silence, the king spoke.

'So if you tend to the people outside the mosque and you deal with the people outside the temple,' said the king, 'you, Lula, must be a Muslim and you, Bhim, must be a Hindu.'

'Yes, sire, bull's-eye,' said the D-10 together.

'You know who should be catapulted from the highest tree and trampled under the heaviest elephants after that?' the king asked.

'Yes, Your Majesty, the two of us,' said the D-10.

'Wrong!' said the king. 'You are clever boys and you've just done me a huge service. It is I who deserve the catapulting, trampling, stretching on a rack, being thrown to the lions etc., etc. And you know why?'

The D-10 was puzzled.

'Because I am a prize idiot. I should at least have my nose tweaked. In my new city I forgot to order the building of temples and mosques. When the people get there and want to go and pray, there'll be no houses of God and they'll be furious. There'll be a riot. There'll be two riots, maybe three! Thank God you boys came along to visit and remind me. Thank you, thank you.'

'We didn't ... er ... exactly come to visit ... Your Majesty,' said the D-10. 'We were brought here to be executed, remember?'

'Executed? What nonsense! Who brought you here for execution? The sergeant of the guard? Call him in immediately, the rascal. I'll give him "execution"! I'll ... I'll have him beaten to death with cannon balls, thrown into a well full of snakes ...'

'I don't think you should do that,' said the D-10.

'Oh,' said the king. 'Can you think of something more horrible?'

'We just thought he should have his nose tweaked.'

The king laughed.

'But there isn't a moment to lose. And, my new friends, just think. If there aren't any temples and mosques, how will you chaps earn your living? There'll be no shoes outside the temple and no carriages and camels outside the mosque. Tch tch tch. How silly of me.'

The king clapped his hands and sent straightaway for the architects and builders of his new city.

When they came, he ordered that they build a temple and a mosque in prominent places in the city immediately. He also sent a very important general to tweak the sergeant's nose.

'I am going to instruct everyone that when the job of slipper-minder and carriage cleaner comes up, the two of you get those jobs.'

'Can we ask one thing?' said the D-10, using both voices.

'Whatever you want.'

'Can the temple and mosque be close to each other?' asked the D-10. 'Then the two of us can see each other every day and help each other, now that we've become friends.'

'Hmmmm. A mosque and temple next to each other. Which means the Hindus and Muslims will meet each other and be friends and that'll stop all these wicked rumours. Especially if they see what good friends you are,' said the king. 'Right, I'll do it. But promise me that every week you'll get the D-10 working and come and see me at the palace for your weekly treat and to tell me what's happening in the town.'

Lula and Bhim promised they would and the king ordered the two of them to be taken on horseback and given a new house in the new city.

'I'll see you there, boys,' the king said. 'The places of worship will be ready very soon. I've told them to get as many people as they can on to the job.'

Three weeks later, when Lula and Bhim had begun their jobs at their new mosque and temple, there arrived a messenger from the king followed by two elephants.

'The king has stopped the practice of trampling people with elephants and wishes to give the trampling elephants as a present to each of you, so you can get about.'

'Thank the king very much,' said the D-10 together. 'And add that we'll keep the elephants, but when we come to see him it'll be in a long soldier's shirt as the Death-Defying D-10.'

∼

Croc Saw-bones and Delilah

IN A NICE HOT COUNTRY, once upon a time, of course, there was a broad muddy river with lots of grass and plenty of trees and jungles growing on its banks. In the trees by this river lived a pack of grey monkeys, and in the river there lived a crocodile. The monkeys called the crocodile Croc Saw-bones, because his teeth were like the teeth of a long and wicked saw.

The crocodile swam in the river and sometimes crawled up on the bank and pretended to be a log and slept there in the sunshine. When the pack of monkeys had nothing else to do, they would tease him and throw stones at him.

If old Croc Saw-bones turned round and waddled up the bank to try and catch them, they would run away and, as he came through the grass, they would climb the nearest trees and throw coconuts and other fruit at him. Poor Croc Saw-bones got pelted with ripe fruit which was soft and splishy. The hard fruit just bounced off him.

He tried to stalk the monkeys by plastering his back with mud and digging himself into ditches under the trees. He'd wait for them, but the monkeys were very cunning. They always saw through his disguises and they knew he couldn't climb trees so they would swing on the branches from tree to tree and get clean away. As they went they would sing a song:

> See you later,
> Alligator,
> Don't you smile,
> Crocodile
> Silly old Saw-bones
> Dirty old croc
> Thick as a plank
> Smelly as a sock!

Only one monkey from the pack felt sorry for old Croc Saw-bones. She was a little monkey girl called Delilah.

She didn't believe in being cruel to the old crocodile and she never threw anything at him at all and tried to stop the others from throwing things, but they wouldn't listen to her. It was their best game.

Poor old Croc would wait for all the monkeys to swing away and then he would go down to the river to wash off the splattered berries and guavas and custard apples from his skin. He would sometimes cry hot crocodile tears because he was very angry at not being able to catch the silly, teasing monkeys.

Delilah didn't run away with the others. She would climb the tree and call out to old Croc Saw-bones.

'I'm very sorry that they teased you,' she would say. 'Did it hurt?'

'Well, not really,' the crocodile would say. 'I've got very thick skin, you see, but it is a great nuisance. I've already had a proper wash this morning.'

Then, after he'd wallowed about and washed, Croc Saw-bones would lie on the bank and Delilah would sit up in the tree and they'd talk.

Delilah liked telling stories. She would remember all the stories her daddy told her the previous night when putting her to bed and she would make up others herself to tell Croc.

All the stories she told were about fairies and princesses and Father Christmas and goblins and castles and all the old favourites like Cinderella and Snow White, and large and small and wonderful magic people. When she finished a story she would say, 'Now, Croc, you tell *me* one.

The old croc didn't know any stories about fairies or magic or castles or faraway places. The only stories he knew were about himself and about what he could see around him. They weren't real stories at all. They were just things that Croc Saw-bones had seen or done.

He would boast about the days when he was young and once he even told Delilah how he ate a whole boatful of sailors.

'I've never seen you eating anything but fish and berries,' Delilah said.

Old Croc Saw-bones only sighed.

'I've eaten all sorts of things,' he said, remembering all

the wonderful meals he'd had. Now that he was old, of course, all he could catch were the fish that swam around him. He didn't know it, but he was a very boastful and boring crocodile.

I'll give you an example. One day, when Delilah asked him for a story, this is the way old Croc began:

'Oh well, yesterday I swam all the way to the other bank. It's quite far but it's easy when you're a big strong crocodile like me and ... and then I had a little snooze in the mud there. The mud is much cleaner there because there aren't any silly monkeys the other side, you know, so they don't throw paper wrappers and junk on the banks and in the water and then I climbed out and had a little ramble around. There's some lovely fruit just coming into season over there. There are bananas, wonderful huge big bunches of yellow bananas. Oh yes, bananas like there was no tomorrow, little monkey, bananas till the greediest gorilla would fall back with a full stomach and plead for mercy ...'

That's the sort of story he told.

Delilah had heard that story before because, one way or the other, every story the old crocodile told was the same. He always managed to bring in, in some roundabout way, his trip that day to the opposite shore. And the story was always about the luscious bananas to be had when one got there.

So Delilah would distract him and make him talk about something else. 'What's your favourite colour?' she would ask.

'Oh brown,' Croc would say. 'Oh definitely, no question. Brown. And what's yours?'

Sometimes Delilah would say 'pink' or 'green', but mostly she liked to make up different shades and colours.

'Lantern blue', she'd say, or 'Evening sky orange.

'What's your favourite sport?'

'Oh wallowing,' the old croc would say. 'No choice there, wallowing every time. A sport for all seasons. The tops, the favourite. Most certainly.'

'You know mine? It's gymnastics! I can do cartwheels and double somersaults in the air and swing from branch to branch.'

'Mmmm, yes!' Old Croc Saw-bones would say.

'And your favourite food?' Delilah would ask. She had told him twenty times that her favourite food was bananas, but somehow the old croc never answered this question. He would just start munching as though he had bubblegum in his mouth and he would roll his eyes and pretend he hadn't heard the question.

One day, Delilah was asleep in a tamarind tree. She was having a lovely dream in which a handsome prince in fairyland was crossing the ocean on a big sailing ship to the land where a princess was waiting for him. Suddenly she was woken up by a terrible sound.

At first she couldn't make it out. It was a sort of crunching and howling and a low croaking sound. When Delilah opened her eyes she saw it was old Croc crying. 'What are you blubbing for, you big baby?' asked Delilah.

'I'm just so sad,' said Croc, his tears dripping with big splashes into the river. 'I've been for a swim these last two days across the river where I saw these beautiful bunches of bananas just waiting to be eaten. And there was no one there to eat them.'

'Well, why didn't you eat them, you wally?' said Delilah.

'Crocodiles don't like bananas, you see,' said Croc, 'and there aren't any monkeys to eat them on the other shore. It's really sad. Such a waste. They'll just wither on the tree.'

Delilah thought for several minutes.

The remnants of the dream of the prince kept coming back to her mind. Then she said, 'I'd really like to go and eat them, but I can't swim.'

'It's a pity,' said Croc. 'I'm sure you'd love them. But if you can't swim, well, that's that … except … er hang on. I've got an idea. Why don't I give you a piggyback across the river?'

'Because you're not a piggy, stupid, you're a crocodile!' said Delilah. She was joking.

What Delilah knew very well was that her father and the other older monkeys had warned her very sternly against two things. The first one was trying to swim across the river and the second was going too near the old crocodile. Delilah really couldn't swim more than five metres, doing a doggy paddle with her arms, so she knew that the warning against swimming in the river was sensible, but she couldn't understand why they had warned her against the poor harmless old braggart of a crocodile.

In fact, old Croc's suggestion struck her as a good idea. 'You mean you can swim with me on your back? And you wouldn't mind taking me across?'

'My pleasure,' said Croc. 'After all, you tell me the most charming stories which make me think of faraway places and grand halls and rich clothes and magic people. It takes my mind right off this slummy old swamp.'

'Well,' said Delilah, getting off the tree and climbing on to Croc's back.' I'll tell you the story of a wonderful dream I was having.'

'That'll be nice,' said Croc, and he turned and swam with his little legs moving in the water and his waist winding and twisting like a smooth piece of rope.

Delilah perched on his back.

She began her story:

'You know, Croc, the story starts where once upon a time there's this very handsome prince. Now, this prince sees an advertisement in the newspaper which makes him very suspicious. What the advertisement in the newspaper says is: WANTED: A HUNDRED WICKED DOGS TO GUARD A DARK TOWER.

'As soon as the prince reads that, he knows that something underhand is afoot. Why would anyone want to set loose a hundred guard dogs in a garden around a tower? Obviously there must be a beautiful princess being kept prisoner in that tower.'

That's the way Delilah began to tell her story. When she got to that point she looked at Croc's scaly head. She had never been so close to it before.

'Can't you go a bit faster?' asked Delilah.

You see, she felt something was wrong, because Croc was not swimming as fast as he had been. He was going more and more slowly and she noticed that every now and then he tried to turn his head. But since crocodiles don't have any necks, he couldn't.

'Is something wrong? Are you tired of carrying me on your back?' asked Delilah.

'Oh, no, no,' said Croc, 'I'm fine.'

'Then are you bored with my story? Shall we play favourites? Come on, let's. What's your favourite food? Mine's bananas!'

Croc didn't answer the question.

'Just go on with your story,' he said.

You see, what Delilah didn't know was that there *was* an answer to her question. It wouldn't be giving any secrets away to tell you that his favourite food was monkeys. The cruel old fellow liked eating monkeys. In fact, the reason he had brought Delilah out into the middle of the river on his back was because he thought that if he got far away from the shore and the other monkeys, he would dip down into the water, swim under it and turn right round and eat up poor little Delilah.

'All right then,' said Delilah. She hadn't even begun to suspect that the old crocodile was thinking evil thoughts. 'The prince called his navy and he got sixteen ships and he ordered every ship of the sixteen to be filled full of lovely cottons and silks and wonderfully carved jewellery and every possible lovely-tasting fruit in baskets full of straw and chocolates and skateboards and dolls and video games and musical toys and anything else that he could think would make a princess happy.'

'Then what happened?' asked Croc. This story was getting very good. Then he thought to himself that he'd just try going underwater once, but as soon as he did so his ears filled with water and he couldn't hear a word of the story Delilah was telling. Quickly he came back to the surface.

'... and so the prince set the pigeon free and it began to fly across the sea towards what must have been land far away,' is what Delilah was saying. Oh dear, thought Croc, I've missed a bit of the story.

'Tell me again from where the prince was ordering ships filled with bottles of Coke and cans of dog meat and all that sort of thing,' he said.

'Why don't you pay more attention, Croc? You usually listen so closely to my stories. What's wrong with you today? And anyway, how long will it take you to swim to that shore now and get to those delicious bananas? Hurry up!' Delilah was getting annoyed. This seemed like a long ride. It was even beginning to get dark. This silly old crocodile was playing some very strange games. He kept snapping his vicious jaws.

'The story, give me the rest of the story,' croaked the croc.

'Oh yes. Well, the prince had sent the pigeon with a message tied to its feet to the princess.'

'Hold on. How did the pigeon know where to go?' asked Croc.

'Because it had come from the princess in the first place, you fool,' said Delilah.

'You didn't tell me that,' said Croc. 'Is it important in the story? What I want to know is does the prince fight the hundred dogs?'

'I'll tell you that when I come to it,' said Delilah.

'That's not fair,' said Croc. 'Forget the rest of the story, just tell me whether he fights the dogs! I'm getting hungry.'

'What's getting hungry got to do with it? We can eat some bananas when we get to the other shore, can't you …' she said and her words trailed away because a thought had just struck her. The old crocodile didn't eat bananas. All this dillying and dallying and diving and ducking, what did it all mean? Only one thing was certain, thought Delilah, he was desperate to hear the end of the story.

'Right,' she said. 'I can't tell you whether he fights the dogs or not, because you wouldn't understand the whole story. That's greedy. It's skipping the main part to get to the end.'

'But does he fight them?'

'What do you think?' asked Delilah. She knew now that she had to play for time and they were only six metres away from the other shore.

'Yes, yes, yes, yes, he does, he does. He fights them, he kills them, he wipes them out, the dirty dogs! Yes, yes,' said Croc. 'And … and tell me, what does he do with the dogs after he kills them?'

'I didn't say he kills them,' said Delilah.

With a great effort, Croc Saw-bones had turned his head sideways and Delilah could see his big teeth and his big wicked eyeball in the corner of his right eye.

'He does, he does. He kills them and … and he eats them!' said Old Croc Saw-bones.

'Nothing of the sort! It's my story, so shut your ugly jaw!' said Delilah.

The croc was just about to say 'Oh' when there was a big crash and Delilah felt herself being flung over the Croc's back and onto the soft grass of the other shore. Old Croc Saw-bones had been so busy listening to the story that he'd forgotten to put his headlights on and in the dark he'd crashed into the other bank. He hurt his teeth, but that's not what he was thinking of. He was thinking of catching little Delilah and eating her up.

'Where are you, you little monkey?' shouted Croc.

But Delilah didn't reply. She was desperate to get at the bananas. She ran off and soon found herself in the banana grove that the old Croc had spoken about.

Quickly she climbed a banana tree.

Croc came scampering up.

'Where are you, Delilah?' he called.

'I'm up here, you bad wicked Croc. I know why you were looking at me and ducking and diving underwater and getting my fur wet. You want to eat me, don't you? I know why you would never tell me what your favourite food was. Because it was me!'

'Yes, yes, yes, yes, a thousand times yes,' said old Croc. 'But what' I mean is no, no, no, no, no, no, no, no, a million times no. That's not what I want you for. I did want to eat you but now all I want is to hear the end of that story.'

'Well, you've behaved very badly, so I'm not going to tell you,' said Delilah.

'I'll give you a lift back to your own shore after you've had your fill of bananas, if you'll just finish the story about the prince and the hundred dogs and the princess,' said Croc.

'I don't trust you an inch,' said Delilah. 'But if you want to hear the end of the story, just lend me some money and tomorrow I'll get on the riverboat and buy a ticket and get home. Then I'll climb safely on to a coconut tree and I'll finish the rest of the story. And if you even yawn at another monkey or open your mouth in front of one, I'll call all the others and we'll pelt you with huge, hard coconuts till you die!' Poor old Croc. He really did want to hear the end of the story about the prince, the dogs, the princess and the dark tower.

'All right then,' said Croc. 'I'll go and get my life savings and give them to you to buy a ticket on the riverboat. How you expect a crocodile to have any cash I don't know. It just so happens that my grandma gave me a gold tooth once that she'd saved from the mouth of an explorer she'd eaten. I've still got it. I can go and get it, but really, Delilah, there isn't any need. I can carry you back.'

Delilah was having none of it.

'No chance,' she said from the banana tree, her mouth full of fruit, 'Once threatened, twice very shy. So buzz off and fetch the tooth. Remember. No story till I'm safely on the other bank.'

So Croc went and fetched the tooth from where he'd buried it. He waited till the morning while Delilah slept up in the tree.

In the morning the riverboat hooted at the shore and Delilah swung across from one tree to the next and jumped on to it. The old croc dropped the gold tooth on the deck from the side without being noticed by the boatman and passengers and Delilah paid for her ticket in gold and got a bagful of change. Old Saw-bones swam behind the boat as it crossed the river.

When it reached the other bank, the rest of the grey monkeys were about. They had missed Delilah. She got out of the boat as they watched, and climbed a coconut palm.

'Are you all right?' asked the head of her monkey tribe.

'Just fine. Leave a girl alone,' said Delilah.

Saw-bones quietly crept up the mud of the bank and sat under the coconut palm and snapped his teeth to call Delilah's attention.

'Now tell me the rest of the story,' he begged.

'Oh very well,' said Delilah and she told him another teeny fragment of the story.

'More, I want more,' said Croc. Delilah said he'd have to wait till the next day and she threw him a bunch of coconuts.

'I don't eat coconuts,' protested Croc. 'No crocodiles do.'

'Oh, is that so?' asked Delilah. 'And no monkeys tell stories.'

'OK, you win,' said Croc and he ate the coconuts.

The next day Delilah told him a bit more of the story.

'The prince ordered a hundred cans of dog food to be opened.'

'And then?'

'Here comes your daily meal of coconuts,' said Delilah throwing him another bunch.

Croc ate the lot. He knew if he didn't he'd never know what happened in the story.

Every day Delilah told him a bit more and made him eat coconuts, peanuts, guavas, mangoes and even bananas. Soon Old Croc Saw-bones began looking forward as much to the coconuts and bananas as to the next instalment of the story.

In fact, fruit became his favourite thing, and by the time they reached the end of that story, old Croc Saw-bones had forgotten all about eating monkeys.

Oxo the Champion

OXO WAS THE FIGHTING CHAMPION of the world. Or he had been before he retired. He could box, wrestle, free-fight, kick-fight, do karate, judo, kendo, the lot. And what's more, according to the World Federation of Fearsome Fighting Creatures (The WFFFC), he was at one time the best in the world at them all.

This wasn't surprising as Oxo was an octopus, and with eight arms or legs he could slap an opponent on both cheeks while sending a powerful drop kick to his chest, punching him in the stomach, fending off blows with two of his arms, tripping him up with one swiftly placed shin and still have a leg left to stand on.

But this story starts when Oxo retired from fighting. It wasn't that he had grown too old or rusty. His last fight had been bad. He fought a kangaroo called Bruce Fisty and, even though Oxo won the fight, he got badly hit in the eye. One of his eyes swelled up and looked like a black snooker ball for ten weeks. Then the swelling went away, but still Oxo couldn't see clearly through that eye. The doctors told him he must never fight again or he'd go blind. So Oxo retired, still champion of all brawls.

Not knowing what to do with himself now that he didn't have to train and run and take on sparring partners for his fights and go into the gym each day, he hung around betting shops and in pubs, generally wasting his time and spending his money. Of course, after a few years of this kind of life, Oxo became very poor and he took to standing on street corners waiting for pork pies to fall from the skies. Fighting had turned him into a tired, battered old octopus.

Eventually, Oxo got fed up with doing nothing all day. He decided he didn't like being retired. He couldn't return to the ring because the doctor had clearly warned him against it, so Oxo thought he'd get himself another sort of job. He went down to the job centre and the man behind the counter said, 'Well, what was the last thing you did?'

'The last thing I did? Oh, I used to sit at my window waiting for a pork pie to drop out of the heavens.'

'Hmmm pork pie, heavens ... er ... let me see. So you're interested in food and religion?'

'You could say that,' replied Oxo.

The man looked through his cards to see what jobs were going.

'Nothing in religion at present. But you could go down to the seafood restaurant, they're looking for someone. I think you'd be ideal.'

'Thanks,' said Oxo. 'Gotta fly, gotta die, gotta get a Gorgon's eye!' It was something he used to say to his mates in the gym in his fighting days.

What a strange thing to say, thought the man. Oxo went off to the seafood restaurant in High Street. Being an octopus, he felt a bit strange walking into a seafood restaurant, but since he needed the job, he plucked up courage and went in.

The manager came out to speak to him.

'I'm sorry, sir. I'm afraid we're closed till twelve o'clock.'

'I haven't come to eat,' said Oxo. 'I've come about the waiter's job.'

'The waiter's job?' asked the manager. 'Have you done that sort of thing before?'

'No. I used to be a fighter, but I bet I'd be good at being a waiter. Having eight arms, I can carry a lot of plates and dishes all at once.'

'I can see that,' said the manager. 'But to tell you the truth we've never had an octopus serving here before. I mean people will think it's strange, because we have octopus on the menu, and it would seem funny for an octopus to be serving octopi, I mean octopuses … I mean serving people octopuses … I really mean serving octopuses to people, get it?' The manager got awfully muddled. 'I mean to say, fishes do eat other fishes, I know all that. But they don't go round serving fish to people in restaurants, do they?'

'You mean you won't give me the job?' asked Oxo.

'Believe me, I'd like to,' said the manager. 'You seem a cheerful enough chap, and once a waiter can whistle we look very favourably on employing him or her. Oh yes.

Very favourably. A whistling waiter is worth his or her weight in gold.'

'I can whistle,' said Oxo and turned his mouth into an 'O'. The most charming sea shanty came dancing out of his mouth on his strong breath.

'Yes, yes, I thought you could. Octopuses sing, don't they? Or is that dolphins? Oh dear, have I got it wrong again? You see, it's not me. I'd have you like a shot. I mean as a waiter, not for my dinner, if you see what I mean, but it's my customers. I don't think they'd like it.'

'Oh well. I know when I'm not wanted. So gotta fly, gotta die, gotta get a Gorgon's eye!' said Oxo, and he turned on all his heels and walked out.

The restaurant manager thought: *Thank goodness I didn't hire him.*

Oxo walked down the street very depressed. He had no job, no money and no food. As he was strolling along looking in the shop windows, he noticed a big sign which said 'Salesman wanted'. It was the window of a shoe shop. A wonderful shoe shop, all glass and glitter. Oxo looked at the neon sign. It said 'The Glass Slipper' and below that it said 'Shoe Boutique'.

Oxo peered in. There were beautiful shoes, beautifully arranged, the right-hand showcase containing men's shoes, the left-hand showcase displaying women's shoes. Oxo stared at the shoes for a few minutes. They were very stylish shoes, all of them. The leather looked so soft and expensive. The designs were very new and the little price tags next to the shoes had enormous numbers on them. *This is a posh shoe shop*, he thought.

He wished he was more smartly dressed, but there was nothing much he could do about that, so he just plucked up courage and walked in.

He went up to the girl at the counter and asked to see the manager.

The girl looked down her long and beautiful nose at him.

'The manageress? Certainly, sir, be seated,' she said, and she went to fetch the manageress, but Oxo could almost hear her thinking, *An octopus in a shoe shop, what next!*

Oxo sat down and very soon the manageress came and asked what she might do for him.

'The job that's advertised in the window,' said Oxo. 'For a salesman.'

'Yes, what about it?' asked the manageress.

'I want the job,' said Oxo.

'But you're an octopus,' said the manageress. 'The sign didn't say sales octopus wanted. It said salesman, or can't you read?'

Oxo thought this was very rude, but he didn't want to say so. Saying so wouldn't get him the job.

'But I can do the job just as well as a salesman, and after a while they won't notice. The customers, I mean. They come here for your excellent shoes not for some parade of salesmen.'

'You are quite right, dear fellow,' said the manageress. 'I wasn't thinking of our customers, I was thinking of you. You see, you won't be able to afford this job.'

'Afford the job? I thought *you* were supposed to pay *me* money,' said Oxo.

The manageress didn't reply. Instead, she clapped her hands gently but with great authority, and three of the young women who were serving customers just left their work and came and stood by the manageress.

'Now look at her feet,' she said. Oxo looked down.

'They are very nice feet, delicate and most becoming,' said Oxo.

'Don't be silly, young fellow, their feet have got nothing to do with it. Can't you see that they are each wearing our Cinderella range of Glass Slipper?'

'They do look very good, the shoes,' said Oxo.

'Precisely, dear boy,' said the manageress.

'Our salespeople wear only the best. They have to, you see. We can't have our girls and boys wearing trashy shoes and working in The Glass Slipper. Can we? Now, can we?'

'No ma'am,' said Oxo. 'It wouldn't do, would it?'

'Right. And do you see any of these girls smiling?' asked the manageress.

Oxo looked from their feet to their faces. They weren't smiling.

'They very rarely smile. You see, they are thinking of all the money they owe this shop and me.' The manageress grinned. 'They have to wear our shoes or they don't get the job and of course our shoes are so expensive we can't just give them away, so they have to pay for them. And if we pay them eleven pounds a week and the shoes cost three hundred times that amount, then they have to spend three hundred weeks of free work to make up the cost of the shoes.'

Oxo made a quick calculation. Eleven pounds by three hundred is thirty-three hundred. That's sixty-six years to pay off. That's a long time. No wonder the young women didn't look happy.

'You have no doubt calculated that it'll take them seventy-two years and eight months to payoff. And maybe a little longer, because we give them a little money each week for themselves and only take ten pounds off their wages for the Cinderella range.'

Oxo gulped.

'I had sixty-six,' he said.

'Ah, that was without the ten per cent interest. Oh, we charge interest here if we lend young people money,' said the manageress. Her voice was crisp and her eyes were like darts. She went on.

'And seeing as you are an octopus, dear boy, we would have to lend you three pairs of shoes and one pair of Shining Prince range gloves. That will be sixty-six four times over plus the ten per cent usual. You don't want to work here that long, do you?'

That would be two hundred and eighty-eight years at least, thought Oxo. He shook his head.

'I thought not,' said the manageress. 'I'm very sorry. For us, not for you, because we are finding it very difficult to fill this vacancy.'

'Well, OK,' said Oxo. He was good at not letting his disappointment show. 'Gotta fly, gotta die, gotta get a Gorgon's eye!' And off he went, leaving the manageress and Maisie, Daisy and Hazy a little puzzled.

Oxo went down the street again. He was very hungry and it was getting dark.

What could he do? He hadn't any money to buy any food.

He walked with some of his hands in his pockets down Piccadilly Circus to Trafalgar Square.

There were crowds of people milling about. Oxo milled about too.

From the centre of the square there came the sound of music. Oxo went towards it.

There, just near the huge stone lions on the north side of Nelson's column, stood a young man. That's not quite true. He wasn't exactly standing. He was half-standing and half-sitting on a stool. One of his feet was on a pedal attached to a lever with a drumstick on the end. The stick beat against a tatty drum. In his hands he held a guitar, and attached to his chest there was a wire contraption with a harmonica on it. The young man was singing, and now and then he'd put his mouth to the harmonica and play a few notes. As he did this, he strummed his guitar and banged the drum with his pedal. With the other foot, the young man occasionally hit a tambourine which was clipped to a spring on the side of the drum.

On the other side of the drum was a sign which said 'Mr Woosnam Woosnam, One-Man Band.'

Oxo watched fascinated as Woosnam Woosnam went from one song into the next and then straight into a third, only pausing to bang the spit out of his harmonica and adjust the spring on the tambourine. While he sang people passed by and dropped coins into the hat that lay just in front of the big drum.

At the end of the third song, Oxo found the man staring at him. He felt a bit uncomfortable. Why was the man staring at him? Of course! He had stopped to listen to all the music and he hadn't paid the young man anything. Poor Oxo. He couldn't because he had no money. He thought he'd better explain.

'Sorry, mate, I haven't got any money.'

The young man paused. 'Not even for a cup of tea?'

Oxo didn't want to answer. He was too embarrassed.

'Gotta fly, gotta die, gotta get a Gorgon's eye!' he said, and turned to leave.

'Oi, poet,' shouted Woosnam Woosnam after him, 'I've finished here, I'm going for a bite myself. Just give me that line and I'll give you a sausage.'

'Thank you, but I can't,' said Oxo, more embarrassed than ever. He began to walk briskly through the crowd.

As he got to the edge of the square he felt a hand on his smooth head.

'Now, wait a minute, buddy, I was talking to you,' said Woosnam Woosnam. On his back were his drum and his guitar and he'd folded the harmonica quite close to his chest.

'I'm sorry, said Oxo, 'Gotta fly, gotta …'

Woosnam interrupted him 'Yeah, yeah, yeah. We know all that. Come and have a sandwich with me, I can see you're looking for work. I've got an idea, a great idea.' Oxo was tempted, so off he went. Woosnam took him into Soho to a café from which he was not banned (because One-Man Bands usually take up so much space that they are told by lots of places not to come in at all).

Oxo ate his sausage and drank his tea.

'That's all I can afford to buy you,' said Woosnam Woosnam. 'You see, I've only collected two pounds today.

The bottom's fallen out of this business. I am an honest One-Man Band, straightforward stuff, guitar, drum, vocals, harmonica and the occasional tambourine or rattle. But it doesn't work any more. The public have got so spoilt by these jugglers and clowns and other street-performing folk who never used to be street-performing folk. All sorts of out-of-work lawyers, architects and gynaecologists rushed into the trade, singing and dancing and playing electronic accordions. It's ruined. The public has turned thirsty for gimmicks.'

Oxo nodded.

'I can't think of a gimmick. I can play any musical instrument but I only have two hands and two feet and one mouth.'

'So do all the lawyers and architects and out-of-work gynaecologists,' protested Oxo.

Woosnam Woosnam just gave a hollow little laugh.

'Can you play any music?' Woosnam asked.

'Not a note.'

'That doesn't matter at first. I'll teach you. You can come into my business and be my partner. We'll call ourselves Woosnam Woosnam and Oxo. Or better still, Oxo and Woosnam Woosnam.'

'And what shall we play?' asked Oxo.

'How can you ask?' asked Woosnam. 'Come home with me and we'll discuss the possibilities.'

Woosnam Woosnam took Oxo home. Oxo was astounded. Woosnam Woosnam had a huge house with ten steps going up, to the front doors and seven bedrooms. When Oxo first walked in, the splendour of the place took his breath away. The drawing room was full of old paintings on the walls and it had antique furniture and two chandeliers. At first Oxo could only just make these out in the dim light.

'Why don't you turn on the lights?' asked Oxo.

'That's a waste of money,' said Woosnam. 'I can see perfectly clearly in the dark.'

Woosnam Woosnam showed Oxo to a bedroom at the top of the house. 'You can stay here for a while if you like,' he said.

Oxo thanked him. It was damp and cold, but even so Oxo could see that it had once been splendid with Persian carpets and Chinese vases.

That very night Woosnam began to teach Oxo the violin, the viola, the cello and the double bass. They went down to the cellar by candlelight and brought out the musty, old cases covered with cobwebs which contained these antique instruments. In a few days' time, Oxo was ready. He knew how to hold the instruments and how to bow them, even though he couldn't play more than a few notes on each.

'Deep end,' said Woosnam, 'I believe in the deep end.'

Off they went with the violin, viola, cello and double bass in Oxo's arms.

In the heart of Covent Garden they set up with two soap boxes. Woosnam gave Oxo three of the instruments and they took up positions, Oxo with the strings and Woosnam Woosnam with his drum and harmonica and cymbals as before.

'Let's go, said Woosnam. 'A-one, a-two, a-three, four.'

They began to play. The sound that emerged was horrible. Naturally, with very little practice, Oxo couldn't play the violin, viola or the double bass.

Still the crowds gathered and threw money after each movement and after each piece. They clapped their hands, laughed and shouted. They had never heard an octopus playing three instruments all at once and Oxo had never heard the clink of so much money in a hat. Each time Oxo got tired, Woosnam Woosnam would ask him to stop and would carry on in his old way, with his honest drum, guitar and harmonica, but however well he sang and played, the crowd melted away and the coins stopped dropping.

Day after day it was the same story. Oxo slowly began to learn how to play the instruments he was holding. He had improved a bit but not all that much. Each evening they would come home and Woosnam Woosnam would gather up all the money they had collected. Together they would go to the corner store and Woosnam would buy a can of beans and a loaf of bread and they'd take it home and eat it without first heating the beans. The rest of the money Woosnam took and hid somewhere in the house.

You see, Woosnam Woosnam, as Oxo found out, was a miser.

'We earned a lot of money today, can't we have a proper meal?' Oxo would ask.

'You want jam, don't you?' Woosnam would reply. 'There are people starving all over the world and you think of proper meals. Be thankful for what you've got.'

'So what are you doing with the money?' Oxo asked one day.

'Never you mind. I picked you up off the street. It's my money . You practise your instrument and keep your mouth shut.'

So every day Oxo and Woosnam returned to a dark house because Woosnam Woosnam hadn't paid the electricity bills and the power had been cut off.

One day Woosnam Woosnam began to cough and wheeze and couldn't play his mouth organ.

'Look, we made a lot of money again today,' Oxo said. 'Let's buy you some cough mixture.'

'Cough mixture? Are you mad? That costs money!' said Woosnam. In the next few days poor Woosnam's cough became worse and his nose got bunged up. He felt very, very ill. So much so that one day when Oxo went to wake him up to go to work, he couldn't even get out of bed.

'Oh well, we can't go and do a gig today,' said Oxo.

'What do you mean ? You go by yourself. Earn some money, you lazy octopus. Humph. Except to be fed for nothing.'

Oxo was distressed. He didn't want to be called a sponger, so he took his instruments and went out to play. He set the instruments up and began. What he noticed was that the strings sounded even worse without the drum and the mouth organ and the cymbals and the whole racket that Woosnam Woosnam made to cover up his squeaky fiddlings.

The crowd did gather, but this time they gathered only to laugh. No one gave him any money.

Just as Oxo was about to pack up, he heard the most fantastic sound coming from the other corner of the square. He looked up and saw that a huge crowd had gathered. He packed up his instruments and just out of curiosity went to see where the music was coming from.

He pushed his way through the crowd. There in the middle of the clearing was a giant centipede. In this creature's hundred hands were twenty violins, three saxophones, three oboes, kettledrums, several flutes, clarinets, a full forty-nine piece orchestra. Around him were six hats and even as Oxo watched the hats were filling up with money.

Without a word, Oxo retreated. He went home to their dank dark house. Woosnam was still coughing and spitting and refusing to call the doctor in case the doctor prescribed some medicine and he had to pay prescription charges.

'How much did we make today?' was the first question Woosnam asked.

'Oh lots,' said Oxo.

'Give it to me and I'll put it away,' said Woosnam, his voice weak and trembling.

Oxo held out his hat, even though there was nothing in it. He was dreading Woosnam's reaction when he found out that he hadn't even got a penny. Woosnam pushed his legs feebly out of the blankets, but as he tried to stand up he fell back onto the bed.

'It's no good, I'm too weak to get up,' he said.

'Tell me where I should put the money,' said Oxo.

'The third floorboard in the dining room, it's loose,' said Woosnam and he sank back into bed.

Oxo rushed down the stairs to the dining room and he heard Woosnam shouting.

'No, no, no, I made a mistake. The money's not there. Not here at all.'

But of course the money was there.

Oxo pulled back the floorboards and found Woosnam's little hoard. There were bundles of notes and a biscuit tin full of coins under the floorboards. Oxo took all the money out and pocketed it.

The next day he said goodbye to Woosnam, took his instruments and the money and went straight to the record shops. He bought a ghetto-blaster with a built-in CD player and twenty CDs of violin pieces and trios and quartets and he went down to Covent Garden. The centipede was performing at one end of the square and Oxo set up at the other.

He turned up the CD with its crystal display, picked up his instruments and mimed to each record he played. The sound was loud and clear and perfect, because the greatest players in the world were playing the instruments on record. The crowds began to gather. They could see the ghetto blaster and they could see the octopus miming to it.

In an hour the crowd around the centipede had deserted him and had gathered around Oxo. They were listening and watching, and they were laughing. They were laughing their heads off. The public could see it was a fraud, but it was funny fraud.

Oxo's hat filled up with money.

Each day he'd go out and play the CD players on the ghetto blaster and gather money. Each evening he would return with some packet soup for Woosnam to drink.

One day, while he was playing to a crowd that stood in a circle round him, a very important-looking policeman pushed his way through the crowd.

'What's going on here? Don't you know that you are on council property and begging is forbidden here?'

'I'm not begging, I'm playing,' said Oxo.

'Leave him alone, officer, he's only miming to the music,' shouted the crowd.

But the policeman was stubborn.

'It's against ... well, it's against something. It's fraud! He's pretending to play music, but I'm very clever. I know the music is really coming from this ... this ghetto blaster.'

'Go on, officer, let him play. We were enjoying it and he never asked for no money,' the crowd shouted.

'What's this then?' the policeman said and kicked Oxo's cap which lay in front of him with the coins that people had given him.

'Oh, must have dropped it,' said Oxo, lifting it up and putting it on his head.

'Let him stay, you old spoilsport flatfoot!' shouted someone in the crowd.

The rest of the crowd took it up and there was a lot of noise, everyone shouting at the policeman.

'Get out of it! Big bully! He ain't done nothing!' and so on.

The policeman was furious.

'All right, all right, all right,' he said and held up his hands for calm.

The crowd quietened down.

'Good. Now tell me why I should let this ragamuffin stay.'

'Because he can play anything you want.'

'Is that a fact?' asked the policeman. 'Well, I bet you he can't play anything *I* want. Not without his silly CD player anyway.'

'Bet you he can!' shouted back the crowd.

'Right then. I'll take your bet. If he can, then I'll let him stay. If he can't, he has to pack it in and never come back on my beat.'

'Done,' shouted the crowd.

'Right then. The piece I want you to play, my ole son, is Beethoven's string quintet!'

'What! Quintet! But that's not fair, he's only got eight hands! As it is, he stands on one leg and leans the double bass against his body.'

'See what I mean? Now clear off. And if I see you back here you'll be arrested.'

The policeman of course had won his bet. There was no way that Oxo could play five instruments, especially an extra viola, and he knew that he couldn't play anything without the CD players and ghetto blaster anyway. Or could he?

'Gotta fly, gotta die, gotta get a Gorgon's eye!' muttered Oxo under his breath.

Woosnam Woosnam was very surprised that he'd come home early. He was well enough now to walk about the house.

'Tell me, Woosnam,' said Oxo, 'what did you do before you became a street musician.'

'Dear boy,' said Woosnam, 'I was the finest classical musician that Tooting ever produced. I played and I taught instruments and the rich and famous flocked to my classes.'

'So why did you become a miser?' Oxo asked, being very direct.

'Miser? How dare you insult me, sir! I was in a string quartet, the most famous, the best. The Tooting String Quartet. We had bookings in Vienna, in Chicago, in Watford.'

'So what happened?'

'You dare ask, dear boy? Just before we were to set out on a world tour, the violinist, wretched girl, ran away with the cellist. The other member of the quartet ... well, she resigned.'

'Why did they run away? Why didn't they stay and be in love and play?' asked Oxo.

Woosnam sighed.

'Have you ever been in love, Oxo? It all went wrong. They ran away because the violinist was engaged to be married to me and the viola player was engaged to be married to the cellist. Then these two found that they couldn't stand me or the viola player, switched partners and had to run away to Venezuela. Since then everything has gone to rack and ruin. I can't see any point in lighting this house or eating good food or living well.'

'I see,' said Oxo. 'But why are you so mean with money?'

'Because I used to have all this, but to tell you the truth, as a one-man band I didn't earn much more than a few pounds a day, and I was saving my money to go to Venezuela to ... to take my revenge on the girl and the partner who betrayed me.'

'So you know how to play all the instruments?' asked Oxo.

'Any piece you like,' said Woosnam.

'Including Beethoven's quintets?'

'Every single one!'

'Fine, we are going to get to work,' said Oxo. 'After all, you have taught me the elements of the strings and I can play simple things.'

Right through the night the two of them practised the quintet. By breakfast time they were perfect.

The next day Oxo persuaded Woosnam to step out. He wrapped him up in a scarf and a great coat and they got to the same spot from which Oxo had been evicted the day before. They set up their boxes and with Woosnam playing the lead, they launched into Beethoven's String Quintet Op. 241. Quicker than usual, a crowd gathered. Oxo and Woosnam Woosnam played for all they were worth and the crowd, some of whom had been there the day before, were enchanted.

As they started the second movement, there was a disturbance at the back of the crowd. Someone was pushing his way in. It was the policeman. He shoved and pushed as he had been trained to do when going through a crowd. *Oh dear, we are going to be arrested*, thought Oxo. The same thought struck people in the crowd.

Still Oxo and Woosnam played on. The policeman pushed his way to the front of the crowd and stood transfixed. He folded his arms and listened. It was his favourite piece of music. And this time there was no CD player or ghetto blaster.

As Oxo and Woosnam played the third movement, he was moved. When they'd finished, the policeman was the first to reach into his pocket and pull out a pound coin to put in Woosnam Woosnam's hat.

The morning was a great success. They had to empty the hat four times because people were giving them so much money.

That night Oxo and Woosnam rehearsed some more pieces and the next day again there was a huge crowd and lots of money. Oxo even noticed that among the crowd was the centipede, clapping with all fifty pairs of hands when they finished.

Oxo stuffed the money into his pockets. By the time they'd finished playing that evening, Oxo was ready to tell Woosnam that he'd stolen the money from the floorboards and bought a CD player. He told him about the policeman and everything that had happened.

'But we've got enough money now for you to go to Venezuela ten times over,' said Oxo.

'I don't want to go any more,' said Woosnam Woosnam, 'I think I'll use it to pay the electricity bills and get some lights back in the house. Then we'll buy a vacuum cleaner and clean the dust up, and we'll buy some clothes, for you and for me. And you know what, Oxo? Tonight we'll go to a restaurant that you choose and have a big, big meal.'

'Hmm,' said Oxo, 'There's a shoe shop I'd like to go to and buy eight pairs of shoes. One set to wear and one for 'best'. As for the restaurant, there's this fish place I'd love to go to. I know the manager. And the next time we have a party, can we invite a policeman and a centipede?'

Damyanti the Rubbish Doll

ONCE UPON A TIME, IN a far-off land, there was a sleepy little town through which ran a long winding river. On the banks of this river there was a rubbish dump and all the dustmen of the town came and dumped their barrows and bins here after cleaning up the streets.

Other people from the town also brought their junk to the dump. It was a place with a little wall running all round it, and from far away you could see the mountain of junk that the townspeople had piled up. There were broken beds, bottles, pipes, sticks, old rubber tyres, bits of rusty metal from cars, pieces of broken-up bicycles, mattresses with their guts spilt out, cardboard boxes, stacks of old newspapers and books, torn, musty old clothes and countless other things.

What the people of the town didn't know, not even the dustmen, was that when the rubbish dump was shut at night and the moon shone down on the mountain of junk, things would begin to move. At first slowly, and then throbbing and pushing from the bottom of the heap upward, would come the rubbish creatures. There was Grubella the rubbish horse, Platty the rubbish duck, Tyro the rubbish elephant and Damyanti the rubbish doll. These were the rubbish people and they lived in the rubbish heap. They were born of rubbish, made of rubbish and rubbish was all they knew. Grubella, Platty, Tyro and Damyanti were, each of them, made of broken bits and pieces. Tyro's trunk was an old Hoover tube, his back was part of an old mattress, his knees were old bed springs and his ears were thrown away bits of ceiling fan. Platty was made of old television sets and Grubella's body was all old tyres.

Damyanti was just as strange. She was tied together with string and stuck together with old hinges. Her eyelids were cracked seashells and her hands were moth-eaten gloves, one bigger than the other. Her nose was a clothes peg and her hair was a discarded mop.

There was only one thing these rubbish folk had in common. All their stomachs were made of plastic bags with supermarket brands printed on them, the sort people do their shopping with and throw away. Tyro had the thickest plastic bag for a tummy and Damyanti had one made of such thin stuff that you could almost see through it. Now the sides of these plastic bags would stick very closely together and flatten out the stomachs of the creatures unless they kept them filled with rubbish. The creatures lived on the rubbish heap and ate off it, stuffing their stomachs and keeping the bags as full as they could.

When they emerged from the rubbish at night, the rubbish people would roam about the town, keeping as quiet as they could so as not to wake anyone up. They went jogging slowly round the town, looking in shop windows and picking up scraps of rubbish from dustbins and from the pavements as they went. During the day they slept.

The diet of the rubbish people was strange. You could call it a very, very mixed diet. They could put almost anything into their hungry plastic bellies. They could crunch broken glass with their teeth, they could swallow old bits of paper, cigarette butts, plastic packets, orange and potato peel, eggshells, you name it, they'd eat it. Damyanti's favourite was sticky old chewing gum that someone had chewed and spat out or stuck in an ash tray or secretly under the top of a table. Some of the things they ate were too disgusting to mention. They never went hungry because the rule of rubbish diet was that they ate what no one else wanted. In that sleepy little town the people weren't very neat or tidy and they did drop things on the pavements and some of them were distinctly litter louts.

One night, as the four of them spread out through the town, Damyanti found a bit of chocolate wrapping paper and of course she gobbled it up. A few steps further on the same pavement she found ten crisp packets and one by one ate them up too. A little further on there were sweet wrappers, ice lolly-sticks, orange peel, the skins of bananas – a never-ending trail of goodies. Damyanti kept her eyes on the pavement and picked up the rich reward. She must have gone a long way, because when she looked up to speak to the others they were nowhere to be found.

'Platty, Tyro, Grubella, where are you?' she shouted.

There was no reply. She walked back the way she had come. The streets were all deserted. No rubbish horse, no rubbish elephant and no rubbish duck. So what was she going to do? She turned another corner. There was another distraction. Someone had dropped a half-eaten ice-cream cone. It was splattered on the pavement. Damyanti licked it up with her leather tongue, forgetting for a moment that she was good and lost.

When she'd licked every bit up, Damyanti looked around. She didn't recognize the streets or the closed shops or the houses. Oh dear! she thought, what am I going to do?

'Grubella,' she shouted again, and then she listened for a reply, but none came.

Damyanti was sad. The sun was coming up and she could hear birds in the trees. She walked this way and that, but she was well and truly lost.

Finally she sat down on the doorstep of a house.

I'll have to wait for the people of the town to wake up and then ask my way to the rubbish dump again, she thought.

She had eaten a lot, her plastic-bag stomach was well stuffed. She felt drowsy. Leaning against the doorpost of the house, she fell asleep.

When Damyanti woke up it was bright daylight and there were cars and carts and people on the streets. When she opened her eyes she got a little shock because there, staring right into her face, was another face. It was the face of a little boy.

'What a beautiful little dolly, it's opened its eyes,' said the boy.

Now, Damyanti had never in her short and happy life been called beautiful and she liked this boy straightway.

'Can you tell me the way back to the rubbish dump?' asked Damyanti but the boy shook his head. He didn't understand Rubbich which is the language that the rubbish people spoke. In fact, even though Damyanti had seen people at the dump before she'd never ever tried to speak to a real person.

'I'm going to take you home,' said the boy and he lifted Damyanti up. 'Even though I can't understand what you're saying. I'll teach you to talk properly.'

The little boy did take Damyanti home. In his room in the large house, there were all sorts of other toys. The boy put Damyanti down next to a very smart robot toy, all metal and silvery. This robot toy could speak too, but it said the same things over and over again: 'I am a robot. I am in the service of the master ...' A lot of nonsense.

There were other toys that spoke. There was a flying saucer full of spacemen who said weird things, a group of monkeys who drank tea and said 'thank you for the lovely cup of tea', a computer which sang songs. No wonder the boy didn't find her strange.

The little boy kept Damyanti in his room for several days. Soon she found out that he was called Fred and that his mother loved him very much. Fred treated her very well, but Damyanti wanted to go home. She knew he wouldn't let her go and she couldn't run away because she couldn't reach the bolt of the front door even if she stood on a chair.

So for days and days Damyanti lived in Fred's house and he played with her and she played with his toys and it was nice and warm and in fact she was very happy in every way except two. Firstly she missed Tyro and Platty and Grubella. Secondly she was constantly hungry.

Fred's father and mother were so tidy and clean that they threw all their rubbish into a chute which reached the bins down in the basement. So poor Damyanti could never find scraps to eat.

No one noticed that Damyanti was hungry. Who ever heard of a doll eating food? Fred shut the door of his room, so Damyanti could never get round the house and explore the kitchen. It was tough.

Several years passed. Fred grew up and he started going out on his own and spending his pocket money.

He also became more and more untidy. He was always rushing here and there. He would come in chewing gum and stick it here and there. He would throw sweet wrappers about his room and he'd leave half-eaten wrappers of fish and chips with cigarette butts stuck in them on his table.

When he went out again, Damyanti would sweep it all up.

As time went by, the sleepy little town began to wake up. The small houses were pulled down and big houses were built. The small winding roads were dug up and big straight ones were built instead. Some of the old shops were replaced with shiny new ones with plastic tables and chairs and big lit-up signs.

Damyanti didn't know any of this because she stayed at home. Fred, however, saw it all happening. One day he was in a hurry to go out with his friends and his mother shouted at him, 'Please eat your dinner before you go out. Eat it while it's hot.'

'Can't, Mum,' said Fred. 'No time. I won't go hungry, I'll pick up some junk food.'

Junk food? Damyanti couldn't believe her ears. He was going to eat junk food? What was this junk food?

That night she stayed awake waiting for Fred to come back home. Sure enough, when he came back and switched on the light, he had in his hand a paper packet with some stuff inside it. He sat on the edge of the bed and took a bite of the stuff.

'Yuk! It's cold,' he said aloud. 'They don't call this junk food for nothing.' He left the packet on the floor by the bed. He was very tired and he changed into his pyjamas and turned the light out and went to sleep.

When Damyanti was sure that he was asleep she crawled out of her corner and peered into the large paper bag. There was all sorts of stuff in it, chips and ketchup, and a burger and a sort of soft bun. She was desperately hungry but she had never eaten a real proper human meal before. She was used to leftovers. Still, she thought she'd try it. After all, Fred had bitten into it and there was a crumpled paper napkin crushed into the bag.

Damyanti put her head into the bag and took a bite. It tasted almost familiar. In fact, it was delicious. Before she could stop herself she'd eaten it all, the plastic container and the napkin and everything except the paper bag. She stopped herself eating that. Instead of gobbling it up she very quietly climbed into the bag and when she was inside, crumpled it up and pulled the top over her.

In the morning, even before Fred woke up, Damyanti heard his mother come into his room.

'Look at that, junk food again!' she said. 'I can't even bear to look at the stuff. It's such a waste, Fred, you buy this stuff and you've left it. I can feel the weight of it. You've hardly eaten any. Still, I suppose the less you eat the better it is for you.' Then she picked up the paper bag with Damyanti in it.

After a few moments Damyanti felt a ticklish feeling in her stomach as she went down the rubbish chute in the paper bag, just like being on a big giant slide and she landed with a thump on her bottom.

Damyanti was used to rubbish, to living in it and being covered by it and sure enough, when she peeked out of the bag, she was in a huge metal rubbish bin and some eggshells and the remains of a tomato-and-bacon breakfast came tumbling down on her head.

Damyanti was quite happy and excited. Her plan was working. In a few minutes' time a truck came and lifted the rubbish bin up as if by magic and emptied all the rubbish into the truck. Then off they went. Damyanti whistled to herself. Soon she'd be back at the old rubbish dump, her old home, and see Platty and Tyro and Grubella and she could be a rubbish person again. She was dying to tell them about the lovely new kind of food she had discovered.

Alas! It was not to be. When the truck reached the dump Damyanti could see that everything had changed. There were no longer great mountains of beautiful rubbish up against the high wall. Several young people in boiler suits were rummaging through a truckload of stuff that had been dumped. It was the same rubbish dump but it now had twenty metal containers and there were signs all over calling the place a 'RECYCLING CENTRE'. The boiler-suit people were directing the motorists who came with their rubbish to sort out their rubbish into metal and bottles and paper and all sorts of other categories.

The rubbish truck dumped the load with Damyanti in it and one of the boiler-suit people came and grabbed poor Damyanti by the arm and threw her into a container with a lot of other damaged and discarded toys.

Damyanti looked around frantically for Platty and Tyro and Grubella, but they weren't here. And what's more there wasn't even the old rubbish to eat. There was plenty of Lego and smashed-up tank engines and teddies whose tummies had burst, but Damyanti had lost her appetite for that sort of junk. She'd have to wait for better things to come.

She didn't have long to wait. The next morning the whole container was taken off to another place, and from there Damyanti was chosen from the broken toys to be sent to an Oxfam shop. That's where poor Damyanti landed up, staring out of the front of a glass case in a shop full of old clothes and toys. It was quite pleasant except for the fact that the two ladies who worked in the shop only ate muesli and thick brown bread and lettuce and they were very clean and never left any rubbish lying about. Every day Damyanti would cross her fingers and hope that one of them would get the urge to have a hamburger or a load of greasy chips or some thick milkshake made out of whipped oils. But no. Each day for lunch the young ladies would eat the same things – brown bread and vegetarian cheese or bowls of muesli.

Damyanti lost count of the number of weeks, months or years she stayed in the Oxfam shop, starved of rubbish, starved of junk food and starved of the company of her old friends.

Then one day Fred and his girlfriend walked into the shop. *My, my, how old he looks and how handsome,* thought Damyanti.

She wanted to wave, but before she could, Fred's girlfriend came and picked her up.

'This is the sweetest thing!' she said.

'My God!' said Fred. 'It's my rubbish doll. For years, Petula, I've been wondering where it went. I thought it was lost for ever and here it is. I thought it had come to life and run away.'

Then Fred turned to Damyanti. 'You weren't unhappy with me and mother, were you, ragamuffin?' he asked.

Damyanti made no reply.

Fred bought Damyanti for a few pence and his girlfriend Petula took her home.

Damyanti wasn't sure she wanted to go with Petula. At least sitting in the shop window she could look out on the street all day and watch the people go by.

But Damyanti was in for a surprise. There in Petula's bedroom on the low shelf next to her wardrobe were all her toys, and amongst them, hurrah, hurray, were Grubella, Platty and Tyro. They'd all landed up here because the recycling policy had sent them off to the Oxfam shop from where Petula always got her toys.

Damyanti was overjoyed and so were the others. They spent all night telling her about their adventures and she told them about hers.

'But what about food?' asked Damyanti.

'There's quite enough of that,' said Platty. 'It's not rubbish, but it's something new and we three quite like it.' Damyanti's heart sank. She had looked around the room and drawn her own conclusions. One of the posters on the wall said 'Smoking Kills'. Another one said 'Save The Rainforests. They Save You!' A third one said 'Killing Chickens Is Wrong'.

'Don't tell me,' said Damyanti, 'she only eats lettuce and muesli and lentil cakes. Oh well.'

Grubella smiled and put her hoof to her lips.

'That's only in the daytime, when Fred and her mother and father and friends are looking. Petula is really a secret junk-food eater. At night she brings in jumbo portions of all sorts of things – junk food like you've never seen before. And she can never eat the lot. See that bin there? That's our larder. She takes a bite from a hamburger or an American fried chicken leg or an instant pizza, and goes 'mmmmm' and throws the rest away. All for yours truly and friends.'

'But doesn't she know you eat up the rest?'

'Of course she does,' said Platty. 'But over the years we've taught her to speak Rubbich and we have a deal. We won't tell anyone about her little habits if she'll bring home generous portions a few times a week.'

'That sounds great to me,' said Damyanti and when Petula came in that evening, and picked up the rubbish doll, Damyanti gave her a big wink.

~

The Bright Princess

ONCE UPON A TIME, VERY long ago, there was a king called Asman and he had a very beautiful daughter called Surya. This princess lived on her own in Asman's palace. She had maidservants to fetch her everything she wanted, but she was kept all by herself and no man was ever allowed to set eyes on her.

There was a very good reason for this. You see, when Surya was born, King Asman gave a very big party and he invited all the people in his kingdom and fed them cakes and ale and crisps, papayas, starfruit and mangoes. There was music and there were games and even party bags for people when they went home. The invitations for the party had been posted to every corner of the country.

Now, in this kingdom there was a wicked witch. Or at least people said she was a wicked witch. Her name was something dreadful. It was so dreadful that people who said her long and complicated name got a sharp pain in their tongues, so instead everyone in the kingdom just called her WW, that's 'double-u, double-u'. King Asman was a very just and straightforward king and he believed that people were only wicked when they had been found guilty of some crime. In other words, he believed that even the wicked witch was innocent until she had been proved guilty. So he sent her an invitation to the party.

When WW got the invitation, she dressed up in her best golden gown, saddled up her donkey on which she used to get about and went to the king's palace at exactly the right time. The king was at the door of the palace greeting everyone. People brought the new baby princess a lot of presents. As always happens in stories about good witches and bad witches, the good ones brought her magic wishes which would come true later on in life. For example, one of them said, 'Thank you for inviting me, King Asman, I wish that your daughter will always love you.'

Another one said, 'Thank you for inviting me, King Asman, I wish that your daughter will be very very clever.'

Then WW turned up and the king said, 'Hello' and asked her to step in and join the party.

WW cackled and said, 'I am so delighted to be invited and I've brought your daughter a wish which will come true.'

'Thank you,' said the king, but somewhere in his mind he was wishing he hadn't invited this person. Even as the shadow of this thought crossed his mind, he was telling himself not to be so silly.

'You know what?' said WW. 'I can see from your face that you don't really want a wish from me, now do you?'

'Well … er … I don't know, you … er … really shouldn't have bothered … er … we would just like your company. No wish, no wish.'

'Don't be silly and don't insult me,' said WW. 'I'm a witch and I have to make wishes for newborn babies, but since you are so sensitive, I'll let you approve of my wish.'

'Oh, all right then,' said the king.

'Well, I wish that your daughter … er … what's her name again?'

'Surya!'

'Ah yes, Surya. I wish that your daughter Surya will be so beautiful that her beauty will shine in the world as brightly as a hundred suns. OK?'

'Well, it's very nice of you,' said the king and then he passed on to his other guests who were queuing up to come inside.

WW went in. She went straight to the food table and there was a great hush as people saw her sweeping in, trailing the end of her golden gown.

'Wow, that's WW herself,' people said to one another softly.

'All right then, where's the rat-and-lizard cake?' asked WW.

'Oh dear,' said one of the footmen who was serving the food, 'there isn't any of that. There's only chocolate cake and a cake with almonds and a cake with raisins, but none of the … the … the thing you asked for.' The poor man went red in the face.

'Hmmmph,' said WW. 'All right, I'll have some frizzled pigtail crisps.'

'I'm sorry,' said the footman, 'we didn't think anyone at the party would want any of those, so we haven't got any.'

'Not got any?' asked WW. 'What kind of a trashy party is this? I want a drink. Get me some sick bull's blood and put a dash of freshly shaved black cat's hair in it.'

This time the poor footman couldn't stand it. He held his mouth and fled from the room.

'What's the matter with that man? What kind of a party is this? Nothing to eat or drink?' shouted WW.

Another footman rushed up.

'What can I get you, madam?'

'Don't you madam me, you chewed-up dog biscuit. Get me a bowl of birds' eye soup, but remember I'm allergic to pigeons' eyes so don't mix them in.'

'But ... but, madam, we ... only have ale, raspberry milkshakes and orange juice and pure apple juice and lassi and bottled water and beer even, but no ... er ... soup ... er of that sort.'

WW stamped her foot. 'This is the worst party I've ever been to,' she said. 'I demand to see the king.'

Everybody was now staring at her as the footman rushed off to call King Asman.

By the time the king came, WW was ranting. 'You invited me, but you didn't think to provide any of the stuff I eat, did you?'

'I'm very sorry,' said the king. This wasn't what he'd expected. In fact, he had no idea what this horrible witch ate. 'Do try some trifle, though, it's delicious and the ice cream comes in seven hundred flavours.'

'I don't eat ice cream,' said WW, 'or anything else at this wretched party. I'm leaving. And I'm taking part of my wish with me, you stupid king. You know I wished your daughter would be so beautiful that her beauty would light up the world like a hundred suns? Well, her beauty will be so bright that no man will be able to go near her. They'll get burnt as soon as they look upon her and turn into pieces of shrivelled crispy bacon – and if they come any closer they'll turn into ash. Hah! There. So she won't have any boyfriends and she won't have any nice princes coming to marry her.'

With this she gathered up her golden gown and swept out into the coach park where her donkey was waiting.

The king was stunned. What could he do? He ordered the musicians to play some happy music. Little baby Surya started crying in her cot. A flock of ravens flew over the palace and grounds to their nests in the high trees of the jungles beyond.

The years passed and Surya grew up and sure enough, she grew prettier and prettier and her beauty was such that when King Asman or any other man, her brothers or the footmen of the palace, looked at her they had to shield their eyes. It was like looking at a very, very bright light or looking at the sun. And as the years passed it became worse.

Soon King Asman had to wear very dark glasses every time Surya came into the room. Finally, when she was no longer a little girl, the king issued orders that no man should go into the room where Surya was. Women could look at her and be safe, but that was only because WW had forgotten to mention women when she put this bad wish on Surya.

When the princess was sixteen years old, King Asman was faced with a terrible problem. It was a tradition in their royal family to have a portrait of every member of the family when they turned sixteen. He sent for his court painter who was called Boss Chitra.

'Do you see the problem?' the king said to Boss Chitra. 'You've got to paint her, but you can't see what she looks like.'

'That's a tricky one, Your Majesty,' said Boss Chitra, 'but there are a few things I can try.'

'Well, you'd better,' said the king, 'or I'll chop your head off. Only joking, only joking!'

'That's not a very funny joke coming from Your Majesty. You had me worried,' said Boss Chitra.

'All you artists ... never take a joke,' said the king. 'But seriously, I haven't seen my daughter for years. I only speak to her on the telephone, so I'd like a portrait of her. I'll give you all the gold you can take away in a wheelbarrow if you do a truthful portrait of her.'

Boss Chitra went away and as he thought and thought an idea came to him. The next day he asked that Princess Surya sit by her window at the palace. He ordered from the glass makers a hundred huge mirrors. He placed the first of them at an angle just outside the princess's window. He placed another a hundred yards away so that it caught the reflection of the first and so that it stood at the corner of the palace outside in the garden. The third one he placed so that it would catch the reflection of the second one round the corner. And so on with the fourth and fifth and sixth and seventh, till he got to the hundredth. Every mirror looked at the one before it, zigging and zagging across the lawns of the palace garden. Then he set up his easel and his canvas in front of the last mirror. If she was too bright to look on with his eyes, he would see her through a hundred reflections, in a mirror.

Surya did as she was told. In the morning she came out and sat by the window and just as she did so there was a blinding flash in the mirrors and Boss Chitra, who was looking at the hundredth one, had a flash of light as bright as a million suns strike his eyes and immediately his eyes clouded over. Surya's beauty was too radiant. It had turned poor Boss Chitra the painter blind.

King Asman was shocked and distressed. His court painter had lost his eyesight through the magic of the wicked witch WW.

'God help me! What have I done?' said King Asman. 'My orders have turned my young friend blind.'

'Just promise me one thing,' said Boss Chitra. 'That you will still allow me to paint your daughter's picture, even though I can't see.'

'How can you do that?' asked King Asman.

'I will call the women who attend upon your daughter and ask them to describe her. Then I shall paint her from what they say.'

The king agreed and Boss Chitra began his work. All the maids came and spoke to him and he asked them questions. Surya's girlfriends and other women who had set eyes on her also came.

'Is she tall?' Boss Chitra would ask.

'Yes, quite tall. Taller than a mouse but not as tall as house,' one of the friends said.

'Does she have large eyes? Long hair? Is her chin round or pointed? Is her hair dark or golden or red or black?'

Boss Chitra spent days and days asking these questions and slowly, from the information he received, he built up a picture. It was a lovely picture. When he had finished, even though he couldn't see it, he had painted the most beautiful girl in the kingdom.

King Asman was very proud. He took the picture and sent it in to Surya's chamber for her to see.

It was the first time Surya had seen a picture of herself and she was very pleased with it.

'Who painted this picture, Daddy?' she asked King Asman on the telephone.

'It was Boss Chitra, my court painter,' said the king.

'But he's a man, isn't he? How did he know what I looked like?'

'The reports of your wonderful looks reached him.'

'What does he look like?' asked the princess.

'Well, he's tall and he's dark and he's quite handsome, but he's a very good artist. Firm teeth, I'm sure he's got … ummm … firm teeth.'

'Isn't there some way I could see him?' asked the princess. 'Come to think of it, Daddy, I've never seen a man.'

The king thought about it a lot. Men weren't even allowed to come close to Surya with their eyes closed because they crumpled and crackled like plastic before a flame. But of course, he must think of a way in which she could see Boss Chitra who'd done such a wonderful painting of her.

Finally he called the attendants of the princess and asked them to get the same hundred huge mirrors that Boss Chitra had used. He instructed the attendants to take them down to the deep lake in the middle of the kingdom. He told Surya to stand on one shore of the lake and he told Boss Chitra to stand many miles away on the other. Then with the huge mirrors he threw the reflection of the young painter onto the water and then back onto the mirror before which the princess stood. There it was, the image of the painter bouncing off the water and onto the mirror. And all the glare and fire that came off the princess's beautiful face was cooled by the deep water of the lake. The princess looked. It was the first time she had seen a man since she grew up. She thought he was wonderful and she wasn't at all shy. 'That's a lovely person,' she said.

By this time everyone in the kingdom had heard that Boss Chitra had painted a picture of the princess and naturally they were curious to see her because she never came out in public. Everyone knew why she didn't come out because very many people in the kingdom had been at the big party when she was born and they knew what WW had wished and done. 'We want to see the princess,' they said.

'All right,' said the king and he ordered that the painting be turned into a postage stamp so that the princess's picture would be seen all over the kingdom.

Wherever people saw it they said, 'So that's what this beautiful princess looks like. It's a pity no man can see her.'

And do you know what? Somewhere in a corner of the kingdom the old wicked witch, WW, was doing her usual business. She got her food, as well as all the stuff she put in her spells, by post. Every day she used to get ten or twelve parcels. Mostly she just tore the wrappers off these parcels and threw the paper away. But when Surya's picture was put on the stamps, old WW began to notice.

At first all she thought was that's a pretty girl, and got on with unwrapping the parcel. After a few days the picture on the stamp began to have an effect on her. 'Whose picture is this?' she asked herself. The question obsessed her. In the end she decided to go down to the post office and find out.

WW dressed up like any old lady and went down to the post office and stood in the queue. When it was her turn she bought fifty first-class stamps and she leaned over the counter and asked the clerk who was selling her the stamps. 'I say, young man, do you know who the girl on the stamps is? I mean, whose picture is it?'

'Don't you know?' said the clerk. 'That's Princess Surya, the one whose real beauty is supposed to burn up men because a wicked witch whose name I can't even say put some rotten spell on her.'

'I see, that's the one …,' said WW, taking her stamps.

All the way home she thought about Princess Surya. She hadn't really meant to turn her into a lonely princess.

For a few days WW thought about it. She didn't want to look at the stamps she had bought because it made her feel bad. So she stopped opening the parcels that were brought to her door by the postman and she started going to the shops instead and listening to the people talking.

'Poor girl,' was what she heard. 'She quite likes this painter who painted her picture which is used on the stamp, but her beauty is so searing, it burnt out his eyes, the poor young man …'

That was part of what WW heard and though she was inclined to feel a little sad she fought off the feeling and tried to tell herself that it served the wretched princess right! In her heart of hearts she knew this was nonsense, because she remembered the party and remembered how she'd lost her temper and put this silly curse on the little child who was quite incapable of doing anyone any harm.

What WW also heard, of course, was people talking about the wicked, nasty old crone who had put the curse on the lovely princess. She knew that she was as unpopular as a jug of castor oil.

When she went home she looked up her book of spells and turned to the page about men who have been turned blind by the dazzling light of beauty. You know what she read there on those pages?

This is what she found first. 'If a girl has dazzling beauty, it becomes real beauty in time. It stops being dazzling and gets deeper and deeper but the shine goes away, just like new silver which shines but gets less and less shiny as it grows older. However, if a witch wants to help she has to say the following spell …'

And then the spell book spelt out the spell.

WW read the spell and repeated it to herself. Here was a princess whom the whole world loved and she, WW, had blighted her life just because the king hadn't got the right kind of food for her at the party.

Quickly WW looked back to the page which dealt with spells to cure the blindness caused by dazzling beauty. She found the spell and repeated the words to herself.

At the bottom of the page on which this spell was written there was, in tiny print, a 'Health Warning'. What it said was

Witches who use the dazzling spell
Must beware of going to hell.

Rubbish, thought WW, scare tactics! It was an old-fashioned book and people were superstitious and wrote all sorts of nonsense in those days.

Still, the thought wouldn't leave her. WW didn't do anything hasty. She hung around her house and was sad about the princess, very annoyed that the story about her had spread and made everyone hate her, worried about the threat in the book and generally jumpy. When she got another parcel with ten stamps bearing the picture of the princess, she couldn't bear it any longer. Off she went to the king's palace on her donkey, repeating endlessly the two spells she had learnt. Of course as she got nearer the palace, the spells began to work.

In her room in the palace, Surya began to feel the light around her becoming more and more normal. And in his special room in the palace, Boss Chitra who was sitting in his chair with his marble eyes could suddenly see the patterns on the wall, the grey and yet warm light of the day, the furniture, the window, the garden and trees and shrubs beyond the window, his own hands … everything.

He was no longer blind. And the princess was no longer dazzling and her beauty was still beauty but it wasn't blinding and burning beauty.

WW reached the palace, parked her donkey and went up to the palace door. She rang the bell and asked to see the king. The footman who answered the door knew who it was and was so scared of WW that he let her in straightaway.

WW went into the king's chamber.

'You know what, Your Majesty? Sixteen or seventeen years ago I said I'd give your daughter a wish and I did. My wish turned into a sort of curse. I was angry because I didn't get my favourite things to eat. But now I've taken the spell off both, your daughter and the painter who painted that beautiful picture.'

'Oh you have, have you?' said the king, because he hardly believed it, but he sent for Surya and for Boss Chitra and found that what WW was saying was true. There was his daughter, beautiful as ever and he could see her. There was Boss Chitra with his sight restored. He could see. Surya's eyes met Boss Chitra's and immediately they fell in love. King Asman was very, very happy.

'How can I reward you? Would you like gold or silver or a free ticket to Disneyland or what?'

'None of that,' said WW, 'just remember that when you send me an invitation for the wedding, see that there's rat-and-lizard cake and sick bull's blood to drink and wild dog samosas, that's all.'

❦

The Beasty Burden

IN THE INDIAN OCEAN THERE'S a very hot island called Kaloristan. On this island there lived a young strongman called Tinbad. His father and grandfather were tailors and Tinbad was learning to be a tailor too.

He would sit on the verandah of their tailoring shop at Main Street of Kaloristan and stitch clothes all day long. It was very boring. Most customers who came to have uniforms and shirts stitched by the firm of Tinbad Senior, Junior and Son were sailors.

Being an island, Kaloristan was of course full of sailors who were always off on voyages and were always in a hurry to have their new clothes ready. They would hang around the shop and sit on the steps of the verandah while Tinbad, his grandfather and father stitched their suits and trousers and other garments and they would chat away.

They told Tinbad fascinating stories of faraway places. When he heard these stories, Tinbad knew he wanted to be a sailor himself. Or that's what he dreamt of being.

So when he was sixteen he plucked up courage and approached his father.

'Dad,' he said. 'I want to go to sea and be a sailor.'

'A sailor? What for? We don't have sailors in our family, only tailors. And anyway, the ports are a long way away and the ships rock and roll on the waters and you'll get sick.'

'Besides, there are a lot of rats on the ships and you hate rats,' said his mother who was listening.

'I don't care,' said Tinbad, 'I just want to sail all the seven seas, or however many there are, and see all the faraway places and bring back wonderful gifts.'

After some argument, his father and mother agreed to let him go. The first voyage Tinbad undertook was from the tiniest port on the island, very close to the village where Tinbad lived. He got a job on a small dhow, a wooden boat with a creaky sail and a cranky motor and they sailed along the coast a distance of twenty miles and came straight back.

For his second voyage, Tinbad tried the port a little further away from home. He caught a boat with an outboard motor that went all the way to another island in the same ocean.

Tinbad was still dissatisfied. He wanted to go on a big long voyage.

The other sailors he met at the little ports and those he worked with told him about Japan and India and Africa and other places. One of the places he heard about was England. An old ship's cook called Hutchinson told him all about it. It sounded very strange to Tinbad. Hutchinson told him that in England there was a big man called Ben who sat in a tower and had to ring a bell every hour. There was a shop as big as a small town named after a man in the Bible who killed baby boys. England had strange kings and queens called Victoria, Euston and Mary the Boney, places which were really pickled circuses, train stations named after bears, pools of black water where people went for holidays, a prince named after a shark, a wax museum named after a woman with two swords … the attractions were endless.

Tinbad was determined to go.

He told his grandfather of his ambition.

'England?' said his grandfather. 'Only the big ships go there. You'll have to cross the whole island and take a ship from the main port, Kalory Bay.'

Tinbad knew that. Neither his grandfather nor his father or mother had ever ventured that far on the island, but Tinbad packed his bags and said goodbye and he set off.

On the way he came to a river.

He thought to himself, *Oh dear, a river, I'll have to swim and get my clothes wet.* But there was no bridge and no boat, so there really wasn't any other way.

Tinbad started to tie his bag onto his back when he heard a voice.

'Oi,' said the voice. 'Young man, can you help an old feller?'

Tinbad looked round. Behind him there was an old man with a long chin smiling at him, showing Tinbad that he had only one tooth. His mouth was smiling but his eyes were anxious.

'I've been sitting by the bank of this river for days and weeks and months, maybe even years,' said the old man. 'I've been waiting for someone young and strong like you to turn up.

'What can I do for you?' asked Tinbad.

'Just give me a piggyback,' said the old man, 'till we get across the river.'

Tinbad looked at the old man. He was wrinkled and sad.

'Come on, then,' said Tinbad and he bent over.

The old man jumped on his back and held tight.

Tinbad waded into the river. The water was cold. The old man was on his back and over the old man's back he had swung his bag.

The water was deep and Tinbad began to swim. He reached the other shore.

'There you are, old man. You can get off now,' said Tinbad.

'Are you crazy? Get off now? I've got my first free ride in ninety-six years.'

'Well, I can't carry you any more, I've got to get to the sea and onto a ship. You see, I'm going to England.'

'Splendid,' said the old man. 'I've always wanted to go to England and look at the queen.' He held on tightly.

'Oh really! Now get off,' said Tinbad, but the old man wouldn't.

'I'm tired, just go on a little way and then I'll get off,' he said.

Oh well, nothing else to do but keep going, thought Tinbad. He walked on and soon came to a tree and decided to sit in the shade.

'OK, old man, that's your lot,' said Tinbad, 'Now get off!'

The old man didn't reply but Tinbad felt his grip tightening round his neck and his bony knees clinging to Tinbad's waist. 'Last chance,' said Tinbad, 'Get off or I'll shake you off, I've had quite enough!'

'Just try it! Try and shake me off, you little beast of burden, you,' said the old geezer, and he let off a little laugh which sounded to Tinbad like 'hyucklety hyuckley hyuck'!

'You asked for it,' said Tinbad and he tried to shake the old man off. The old man clung tighter until Tinbad was choking and coughing.

'Stop it, let go!' said Tinbad.

'Stop jumping up and down and trying to shake me up, it won't do any good. I may be old but my arms and knees are strong and I like it on your back, actually,' said the old man.

'If you don't get off, I'll roll on my back and you'll be crushed,' said Tinbad.

'Don't be silly, beasty burden,' said the stubborn old man, 'you have no idea whom you are dealing with. Hyucklety hyuck! I am the leech of ages, the spirit of gum, the grandfather of all super-duper-zooper-pooper-grouper- shmooper-glueper-GLUE.'

'I don't care who you are, I'm going to get you off,' said Tinbad and he fell backwards and tumbled over and over.

The old man wasn't perturbed. He took the rolling and crushing as though nothing was happening.

'You can't really hurt me, stupid, stupid beasty burden,' said the old man and then he let out a shriek which made

Tinbad jump. He shrieked like an eagle, then he barked like a dog and howled like a wolf, laughed like a hyena and then just said 'gyuk gyuk gyuklety gyuk, I'm off to see the K-K-K-K-K-veen!'

Tinbad checked his watch. In half an hour the ship would be leaving for England and if he missed it he'd have to wait another year for a booking, so he thought he'd just try and forget about the old man being on his back and get on with it.

In twenty-nine minutes Tinbad had reached the ship with a minute to spare. He went on board.

Soon the ship sailed. It was a long voyage lasting several weeks and all through it the old man clung to Tinbad's back. He wouldn't get off. Not even when Tinbad was having his dinner or going to bed. There he was, clamped onto his back.

At first Tinbad thought that if he pretended to go to sleep the old man would fall asleep too and then he could shake him off. But no. The old fellow was a wily old soul and he slept with his bulgy eyes open and his knees and arms as tight round Tinbad as they were when he was awake.

Soon Tinbad learnt to sleep and eat and walk and talk while ignoring the old man on his back. Poor Tinbad thought he now knew how a snail felt, having to carry a shell on its back.

When they reached England and got off the ship, Tinbad took a train to London. He had to pay half fare for the old fellow.

'Look, you rogue,' he said to the old man, 'this is London. Now will you get off?'

'I'll never get off,' said the old man 'and if you don't stop asking me to get off I'll start my shenanigans again. I'll screech and growl and laugh and scream and grunt and yelp and go "gyuk, gyuk, gyuklety gyuk or hyuck, hyuck, hyucklety hyuck"!'

'No, no, anything but that,' agreed Tinbad, 'I can't stand that racket, I won't mention getting off my back again.'

Whatever Tinbad did, shopping, getting on a bus, eating, drinking or sleeping, the old man was always with him. (How did Tinbad change his clothes, you may be wondering? The answer is that when he changed his shirt the old man would relax his grip on his neck and when he changed his trousers he would loosen his knees to allow him to slip on fresh ones, but during both changes, he would tighten his bony-fingered grip on Tinbad's throat.) Tinbad was very unhappy. He didn't know what to do.

For one thing, England wasn't at all like the old cook Hutchinson had said. Everything was ordinary – the fish fingers weren't fish's fingers at all, there were no liquid fairies in Fairy Liquid. Hamburgers weren't made of ham. Besides, people laughed at him when he couldn't say 'Knightsbridge' and 'Leicester' and 'Worcester' and 'Holborn' and a hundred other names he just couldn't work out.

The old man, on the other hand, was quite happy. Every time Tinbad said k-nigh-ats-brid-gay instead of 'Knightsbridge', the old man would do a very teeny hyucklety hyuck on his back. He loved England too. There were three things the old man loved especially. He loved the game shows on telly, he loved cream buns and he loved the queen.

Tinbad was desperate to get rid of him. He couldn't even take a ship back home because he was stuck with this load. Tinbad thought and thought and thought.

Then he had an idea.

You know what he did? He sent his TV set back to the shop from which he'd hired it. Whenever they passed an old people's home, Tinbad would say, 'Oh I'd love to live there when I'm old because they've got beautiful colour television sets in there, and the people who live there can watch TV all day long.'

But it was no good. The old man would just whistle *God save the queen* and pretend he hadn't heard.

Tinbad tried to go to places where he thought the old man wouldn't want to go, frightening places and gruesome museums, thinking that maybe the old man would say, 'I'm not going in there, you'd better go by yourself.'

No such luck. The old man just yawned and giggled right through the frightening bits and said 'Gyuk gyuk gyuklety gyuk squared!'

Tinbad tried bribing the old man with cream buns.

'Will you get off my back if I buy you twenty-four buns?' he'd ask.

'Make it thirty-six,' the old man would say. Then Tinbad would buy thirty-six cream buns and the old man would gulp them down one after the other.

'OK, you've had your bun feast, now get off my back. You promised!' Tinbad would say, but the old man would only hold tighter and tighter and whistle *God save the queen* louder and louder.

'Foolish boy, beasty burden, promises were made to be broken. Hyucklety hyuck and shyuck shyuck shyuck!'

One day, when Tinbad was pouring himself and the old man some milk for their morning breakfast, the old man said, 'It's my birthday today.'

Tinbad was surprised. He'd never thought of the old man having ever been born, let alone having a birthday! He had thought of him as an everlasting demon.

'So how old are you, guv'nor?' Tinbad asked.

'Mind your own business,' snapped the old man and he mumbled things to himself as he did when he was annoyed with Tinbad, just to make Tinbad feel bad.

Just then there was a knock on the door and Tinbad answered it. Who should be standing there but a special postman? With a big grin, the postman handed an envelope over to Tinbad.

'What's this?' asked Tinbad.

'A telegram,' said the postman.

The old man lunged for the telegram, trying to grab it from Tinbad.

'Hold your horses! It's for you, you impatient old bother!' said Tinbad and he handed the envelope over.

The old man opened it.

'I can't read,' he said, 'What does it say?'

'If you get off my back, I'll read it to you,' said Tinbad.

'I'll pretend you didn't say that,' said the old man. 'I'm not getting off your back till doomsday and I don't care what the silly old telegram says!'

'Oh, you will,' said Tinbad. 'It's from the queen.'

'From the queen?' asked the old man jumping up and down on poor Tinbad's back, and he laughed, 'Hyucklety hyuck hyuck.'

'You never told me you were about to be a hundred years old,' said Tinbad.

'Because it's none of your business,' said the old man.

'Well, happy birthday,' said Tinbad. 'And do you know what? The queen has invited you to tea.'

The old man was very excited.

'Let me see, let me see, hyuck hyuck,' and even though he couldn't read he grabbed the telegram and held it upside down and gave it two or three kisses.

'I love the queen,' said the old man. 'Now come on! Get my best clothes out and yours, we're going to see the queen for tea. After all, you're only a hundred years old once.'

'Quite right,' said Tinbad. A little plan was forming in his head. He helped the old man dress up that afternoon and he put on his own best sailor's cap, and off they went, piggyback, to Buckingham Palace.

Oh, the old man was excited. He kept striking Tinbad on his ribs and shouting 'Giddyup, giddyup, giddyup!'

Finally they got to the palace. At the gates were two soldiers in tall hats and red coats. Tinbad went up to the gate.

'What do you want?' said one of the soldiers and Tinbad knew from the three stripes on his sleeve that he was a sergeant.

'To see the queen,' he said. 'We've got an invitation to tea.'

The sergeant turned up his nose. 'You've got an invitation? To see the queen? For tea? Whatever for?'

'Because, sonny boy,' the old man chirped in, 'I am a hundred years old today and the queen wants to see me. So 'hyuck hyuck and double hyuck. Stand aside, we're going in.'

'And I suppose this young sailor is also a hundred years old?' the sergeant asked.

'A hundred years old?' the old man said. 'Hyuck. He's only a beasty burden, and a bit of an idiot.'

'Well then, he's not invited to tea, is he?' the sergeant asked.

'Oh, I suppose not,' said the old man and he scratched his head. 'But I do really want to see the queen.'

'Nobody's stopping you,' said the sergeant, 'but we're stopping *him.*'

Tinbad was smiling to himself.

'You mean I can't go in?' he asked.

'I mean exactly that. The old man will have to dismount and quick march by himself.'

The old man began to frown.

'Oh dear,' he said, 'can't I just take him in and put him in the bicycle shed or something?'

'I'm afraid not,' said the sergeant and he looked at the telegram which Tinbad had handed to him.

'This invitation is for four o'clock and it's one minute to four now,' said the sergeant. 'You'll have to decide who's going and who's not very, very soon.

'Now, Tinbad,' said the old man, 'I think I'll just go in and pop out again as soon as I've had tea. You'd better wait for me right here.'

'Sure thing, guv'nor,' said Tinbad.

As he said these words he felt the old man loosening his grip on his neck and on his hip and climbing down. Tinbad couldn't believe it. There was the old man standing on his own two feet. He had crooked bow legs and a bent back and one of the soldiers lent him a stick. He hobbled off through the gates.

'Here I come, Queen, hyuck hyuck hyucklety hyuck!' he said with a grin as big as a melon slice.

Tinbad watched as the old man went up to the front door of the palace and rang the bell. Then he turned round and ran as fast as he could.

He didn't turn back till he had got to Victoria and got a train to Southampton and then a ship across the ocean, far far away from the hyucklety hyucking old demon.

~

Chew Chew

IT HAD BEEN A VERY strange evening for Solly, full of surprises. First of all, this friend of his mum's and dad's turned up at the front door with two baskets.

'Oh hullo, hullo, hullo, hullo, I am Mr Muttoo, friend of father and mother and extraordinary delivery boy for intercontinental fruity trips,' he said when Grandpa answered the doorbell, 'Two baskets. One for Suleiman and one for big daddy and big mummy.'

Mr Muttoo beamed like a crescent moon. Suleiman was Solly's real name but only his family called him that.

'There are letters for all of you inside the mango baskets, happy eating, happy reading. Your parents are such dear people, such lovely human beings. I love them,' Mr Muttoo said.

'How are they?' Solly's grandpa asked, meaning Solly's mum and dad. He invited the man in. 'Please come and tell us all about Karachi.'

'Can't stop at all,' said Mr Muttoo. 'Business calls, busy busy buzz buzz, just passing by. Oh oh, one thing, one thing. I told Suleiman's mother I would deliver the basket with a kiss from her.'

The last thing Solly wanted was a kiss from Mr Muttoo, but he got one anyway. Before Solly could step back far enough to dodge, Mr Muttoo stepped through the door, grabbed him, half lifted him up and, saying 'mmmmmmm' through his cheeks, gave him a big sloppy kiss.

Still, his mother and father had sent mangoes, and a basketful of his favourite fruit was probably worth the humiliation.

As soon as Mr Muttoo went, Suleiman took the basket upstairs. It was very heavy, but he dragged it one stair at a time to his room in the attic.

The basket was tied with string and had a plastic bag around it. Solly cut the string and the plastic, took the wicker lid off and looked inside.

He could see a mop of what looked like black hair. He put his hand in and pulled. There was a little scream from the basket.

'Youch!' said the voice.

Solly was startled. He looked closer. There weren't any mangoes in this basket, there was only a girl. She was crouched inside and wouldn't stand up till Solly grabbed her hair and pulled. The girl stood up.

'What are you doing in the basket?' Solly asked.

'This is Captain Dinesh Mehta. We are cruising at twenty-two thousand feet. In a moment we'll be crossing the Bosphorus, with the city of Istanbul directly on our left,' she said. She spoke in a man's voice. Maybe she's using some kind of tape recorder, Solly thought.

'Where are my mangoes?' he demanded. The girl didn't reply.

'This is my basket, who gave you permission to get in?' Solly asked.

'We shall be landing at Heathrow Airport, Terminal 3, in approximately five minutes. The captain has switched on the no-smoking sign, so please extinguish all cigarettes. Thank you,' said the girl in a woman's voice this time. It sounded as though she was talking through a tube.

'Get out then. There might be a letter for me, even if you've eaten all the damned mangoes. I could tell the police, you know.'

The word 'police' sparked the girl off.

'Police?' she asked, in a gruff man's voice, 'I am very good with the police. I slip through their hands like a slimy fish.' This time she was speaking Urdu, a language Suleiman knew well.

'Don't think I don't understand that,' he said. 'I'm Pakistani, or my mum and dad are.' The only word the girl understood was 'Pakistani'. Solly could see that, so he began to speak to her in Urdu.

'You better get out of the basket,' he said.

The girl got out. She was short and she wasn't very pretty. She had wide nostrils and bushy eyebrows, matted, raggy, black hair and her dress barely covered her brown skin. Solly couldn't even tell what colour the dress was or if the fabric had a pattern because it was brown with mud and grime. And she stank.

'Where did you come from?'

'I'm completely lost and dizzy and I just want to sleep now, right here, so leave me alone, little boy, or I'll bite you,' the horrible girl said. She jumped onto Solly's bed.

'You're not lost. You're in England and you've just smuggled yourself in from Pakistan, I think. That's illegal! So don't try and run away. And get off my bed!'

Now the whole room was full of the horrible stink.

'I think you'd better go,' said Solly, resisting the urge to hold his nose because it would seem rude, and he was a well-brought-up young man.

'No,' said the girl and she drew back the duvet on Solly's bed and got in. She pulled the duvet up to her chin so that her feet stuck out from under it at the end of the bed.

Solly saw them and his eyes were transfixed. The girl was lying on her back, but her feet pointed backwards towards the floor at the end of the bed.

'How do you do that?' he asked.

'Now let me sleep. It was horrible in that basket,' the girl said.

'But your feet,' said Solly. He wanted to pull the duvet off the girl. She couldn't have twisted her body in the bed to turn her feet backwards. This was very strange.

Just as he was thinking this, he caught the girl's eye. She was staring at his feet.

'What's wrong with your feet?' the girl asked.

'My feet?' said Solly. 'Look at yours!'

'They are turned around,' the girl said. 'They are pointing forwards.'

She jumped out of bed.

Solly stared. His mother had always ticked him off for staring or even looking curiously at people who were disabled, and this girl ... well, she didn't look disabled. It really looked as though her feet were intended to be that way.

'I told you, I'm not going anywhere. I'm tired,' she said and she sounded as though she meant it.

'All right then, I think you should have a shower,' Solly said. The stink was becoming unbearable. 'And get out of those torn clothes. Look, I'll lend you some proper ones.'

The little girl made no response. She just stared at his feet with her huge, round, dark eyes.

'Look, try my shoes first,' Solly said, bringing her his trainers. He was curious to see how she'd put on a pair of shoes.

Maybe if she got used to the idea of his shoes then she'd take a T-shirt and jeans and change into them, Solly thought, but what if Grandma or Grandpa came up the stairs now?

'Go on, try them on.' Solly threw the shoes to her in desperation.

She put them on, lacing them up with both hands behind her ankles as Solly watched, amazed. It was all he could do to lace up trainers the right way round.

'They fit you. Good.' he said. 'Now try the T-shirt and the sweater, it'll be nice and warm.

He went and got some jeans out of his chest of drawers. He didn't know whether to offer her a pair of knickers or socks. He decided this would be too embarrassing.

'You can have a nice hot shower if you like.'

The girl didn't seem to understand. She looked at the clothes he offered her and put them beside her on the bed.

'Now go and have a shower or I will call the police,' he said.

The girl went into the bathroom. Solly waited. Soon she came out in his clothes with her hair long and wet and black, hanging down over her face and back.

'Tell me how you got here, or I'll call Grandpa. He doesn't like stowaways and smuggling and all that sort of thing.'

The girl understood. She picked up a brush and ran it through her hair.

'You see, we went at night to the fruit market in Karachi where they sell fruit …'

'What else would they sell?' asked Solly. This girl was silly.

'And why does your voice keep changing? If you want to talk to me, talk straight, don't play the fool, you know.'

'I'm not,' said the girl, 'I'm telling you the truth. 'And this time her voice was just like Solly's. He couldn't believe his ears. She was making fun of him.

'Say that again,' he demanded.

'I was telling you', if you'll only be patient, little boy,' the cheeky girl said. 'Our whole tribe went to the fruit market and I climbed right to the top of a mountain of mangoes as tall as your ceiling. It was pitch-dark and suddenly the police whistles began to blow.' The little girl blew a very shrill whistle with her bare lips.

'Stop that, you idiot! Grandma and Grandpa are watching telly and they'll be up here like a shot.'

'Sorry, sorry, sorry. But I really don't know what happened to me after I tumbled down the hill of mangoes and fell into the basket.'

'What about the rest of your "tribe", as you call them?'

'I heard them running away and, as I tried to get down the mango mountain, I slipped into the basket.'

'So you and your tribe are mango thieves?'

'No, we don't eat mangoes really, we'd gone to the fruit market to … to … I don't know why. But we go places at night and come back by dawn.'

'Oh you do, do you?'

'Yes, it's … it's what we do.'

'Like your job?'

'That's right.'

'Doesn't sound like much of a job to me,' said Solly.

Well, you'd better disappear before dawn from here was what Solly was thinking, and he was about to say it out loud.

'Have you chewed up my mum's letter too?'

'Not the kind of thing we eat, you silly boy,' said the insolent little girl.

Solly looked in the basket. There was a bundle of straw

in the bottom of it and on top of that was an envelope. He pulled the envelope out. It had his name on it, and inside there was a pendrive.

He transferred the music file onto his MP3 player and turned it on. It was his mother's voice: 'Dear Suleiman, we hope you like the mangoes …'

And the letter went on.

Just as Solly was settling into listening to his mum's voice, the dog began to wail at the door. Their dog was called Burger because he was a fat, flat, dark-brown dog.

'Oh no, I forgot to take Burger out. Now he'll go and do his mess somewhere in the house.'

Grandma shouted up the stairs, 'Are you eating the mangoes? Or reading Mummy's letter, Suleiman?'

'The letter,' Solly shouted back.

'What does she say? Are they all right?'

'The usual stuff about missing me and going to Lahore to see aunty and lots of love and junk,' said Solly, even though he had only heard a bit of it.

'You must write to them straightaway. And you forgot to take the dog out. Now it's too dark. You'd better have your bath and come down to say goodnight before bed.'

'Can Grandpa take him out? He's desperate!'

'Grandpa's tired. Leave him.'

Solly could hear her going back downstairs.

He hadn't said anything about the girl, Solly was thinking, so now it was a secret from Grandma.

'I'll take your dog out,' said the girl.

'It's dark. Children don't go out in the dark here.'

'I go out only when it's dark. The daylight hurts my eyes. And I'm not a child, you boy!'

This was a very funny girl.

'Then you can take him out. But wait till Grandma and Grandpa go to bed.'

Next to Solly's room was the prayer room where Grandpa kept a copy of the Koran and a prayer mat. Maybe she could sleep on the floor there, Solly thought, but then he changed his mind. Grandpa went in there at odd times of the day and he would find her.

If he really wanted to hide her, she should sleep in Mum and Dad's room because no one went in there. Or very rarely.

'You can wait here,' Solly said. He didn't want to say anything about hiding her yet, but looking at her in a sweater that was too large, in his muddy trainers, her hair loose, he felt sorry for her.

'If you're a stowaway, I'll help you get back. Only stowaways don't want to get back, do they?'

After Solly helped the girl sneak out with Burger on a leash, he ran himself a bath. He had the feeling that even though the stink of the girl had gone, some of it still stuck to him, and he wanted to wash it off. Sitting in the bath, he thought it was quite exciting, meeting a stranger out of a basket. He couldn't really tell Grandpa. They'd call the police and she'd be locked up.

And besides, the girls and boys in Enid Blyton stories or other adventure stories didn't tell on stowaways and fugitives and people like that. They always helped them.

A couple of hours later, as Solly lay awake in bed, he heard stones on his windowpane. It must be her. He tiptoed downstairs and let the strange girl in.

They climbed the stairs quietly in the dark until they came to Solly's attic.

'Are you hungry?' asked Solly.

'Just a bit chewy.'

'Shall I get you some bread from the kitchen?'

The girl shook her head.

'You'd better eat something,' said Solly. 'You say what you want and I'll go and get it. I've got nothing here but chewing gum.'

'What's that?' asked the girl.

'It's not to eat, really. It's just to chew.'

The girl nodded vigorously, indicating that she wanted some of that.

Solly shrugged. He picked up the packet of sugar-free gum and gave it to her.

The girl fell upon it and stuck it in her mouth. She chewed it and chewed it as though there was no tomorrow.

'You like that, huh?' asked Solly.

The girl didn't reply, she kept chewing the gum.

'So what is your name?'

Again, she didn't reply. Just kept chewing.

'Stop all this chew, chew! What's your name?'

'Chew Chew,' said the girl.

'Right, Chew Chew. If that's what you want to be called, fine. Now. You can sleep in Mum and Dad's room.'

Solly showed her downstairs, trying to hold her hand and guide her, but the girl avoided his touch. She seemed to be able to see in the dark. He showed her into his parents' room and gave her two blankets to make herself comfortable under Mum and Dad's bed.

The next day, before going to school, Solly crept into the big bedroom and left Chew Chew with strict instructions to hide and make no noise.

'They don't come in in the morning, but if anyone does, get into the wardrobe, no one looks in there.'

All day at school he wanted to tell his friends about the strange girl with turned-back feet, but he didn't dare. They might think he was just boasting. Worse, his friends might say they wanted to come and check it out for themselves!

A week passed and Chew Chew was still there. She never went out in the day. She said the sunlight hurt her eyes even though Solly got a pair of Grandpa's dark glasses and gave them to her. She'd get active at night when the house was still, and wander about the town with Burger.

She'd taught herself to bark like Burger and to make the whining sounds he made when scratching at Solly's door.

Solly was getting anxious about keeping this girl in the house, but he couldn't think of anything else to do with her. It wouldn't be right, he thought, to turn her out.

Besides, Solly felt they were becoming good friends. After Grandma and Grandpa went to bed, which they did straight after watching the news on telly, Chew Chew would come up to Solly's room and tell him stories. Solly had bought her a stack of chewing gum, because that was all Chew Chew would eat. When he asked her if he should smuggle a sandwich or something else to her from the fridge, she always said she'd eaten and she wasn't hungry.

One evening, Solly was watching a video in his own room. Chew Chew wanted to watch it too and Solly allowed her to sit in the bottom of the wardrobe with the door ajar so she could see. If anyone came in, he would push the door and lock her in. Chew Chew liked videos, and she would learn the voices and words from them. 'Keep the change, you filthy animal' was what she kept repeating in a severe American accent after she'd seen *Home Alone*. And 'We're all prisoners, Chickie Baby, we're all locked in,' from a film called *The Love Bug* which was one that Solly watched over and over again.

This evening, they were watching *The Love Bug* once again and, as they watched, Solly noticed that the girl was beginning to smell again. Solly decided he wasn't embarrassed to point this out to her.

'Look, Chew Chew,' Solly said, 'You've been here days and you've only had one shower. I think you'd better have a bath because you stink.'

Chew Chew was insulted and began sulking, but when the film was over, Solly went into the bathroom down the corridor and ran the bath for her.

'Come on, now,' he ordered, 'I'll give you a nice fresh shirt too.'

Chew Chew went to the bathroom while Solly stood guard in the corridor to see that she wasn't discovered.

While she was in the bath, what he was dreading happened. He heard Grandpa's footsteps coming up the stairs. Solly dashed into his room and left the door open. Grandpa came to the landing and Solly could hear him knocking at the bathroom door.

'Solly, are you in there?'

Solly held his breath as Grandpa knocked again.

'Solly?'

Then suddenly, Solly heard himself singing, at first very softly and then louder and louder. Chew Chew was singing in his voice. It was the Cowboy Carol he had been rehearsing for the Christmas choir: 'There'll be a new world beginning from tonight ...'

'Stop that cacophony, boy,' Grandpa said, but the singing carried on louder than ever.

'The mischief, he can't even hear me,' Solly heard Grandpa mutter as he went down the stairs again.

'Just one minute, Grandpa, I've got soap in my eyes. I'll call when I've finished,' Chew Chew shouted, imitating Solly's voice. And she sang, 'Yi yippee, we're going to ride the trail!'

'It's all right, dear, call me when you're done. I just want my tooth tumbler,' Grandpa called, 'and I do like your song. Strong stuff.'

When the coast was clear, Chew Chew came out, smelling sweet but still frowning.

'These clothes stink, you should take them out with you at night and throw them away,' said Solly, bundling up the T-shirt she'd changed out of. 'But you look smart.'

Chew Chew smiled. She wasn't used to compliments.

'What do you get up to on your walks?' Solly would ask sometimes, but Chew Chew wouldn't reply. One day when he asked her again, she said: 'We miss you very much, darling, and you do understand that we were going to be so busy that we couldn't really have brought you with us, and Daddy didn't want you missing any school. So work hard, and do all your homework. And try and write every week, once at least. I know it's a bore, but please, please, Solly, I miss you so much.' She was saying it in his mother's voice.

'You've been listening to my MP3 player and my mum's letter! It's rude to listen to other people's letters you know.'

Chew Chew just grinned. She was very odd, and she had no idea of good manners.

'None of the tank engines volunteered. The fat controller was annoyed ...' she said.

Solly could have sworn the voice came out of his player.

'And you've been listening to my baby tapes! Actually, that's a good idea, if you're such a baby, you can take those into your Chew-cubby with you and listen to them all night. Keep you amused. Just your sort of stuff. You've got the mind of a four-year-old.'

'I'm hundreds of years old, I think' said Chew Chew, again using the voice she'd learnt from the Thomas tapes, the voice of Ringo Starr.

'Don't you know exactly? When's your birthday?'

'Don't know,' said Chew Chew.

'You don't know your name, you don't know where you come from, how old you are, who your family is ...'

'Oh, I know who my family is. It's Mum, Dad, my brother, he's horrible, and Grandma and Grandpa and another Grandpa and Grandma and Great Grandma and Great Grandpa and Great Grandma two and Great Grandpa two and Great Grandpa three and Great Grandma three ...'

'There's four Great-Grands,' said Solly, 'and when you get to the Great Greats, there's Great Great Grandma One, Two, Three, Four, Five, Six, Seven and Eight?'

'That's right. Do you know my family?'

'Don't be silly, I just worked it out. But ... are they all alive?' asked Solly.

'What do you mean? Of course they're all alive!'

'I mean, aren't any of them dead?'

'Of course not.'

'Then where do they live? We know it's Pakistan, but where?'

'I don't know.'

'You don't remember the address?'

'There isn't an address. No one can find us. We call on them, they don't call on us. That's what my mum taught me when I was very young.'

'Did she? When you were just a few hundred years old, right?'

'Maybe.' Sarcasm was wasted on this girl.

'Then you're stuck in England until they come and get you, aren't you?'

'I don't want to be stuck, Solly,' Chew Chew said, chewing furiously on her twentieth packet of gum that day. 'It's too cold.'

One morning, when Solly went down to breakfast, Grandpa was reading the *Gazette,* their local newspaper.

'Look at this,' he said to Grandma, 'a very curious story.'

'Can I see?' asked Solly.

'Grandma can read it out.'

Grandma took the paper and read the story out loud.

'"Mr Shah, of 3 Barley Crescent, opened his shop very early last Friday and got an awful shock. A little girl came into his shop just as he'd raised the shutters. It was his first customer for the day and Mr Shah was his usual merry self.

Then, as he was bringing the milk crates in, he thought he heard his wife call to him from the back room. This was odd because his wife had gone to India the day before. When Mr Shah went towards the back room, the little girl grabbed something from the sweets counter and ran. Mr Shah ran after her, but didn't catch her because he slipped in the snow and fell. By the time he got himself together, the little girl had gone. He followed in the direction in which she'd gone and then turned back because he'd left the shop unattended. 'What was very curious,' said Mr Shah, and we reproduce the photograph he sent to us, 'was that the footsteps of the girl in the snow were not going away from the shop but coming towards it.' Note also that alongside the girl's footprints where the footprints of a dog, apparently going in the opposite direction to the human prints.

'"Mr Shah, who reported a dozen packets of chewing gum missing, has reported the incident to the police and is at present being treated for shock by his doctor."'

Grandma showed Solly the photograph of Mr Shah's shop and the footsteps in the snow. There was also a picture of Mr Shah by his shop later on that day.

'These shopkeepers try and get free advertising for themselves by making up these preposterous stories. Monstrous, preposterous, ridiculous stories!' Grandpa sounded annoyed.

Solly rushed to school. When he got back in the afternoon, Chew Chew was still hibernating. She woke up when it got dark and stole into Solly's room. She would often play a nasty trick on him. She'd wait outside the door and call out in his mum's voice, or Ringo Starr's voice.

It never failed to fool Solly, and it made him angry with himself for being fooled, even though he had to admit that her voices were pretty perfect.

'I know you've been stealing chewing gum. It's got into the papers. Look, I've only got twelve pence left. Grandpa is very strict with pocket money, so that's all we have till next week. You can have it if you promise to stop stealing. It's wicked.'

Chew Chew nodded.

The next day there was more stuff in the papers. This time a milkman on his rounds had seen a little girl with dark hair and wearing four sweaters one on top of the other, with wellies turned round so her feet stuck out backwards, and with a pair of dark glasses, running across the common. The police had been informed and had advised the milkman to see a psychiatrist.

'You see how superstition catches on. If the papers say that one man has seen a spaceship landing, a hundred clowns come forward and say they saw them too. Bull and poppycock! Then they'll insist that they were green-skinned and their eyes were like mushrooms on stalks. Balderdash and codswallop, my boy. Damn fools!' Grandpa said.

'You never know, it may be true,' Solly protested.

'You see how this boy is learning cheek,' said Grandpa. He hated any sort of contradiction.

'I'm not being cheeky. I'm sorry.'

'This is all nonsense, superstition, gobbledygook, mumbo-jumbo and wishful thinking. People trying to make themselves more important than they are.'

'But maybe they did see a girl with turned-about feet.'

'Have you ever seen a girl with turned-about feet?' Grandpa asked and before Solly could answer, he added, 'Of course you haven't! You know science was born in India. We invented the zero and Muslims invented algebra and inquisitiveness. Now these people here are reverting to rubbish and barbarism. A woman couldn't balance if her feet were turned backwards!'

'How do you know if you've never seen one?' Solly said. Even as he said it, he knew it was wrong to argue with Grandpa. He was very short-tempered and wouldn't like it.

'The possibility doesn't exist,' said Grandpa.

'It does.' Solly said.

'Insolence. I owe the boy two pounds in pocket money but I shan't give it to him till he writes out a hundred times that girls with feet turned backwards don't exist.'

Then Grandpa got up from the breakfast table, took his scarf, coat and stick, and went out for his morning walk.

That evening, Solly had to tell Chew Chew that he couldn't help her by giving her his pocket money for chewing gum. She'd just have to make what she had last longer.

Actually he was getting a bit fed up with her. Why should he have to look after her? How was he going to tell her to leave the house? It was embarrassing. What was worse, he couldn't tell anyone else about it or get advice.

The next day, as Solly was watching telly with Grandpa and Grandma, something sensational happened. The local news came on and the announcer said that police were looking for a chewing gum thief. They believed she was a little girl who had pulled off twenty-three raids in the last few days.

'The thief has a peculiar way of operating. She is a perfect mimic and calls out to her victims in voices which they recognize. When the victims answer the calls, she slips into the shops and steals the gums and runs. Earlier reports that she wears her boots the wrong way round have been confirmed by all twenty-three shopkeepers who were robbed. A postman said he saw such a girl, with dark skin, black hair, not more than three feet and six inches tall, running in the snow dragging a fat dog with tiny feet. The dog's footprints were going forward but the girl's pointed backwards.'

'That postman should be sacked. He shouldn't be in government employment if he gets hysterical like these shopkeepers,' Grandpa said.

When Solly went up to his room he was angry. Chew Chew was sitting under his bed.

'I thought I told you not to steal!'

'I can't help it,' she said, 'I knew all those people had seen me, but if I don't chew gum I have this feeling that I'll do something very, very bad.'

'You mean you'll go back to smoking? When my mum gave up smoking she chewed gum for months. Then she gave it up and started smoking again.'

'Not smoking. Something even worse.'

'What's worse than smoking? My class teacher, Ms Tite, said smoking is the worst bad habit one can have.'

'Idiot child. I can't even explain it. This is much worse.'

'Whatever you're thinking or not thinking, it can't be worse than stealing. I've a good mind to throw you out, you know. If I knew who you were I'd definitely do it.'

'If I knew where to go, I'd go myself,' said Chew Chew.

The next day was Sunday. Grandpa bought five Sunday newspapers. The story was in two of them.

'Would you believe what these idiots are now saying?' asked Grandpa, as he sat in the front room downstairs with his coffee and his pipe and read the newspapers in his dressing gown.

Solly pretended he hadn't heard, but when Grandpa put the papers down he borrowed them and took them upstairs. They were fascinating.

There was a fellow in one of them called Swami Tikoo who said that what the postman and milkman and shopkeepers had seen was something very well known in India and Pakistan. Solly read the article three times.

'Do you know what you are?' Solly asked Chew Chew.

'I don't care what you call me,' said Chew Chew, 'but I really want to go home.' For the first time she looks sad, Solly thought.

'Well, I don't know if I can help with that, but I can tell you what you are. You're a Churail. A kind of witch. And all of you have three things in common: you have your feet turned backwards, you live for ever and you imitate people's voices. That's what it says in the article.'

'It all sounds quite familiar. What else does it say?'

'Some horrible stuff.'

'What stuff?'

'You really want to know?'

'I shall sooner or later.'

'Your mum and dad should have told you already, but maybe you're too young to know these things. Maybe you're only a few thousand years old and have to grow up and then they'll tell you the real McCoy.'

'What does the article say? Anything about chewing gum?'

'Not a word. What it says is that Churails call out to people from outside their windows. They deceive them and make them come out alone. Then they attack them and tear open their stomachs and eat their guts.'

'I knew it was something like that,' Chew Chew said. 'Mum and Dad didn't give me any real guts to get going on, but they used to give me this stuff to chew. Some kind of blubber. But I suppose I'll grow into guts as I get older.'

'I gather you will, but you're not going to be anywhere near me when you do,' said Solly.

'If you like I'll leave,' said Chew Chew.

'And where would you go? There isn't a Home for Lost Churails like there is for dogs and cats, you know. And I very much doubt if the National Society for the Prevention of Cruelty to Children will recognize you as a child. Then there's another problem. In a few days it's Christmas and I'm off to Pakistan because my dad sent me a ticket. Pity he didn't send you one.'

'So what am I going to do?'

'Don't ask awkward questions, we'll think of something,' said Solly.

That night Solly couldn't sleep. As he lay awake, a thought came to him. He got out of bed and sneaked down to his mum and dad's room. Chew Chew hadn't gone out. She was there, sitting under the bed.

'Come up to my room,' Solly said.

They tiptoed up.

'Dad's asked me to take two computers to Pakistan and Grandpa is buying them. If you can be smuggled into the country, you can be smuggled out again. Right?'

Chew Chew still looked glum.

'I read the article just now. It said Churails live in graveyards. There must be millions of graveyards in Pakistan. How will I ever find my people?'

'Remember what your mother told you? "Don't call us, we'll call you?" Well, I've got an idea. You have to do exactly as I say.'

Chew Chew nodded.

The next day, Solly went to the shop which specialized in Indian and Pakistani videos where Grandma had an account. 'I want twenty of the most popular videos in Pakistan, the whole top twenty,' he said.

Solly took the bagful of videos home.

'You're not going thieving tonight,' he told Chew Chew. 'Instead, you're watching videos. I've got nine films, ten soap operas and one politics thing with the news. In the next three days you have to watch them all on Mum and Dad's video. Lock the door and keep the sound down.'

For three nights poor Chew Chew stayed in and watched Pakistani videos one after the other.

Then the Christmas holidays began and Suleiman was sent upstairs to pack his clothes in preparation for his trip.

That evening Mr Muttoo, the same friend of Solly's mum and dad's who'd brought the mangoes, turned up with the computer boxes. This time he was wearing a large tie with palm trees and a boat painted on it.

'I've brought the technology and I want a kiss from the dear little boy,' he said, showing his startlingly red tongue. There was no escape. He grabbed Solly with his big hands and gave him a kiss. 'What a dear boy, take that back from me for your daddy and mummy. Give my regards to Clifton,' he said. Solly knew that Clifton was the place where Dad and Mum had their house.

There were five computer boxes in all, two of them with computers, two with printers and one with wires and attachments and books.

Solly had seen computer packing cases before. He knew there'd be a lot of stuffing and packing in them.

Late that night he crept down to Chew Chew, and they both went into the front room. Solly pulled one of the printers out and asked Chew Chew to try the box for size. She got into the box and he shut it over her.

'I can pack it up to make it look just like new, I think.'

'Then what do I do?'

'It'll be a bit uncomfortable, but tomorrow evening you'll be in Karachi. Then you can leave it to me. Just do one more thing. When you go out tonight, take this wretched printer and leave it outside one of the shops which you've robbed and write them a note saying you've donated it in payment for the chewing gum. And one more thing, if you're taking Burger, can you please walk backwards so that your footprints go in the same direction as his?'

Chew Chew agreed. Solly went upstairs to await her return. Chew Chew picked up the printer and went out for her last adventure in the snow. When she came back, Solly said goodbye to her and made her climb into the printer box. Then he taped it up.

In the morning, the boxes were loaded into the car together with Solly's one suitcase and one piece of hand luggage. Grandpa and Grandma drove him to the airport.

Grandpa made a silly fuss and asked the air hostesses to keep an eye on Solly, which was a bit embarrassing considering that he was nearly eight years old. His grandparents weren't allowed beyond the Departure gates, so Solly waved goodbye. He was checked at the security gate for guns and bombs and, not having any, was taken by an air hostess onto the plane.

At Karachi airport Dad and Mum were waiting. Karachi was hotter than London but not as hot as he had expected.

Throughout the flight and at Karachi airport Solly kept thinking about Chew Chew and how uncomfortable she must be, crouched up in the box. Of course, she was used to being without food and water and air. She was a witch, wasn't she? But quite a nice one, or more like a little, lost girl with backward-pointing feet.

'What have you got a bag full of chewing gum for?' his mum asked Solly.

'To give to any new friends I make this holiday,' Solly replied.

At their large house in Clifton, Solly got to work unpacking poor Chew Chew and putting the printer back into its own box. 'I love being back in the warm, I'm going to wander about all night and lay tricks and maybe eat someone's guts or get up to some more mischief.'

'You're not going to do anything of the sort,' said Solly. 'You're going to sit under the bed and tomorrow I'm going to put my plan into operation.'

The next day Solly went out to the bazaar with his mum. It was not the first time he'd been in Karachi, but it all looked fascinating and new. Solly was looking at the little girls. He noticed that all of them wore baggy trousers and long shirts and some of them wore scarves round their heads.

That's what Chew Chew should wear, Solly thought, to cover up her feet. Only the trousers shouldn't bunch up at the ankles, but trail along the ground. The people of Karachi know all about Churails and they don't like them, so they'd probably start throwing stones if they noticed her feet.

'Tomorrow we are going to start our mass confusion, so be ready,' he told Chew Chew when he got back from the bazaar.

The next day, when Dad went to work and Mum went out, Solly got going. He took Chew Chew into Dad's study, where the phone was, and got to work.

First they phoned up the chief of police. Chew Chew put on the prime minister's voice and demanded that all traffic be stopped in the centre of Karachi as the prime minister and some very important foreign guests were going to go on a tour. The chief of police was very surprised to get the phone call, but he recognized the voice and immediately said, 'Yes, Prime Minister, no, Prime Minister, of course and anything you say, Prime Minister.'

'Next, I think you should put on the voice of TV stars and phone the newspapers.'

'What shall I say?' Chew Chew asked, still in the voice of the prime minister. She was enjoying this game.

'You say: "This is so-and-so, you know me, I appear every week on such-and-such programme. Well, I've been a very bad girl, I've dodged paying any tax for years and I've got all this money saved up which I feel very guilty about and am now going to donate to charity. Call at my house and I'll give you a full interview." Then ring up another newspaper as another star and say, "I'm giving up my acting career and turning into a Christian nun and you can have an exclusive interview." That'll bring them out.'

It did bring them out. The police stopped traffic in Karachi for hours before they realized that the phone call was a hoax. Reporters from the newspapers had to be dragged away from outside the houses of the TV stars whose voices Chew Chew had imitated. They weren't very happy when the police smashed their cameras and bodyguards snatched their notebooks and tore them up. The papers the next day were full of reports: 'TV star repents tax fraud and then changes her mind.'

And: 'Reporters beaten up by star's bodyguards'.

'I don't think that's quite enough,' Solly said. 'We've got to think up more tricks.'

Next day they were at it again. From the videos Chew Chew had picked up the voices not only of film stars, TV stars and politicians, but also of the leading religious men of the country. Their little trick made the TV news that evening.

'A leading religious leader has called for a complete ban on all TV. Sheikh Mahdood Hadood has called for a withdrawal of all television as an instrument of the devil.

He told this TV station that unless transmission stops after today, he will call on the whole population to march on the TV stations and force them to stop.'

An hour later Sheikh Mahdood Hadood himself called the station and said he enjoyed TV a lot himself, he watched all the programmes, especially the satellite stations with American soap operas, and he hadn't called for any ban at all.

After two days there was a nationwide hunt for the hoaxer. The newspapers began calling Chew Chew 'Thousand Voices'.

On the third day the headlines said, 'Police search all major cities for Thousand Voices' and 'Thousand Voices pulls off major hoax on phone-in programme.'

The report told of how Chew Chew had rung up the live phone-in TV programme pretending to be the Sultan of Brain who was visiting the country and had been interviewed on TV the day before. He offered to buy up the Pakistani Air Force.

'What shall we do next?' asked Chew Chew. She was having a whale of a time.

'I'm going to use the phone this time,' said Solly. 'You put on the baggy salwar and dark glasses and the scarf on your head.'

Then Solly picked up the phone and dialled.

'Is that the central Karachi police station? May I speak to the chief of police please? …Yes. Hello. My name is Suleiman Afridi. I live in Clifton and I can give you the address. I'm calling because I've got hold of the person the papers call a Thousand Voices. She is going to prove that she is Thousand Voices and give herself up if you promise that she won't be sent to jail and if you can keep her at one of the best hotels for two nights and if you tell the newspapers and TV exactly where she is ... That's agreed, then. All right, she'll be round at your police station in half an hour. Be sure you are there personally to receive her ... No, this is not a hoax and if you don't agree immediately, we'll cancel the offer to surrender ... No, I am not looking for a reward. You can please give the offered reward to a charity for orphaned children.'

'What did you do that for? You are sending me to the police?'

'Not to the police, you idiot. Remember what you told me? You'll be at a luxury hotel where no one will bother you under police protection and, with all the publicity, your people will know exactly where you are.'

Chew Chew got it. She came across to Solly and much to his embarrassment gave him a big sloppy kiss on his cheek. 'Thank you,' she said.

Solly didn't tell his mum or dad, but he called a taxi and Chew Chew and he sped away.

The police chief was very wary, but when Chew Chew did ten different voices for him he knew he'd got his girl.

'Which hotel would you like?' he asked.

'Have you told the reporters?'

'Yes, they're waiting to hear where and when they can meet Thousand Voices.'

Solly named the most expensive hotel in the city and the police chief said 'fine'.

They set off by police car with outriders on motorcycles clearing the way.

There was a crowd of TV crews, reporters, photographers, and radio interviewers waiting. When they saw Chew Chew with the police chief a cry went up.

'Where's Thousand Voices? We want Thousand Voices.'

'Ladies and gentlemen of the Press, this is Thousand Voices.'

Proudly, like a ringmaster presenting a favourite act, the police chief turned to Chew Chew and Chew Chew began her speech as prime minister, then as Sheikh Mahdood Hadood and then as the several TV stars she'd imitated and even some she hadn't yet imitated. The reporters clapped and the photographers' bulbs flashed.

It didn't take long. Solly was right. The Churail tribe saw the photographs, or perhaps they were watching TV at their favourite shrine. Chew Chew the Churail only stayed at the hotel for a day. Then she was gone. She left a note for Solly.

You were right. Dad and Mum and Grandad and Great Grandad Eight and Great Great Grandma Fifteen came and got me. They came to the window of my room and guess whose voice they used to call me out? Yours! Till I opened the window, I was completely taken in. I thought it was really you. And if you hear of more chewing gum robberies you know whom to blame. I think I prefer it to blood and guts.

Lots of thanks and love,
Chew Chew the Churail.